Lachlan felt himself pulled by the strange emotion he saw in her eyes. Curiosity. Attraction. And most dangerous and tempting of all: possibility.

He could almost believe she meant it.

His gaze dropped to her mouth. He leaned closer. Her lips parted instinctively at his movement. He smothered an oath. Knowledge surged inside him, hot, primitive, and raw. He could kiss her. And God, he wanted to. Wanted it so badly it scared him. Christ, he could almost taste her on his lips.

He'd been careful to hide his desire after that night by the loch, but it was still there, simmering just under the surface. And he felt it now. Felt it rise up and grab him in its steely grip, trying to drag him under.

His hand reached out. Slowly. Carefully. As if she were the most delicate piece of porcelain, his finger grazed the side of her cheek.

His heart jammed in his chest. *Jesus!* He groaned. So damned soft. As smooth and velvety as a bairn. His big, battle-scarred hand looked ridiculous against something so fine.

He tipped her chin, feeling himself falling, lured by the promise in her eyes. His mouth lowered . . .

He caught himself at the last moment.

## By Monica McCarty

*The Viper*
*The Chief*
*The Hawk*
*The Ranger*

*Highland Warrior*
*Highland Outlaw*
*Highland Scoundrel*

*Highlander Untamed*
*Highlander Unmasked*
*Highlander Unchained*

# THE Viper

A HIGHLAND GUARD NOVEL

# MONICA McCARTY

BALLANTINE BOOKS • NEW YORK

*The Viper* is a work of fiction. Names, characters, places, and incidents are the products of the author's imagination or are used fictitiously. Any resemblance to actual events, locales, or persons, living or dead, is entirely coincidental.

A Ballantine Books Mass Market Original

Copyright © 2011 by Monica McCarty
Excerpt from *The Saint* copyright © 2011 by Monica McCarty
All rights reserved.

Published in the United States by Ballantine Books, an imprint of The Random House Publishing Group, a division of Random House, Inc., New York.

BALLANTINE and colophon are trademarks of Random House, Inc.

This book contains an excerpt from the forthcoming book *The Saint* by Monica McCarty. This excerpt has been set for this edition only and may not reflect the final content of the forthcoming edition.

ISBN 978-0-345-52839-1
eBook ISBN 978-0-345-53147-6

Cover design: Lynn Andreozzi
Cover illustration: Franco Accornero

Printed in the United States of America

www.ballantinebooks.com

9 8 7 6 5 4 3 2 1

Ballantine Books mass market edition: November 2011

To Jami who has been eager for Lachlan's story from day one. Squirrel? Thank you for . . . everything.

# ACKNOWLEDGMENTS

*The Viper* is a milestone for me, as it marks the publication of my tenth novel—all ten published with Ballantine in a little over four years. I truly appreciate the opportunity, support, and hard work undertaken by everyone at Ballantine to enable that to happen, including, to name a few: Gina Centrello, Scott Shannon, Libby McGuire, Gina Wachtel, Kim Hovey, Linda Marrow, Penelope Haynes, Junessa Viloria, and all of the fabulous copy editors and production assistants. Also Lynn Andreozzi and the Art Department for the stunning covers (where do you find all these guys and can you pass on the number?—only kidding Dave . . . really) and the Sales Department for making sure readers can find my books in their favorite stores.

A special thanks to Kate Collins, my editor for the last seven books. You make work not feel like work. Whether it's discussing a book, kids, or the Red Sox, I always look forward to our phone calls. Thanks for making my stories better.

I'm fortunate to have not one, but two fantastic agents, Andrea Cirillo and Annelise Robey, to help me navigate the business side of writing, as well as be that extra pair of eyes when called upon. You guys are the best.

As always to the Wednesday lunch gang, Emily Cotler, Estella Tse, and the wonderful designers at Wax Creative.

And finally, to my (almost always) supportive family. Dave, Reid, and Maxine I'm looking at you. Okay, I'm done. Now leave me alone, I need to write. Kidding. Really.

# FOREWORD

The period from March 1306, when Robert Bruce makes his desperate bid for the Scottish crown, to the late summer of 1308, when he defeats the MacDougalls at the Battle of Brander, marks one of the most dramatic falls and subsequent comebacks in history.

By September 1306, six months after Bruce is crowned king at Scone by Isabella MacDuff, Countess of Buchan, his cause is all but lost. He is forced to flee his kingdom a fugitive, taking refuge in the shadowy mists of the Western Isles.

Yet from the jaws of certain defeat, with the help of his secret band of elite warriors known as the Highland Guard, Bruce returns to Scotland six months later and defeats not only the English, but also the Scottish nobles who stand against him.

Yet this is only half of the story. Not all of Bruce's supporters have escaped the wrath of the most powerful king in Christendom: Edward Plantagenet, King of England, the self-styled "Hammer of the Scots." Many have paid the ultimate price, but others still are suffering for freedom's call.

In these merciless times, when the line between life and death is merely a shadow, once again Bruce will call on the legendary warriors of the Highland Guard to set them free.

# Prologue

✣

"Because she has not struck with the sword, she shall not die by the sword, but on account of the unlawful coronation which she performed, let her be closely confined in an abode of stone and iron made in the shape of a cross, and let her be hung up out of doors in the open air at Berwick, that both in life and after her death, she may be a spectacle and eternal reproach to travellers."

*Order of Edward I imprisoning Isabella MacDuff, Countess of Buchan*

*Berwick Castle, Berwick-Upon-Tweed, English Marches,*
*Late September 1306*

They'd come for her.

Bella heard the door open and saw the constable flanked by a handful of guardsmen, but her mind still didn't want to accept the truth.

This wasn't happening. This *couldn't* be happening.

In the weeks it had taken them to build her special prison, she'd told herself that someone would intervene. Someone would put a stop to this barbarity masquerading as justice.

Someone would help her.

Perhaps Edward would relent, as he'd done for Robert Bruce's daughter and wife, and send her to a convent instead? Or maybe Bella's erstwhile husband, the Earl of Buchan, would see beyond his hatred and plead for mercy on her behalf?

Even if her enemies did nothing, surely she could count on her friends? Her brother might use his influence as a favorite of the king's son to help her, or Robert . . . Robert would do *something*. After all she'd risked to crown him king, he would not forsake her.

In her weaker moments, she even convinced herself that

she might have been wrong about Lachlan MacRuairi. Maybe when he heard what Edward planned to do to her, he would come for her and find a way to get her out.

She told herself these men wouldn't leave her to this horrible fate.

But no one had come for her. No one had intervened. Edward intended to make an example of her. Her husband despised her. Her brother was a prisoner, even if a favored one. Bruce was fighting for his life. And Lachlan . . . he was the one who'd put her here.

She was alone, but for her cousin Margaret, who would serve as her attendant. The one concession Edward had made to her noble blood.

The constable of Berwick Castle, Sir John de Seagrave, one of Edward's commanders in the campaign against Scotland, cleared his throat uncomfortably. He wouldn't meet her gaze. Apparently even Edward's lackey didn't approve of his king's "justice" this day.

"It's time, my lady."

The flash of panic came so hard and fast it stopped her heart. She froze like a doe in the hunter's sights. But then instinct set in, and her pulse exploded in a frantic race. She felt the overwhelming urge to run, to flee, to save herself from the arrow aimed at her heart.

Perhaps guessing her thoughts, one of the guardsmen stepped forward to grab her arm and hauled her to her feet. She flinched at his touch. Sir Simon Fitzhugh, the cruel captain of the guard, made her skin crawl with his florid, sweaty face, stale breath, and lecherous stares.

He pulled her toward the door and for a moment her body resisted. She leaned back, her feet planted firmly on the stone floor, refusing to move.

Until she saw him smile. The excited spark in his eye told her this was what he wanted. He wanted her to resist. He wanted to see her fear. He wanted to drag her across the bailey in front of all those people and see her humiliated and humbled.

The stiffness slid from her limbs as the resistance went out of her. She gave him an icy stare. "Get your hands off of me."

He flushed with anger at the haughty contempt in her voice, and Bella knew goading him had been a mistake. She would pay for her words later, when she was completely at his mercy. He wouldn't abuse her person. Though she'd been branded a rebel and found guilty of treason, she was still a countess. But he would find millions of ways to exact his punishment and make her life miserable over the next . . .

Her heart caught in another hard gasp of panic. Days? Months? She tried to swallow. God help her, *years*?

She pushed back the bile that rose in her throat, but her stomach clenched as she followed the constable out of the small room in the guardhouse that had served as her temporary prison.

The first thing she noticed on stepping outside after over a month of imprisonment wasn't the brightness of the daylight, the freshness of the air, or the vastness of the crowd gathered to watch her torment, but the sharpness of the wind and the piercing, bone-chilling cold. The heavy layers of wool she'd donned as protection felt as gossamer as the linen of her chemise.

It was freezing, and it was only September. What would December be like—January?—when she was perched high on the tower with nothing to protect her from the brutal east wind but the cold iron bars of her prison cage? A shiver ran through her.

Her tormentor noticed. "Feels like an early winter this year, doesn't it, *Countess*?" Simon sneered the last, and then pointed up in the direction of the tower. "Wonder how cozy that cage of yers will feel in the sleet and snow?"

He leaned closer, his fetid breath singeing her skin. "I might be willing to help keep you warm, if you beg real nice."

His eyes dropped to her breasts. Though she was covered to her neck in layers of thick wool, she felt unclean. As if the lust in his eyes had somehow touched her, and no amount of bathing would remove the foul stench.

She shuddered with revulsion and fought the urge to follow the direction of his hand. *Don't look.* She couldn't look. If she looked at the cage she would never be able to do this. They would have to drag her across the courtyard after all.

She swallowed the knot of fear, refusing to let him know that he'd gotten to her. "I'd rather freeze to death."

His eyes blazed, hearing the truth in her words. He spit on the ground, inches from the gold-embroidered edge of her fine gown. "Haughty bitch! You won't be so proud in a week or two."

He was wrong. Pride was all she had left. Pride would keep her strong. Pride would help her survive.

She was a MacDuff, from the ancient line of Mormaers of Fife—the highest of all Scottish noble families. She was the daughter and sister of an earl, and the disavowed wife of another.

An English king had no right to pass judgment on her.

But he had, in a particularly barbaric fashion. She was to be an example. A deterrent to the "rebels" who'd dared to support Robert Bruce's bid for the Scottish throne.

Her noble blood hadn't saved her, nor had her sex. Edward Plantagenet, King of England, didn't care that she was a woman. She'd dared to crown a "rebel" king, and for that act she would be hung in a cage on the highest tower of Berwick Castle, open to the elements so that all who passed by could see her and be warned.

Bella never could have imagined how much that one act would cost her. Her daughter. Her freedom. And now . . . *this.*

She'd wanted to do something important. To help her country. To do the right thing. She'd never wanted to be a symbol.

It wasn't supposed to be like this.

God, what an idealistic fool she'd been. Just like Lachlan had accused her. She'd been so smug. So self-assured. So bloody certain that she was right.

Now, look at her.

*No!* He wasn't right, he wasn't. She couldn't let him be. Then it would all be for nothing.

She couldn't think about the brigand. It hurt too much. How could he have done this?

*Not now.* Later, there would be plenty of time to curse Lachlan MacRuairi back to the devil that had spawned him.

She fisted her hands at her side, trying to muster strength. She wouldn't show fear. She wouldn't let them break her. But her heart drummed in her throat as she marched slowly across the courtyard.

It took her a moment to realize what was wrong. The crowd gathered to witness her punishment should be shouting, jeering, taunting, calling her names, and throwing rotten fruit and scraps of food at her. But it was deathly quiet.

The people of Scotland's once greatest market town were intimately familiar with the King of England's ruthlessness. Ten years ago, Berwick had been destroyed and its people massacred in one of the greatest atrocities committed in the long and destructive war between Scotland and England. Women, children—no one was spared in the sacking of Berwick, which had lasted for two long, bloody days and claimed the lives of thousands.

The crowd's silence was a protest. A condemnation. An admonition to King Edward of the horrible wrong being done this day.

Emotion swelled in her chest. She felt the heat of tears

burn at the back of her eyes, the unexpected show of support threatening to snap the fragile threads of pride barely holding her together.

Not everyone had deserted her.

Suddenly, she caught the flash of a movement out of the corner of her eye. She flinched instinctively, thinking someone had finally decided to throw something at her. But instead of an apple or a rotten egg, she glanced down at her feet and saw the bud of a perfect pink rose.

One of the guards tried to stop her when she bent down to pick it up, but she waved him off. "It's only a rose," she said loudly. "Does Edward's army fear flowers?"

The jab was not lost on the crowd, and she heard the murmur of jeers and snickers. Edward's knights were supposed to be the flower of chivalry. But there was nothing chivalrous about the deed being done this day.

Simon would have ripped it out of her hand, but Sir John stopped him. "Let her keep it. For pity's sake, what harm will it do?"

Bella tucked the rose in the MacDuff brooch that secured her fur-lined mantle, and then bowed her head to the crowd in silent acknowledgment of their solidarity.

The rosebud—insignificant though it might seem—gave her strength. She hadn't been forsaken by everyone. Her countrymen were with her.

But when she entered the tower, she did so alone. The sudden darkness enveloped her like a tomb. Thoughts of what awaited her closed in on her. Each step became slower, heavier, harder to make as they led her up the stairwell. It felt as if she were walking deeper and deeper into a bog, drowning, and helpless to get out.

She tried to push aside the fear, but it was nipping at her like a pack of hungry wolves.

Somehow she made it to the top. She stood in the crowded stairwell as the constable fumbled with the new lock on the door to the tower battlements. A guard would be posted as well. They weren't taking any chances of her escape.

Finally, the door swung open. The sudden gust of wind knocked her back.

*Dear God!* It was so much colder than she'd feared. Instinctively, she jerked back, not wanting to go any farther, but the guards behind her started to walk, compelling her forward onto the roof.

The wind whipped around her, nearly tearing the mantle off her shoulders. She gathered it around her, gripping it tightly, and followed the guardsmen onto the battlements.

When they stopped, she knew the time had come. She could avoid it no longer.

Slowly, she lifted her gaze to view Edward's punishment for the first time.

A startled cry emerged from her throat. She'd known what to expect, but her knees buckled all the same. There, built into the parapets, was her stone and iron cage in the shape of a cross.

But Christianity was the farthest thing from her mind as she gazed upon the monstrosity. The walls were of latticed wood, crossed by bars of iron and secured to the parapet wall with stone and iron. It was so small—so confining—no more than six feet wide by four feet deep. Good God, she'd barely be able to move around. There wasn't even a bed, only a pallet to lie upon. The single small brazier would provide little comfort against the bitter cold. A crude bench was built into one corner, and in another stood a strange wooden box . . .

Her stomach dropped, realizing what it was. She would not even be permitted to leave the cage to use the garderobe. The box was a privy.

She staggered, overwhelmed by horror. By the fear that not even her formidable will could keep in abeyance.

Instinctively, she stepped back, but her jailor was there to prevent her. "Second thoughts, Countess? I'd say it's too

late for that. You should have known better than to defy
the greatest king in all of Christendom."

Bella was ashamed to admit that as she stood there looking at the horrible cage, knowing that she had to go in and
not knowing when she might come out, she wondered if
the brute was right. At that moment her beliefs, her conviction in what she'd done, wavered under the force of fear.

But only for a moment.

It was only a cage, she told herself. She'd weathered
worse. Her husband's accusations and suspicions. Being
hunted across Scotland like a dog. Betrayal by a man she
never should have trusted. And the worst of all, the separation from her daughter.

Her daughter would give her strength. She had to survive
this to see Joan again.

She looked the foul fiend straight in the eye. "He's not
my king." And then, head high, Bella MacDuff, Countess
of Buchan, walked through the iron gate of the cage.

# One

🌿

*Balvenie Castle, Moray, Six Months Earlier*

Bella was distracted, her mind whirling with all that she had to do before she left. *The brooch!* She couldn't forget the MacDuff brooch for the ceremony.

She didn't notice the guard missing outside her door until it was too late. A man took her by surprise, grabbing her from behind as she entered her chamber.

Her heart jumped to her throat in shock and panic, immediately sensing the danger radiating from the intruder. He was big and strong and about as pliable as rock.

But she wouldn't be taken without a fight. She lashed out trying to break free, but it only made his hold clamp down on her tighter. She tried to scream, but his hand muffled any sound.

"Calm down," a rough voice whispered in her ear. "I mean you no harm. I'm here to take you to Scone."

She stilled, his words penetrating through the haze of terror. Scone? But she was to leave for Scone tomorrow. And Robert's men were to come to her in the woods, on her way back from church, not in the castle.

Her heart pounded wildly as she tried to sort it out, tried to decide whether to believe him, all the while conscious of the steely strength of the leather-clad arm wrapped tightly around her chest. Good God, the brute could snap her in two with one hard squeeze!

They stood there like that for a minute in the semidarkness, unmoving, while he waited for his words to sink in.

"Do you understand?"

The gravelly voice did little to reassure her, but what choice did she have? She couldn't breathe with his hand covering her mouth so tightly. Besides, he could have killed her already if that was what he intended.

With that pleasant thought filtering through her mind, she nodded.

Slowly—cautiously—he released her.

Once the air had returned to her lungs, Bella spun in anger and indignation. "What is the meaning of this? Who—"

She gasped at the sight of him. Though little light streamed through the tower window with night almost fallen, there was enough to know that she'd been right to fear him. He was not the kind of man any woman would want to be alone with in the dark—or in bright daylight, for that matter—and her heart gave an involuntary start.

Good God in heaven, could this man really have been sent by Robert?

Built to intimidate, he was tall, broad-shouldered, and packed with layers—and layers—of muscle. He was every inch a powerful warrior: solid, strong, and deadly.

But he was no knight. One glance told her that. He had the look of a man born to fight. Not on a steed of white, clad in mail, but a brute who liked to brawl in the dirt.

He seemed to have enough weapons strapped to his body to equip a small army, including the hilts of two swords she could see worn across his back. He wore little armor: only a black leather *cotun* and chausses studded with small rivets of steel. His mail was limited to a blackened coif to protect his neck.

But it was his eyes that stopped her. Beneath the ghastly steel nasal helm they were unnaturally vivid, the color so piercing in the darkness, they seemed to glow.

She'd never seen eyes like that in her life. A shiver ran down her spine, spreading over the surface of her skin like a prickly sheet of ice.

*Cat eyes,* she thought. *Feral* cat eyes. Chilling in their intensity and undeniably predatory.

"Lachlan MacRuairi," he said, answering her unfinished question. "I'm sorry for surprising you, Countess, but it couldn't be avoided. We don't have much time."

For the second time that night Bella was stunned speechless. Lachlan *MacRuairi*? Her eyes widened. *This* was the man Robert had sent to see her safely to Scone? A mercenary? And not just any mercenary, but a man whose exploits in the Western Isles had made him the most notorious gallowglass in Scotland. The greatest scourge of the seas in a kingdom of pirates.

Surely there must be some mistake. Lachlan MacRuairi would sell his mother to the highest bidder—if a woman could be found who would claim him. He was a bastard, but for his blood, heir to one of the largest dominions in the Western Isles. Though the clan lands had gone to his legitimate half-sister, Christina of the Isles, he was still titular chief. But he'd ignored his duty and responsibility, forsaking his clansmen, to pursue his own ends.

He was a black-hearted villain if ever there was one, rumored to have murdered his wife.

Bella was incredulous. With everything she was risking, she couldn't believe Robert had sent this . . . this . . . why, he was no more than a brigand!

She peered into the shadows, taking in the details she'd missed before. Saints preserve her, just look at him! He even looked like a brigand. She'd wager his jaw hadn't seen the side of a blade or razor in a week. A thin scar lined the underside of one cheek, and his sharp, slitted gaze was hard enough to cut rock. Below the edge of his helm, his dark hair fell in thick, disheveled waves to his chin.

What she could see of his face seemed cut from cold, hard granite. With some surprise, she realized that the hooded gaze, square jaw, high cheekbones, and wide mouth might have been considered handsome—*exceedingly* handsome even—were they not set at such a menacing angle. What a shame to have such a face destroyed by a black heart.

Their eyes met, and Bella realized that she was not alone in her study. He was watching her with equal intensity. She could feel his eyes rake her in the shadowy twilight.

The sudden flare made her uneasy, though she didn't know why. Bella was used to seeing that spark in men's eyes.

She'd been barely three-and-ten when it started. It was exactly the same time her breasts had filled, her hips had curved, and her face had lost its youthful roundness. Since then, men had looked at her differently. As if they wanted only one thing from her.

She'd learned to ignore it. But with him, it felt different. It felt threatening in a way she'd never experienced before. Her pulse spiked, and a strange flush skimmed over the surface of her skin.

Instinctively, she took a step back.

He noticed her reaction, and his gaze hardened. "Lachlan MacRuairi," he repeated, not hiding his impatience. "Bruce sent me."

"I know who you are," she said, unable to keep the distaste from her voice.

The tight seam of his mouth seemed to get a little tighter. "I know you were not expecting me tonight, but there's been a change of plans."

Bella almost laughed at the absurdity. To say that she was not expecting him was to put it mildly. What could Robert have been thinking to send such a man to her?

She was risking everything to go to Scone and place the crown upon his head. To do the duty her brother, a virtual prisoner in Edward's English court, could not.

When her mother, Joan de Clare, had first come to her with the proposition about a week ago, Bella had been dumbfounded. To place the crown on Robert Bruce's head—a man who'd been declared a rebel and an outlaw—would be to defy not only the most powerful king in Christendom, Edward of England, but also her husband.

John Comyn, Earl of Buchan, hailed from one of the most powerful families in Scotland who were the Bruces' fiercest rivals and foes. That rivalry had turned deadly a few weeks ago when Robert had stabbed her husband's cousin, the Lord of Badenoch, before the high altar of Greyfriars Monastery in Dumfries.

Even now her husband was in England demanding justice for his cousin's death from King Edward. Buchan despised Bruce and would rather see Edward as his master than Robert Bruce on the throne. He wouldn't listen to reason. The good of Scotland paled in the force of his hatred.

By doing this, her husband would never forgive her. He would consider her duty a betrayal. It would be the end of their marriage—such as it was.

But the MacDuffs held the hereditary right to enthrone Scotland's kings, and without one some would question the validity of the ceremony. As it was, Robert's claim to the throne would be contested by many of the important noblemen in Scotland, including her husband. To establish the legitimacy of his kingship among the rest, Bruce would need all the symbolism and adherence to tradition that he could find.

Even then it would be a challenge. Robert was in for a long, difficult struggle. His cause was anything but certain. Bella did not delude herself: in doing this, in aligning herself so publicly with Bruce, her future would be uncertain as well. She would be branded a rebel by the English king who claimed Scotland as his dominion.

If Robert lost, if he failed to gather enough support from Scotland's nobles, he would stand no chance against Edward. And defying Edward Plantagenet was a grave risk indeed.

Bella had looked to her mother for guidance. Though her mother had recently married one of Bruce's men, she would not be asking Bella to crown Robert for that alone. Like Bella, her mother wanted to see Scotland freed from English tyranny, and both believed that Robert Bruce was the man to see it done. Her mother's conviction in Bruce's cause was just as strong as her own. Edward Plantagenet had tightened his iron fist around the neck of Scotland, and Robert Bruce was its last breath. If anyone could do this, he could.

She had to take the risk. In many ways this was the moment she'd been waiting for throughout her entire life. A chance to do something truly important. A chance to stand up for what she believed in. Duty, loyalty, putting her needs behind the good of her family and Scotland. These weren't mere words or ideals, but something real. Something worth fighting for.

Duty had kept her by her husband's side for so long, but Buchan had never earned her loyalty. For the sake of their daughter she'd weathered his storm of jealous rage, suspicion, and obsessive lust.

To protect her daughter she might have had second thoughts, had her husband not mentioned that he was considering betrothing the twelve-year-old Joan, named after her grandmother, to one of his cronies, a man four times her age.

Bella would die before she let that happen.

Once her mother had assured her that Joan would be able to come with her, Bella had agreed.

But seeing the man he'd sent for her, she wondered what

she'd gotten herself into. If Lachlan MacRuairi was the sort of man Robert was relying on, the rebellion was doomed before it had begun.

How much had he had to pay him? She doubted there was an amount high enough to ensure the loyalty of a brigand like MacRuairi.

MacRuairi folded his arms across his chest, an impatient gesture made threatening by the massive size of his arms. Muscles like that could be earned only on a battlefield. *Many* battlefields.

"Is there a problem?"

"I was expecting . . ." She glanced into the darkness behind him, hoping to see a party of shiny, mail-clad knights rush out of the shadows.

His eyes narrowed to slits, almost as if he knew exactly what she was thinking.

"Where are the rest of the men?" she finished lamely.

Her question seemed to amuse him, if the twist in his mouth could be construed as a smile. "Waiting below."

"How did you get in here? What happened to the guard?"

"Guards," he corrected. He gave her a hard look. "I thought Buchan did not suspect anything?"

Bella almost laughed. All her husband did was suspect. Falsely—not that it mattered anymore. But she knew that Lachlan was referring to her plans to crown Bruce. "That's not why he has me watched."

He gave her a questioning look but didn't ask what she meant. She wouldn't have told him anyway.

The brigand had extinguished his pleasantries—if they could be called such—and was obviously anxious to get on with his reason for being here. He moved to the window, careful to stay out of sight but sneaking a glance at the courtyard below. "Come." He took her elbow, and every nerve ending sparked at his touch. "We have to go. There isn't much time. Fetch your cloak and anything else you wish to take with you. But be quick about it."

What was he talking about? They weren't supposed to leave until tomorrow. Nothing was ready. She'd left the evening meal early to start gathering their belongings.

Bella jerked her arm from his hold, having no wish to go anywhere with him. "I'm not going anywhere until you tell me what this is about."

She didn't think it was possible for his face to grow more menacing. He leaned closer, his eerie, piercing eyes pinning her. Green, she realized. Even in the darkness his eyes glowed like two golden emeralds in the sun.

"What this is about?" he repeated. Grabbing her by the shoulders, he thrust her toward the window. "It's about those banners in the distance just beyond the trees. In about ten minutes your husband and his men are going to ride through that gate, and if I were you I wouldn't want to be here when he arrives."

She gasped, the color draining from her face. Her eyes searched the brigand's hostile, merciless gaze and read the answer to her question: Her husband knew. Somehow, Buchan had learned of her plans.

And God help her, he was going to kill her.

Lachlan saw her blanch and almost regretted his harshness. Almost. But the way the haughty little countess looked at him, the way she flinched from his touch, pricked.

It shouldn't.

God knows he was used to suspicion and disdain—hell, it was warranted. Bastard. Ruthless. Predatory. Opportunistic pirate. Those were a few of the more flattering things he'd been called. Most of them were true. Even among the other members of the newly formed Highland Guard he was suspect.

He didn't give a shite what anyone thought. Usually. But the scorn in those big, flashing blue eyes set him on edge. Actually, a number of things about Bella MacDuff set him on edge.

*Christ.* He could still feel the bolt of lust reverberating through his body. He hadn't felt anything like that since . . .

His mouth flattened. Not since the first time he'd seen Juliana. If there was anything guaranteed to chill his blood, it was the thought of his deceitful bitch of a wife. But Juliana was no longer his concern and hadn't been for eight blessed years. She was where she belonged: in hell, tormenting the devil.

On the surface, Bella MacDuff didn't look anything like his dead wife. Juliana had been tall and slender, with delicate features, and hair as pitch black as her heart. The countess was fair, with hair the color of flax and bold features, of medium height, and curvy. *Very* curvy, if the weight of those breasts on his arm had been any indication.

Both women were attractive—beautiful even—but that was not what made them alike. It was that indefinable quality, that *je ne sais quoi* as the French called it, that stirred the blood. It was the slant in the eyes, the curve of a mouth, the raw sensuality that grabbed a man by the bollocks and didn't let go.

They were the kind of women men wanted to fuck.

Had he left it at that with Juliana, he would have saved himself a lot of trouble. But lust had blinded him to the truth about his wife until it was too late. His cock had made him a fool once. It wouldn't happen again.

"Have care with the countess," Bruce had said with an enigmatic smile. "She can be . . . distracting."

At least now he understood Bruce's warning. But the king had no cause for concern. Lust was the last thing Lachlan would ever let get in the way of a mission.

He had enough problems as it was. Their fairly straightforward job had taken a complicated turn about an hour ago when MacKay intercepted two of Buchan's guardsmen on the way to the castle to prepare for the earl's arrival.

Buchan's return by itself wouldn't have been much of a problem. They still would have been able to proceed with their prearranged plan to intercept the countess and her daughter on their way back from Sunday services—the one time the countess was certain to be permitted to leave the castle.

But Lachlan better than anyone knew that missions rarely went according to plan. MacKay had also learned from his interrogation of the riders that the earl had gotten wind of the coronation and the countess's part in it.

That changed everything. Once the earl returned, the castle would be locked up tight as a nun's thighs, and he doubted there would be any outings for the countess for months to come, even to church.

MacKay figured they had about an hour.

Lachlan had needed a quarter of that to breach the castle gate and nearly twice as long to find the countess. Leaving him with five minutes—give or take—before Gordon set off their escape.

He sure as hell didn't have time to ease his haughty little companion's misgivings about his suitability as an escort.

His harsh words, however, seemed to work a miraculous change in her manner. Fear was a powerful motivator. She raced to the ambry, pulled out a dark cloak, which she hastily tossed around her shoulders, and retrieved a small, intricately carved wooden chest from a shelf.

Lachlan's guess that it was her jewelry was confirmed when she opened the lid to reveal a sultan's treasure trove of gold and jewels. *God's blood!*

He expected her to stuff the contents in the finely embroidered purse she had tied around her waist, but instead she retrieved one item, closed the lid, and returned the box to the shelf.

Once her task was done, she turned back to him. "I'm ready."

Lachlan glanced to the box. "Is that all you're taking?"

Her eyes narrowed as if she expected him to take the box

himself. Hell, he was more than half-tempted. Jewels like that would pay a lot of debts.

"The rest belongs to my husband. This is the only piece that matters."

Spoken as only someone who'd been rich her entire life could say. It was easy to be sanctimonious when you were dressed in finery that would feed an entire village for weeks. He scanned from the thick gold circlet that secured her long, lustrous hair to the rich, gold-embroidered fabric of her surcotte, the fur-lined cloak, the heavy pearl and sapphire necklace, the slim, milky-white fingers laden with rings, and the tips of her dainty silk slippers.

He could see by the way her cheeks flushed that she knew what he was thinking.

She lifted her chin. "If you are done, we can go fetch my daughter."

Ah hell, he'd forgotten about the brat. Why anyone would insist on dragging a young girl halfway across Scotland into war, he didn't know.

But it wasn't his job to ask questions.

For three years he would do whatever task Bruce put before him—pleasant or unpleasant, it didn't matter. Though he suspected it was the latter that had helped to earn him his place among the elite warriors of Bruce's secret guard. There were other qualities—he was ruthless in battle, skilled with a blade, and unusually adept at getting in and out of places—but a man with few qualms was prized highly in war.

He did whatever it took to get the job done.

War was a cesspit. Everyone got dirty. Everyone. The only difference between him and other people was that he didn't pretend otherwise or cloak his excuses in noble causes or patriotism.

Lachlan didn't give a damn about politics. Hired swords didn't have room for convictions. It was easier that way.

He'd agreed to fight for Bruce for one reason: he had

debts to pay, both personal and financial. His agreement with Bruce would satisfy both.

He was tired of doing other people's dirty work. If all went well, he wouldn't have to again. He'd collect his reward, pay back his debts, and have enough money left to go someplace and disappear. A remote isle in the west would do fine. He would answer to no one but himself.

But for that to happen, Bruce had to be king. If Isabella MacDuff could help make that happen, Lachlan would damned well get her there. And her daughter.

"Where is she?" he asked.

The countess bit her lip. An innocent gesture that with a mouth like hers became distinctly erotic. *Christ*. Not the time to think about that soft pink mouth wrapped tightly around . . .

He felt a heavy swell in his loins and quickly shifted his gaze, annoyed by the rare lapse.

"I left her in the Hall." He could hear the anxiety rising in her voice as she sought to explain. "She was still finishing her meal. I didn't know . . ." Her voice drifted off. "I thought we had until tomorrow."

She grabbed his arm. His body leapt to attention, every muscle jumping at the contact. It felt as if he'd been hit with a lightning bolt. It was the first time she'd voluntarily touched him, but he doubted she even realized what she was doing. Her fear for her daughter had taken over.

"We can't leave without her," she pleaded, anticipating his argument. The appeal in her beautiful upturned face wasn't without effect. Big blue eyes framed by dark winged brows and sooty long lashes, a straight nose, flawless, creamy skin, a sensually curved mouth a whore would envy . . . most men would be hard pressed to resist.

But he wasn't most men.

Lachlan's mouth tightened. He wasn't one to mince words. He should tell her that the distraction that would enable their escape was between them and the Hall and was set to go at any minute. That there was one chance in twenty that they'd be able to reach the girl before all hell broke lose.

But the desperation in her voice stopped him.

Isabella MacDuff might be about to betray her husband to crown his rival, but she obviously loved her child. Since he was the last man in the world to be moved by sentiment or a pretty face and a fantastic pair of breasts, he knew there must be another reason he held his tongue: the mission. Instinctively, he realized that if he told her the truth she would put up a fight. And they couldn't afford the delay. Any delay. They'd be riding out with a perilously small head start as it was.

"One of my men will get her," he said, remembering how anxious she'd been to find someone—anyone—else lurking in the shadows to escort her. He wondered what she'd say when she discovered there were only three of them.

He even might have meant what he said . . . for a minute. But they'd barely made it outside before a blast of booming thunder shattered the evening air.

Time had just run out.


Bella cursed herself for leaving Joan behind in the Hall while she returned to their rooms to ready their belongings for the morrow. She couldn't have known, she told herself. But it didn't help ease the tide of anxiety and fear rising in her chest.

She hadn't wanted her too-curious daughter to start asking questions. It was safer for Joan—for them both—if her daughter didn't know what she planned. A stray slip of the tongue could have been disastrous.

But disaster had come anyway. How had her husband found out?

It didn't matter. All that mattered was that he had. Buchan's rage would know no bounds. After all those years of baseless accusation and suspicion that she'd betrayed him, she'd finally done something to warrant his anger.

Shuddering from the sudden chill in her blood, she followed Robert's hired sword of disrepute down the torchlit corridor, into the donjon stairwell, and out into the courtyard. She didn't ask what he'd done to the guardsmen her husband left to watch her, not wanting to know, but was grateful when they made it out of the tower without incident.

But she'd barely stepped onto the cobbled stone of the courtyard when a boom shattered her ears and shook the ground under her feet. A moment later a second boom followed and an inferno of flames lit the darkening sky.

Pandemonium broke out. People flooded out of the buildings lining the castle walls into the courtyard. She could hear women's screams. Men's shouts. The thunder of . . .

"Watch out!" MacRuairi yelled, pulling her to the side as a stampede of terrified horses tore by them.

. . . hooves. Her heart thumped at the narrow miss.

The stables, she realized. They'd set fire to the stables, and the wooden building stuffed with hay was going up like kindling.

The fire seemed to consume the night. Smoke filled the air.

*Joan!* Dear God, her daughter!

She lurched toward the Hall, but Lachlan anticipated her movement and held her back.

"The lass will be taken care of. We have to go. The guards won't be distracted for long."

The cold grip of panic clenched her heart in its icy fist. She pulled against him, but his hand was clamped down on her so tightly she didn't move. "I can't leave without my daughter."

He jerked her around harshly, his mouth pulled in a thin white line. She sucked in her breath, for the first time realizing just how dangerous this man could be. He looked every bit as mean and menacing as his reputation warned.

She should be terrified, but her skin prickled with a strange flush. In the midst of chaos, she felt the unwelcome shock of awareness. Her breath stilled. She could smell the leather of his *cotun,* the wind on his skin, and the warm spiciness of his breath. But most of all she was distinctly aware of the heat and rock-hard strength of the body against hers. A warrior's body.

Alarm flared through her like a bell. Her cheeks flushed with mortified heat. What was wrong with her? After years of feeling dead to sensation, her body decides to come alive now? To react to such a man was beyond shameful.

The hard clip of his voice brought her harshly back to reality.

"Look, Countess. If you want to get out of here before your husband arrives, we have to go now. Your daughter isn't in any danger. The flames are nowhere near the Hall. I signaled to my men as we left the tower; they are fetching the gel now."

"But—"

He cut off her protest. "Decide now. If you are getting out of here it's right now. Are you going to do this or not?"

Helplessly, she gazed back across the courtyard, wishing that her daughter would somehow materialize out of the smoke. Every instinct urged her to race into the chaos to find her. But now that the initial panic had passed, she could see that he was right. The fire was not as big as it had originally seemed and wasn't near the Hall.

She turned back to him. "You're sure your men understood? Someone will get her? They won't leave without her?"

His face hardened, but he met her gaze unflinchingly. "Aye."

Bella held his gaze, knowing that she had no reason to

trust him. Indeed from what she knew of him, she had every reason not to.

But she didn't have a choice. Her decision had been made when she'd agreed to crown Robert.

She nodded. God help her, she nodded, hoping she hadn't made the worst decision of her life.

She allowed him to drag her out of the castle gate and be herded with the stream of other terrified onlookers. The guards didn't look at them twice, too busy trying to put out the fire and catch her husband's valuable horses before they disappeared into the countryside.

The brigand pulled her along beside him toward the trees. She kept looking behind them, trying to catch a glimpse of her daughter in the crowd. Joan had been wearing red. A deep garnet gown embroidered in gold thread and pearls.

"Where is she?" she asked at one point. "I don't see her."

He didn't answer, pulling her deeper and deeper into the forest. Soon she wouldn't be able to see the castle at all.

"Stop," she said, jerking back and digging her heels into the ground. "Where are your men? Where is my—"

The sharp sounds of a whistle behind them stopped her. Lachlan returned the sound and a few moments later two men rode up behind them, leading two additional horses—one of which she recognized as her husband's.

"You have her?" one of the riders asked.

Like Lachlan, the two men were not dressed as knights and wore darkened nasal helms, padded black leather war coats studded with pieces of steel, and strangely fashioned dark plaids.

"Aye," Lachlan responded.

"Any trouble?" the other man asked.

"Nothing I couldn't handle," Lachlan said, taking the reins of one of the horses.

Bella looked around, expecting to see more men joining them. "Where *are* the rest of your men?"

The smaller of the men on horseback—the one who'd spoken first—grinned. "We *are* the rest, my lady."

Her gaze shot to Lachlan. "Then who is getting my daughter?"

His expression didn't flicker. Nothing betrayed even the barest hint of discomfort. He looked like exactly what he was: a mean, ruthless brigand.

He shrugged indifferently. "It was impossible. We didn't have time. Look," he said, pointing back toward the castle, "they've already gotten things under control. The guards are back at the gates."

But she didn't want to look. Bella felt the horror rise inside her as she realized what he was saying. What he'd done. Her eyes bit into his, and her voice shook with anger. "You *lied* to me."

Her anger had no effect on him. "I did what I had to do to get us out of there." No apology, no regret, just a calm take-it-or-leave-it explanation. "The girl is better off at the castle. Where we are going is no place for a child."

Anger surged within her like a maelstrom. How dare he! She was the one who decided how to keep her daughter safe. "That wasn't your choice to make."

"Aye, it was. It's my duty to get you to Scone."

"It's your duty to get me *and* my daughter to Scone."

His mouth tightened infinitesimally, but he seemed otherwise unmoved. While her heart was tearing apart into a thousand tiny pieces.

She glanced back at the castle, seeing the guardsmen swarming the gate. Every bone, every fiber of her being urged her to go back in there. No matter how foolish.

Joan was the most important person in the world to her. She needed her. How could she possibly leave her behind? It wasn't supposed to happen like this. She'd never intended . . .

She looked at the two other men for help but saw only pity in their eyes.

The brigand had tired of waiting. "What's it to be, Countess? Will you ride with us to Scone and keep your promise to Bruce, or will you return to your daughter and husband?"

Clearly it made no difference to him.

Bella had never despised anyone as much as she did at that moment. She heard the subtle taunt in his voice. He knew she was trapped. Even if she could ignore her duty and turn her back on Bruce and her country, she couldn't go back. If her husband got hold of her . . .

She wouldn't be able to protect her daughter from the grave.

Emotion rose inside her, burning her throat. Her eyes. Her chest. She'd been a fool to believe one word out of Lachlan MacRuairi's deceitful mouth. She wanted to curse him. To strike him. To rage at him like a madwoman.

She wanted to collapse in a ball and weep with despair.

But years of controlling her emotions were not without effect. *Never show weakness. Never give him the power to hurt you.*

As Bella forced her anger to cool, she swore that one day she would wipe that sneer from Lachlan MacRuairi's cruelly handsome I-don't-care-about-anything face.

Without another word, she took the proffered reins and allowed him to help her mount the horse.

As they rode away, Bella's back was a rigid wall of steel, giving no hint of the shattering emotions tearing her apart inside.

*It won't be long,* she told herself. Once Robert was king he would find a way into the people's hearts. Just as he had into hers.

But she wouldn't rest until her daughter was safely in her arms again.

# Two

❧

Lachlan sat on a low rock next to Gordon and MacKay, eating the simple meal of dried beef and oatcake with relish. The glare of the woman shooting daggers at his back from the rear of the cave didn't sour one bite.

He didn't give a shite what she thought. He did what he had to do to get her the hell out of there. Lying, cheating, stealing—they were all part of war. With what she was about to set in motion, she'd better damn well get used to it.

It wasn't as if she was in any position to judge. For Christ's sake, she'd just fled her husband to put a crown on his bitterest rival's head.

If Buchan wasn't such an insufferable arse, Lachlan might actually feel sorry for the bastard. He better than any man knew not to expect loyalty from anyone, especially a wife. If Lachlan needed any more reasons to never get married again—which he sure as hell didn't—this was yet another glowing example.

To hell with her. He'd done what he needed to do to salvage the mission. There had been no way to reach her daughter in time. They'd ridden barely a minute before they'd heard the thundering hooves of the approaching army. He had nothing to feel guilty about. He'd made a mission decision. Getting the job done was the only thing that mattered.

He'd do it again, damn it.

Though next time he wouldn't look at her face. Pride couldn't mask the look in her eyes when they were riding away, leaving her daughter behind . . .

He'd seen enough men being tortured to recognize it. Agony. Pure, raw, and unadulterated agony.

He bit off another piece of beef to stave off the slight tightening in his chest, even though it was too high to be hunger.

Suddenly he grimaced and reached for his skin, taking a long swig of the *uisge-beatha* to wash it down.

Gordon was watching him "Something wrong with your food?"

"Damned beef is rancid."

"Mine tastes fine."

Lachlan shrugged, taking another long drink. The liquid fire of the whisky burned away the taste of everything.

He could feel MacKay's eyes on him, but the fierce Highlander didn't say anything. He didn't need to. His disapproval rang out loud and clear.

Magnus MacKay hailed from the mountains of Northern Scotland. Tall, heavily muscled, and almost as strong as Robbie Boyd, he was one of the toughest son-of-a-bitches Lachlan had ever met, able to survive in the most varied and extreme of conditions.

About the only place he didn't seem comfortable was on a horse. Not the most graceful of riders in the best of circumstances, in the worst he seemed to hold his seat by sheer force of will. After the harrowing night of riding they'd just had—the last half of which had been in heavy rain—the countess wasn't the only one who'd needed a rest.

MacKay didn't like him, but that was hardly unusual. As long as he didn't get in Lachlan's way, they'd be fine. He sure as hell hadn't been looking for camaraderie when he agreed to join Bruce's secret band of phantom warriors.

It was an intriguing concept, he had to admit. The best warriors in each discipline of warfare joined together in one elite force. He'd already seen what they could do. But they couldn't win the war alone, and he was skeptical that knights like Robert Bruce, engrained in the chivalric code, would embrace the furtive tactics of Highlanders.

Undoubtedly they were the best men Lachlan had ever fought with. But that didn't mean he wanted them to rely on him or that he would rely on them. His wife's betrayal had taught him a hard lesson in trust that had left the men who followed him dead, himself unjustly disgraced, and his holdings forfeited. He'd turned to what he had left: being a trained killer who lived by and for the sword.

"Something to say, Saint?" he challenged, using the name MacSorley had taken to calling the big man in jest. It wasn't because of his piety. Unlike the other men, MacKay never seemed to talk about the lasses. Whereas on missions, in battle, away from home and sitting by a campfire at night, most warriors talked about nothing else. Lachlan intended to find out why.

"The countess is right," MacKay said, putting down the strange implement he'd been working on. He was always trying to come up with ways to make weapons more efficient—in other words, deadly. "We were supposed to bring her *and* the lass."

"He explained what happened," Gordon interjected before Lachlan could tell him to bugger off. "There wouldn't have been time."

William Gordon possessed a unique skill—and it wasn't just that he was one of the few men who seemed to like Lachlan. He knew how to make thunder and flying fire with the secret recipe of black powder brought back from the holy lands by his grandfather.

"Maybe not," the stubborn Highlander conceded. "But if he'd told us his plan, we might have been able to help."

"How?" Lachlan challenged. "Nothing you could have done would have changed anything. My job was to sneak us in the castle and find the lass. You and Gordon provided the distraction. I don't need you or anyone else looking over my shoulder." They would have only gotten in the way. They knew that as well as he did. "I got her out, didn't I?"

MacKay stared back at him. "Aye, you got her. But if I were you I'd watch my back for a while."

On that, at least, they could agree.

Gordon had taken off the plaid that he wore around his shoulders to blend into the night and twisted it into a thick rope between his hands, squeezing the water from the rain onto the dirt floor at his feet. "You were right about something else," he said to Lachlan in a low voice. "This is no place for a child." He shivered. "Damn, I wish we could light a fire."

They couldn't risk it. Though Lachlan hoped they'd put distance between them and Buchan, they couldn't be sure how long it would take for him to discover his wife had fled.

Realizing he no longer felt two holes burning in his back, Lachlan stole a glance toward the back of the cave and saw that the countess had taken his advice to rest while she could. They wouldn't be staying for long.

Gordon followed his eyes. "She's got a lot of courage," he said with obvious admiration. "I wonder why she's doing it?" Lachlan had wondered the same thing. "A remarkable woman."

Lachlan scoffed sharply. "I think her husband might disagree with you."

"Buchan's a belligerent arse. Almost as much of a spiteful tyrant as Edward. He's old enough to be her father, and she's . . ." His voice drifted off and Lachlan felt an irrational twinge of annoyance, knowing exactly where Gordon's mind was headed. The same place it did every time Lachlan looked at her: to his cock. Which was why he avoided looking at her. "There's something about her that's hard to put into words."

Sensual. Seductive. Cock-hardening.

Gordon shrugged, giving up. "Seems a waste on an old man. Buchan doesn't deserve such a boon."

Lachlan quirked his brow. "So youth and beauty are an excuse for betrayal?" Time to test his theory. "I hope you are as forgiving of your wife." Though he was speaking to Gordon, he was watching MacKay and saw the big Highlander still. "It's not too late to reconsider those vows, you know. You won't be married for . . ."

"No date has been set," Gordon filled in. "We were betrothed just before I left for training on Skye."

MacKay hadn't moved. Usually when the subject of Gordon's impending nuptials arose, he immediately got up and walked away.

Maybe Lachlan had guessed wrong.

"Then you have plenty of time to get out of it," Lachlan said. "Take my word for it, marriage is a black plague on the soul; a wife will only make you miserable."

Gordon was impossible to rile. He only smiled. "One bad grape doesn't sour the whole barrel of wine. Not all women are like your wife."

"Thank God," Lachlan said with a shudder. Gordon was right. Bad shite happened to everyone. He didn't dwell on Juliana's betrayal, but it had cost too much for him to forget. And it sure as hell didn't mean he ever wanted to jump back in the cesspit again.

Gordon smiled, shaking his head. "Besides, I couldn't get out of it even if I wanted to. The betrothal contract is as binding as a marriage contract. I'm honor bound to go through with it."

Lachlan made a harsh sound that was supposed to be a

laugh. "Honor has nothing to do with marriage." He fixed his gaze on MacKay again. "What's she like, your betrothed? Ugly as a sow or fair like the little countess over there?"

Gordon shrugged. "I don't know."

That surprised him. "You've never met her?"

Gordon shook his head. "It was arranged by our fathers." Both of whom, Lachlan knew, opposed Bruce. "I fostered with her brother," he added by way of explanation.

Perhaps Lachlan hadn't been wrong after all. MacKay started to get up. But Lachlan stopped him. "The Sutherlands are friends of yours, aren't they, Saint?" he said sarcastically. Gordon's betrothed was Helen of Moray, the daughter of the Earl of Sutherland, and there were few feuds longer or more intense than that between the MacKays and the Sutherlands. "Have you ever seen the bride?"

MacKay's hand tightened around the hilt of the eating knife he still held in his hand. *Interesting.*

"Aye," he said with all the enthusiasm of pulling teeth.

Gordon didn't hide his surprise. "You never said anything."

MacKay shrugged indifferently, though Lachlan suspected he was anything but. "It didn't seem important."

Lachlan sensed the weak spot and went in for the kill. "So what do you think, Saint? Is Gordon here going to need a few tankards of whisky to stomach fucking his bride, or is he going to be eager to plunge his cock between her soft, velvety thighs?"

For a moment Lachlan wondered if he'd gone too far. MacKay looked as if he might kill him. But the look was gone so quickly, he could have imagined it.

He hadn't, though.

"You're a crude bastard, MacRuairi. I don't know why the hell Bruce thought you could be a part of this team. You're poison."

Lachlan smiled. "That's exactly why he wanted me." Silent and deadly. The perfect weapon.

He would have said more, but Lachlan saw the troubled look on Gordon's face and let the subject drop.

Bella woke with a start. She looked around, seeing the unfamiliar stone walls, and for a moment didn't know where she was.

Then suddenly the memories returned, and all the despair and heartache of the night before crashed over her in a fresh, heavy wave.

*Keep her safe. Please keep my daughter safe.*

Buchan wouldn't hurt her. Not physically at least. Joan was the one good thing that was between them. Her husband's angry tirades, his jealousy, his irrational suspicions had never spilled over to their daughter.

Buchan cared for the quiet girl with the big, soulful eyes as much as he could care for anyone. Joan bore the mark of her father in her dark hair, blue eyes, and classically shaped features.

Thank God.

Her husband had accused her of many horrible things over the years, but bearing a bastard wasn't one of them.

Bella had just turned sixteen when she'd had Joan—a child still herself. She could remember sitting up in the big wooden bed, holding her babe, and waiting for her husband to come see the tiny miracle bundled in her arms.

She might have forgiven him everything at that moment. Even the brutal way he'd taken her virginity on the first night of their marriage. At fifteen she'd been too young to bed. But he was like a dog in heat and couldn't wait to rip off her clothes, to throw her down on the bed, to force her legs apart and plunge his hardened member inside her with no care for her innocence or youth.

To think before they married, she'd thought him so handsome with his dark hair and light eyes. Older, yes, but still in the prime of his manhood. He wasn't particularly tall, but he'd been a knight for over twenty years. Knighted by King Alexander himself when he was only one-and-twenty. And he was strong, with a warrior's thick, muscular body.

But she'd come to hate the physical strength that initially had attracted her. Hate the way he could dominate her so completely.

Still, she might have put aside the disappointment of her first year of marriage on the birth of their daughter if he'd shown one smidgen of kindness toward her. If he'd given one word of praise. If he'd looked at her with one hint of affection rather than possession and lust.

Instead he'd taken one look at her and said, "Perhaps I shall keep you with child. You're as fat as an old cow. No one will want you like this."

His words had killed any thoughts of happiness. From that moment on, Bella knew exactly what her marriage was: She was his whore and he was her jealous master.

She'd fought back the only way she could, by submitting to his demands with stoic indifference, as was her duty. The more he tried to humiliate her—tried to provoke a response from her—the colder she became, until she stopped feeling anything.

But the hardest part was the jealousy and suspicion. It wasn't her fault men looked at her. She dressed modestly, even severely. Arranged her hair in unflattering styles. But still he accused her of flirting. Of enticing men with her eyes and her smile.

She stopped going with him to court. Retreated to the background when other men came to visit. Kept her eyes downcast and never smiled. But he saw her efforts as furtive, accusing her then of sneaking off to meet imagined lovers.

No matter what she did, he accused. She grew tired of defending herself, and eventually stopped trying.

She dressed the way she wanted, wore her hair the way

she wanted, and talked to other men if she wanted to. She grew deaf to his accusations and learned to live in a prison of suspicion, dreaming of the day she would be free of him.

But she'd never dreamed it would come to this.

She took what solace she could from the situation in the knowledge that no matter how much her husband would hate her for what she'd done, he wouldn't take it out on their daughter.

She hoped. But what would Joan think when she learned her mother had gone without a word? Buchan could be so cruel and calculating. So vengeful. She feared her husband would try to poison the girl's mind against her. If only she'd told Joan her plans, she would know she hadn't intended to leave her.

Bella sat up and shook off the exhaustion that the short nap had done little to alleviate. It was hard to relax when she knew her husband was out there somewhere looking for her. The knot of fear in her stomach that she'd had since leaving Balvenie was her constant companion.

He would be mad with rage. The fact that it had to do with Robert Bruce would make it worse. Her threats to geld him when he slept if he ever hit her again wouldn't forestall him this time.

Glancing around, she saw William Gordon huddled against the wall by the mouth of the cave. She followed the direction of his gaze and stiffened, seeing what had drawn his attention. Lachlan MacRuairi and Magnus MacKay were a short distance away, standing in a small clearing in the trees, and from the looks of it arguing. At least MacKay was arguing. MacRuairi wore a lazy smile on his face, as if he didn't have a care in the world.

Her anger toward the brigand had not dulled any over the long, strenuous ride of the night before, and dawn brought no new light. God, she couldn't wait to be rid of him. Not much longer. The men said it would take two days of hard riding to reach Scone, which would get them there the night before the coronation.

Bella stood up and walked over to Gordon. Taking a seat on a small stone opposite him, she said, "Your friend doesn't seem to like him very much."

The young warrior broke out into a friendly smile. He was boyishly handsome, with floppy, light-brown hair, twinkling blue eyes, and straight white teeth. Under normal circumstances she would have thought him imposing, but compared to MacRuairi and MacKay he seemed far less physically intimidating.

Bella's first impression had been of an affable, good-natured sort. The kind of man who liked everyone. An impression that was borne out by his next words.

"MacRuairi? Ah, he's not as bad as he seems."

Bella resisted the unladylike urge to snort, suspecting he was much worse.

"I'm afraid he didn't get a chance to make a good first impression, but his hands were tied."

Bella waved him off. "You don't need to apologize for him. I just wonder that Robert would involve himself with a man of his ilk. Allying himself with a freebooting pirate and opportunist like Lachlan MacRuairi won't endear him to any of the other nobles. I wonder how much it cost him to buy his loyalty—or rather, his temporary loyalty."

All of a sudden, she stopped. Her skin flushed, tingling with heat, and her blood seemed to race a little faster through her veins.

Instinctively, she knew he was behind her.

"Not enough," MacRuairi said flatly. He turned to Gordon. "Ready the horses. We're leaving as soon as MacKay gets back."

The young warrior bounded off to do his bidding.

She stood up, scanning his face and seeing nothing but sincerity. "So you don't deny it?"

He met her gaze. He'd removed his helm, and in the cold

light of dawn she had to admit he was an impressive sight—
if your tastes ran to dark and dangerous brigands oozing
virility, which, humiliatingly, hers appeared to. With his
dark, wavy hair, striking green eyes, and chiseled, perfectly
aligned features, he was sinfully handsome.

Even noticing it felt sinful. Because as much as she
wanted to pretend otherwise, it wasn't an abstract observation of the sort she'd made over the years when a handsome man had been allowed near her. The spike in her
pulse, hitch in her breath, and prickle on her skin told
her that.

Good God in heaven, what was wrong with her?

Perhaps her husband had been right. One night out of his
prison, and her body was reacting like an awestruck young
girl who'd seen her first handsome knight. Except Lachlan
MacRuairi wasn't a knight, and she was a grown woman
who should know better.

It was disconcerting that she—or her body at least—
could be so shallow. No matter how objectively pleasing to
the eye, there was nothing remotely attractive about Lachlan MacRuairi.

"Why should I?" He shrugged matter-of-factly. "Money
is as good a reason to fight as any. Better than most, actually."

The man had no shame. "Do you care nothing about
what is going on around you?"

His mouth curved in a wry smirk. "Oh, I care about a lot
of things."

She nudged her chin up disdainfully. "Things that aren't
gold and silver?"

"I'm partial to land as well." His smile infuriated her,
although why, she didn't know. She wouldn't expect a man
loyal only to his purse to understand.

"Is there nothing you would fight for? Sacrifice for?
What about integrity and beliefs? What about duty and

responsibility? What about the good of your clan and Scotland?"

He laughed in a way that made her feel as if she'd just walked out of a convent. "God, you're priceless, Countess! Such passion and conviction. But let's see how well those lofty ideals of yours hold up in a month or two."

Bella fisted her hands at her side so she wouldn't give in to the childish urge to slap that condescending smirk off his face. His cynical, self-serving attitude was everything that was wrong with Scotland. "Don't you believe in Robert? Don't you think he can win?"

He shrugged indifferently. "Bruce has a chance if everything goes right. But it's a gamble against a very powerful enemy." He gave her a hard look. "Edward won't be so forgiving of those who defy him." His eyes slid over her coldly, but it seemed to have the opposite effect on her as heat spread over her skin. "Even pretty countesses."

She flushed. "I know what I risk."

If she didn't fight for what she believed in, how could she expect anyone else to? If everyone were like him, they would never have a chance to rid Scotland of Edward's grasping iron fist. Sometimes there were things bigger than yourself. This was one of them. She believed in Robert Bruce. Believed that Scotland should be freed from English domination, and that he was the man to do it.

What she was doing was right.

"Do you?" He gave her a long look. "We'll see."

He turned at the sound of an approaching rider. It was MacKay, and from the frown on his face, she could tell something was wrong.

"We've got a problem," he said.

Though not as menacing-looking as Lachlan, the gruff warrior was equally imposing. But he wasn't threatening—not in the way MacRuairi was. And he was one of the rare men who looked at her without the taint of lust in his eyes.

Lachlan swore. "Buchan?"

The big man nodded grimly. "Aye."

"On our tail?" Gordon asked, coming up and leading the horses.

"Aye, and ahead of us. He has the road blocked about a half-mile from here."

Bella tried to calm the sudden burst of panic fluttering in her chest. "But how did he find us?"

She'd directed her question to MacKay, but it was Lachlan who answered. "He knew the road we'd take to Scone. Our path wouldn't have been too hard to follow. I hoped the rain would help." He looked back to the other two men. "He must have discovered her missing right away."

A trickle of ice shivered down her spine. "So he knows where we are?"

"He's guessing we're in the area," MacKay said.

"Then we will stay off the road and go in a different direction?"

Neither of the men said anything, and her heart took another jolt of fear. "What's the problem?"

The brigand spoke first. "It isn't that easy. There's a river to the south and bogland to the north. With all the rain, it's too dangerous to try to get the horses through."

"So you chose to rest in a place where we have no escape?"

She'd directed her question to Lachlan, who, from what she could tell, was in charge. His expression didn't change, but she knew her criticism had angered him. His golden-green eyes glowed even hotter.

"I stopped because the horses needed to rest and you were about ready to fall off your horse. This cave is hidden and is the only place I knew we'd be safe in the area. It's also dry, which I assumed you'd appreciate."

Her cheeks fired, knowing he was right. "So we're trapped?"

"For now."

How could he sound so calm, when she could feel hysteria beckoning? "That's it? Don't you have a plan?"

He smiled, actually *smiled*! If she weren't so angry, she might have noticed the way his eyes crinkled at the edges. "Aye, to stay put."

"For how long?" The coronation was only two days away.

"Until he gives up, or—" He stopped.

"Or what?" she demanded, not sure she wanted to know.

"Or gets too close."

# Three

❦

It was dusk as Lachlan approached the cave. After a long day of scouting, following Buchan's men to make sure they left, he knew he should be exhausted, but his body teemed with restlessness.

Though it would have been foolish to attempt to outrun Buchan's men with the countess in tow and without extra horses, after nearly two days of waiting, he felt like one of King Edward's menagerie lions in a very small cage. Not for the first time, he wished that he'd been the one to ride ahead to warn Bruce of the delay, rather than Gordon.

There'd been no question of sending MacKay. They needed a skilled rider to sneak past Buchan's defenses. Lachlan qualified, but Bruce had put him in charge.

This was his mission, curse it.

Or what was left of it, anyway. The coronation was set for tomorrow, and they were still nearly a two-days' ride away.

He'd underestimated Buchan's resources and his determination. He must have half his men scouring the countryside for his wife. The hunt had gotten perilously close for a while, but Lachlan had chosen their hiding place well, and it appeared that the last of Buchan's men had finally moved off.

They'd wait a few hours before leaving, just to make sure.

It was almost over—thank God! He couldn't wait to have this job behind him.

The past two days had been hell, and Bella MacDuff was his own personal demon. He wished he could say it was because she was a pain in the arse: making unrealistic demands, criticizing, or otherwise complaining about their situation.

But he couldn't.

Actually, he was forced to admit that she'd adapted quite well to their less-than-luxurious accommodations. Most noblewomen he knew would have sat on a rock and expected to be waited on when not bemoaning their wretched fate. But the proud little countess had taken it upon herself to sweep out the cave, dust off the spiderwebs, and wash their meager eating supplies, offering to help—MacKay, that is, not him—whenever she could.

She might look soft and vulnerable on the outside, but she had spirit. Bold, strong, and proud, he suspected there was very little that would defeat Bella MacDuff. Hell, with what she was about to do, she was going to need that strength.

It wasn't a shrewish or demanding personality that set him on edge. What set him on edge was his own damned reaction to her. One glimpse of those substantial curves, one word from that sensual mouth, or one sniff of that sweet feminine scent and he was hit with a bolt of lust that was getting harder and harder to ignore.

The cave was too bloody small. He'd made the mistake of bumping into her once and nearly jumped out of his damned skin.

She might despise him, but his cock didn't care. The weakness infuriated him. It was as if eight years of control had caught up with him all at once.

He steeled himself for entering the cave and was about to

give the whistle that indicated his approach, when a tinkle of laughter stopped him in his tracks.

The soft, husky sound floated through the darkness, shimmering over his skin like a hot caress, setting his nerve endings on edge. Every muscle in his body went rigid. His hands fisted at his side as he fought to cool the surge of heat that had become almost reflexive when he got within fifty feet of her.

"This is delicious," he heard her say.

Even her voice was seductive. Smooth and soft as warm cream.

MacKay mumbled some reply, and Lachlan felt his anger spike, imagining the fierce warrior preening under her praise.

He took a few more steps toward the cave, enabling him to get a glimpse inside. The soft cascade of blond waves falling down her back caught the light in a golden glow. He could imagine it pouring over his skin like a warm satin veil. He wanted to dig his fingers through it. Rub his face in it. Inhale the deep, fragrant scent.

*Hell.* The cold burn was beckoning. Again.

"Who could have imagined that raw fish could be so delicious?" She used her dainty fingers to pick up another chunk from the plate MacKay had fashioned from a piece of wood plank. Considerate bastard. "What is this sauce that you've put on it?"

MacKay's mouth curved, and Lachlan felt his fists clench even tighter. "It's just some herbs and a bit of wine."

"And you found all this nearby? You are a man of most useful skills, Magnus MacKay."

Lachlan felt a hard spike of irritation. MacKay picked a few herbs and she lavished praise on him as if he'd turned water into wine. Whereas Lachlan had spent hours—days—in the rain ensuring that no one approached to kill them, and all he got was a few angry glares when she was forced to acknowledge his existence.

He didn't like this dark feeling simmering inside him. A feeling that made him want to slam his fist into MacKay's formidable jaw for no reason.

There was nothing improper about their behavior. She just seemed to genuinely like the big Highlander, which was in stark contrast to the loathing she felt for him.

Being loathed was nothing new, so why was it bothering him now?

MacKay shrugged, obviously embarrassed but just as obviously pleased. "It isn't difficult, if you know what you're looking for."

She laughed again. "But that's it, isn't it? I'd ask you to show me, but I fear I'm hopeless when it comes to discerning plants. Joan is the one—"

She stopped suddenly, and Lachlan braced himself. He felt that annoying pinch in his chest again. If he thought he was capable of it, he would think it was guilt. But he didn't waste his time beating himself up over things that couldn't be changed.

He could hear the emotion thick in her voice when she finished, "My daughter is the one who is good with plants."

The rough Highlander's voice was surprisingly gentle. "You're worried for the lass."

The countess nodded. Though her face was turned away from him, Lachlan knew her eyes were filled with tears. It was that way every time the girl's name came up.

"Buchan won't harm her?" MacKay asked, the edge of steel in his voice.

She shook her head. "Nay. At least I don't think so. But I didn't tell her what I had planned. I never told her I intended to take her with me. And I fear he'll fill her head with all kinds of horrible lies. I just wish . . ."

Her voice fell off. But then her jaw clenched, and her mouth tightened.

Lachlan wasn't the only one who'd guessed her thoughts. "I don't like him any better than you do," MacKay said, "but there was nothing else that MacRuairi could have done—or that anyone could have done—to get your daughter out in time. Not with the explosion set and your husband so close. I've seen him get out of some impossible situations, but even he'd be hard pressed to sneak a woman and a child out of a fortress like Balvenie with your husband and his men looking on."

*God damn it!* Lachlan didn't need MacKay to defend him. He strode angrily into the cave, ignoring MacKay's chastising frown for not giving the signal, and stopped a few feet away from where they were sitting.

He resisted the urge to inhale. How the hell did she still smell so good after two days in a cave? He cursed MacKay again, this time for giving her that blasted soap.

She gave him a quick glance, her eyes still watery with emotion. The annoying pinch in his chest nipped harder.

"I'm sorry," he said angrily, not knowing what in the hell he was doing. "I'm sorry we were forced to leave your daughter behind."

He swore he could hear MacKay's mouth drop open.

The countess looked just as surprised. She lifted her gaze to his again, but this time did not turn sharply away.

She studied his face. Even though he knew his expression betrayed nothing, it still made him uncomfortable. Damned uncomfortable.

"But not for lying?" she asked.

He shook his head. "Nay. I had to get you out of there. You would have protested, and we didn't have time for a delay."

"What if I didn't want to go without my daughter? Did you ever consider that?"

He gave her a hard, steady look. "Maybe you should be thanking me for not forcing you to have to make that decision."

She gasped, her eyes widening a little as his words struck with pointed precision. She'd been so angry at him for lying that she hadn't thought about what would have happened had he told her the truth: She would have been forced to choose between her daughter and keeping her promise to Bruce. All those lofty ideals of hers would have been held to the test of a mother's love.

The stricken look on her face told him that she'd reached the same conclusion.

"Try to get some sleep," he said gruffly, looking away. "The last of your husband's men left this afternoon. We'll leave in a few hours and ride straight through. I'm not sure how long Bruce will wait."

She seemed relieved by the change of subject. "You're sure William made it to Scone?"

"Aye, but I didn't think Buchan would delay us for so long. Bruce may decide waiting to become king is too risky."

She nodded, then excused herself for a few moments of privacy. He tried not to watch her as she left.

MacKay stood up from his seat and started to gather his things. He'd take the watch while Lachlan slept—or tried to sleep with her so close.

Lachlan could feel his eyes on him. Finally, the other man spoke. "Leave her alone, MacRuairi. The lass has been through enough. Buchan has made her life hell."

Lachlan stepped forward, seeing a blast of red. "What do you mean? Does he beat her?"

MacKay gave him a long look, appraising the vehemence of his reaction. "I don't know. But the lass was tormented. He kept her under guard at all times."

He supposed that explained the guard at her door and the two at the foot of the stairs. "Why?"

"Because he's a controlling bastard who wanted to keep a tight rein on his wife."

Lachlan frowned. He better than anyone knew the destructive force of jealousy. Whether warranted or not. He wondered whether it was.

He eyed MacKay suspiciously. "Why did she tell you all this?"

"She didn't. I pieced it together from some things she's said. As for why, I don't look at her like you do." He paused, the look intensifying. "Why does it matter to you?"

"It doesn't." But it put a new slant on why she would betray her husband.

Clearly, MacKay didn't believe him. "I've seen the way you look at her. She's a nice lady—a nice *married* lady—who will be in enough trouble with what she's about to do without you panting after her."

Lachlan didn't need a lecture from MacKay—or anyone else for that matter. Sure, he lusted after her. A man would have to be a eunuch not to. But Lachlan had already lost his head for one woman he'd lusted after. Once was enough.

And from what he could tell, MacKay should worry about himself. "*If* I wanted her, what makes you think a marriage contract would stand in my way?"

MacKay shot him a look of disgust as he was about to walk out of the cave. "MacLeod is right. You have the morals of a snake."

A viper, MacLeod had called him. Hell, maybe the leader of the Highland Guard was right. That's why he was here, wasn't it? Get the job done, no questions asked.

Lachlan smiled, unable to resist. "Maybe, but at least I'm not lusting after my best friend's betrothed."

He knew his arrow had struck when MacKay flinched. Lachlan watched for any sign of movement, not taking his eyes from MacKay's hands. The second he reached for a weapon, Lachlan would be ready.

Though he could sense the dark rage that had come over the other man, MacKay was too good a warrior to let Lachlan's goading get to him. "Stay out of my way, MacRuairi. Spread your damned venom someplace else."

He left the cave without another word.

* * *

Bella loved to ride. It was the one freedom her husband allowed her—albeit under the careful watch of a dozen guardsmen whose presence was not to protect her but to prevent her from sneaking off to some illicit liaison with a bevy of waiting lovers.

But after forty hours straight in the saddle—half of that in rain—she didn't think she'd ever want to see a horse again.

She'd thought she was a good rider. But forced off the roads into difficult and uneven terrain, and pushed at an unrelenting pace, she'd reconsidered. Compared to the two warriors who accompanied her, she felt like a bairn on lead-strings.

Their occasional stops, she knew, were for her benefit as much as that of the horses. MacKay had begun to show signs of weariness, but MacRuairi looked as though he could ride another forty hours.

How did a pirate learn to ride so well? The *Gall-Gaedhil* descendants of Somerled were expert seafarers, practically born in their galleys.

She glanced to the side, where MacRuairi rode slightly behind her, and instantly regretted it. Though he'd averted his gaze the moment she turned, it wasn't before she'd caught a glimpse of the look in his eyes. It was hot, intense, and fierce. Lust in its most raw and primitive form.

It startled her, and she had to smother the sharp gasp that rose in her chest. Though she pretended not to notice, her insides felt singed by the blast of heat, her stomach fluttered nervously, and she felt a tickle of heated awareness in a place that she shouldn't.

It wasn't the first time she'd caught the edge of one of those looks. He wanted her, but he didn't want her to see it. He was like every other man that looked at her with one thing on his mind. He just controlled it better.

Bella had been the subject of one man's frenzied lust already; she didn't need another. From the first, her lack of response had angered her husband. It was almost as if he thought he could force a response from her with his increasingly base demands. No matter what he asked of her, or what he did to her, she refused to be cowed, refused to give him the satisfaction of shame.

Only later did Bella realize he'd actually thought he could force her to feel pleasure. When she didn't, he blamed her, accusing her of being unnatural and cold.

Ironically, one smoldering look from Lachlan MacRuairi had elicited more response from her than any of the things her husband had done to her.

As disconcerting as her reaction was to him, she was pleased to see that he seemed just as eager to ignore it as she was. Apparently, she wasn't the only one who couldn't wait for this journey to be over.

They rode for a few more hours, the men taking turns riding ahead and behind. They rode until she didn't think she could go on.

She shifted in the saddle. He must have been watching her again because he said, "We'll stop up ahead to water the horses. We should be on the outskirts of Scone in a few hours."

The relief that she felt on hearing that not only would they be stopping, but that her ordeal would soon be over, pushed aside everything else. Forgetting whom she was speaking to, she heaved a heavy sigh and smiled. "Thank God!"

He looked momentarily stunned, confused even.

It was the first time she'd ever smiled at him. Actually, it was the first time she'd ever looked at him with anything other than suspicion or anger.

She realized it at the same time he did.

Their eyes held for an instant too long before she looked away, feeling oddly self-conscious and extremely aware that they were alone.

His voice when he spoke seemed unusually cautious—as

if he were taking care not to upset this tentative truce. "I think we will all be glad when this is over." His eyes found hers once more, and she felt that strange buzz go through her. His eyes were . . . *intense.* Piercing, nay, riveting, they were so crystal clear, so vibrant in color that they didn't seem real. "You've held up well, my lady. I regret having to push you so hard, but if there is to be any chance of reaching Scone in time, it's necessary."

Bella was just as taken aback by his second apology as she had been by the first. Lachlan MacRuairi seemed to be the last man who would apologize for anything, and she didn't quite know what to make of it.

She didn't quite know what to make of *him.*

She was forced to admit that he was right about one thing. He'd saved her from having to make a horrible decision in choosing whether to leave her daughter. He'd still lied to her, and she knew better than to trust him, but maybe he wasn't quite the heartless brigand she'd first imagined him.

Heartless brigands didn't cover you with a plaid at night when you were sleeping in a dry cave while they spent hours in the cold rain. When she'd woken yesterday morning, warm and cozy, she'd recognized the dark blue and gray plaid right away as the one he wore around his shoulders. But it didn't explain how—or why—it had ended up on her.

It was also hard not to admire the cool efficiency with which he did his job. Except for short breaks, he'd taken the lion's share of the watch, sleeping little and spending hours on end in the cold and rain. When one of the horses had gotten loose and wandered into a bog, it had been Lachlan who'd gone in after it, spending over an hour in the bone-chilling, foul-smelling muck.

She wondered what had made him so cynical. Could he really care so little about everything? He was a mystery, and she couldn't help but feel mildly curious. She frowned. Nay, very curious.

"Do you think they'll wait?" she asked, returning to what she *should* be thinking about.

He lifted a brow. "Do you want them to?"

The question took her aback. After all she'd gone through to get here, of course she should want to see it through. But after days of being hunted by her husband's men, she wondered if she was prepared for what was to come.

Realizing that her thoughts were sliding dangerously toward MacRuairi's earlier warnings, she drew herself up and met his gaze. "Of course I do."

It wasn't just her duty, it was the right thing to do. Robert Bruce was not only the best chance Scotland had of being free from English tyranny, he was the one man who just might be able to unite Scotland behind him. She would do her part to help that happen. It was her chance to do something important.

She was worth more than a pair of spread legs to sate a man's lust.

He dismounted, tied his horse to a tree, and then helped her down.

She did everything she could not to notice the feel of his hands on her waist. She wished Magnus were here instead. He didn't make her feel so . . . jittery.

Magnus looked at her like a friend.

MacRuairi looked at her like he wanted to strip her clothes off and lick every inch of her.

The thought should disgust her. Instead it made her pulse quicken and her skin flare with heat. Whatever this feeling was, it seemed to be growing more persistent and demanding, and she didn't like it.

"Will Magnus know where to find us?" She could hear the slight breathiness in her voice.

A dark look crossed his face at the mention of the other man's name. He released her so suddenly, she wobbled, her legs feeling like jelly after the long ride. "Aye. He'll find us. Be ready to go when he does."

He dismissed her with a curt nod and began to tend to the horses.

She frowned, watching him, wondering what she'd done to spark his anger. For a moment they'd actually been conversing normally.

She removed a few items from the pack tied to her saddle and started to walk down to the edge of the loch.

"Where are you going?" he asked.

"To wash." When he seemed about to argue, she cut him off. "I'm not going to crown Scotland's next king looking like a beggar woman."

He narrowed that eerie slitted gaze on her. "Be careful. Stay where I can see you."

Bella was glad her back was already to him so he couldn't see her blush. She intended to get good and clean and had no intention of letting him watch.

She quickly tended to her more pressing need, and after a quick glance around, removed her clothing. Gritting her teeth, she jumped into the freezing loch.

She was in and out in no more than two minutes, washing her hair as best she could with the thin sliver of soap MacKay had given her, and then using a cloth to scrub as much of her skin as she could reach.

"Countess!"

She winced; he sounded furious.

"I'm here," she said, frantically rubbing her hair with a fresh cloth and then drying herself as best she could with the now-sopping toweling. "Just give me a minute."

Her body wracking with shivers, she reached for her chemise. But before she could slip it over her head, someone grabbed her from behind.

The fleeting thought that it might be MacRuairi was gone the instant she inhaled. For a brigand, MacRuairi seemed to have an unusual penchant for cleanliness. He always smelled . . . nice. Warm and leathery, with a subtle masculine spice. This man smelled like sweat and stale onions.

Dear God, she'd been captured!

Her blood ran cold, and terror jumped inside her, her senses sharpening with awareness.

She was painfully aware of her nakedness, but her first impulse was escape. She tried to kick and scream, but the man had his hand over her mouth and his other arm locked around her waist as he dragged her deeper into the woods.

"Don't make it harder on yourself than it already is, my lady," he warned in a harsh whisper. "The earl is eager to see you." He laughed. "Though I wager he'll be surprised to see so much of you." Bella stilled, hearing something in his voice. She knew it wasn't a mistake when his gauntleted hand slid up to squeeze her breast.

An entirely different kind of fear ran through her.

"Oops," he whispered. She tried to wrench away from his disgusting touch, but it only made his hand squeeze harder. "I can see why your husband is so anxious to get you back. I've never seen tits like these. If you weren't married to Buchan, I'd take my reward right now."

Suddenly, she jerked toward the sound behind her. Her heart dropped, hearing the unmistakable clang of steel on steel.

Her captor had heard it as well. "After the rest of my men take care of the rebel, you can scream all you want."

*Oh God, Lachlan!* The pang in her chest was surprisingly strong.

He wasn't the man she would have chosen to escort her, but the thought that he was fighting for his life—or possibly already dead—right now proved . . . distressing. Suprisingly distressing.

Bella went slack, as if the fight had gone out of her. Even if MacRuairi couldn't help her, she had no intention of allowing this man to take her back to her husband. She would fight until she couldn't.

Her apparent submission worked. That, and the fact that the forest had suddenly gone quiet resulted in her captor loosening his hold.

She had her opportunity and took it. She bit down as hard as she could on his meaty hand, stomped her heel on his instep, and thrust her elbow deep into his beefy belly.

Caught unaware, he let go with a grunt, more from the shock than the force of the blows.

She lunged toward the nearest gap in the trees, knowing she had only a few seconds before he recovered.

"You little bit—"

The rest of his curse was cut off by a sickening thud.

She chanced a glance behind her and saw him teetering like a big oak tree about to fall, the hilt of a dagger protruding from his neck.

Before he'd hit the ground, MacRuairi emerged soundlessly from the trees. He bent over the dying man, pulled out the dagger, and drew it across his throat with cool efficiency, putting a decisive end to the threat.

His gaze found hers through the filter of leaves, branches, and bracken. "Are you all right?" His voice was surprisingly thick. It made her feel the strange urge to cry the way she had as a little girl when her mother asked her the same thing after something horrible had happened.

Her throat tight with emotion, she could only nod.

"It's safe now; you can come out."

The rush of relief that hit her was so profound that Bella felt tears spring to her eyes. She stepped into the clearing.

He took one look at her and went as rigid as stone. She'd forgotten she was naked until that moment. His eyes never left hers, but she sensed he saw everything.

Still, she would have run to him. Done something incredibly foolish and launched herself into the warm solidness of his chest and arms, wanting nothing more than to feel safe. But the look in his eyes stopped her.

If she thought she'd seen him angry before, it was clear she hadn't. His mouth was white, his jaw was clenched in a tight line, and his eyes were as cold and hard as chips of green ice. She could see his hand squeezing around the hilt of the dirk he still held. Every muscle in his body seemed drawn up tight, rigid with rage. She couldn't look away from the muscle flexing ominously below his jaw.

There was something infinitely more dangerous about his cold control than the hot rage she'd met with before.

What was wrong with him?

She shrank back, but in two long strides he was at her side.

Taking her by the elbow, he hauled her up against the hard muscular wall of his chest. Heaven help her, she felt every ridge, every plane, every hard shard of muscle. Her heart pounded, not just with fear.

"If you'd wanted a man to help you bathe, you only had to ask." She gasped, shocked by his accusation. "I told you not to leave my sight." He was shaking her. "Why did you sneak away? What did you think you were doing?"

A ball of tears rose in her throat and burned behind her eyes. She didn't understand why he was so angry. He sounded just like her husband. Yelling at her. Accusing her. Bullying her. "I just wanted to get clean. I didn't think—"

"You didn't think at all. God damn it, don't you know what could have happened? You could have been killed!"

He shouted the last, the sound lingering in the thick forest air. It seemed to shock him out of his rage.

He dropped her as if scalded.

They stood there staring at each other in silence for a long heartbeat. Her chest rose and fell with the unevenness of her breath. He didn't appear to notice, but to her shame, her nipples tightened and her breasts filled with a strange heaviness. He flinched as if with pain, but recovered quickly.

When he spoke, his voice was once again even and dispassionate. Indifferent. Not laced with . . . fear? Nay, it couldn't have been fear. Fear would mean he cared. But Lachlan MacRuairi was incapable of caring about anyone.

"Next time, do what I say and there won't be any problems."

Angry tears pricked her eyes. How dare he try to blame this on her! She hadn't wandered off and gotten herself captured. Those men had obviously been lying in wait for them. They would have taken her whether she'd been in his sight or not. "Maybe if you do your job a little better there won't be a next time."

She regretted her words before they'd left her mouth. It was just as unfair to him as his anger had been to her. He'd been protecting her, not scouting ahead for danger. MacKay had been scouting, but they'd anticipated being followed, not having men waiting ahead of them this close to Scone.

He cocked a brow. Rather than anger him, her remark seemed to have impressed him. "Keep up that spirit, Countess. You're going to need it."

Her mouth clenched. She hated when he talked to her like that. As if he knew something she didn't. The cold, calculating mercenary to her naive idealist. It was easy to be cynical when you didn't believe in anything.

Her fists balled at her side, resisting the urge to slap that mocking look off his face. "Go to hell, MacRuairi."

He laughed. "You're too late, Countess. I've already been there." His eyes dipped infinitesimally, his expression as hard as ice. "For Christ's sake, put some clothes on."

If he meant to shame her with her nakedness, it didn't work. She'd lost her modesty long ago. Her husband had forced her to stand before him naked for hours, commenting about every inch of her body, touching her, telling her in crude detail what he wanted to do to her, trying to humiliate and force some emotion from her. She was invulnerable. These naked breasts, hips, and limbs weren't her. MacRuairi didn't see her at all.

Refusing to shrink from the scorn in his voice, Bella held her head high and walked—not ran—back to the edge of the loch. She could feel his gaze on her as she dressed, but when she glanced at him, his face was a stony mask.

When she'd finished, she followed him back to the horses in silence. Everything, it seemed, had been said.

But when she saw the half-dozen men he'd killed—single-handedly—she stopped with a horrified gasp.

He mistook her shock for condemnation. "War, Countess, in all of its vivid color. Get used to it—you'll be seeing a lot more."

She slammed her mouth shut, having been about to thank him for what he'd done to save her. Why bother? He would probably only yell at her again or taunt her with that barbed tongue of his.

Even if at times it seemed differently, Lachlan MacRuairi was a mean, vicious scourge, and she'd do well to remember it.

But she finally understood why Robert had hired him. She might question his loyalty, but a man who could kill so effectively was a valuable addition to any army.

MacKay caught up with them about an hour later, but she and MacRuairi didn't speak again.

When they finally arrived at the Scone Abbey, it was to the disappointing news that the coronation had taken place two days before, on the Hill of Credulity. But their disappointment was short-lived. A second ceremony was being held—a secret ceremony set amongst the ancient stones of the Druids. If they hurried, they might make it.

With MacRuairi leading, the three raced across the countryside, traveling the short distance east from Scone Abbey through Scone Wood to the circle of stones. The setting chosen by Bruce for the ceremony did not surprise her.

Edward had stolen Scotland's famous Stone of Destiny, the traditional seat upon which its kings were enthroned, ten years before. The Druids' stones were a link to Scotland's past, and a symbol—just as she was—of the strength and continuity of the realm.

The haunting drone of the pipers drifted through the wind, stirring the soul, as they crested the hill and the stone circle came into view. Bella sucked in her breath, awed by the sight before her. Golden rays of sunlight streamed like fingers between the mysterious stones, as if the hand of God himself were reaching down from heaven to bless this sacred event.

Robert stood before the largest stone, magnificently attired in his royal vestments. Only a handful of witnesses were gathered around him. She recognized William Lamberton, Bishop of St. Andrews, at his left, but not the formidable-looking warrior to his right. As they came to a stop, she noticed Christina Fraser among the gathering of warriors lined up before him.

Ignoring MacRuairi's attempt to help her down—and the resulting look of fury on his face—Bella hopped off her horse and hurried toward Robert. "Your Grace," she said, with a curtsy. "I came as soon as I could. I hope I am not too late?"

She couldn't resist the pointed look at MacRuairi, nor the resulting satisfaction when his mouth tightened.

Robert gave her the broad, brotherly smile that had earned her eternal loyalty all those years ago. "Nay, Bella, not too late. Never too late. Not when you have risked so much to be here."

Bella smiled back at him. She might never want to see Lachlan MacRuairi again, but at least he'd done his job. He'd gotten her here in time.

A short while later Bella stood opposite Scotland's last hope, the man she believed in with all her heart, and listened to the bishop recite his descent from the great King

Kenneth MacAlpin, the first King of Scots, establishing Robert's lineage and right to the throne. When the bishop had finished, Bella stepped forward—the MacDuff brooch displayed prominently on her cloak—to take her place in history, claiming the hereditary right held by her family: the right to crown a king.

The bishop handed her the crown. The weight of responsibility felt heavy in her hands; she knew the import of what she was about to do.

But when the moment came, Bella did not pause or hesitate. Hands steady, she lifted the circlet of gold high in the air, letting the sun catch it in a halo of blazing light before setting it upon Robert's head. With the full force of her ancestors behind her and the absolute certainty in the righteousness of the cause for which she'd defied a husband and a king, Bella repeated the words that had been said two days earlier, *"Beannachd De Righ Alban."* God Bless the King of Scotland. The words might be the same as those said at the first ceremony, but there was one important difference: this time they'd been said by a MacDuff.

Bella felt a wave of relief crash over her. It was *done*. There was no going back.

Her duty done, she stood to the side, watching as the witnesses came forward one by one to bow before the king. When it was Lachlan's turn, she stiffened, instinctively bracing herself. It didn't help. The brigand shot her a glare, then lifted a brow with a cynical smirk.

She flushed, feeling the heat of anger spread over her skin. Damn him, she knew what she was doing.

But whatever events this day set in motion, she was glad it was over. She was even more glad that she would never have to see Lachlan MacRuairi again.

# Four

❧

"Never" came four months later.

With all that had gone wrong—and so much had gone wrong—Bella could never have dreamed it would come to this. Fleeing for their lives like . . . outlaws. King Hood, the English called Robert. It was painfully true.

She gazed at her terrified cousin Margaret's big blue eyes, wide in her pale face. "You're sure, Margaret? The queen said we are to leave the king and the rest of the army?"

Margaret nodded, tears streaming down her cheeks. "She told me to gather our things. We'll depart within the hour."

The fear in her cousin's face was palpable. Not for the first time, Bella regretted taking Margaret as her attendant. The timid, sweet lass wasn't suited for this.

*No one* was suited for this.

Over the past month they'd seen more war, death, and blood than she wanted to see in a lifetime.

The fragile support Robert had built in the months after the coronation while Edward mobilized his forces to march against the "rebels" had collapsed after the devastating defeat at Methven. In agreeing to meet the English at Methven, Robert had been looking for vindication. Instead he'd met trickery, when Aymer de Valence set aside the rules of chivalry and attacked before the agreed-upon time for battle.

The gamble for the decisive victory that would establish Robert's kingship had failed miserably and disastrously. The king's remaining supporters had been sent reeling, forced to take refuge in the hills of Atholl while trying to recover and rally more men to his banner.

But few heeded the call. Before Methven, Robert's support had been tenuous at best. More than half the country had aligned against him with her husband and many other powerful nobles. After Methven, even those sympathetic to Bruce were too scared to stand against Edward's fury and the promise of retribution. Simon Fraser's capture and subsequent execution in a hideous manner similar to Wallace's reminded them all of the consequences.

Bella, Queen Elizabeth, Robert's daughter Marjory by his first wife, and two of his sisters, Christina and Mary, had been forced to take refuge along with them. For the past month they'd been living off the land like outlaws, in hastily constructed huts surrounded by a simple wooden palisade in the woods near the banks of Loch Trummel, sheltered by Duncan the Stout, the Chief of Clan Donnachaidh.

Yesterday, with the hunt closing in from the English in the east, Robert had tried to push westward. But he'd found his path blocked at Dal Righ by John MacDougall, Lord of Lorn, and one thousand of his clansmen. With the few hundred of his remaining men, the king had fought them back, barely escaping with his life. One of Lorn's men had him in his grasp, literally ripping the cloak from Robert's shoulders, taking his brooch along with it.

Now, even their temporary shelter couldn't protect them. They were fleeing again.

Thank God, Joan wasn't here. MacRuairi had been right: This was no place for her daughter.

It turned out he'd been right about a number of things.

She'd vastly underestimated King Edward's fury at his re-
bellious "subjects." The full force of his hammer had come
down upon them. Even she had a price upon her head.

And now, the infamous "dragon banner" had been
raised. The flag promised no mercy for the rebels. They
could be killed without trial and raped with impunity.

She smothered a shiver of fear and turned back to consol-
ing her cousin, pushing aside thoughts of Lachlan MacRuairi.
She'd heard little of the brigand since the coronation—not
that she'd been listening for word of him. With the way the
war had been going, the opportunistic pirate had probably
changed sides already.

She clenched her jaw. The only thing she should be thinking about was getting to safety so that she could find a way
to get her daughter back. Four months seemed an eternity.
But at least Joan hadn't been forced to marry. Bella's "treason" had taken care of that threat.

She stroked her cousin's hair, as the terrified girl wept on
her shoulder.

"What will become of us?" Margaret sobbed. "How will
we make it to Kildrummy with only a handful of men to
protect us?"

Bella didn't say anything. What could she say, when she
didn't know? The king sending the women away with only
a small band of knights to protect them sounded terrifying
to her as well.

Her cousin lifted her head, eyes red-rimmed and swollen.
"I've never even heard of the man who will be leading us.
Lachlan Mac . . . Mac—"

Bella stiffened. "MacRuairi?"

Her cousin nodded furiously. "That's it—do you know
him?"

Her mouth fell in a grim line. "He was one of the men
who brought me from Balvenie."

In the months of frustration and forced separation from
her daughter—her husband had dared her to try to come

and fetch her—Bella had told her cousin most of what had happened. The heartbreak hadn't lessened; it had only grown worse as each day of their separation passed. She dared not ask herself when she would see her daughter again; the answer was too painful to contemplate.

But at least Joan knew Bella had not intentionally left her behind. A few weeks after the coronation, Robert told her that a message had been taken to her daughter. He wouldn't tell her the details but assured her Joan had been told everything. Bella had been touched by the king's thoughtfulness.

Margaret gasped. "The one who lied to you about Joan?"

She nodded, and her cousin looked appropriately horror-struck.

Bella couldn't believe it either. Not only was the king sending them away, he was entrusting his family to a man who made no qualms about being loyal only to his purse. MacRuairi's untrustworthiness wasn't her only objection. After their last meeting, she didn't want to have to rely on him again for her safety—or for anything, for that matter. And perhaps most significantly, she didn't like her own reaction to him.

Lachlan MacRuairi made her uneasy.

"Don't worry, cousin, I'll speak to Robert and get to the bottom of this. There must be some mistake."

Leaving Margaret with the task of gathering their meager belongings, Bella went in search of the king.

He wasn't at the King's Hall—how the army had taken to referring to the royal hut. After Queen Elizabeth confirmed Margaret's story, she directed Bella to the banks of the loch where what was left of the king's army camped.

Bella hurried to the loch. But the sight that met her only increased her anxiousness. What was left of the army was in disarray. Perhaps only two hundred men remained, many of them wounded and bleeding, some with limbs barely attached, lying on the ground where they'd collapsed or been dumped after yesterday's retreat.

The stench was horrible. She covered her mouth to try not to retch. She should be used to it. But the scent of blood, sweat, and other bodily fluids simmering together in a sickly mess was something she didn't think she'd ever get used to.

Men were rushing everywhere. Tearing down tents. Packing their belongings. They didn't notice her. Or if they did, they were too busy to care. The army was disbanding, fleeing for their lives. Sweet Mary, how could this have happened?

Finally, she caught sight of Edward Bruce. She didn't much like Robert's younger brother. Quick-tempered, volatile, and arrogant, Sir Edward was nearly his brother's equal on the battlefield, but he lacked Robert's gallantry and natural chivalry.

"The king," she asked. "Where is he? I must speak with him."

Edward's eyes slid over her. Though the hard, ebony-like gaze betrayed nothing, she sensed the crude thoughts. "He's busy. What do you need? Perhaps I can give it to you?"

Her eyes narrowed, hearing the suggestion in his words if not his tone. She knew what was being said. The vicious lies started by her husband as a basis for setting her aside had spread even through their own camp. That Edward Bruce would even hint at Buchan's lies infuriated her. He should know better.

"I need *the king*," she said in a tone that suggested a substitute—especially a younger brother—would not do. She knew how sensitive Edward was to comparisons to his royal brother. "It's *important*."

He gave her a scathing look; her jab had struck. "He's over there." He pointed to a circle of men standing apart from the rest near the shieling that was housing the king's precious few war horses. "But I'd wait until he's done."

The king looked to be in an important meeting. She recognized some of Robert's most trusted knights: Sir Neil Campbell, Sir James Douglas, the Earl of Atholl, and a few others, including William Gordon and Magnus MacKay.

Though the sight of the last two men always pleased her, and she'd enjoyed speaking to them when their paths had crossed over the past few months, something about their place in the king's army confused her. For ordinary men-at-arms, they seemed to keep unusually important company.

She often saw them with a few other men, including one who seemed unusually close in the king's confidence: a West Highland chieftain from the Isle of Skye named Tor MacLeod.

Something about these men stood out. Not just their impressive size and strength—Highlanders were a tall, muscular lot—but the command and air of authority that surrounded them.

They ate with the other regular men-at-arms, barracked with them, and fought beside them, but then they would disappear for days, even weeks, on end without explanation. It was odd.

She followed Edward's advice. Fortunately, she didn't have long to wait. The meeting broke up a few minutes later, and the men started to disperse. All except for one.

She felt a strange shock reverberate through her. Her heart pounded hard in her chest. Lachlan MacRuairi hadn't changed in the months since she'd seen him last. If anything, he only looked more disreputable. His hair was longer, his jaw more stubbled, his black leather *cotun* dustier and stained with blood, and he appeared to have added a few weapons to the armory already strapped to his back.

His face, too, looked leaner and harder.

But if anything, it only added to his dangerous appeal.

Her mouth pursed with annoyance. Obviously, some things hadn't changed. The brigand was still a handsome devil who exuded some kind of base masculine virility. And if the erratic race of her heart meant anything, she still no-ticed it.

She needed to put a stop to this. Set-aside wife or not, her inexplicable attraction to Lachlan MacRuairi was wrong. She'd had enough trouble in her life; she didn't need any more from a notorious pirate bastard who looked at her as if all she was good for was what she could do to pleasure him. And she knew exactly how to do that. She'd been in-structed well.

She crossed the clearing, weaving through the chaos, and approached the shieling from the side. Unsure whether to interrupt, she hoped to catch Robert's attention, but the two men were too busy arguing to notice her hovering nearby. She didn't mean to listen, but they weren't exactly keeping their voices low.

"Find someone else," Lachlan bit out. "Put Douglas or Atholl in charge. I'll serve you better in the west with Hawk."

Bella frowned, wondering who this Hawk was, until she realized what he was saying. Then, were the situation not so dire, she would have smiled. MacRuairi was doing the objecting for her. He didn't want to lead them.

"I decide how you should serve me, not you. Are you refusing my orders?"

Bella stilled, watching Lachlan's reaction to the king's challenge. His jaw clenched so hard his mouth turned white, and his eyes sparked with defiance. He held very still. Almost too still. Like a coiled snake ready to strike.

She could hear the grudging tightness in his voice when he replied. "Nay, I'm not refusing. I'm asking you to recon-sider. This isn't what I signed up for."

What, duty and responsibility? She shouldn't be sur-prised. A man who ignored his own clan was hardly a leader.

But as menacing as MacRuairi could be, Robert Bruce was one of the greatest knights in Christendom and not a man to back down from anyone—even a mean, overly muscular cutthroat. "This is exactly what you signed up for. Why do you think I want you in charge?"

The two men stared at each other for a long moment. Bella could practically feel the tension crackling between them.

Finally, Lachlan nodded. "I'll ready the horses."

Bella watched in frustration as he ducked into the shieling. It would have been nice if he could have convinced Robert, but it was going to be up to her to make him see reason.

The king started walking toward her and was so distracted that he might have walked right by her had she not stopped him.

"Sire, a word if you please."

He glanced up and saw her. The hint of a smile attempted to break through the mask of strain. Her heart clenched with sadness, seeing the change that had come over him.

Robert Bruce looked like a man who'd suffered defeat. Who'd nearly been killed—twice. Who'd seen countless friends die at his side. He looked like a man who was being hunted and knew there was no safe place left to hide.

Bella felt the tears gather in the back of her throat. As long as she lived, she'd never thought to see such dejection on Robert Bruce's face.

She'd been a girl no older than Joan the first time she'd met the handsome, young squire who'd come to train with her father. Even at ten-and-seven, he'd seemed larger than life. Gallant and charming, he'd tweaked her nose and told her she'd be trouble some day. Spirit to spare, he'd said.

Little did he know she'd need every ounce of it when she'd married.

Robert was the only man who'd ever made her think her opinions mattered. He was like the older brother she'd always wanted. Patient. Interested in what she had to say. Kind. And most of all, a fierce protector.

In those months he'd spent with them before her father's death, he'd saved her from countless beatings at her father's hand. Bella's father was a cruel man with a volatile temper, prone to striking her whenever she displeased him—which was frequently. But Robert had an uncanny ability to distract him. To turn his attention from the awkward girl who'd dropped the bread, or dribbled her soup, or laughed too loud.

When some of his kinsmen had murdered her father, she'd been heartbroken. Not in mourning the death of a man who'd seemed a tyrannical stranger to her, but because she knew it meant Robert would have to leave.

She'd seen little of him once she was married, until a few years ago when they were both in London. Her face darkened at the humiliating memories. It was the one time her husband had struck her. He'd caught her and Robert in the garden talking and saw their friendship as something else. She loved Robert like a brother, and now as a loyal subject loved her king, nothing more. But her husband had tried to make it into something illicit.

"Is it true, Robert? Are you sending us away?"

The sadness in his eyes broke her heart. "Not sending you away, Bella, giving you a chance." When he saw her questioning look, he explained. "They'll follow me."

Of course. He hoped to draw their enemies away, giving the women a chance to escape. Even now, he was still trying to find a way to protect them.

"Nigel is holding Kildrummy," he said, referring to his youngest brother. "You should be safe there for a while. But if the English get too close, I've instructed Vi—" He stopped himself. "MacRuairi to take you to my sister, the queen, in Norway."

He noticed her expression, but put up his hand to cut her off.

"I know you don't like him, but he spent many months in Norway in his youth." It didn't surprise her. Of the *Gall-*

*Gaedhil* half-Norse, half-Gael descendants of Somerled, which included the MacDougalls, the MacDonalds, and the MacRuairis, the MacRuairi branch was the most closely aligned with the Norse. "He knows it, and if need be, he can get you there. You know how these West Highlanders are in their galleys."

Pirates were excellent seafarers, but that didn't mean she wanted to entrust her life to one. "It's not that I don't like him," she explained. "I don't trust him."

Robert studied her face, his expression darkening. "Is there something you haven't told me, Bella? Did he do something to offend—"

She shook her head furiously, cutting him off. "Nay, it's nothing like that." A few heated looks didn't signify. No matter how they affected her.

"Then is it his skills you object to?"

She shook her head again, recalling the half-dozen men littered on the forest floor. She could hardly complain of that. "It's his loyalty that I question. How can you be certain of his allegiance? The man is little better than a brigand."

His mouth curved, the first sign of amusement she'd seen on his face in a long time. "Aye, he is that. But you have nothing to fear, Bella. If MacRuairi says he'll do something, he does it. It's getting him to agree that can be tricky."

The distinction did little to reassure her. "Please, Robert." She put her hand on his arm, her cheeks pinkening. "I couldn't help but overhear . . ." She bit her lip. "He doesn't want to go with us either. He's forsaken his own clansmen; what makes you think he can lead us? Isn't there someone else who could take us?"

Robert shook his head. "I've made my decision, Bella. I'm not asking you to trust him, I'm asking you to trust me."

She did trust him. Even with everything that had happened, she believed in him. Her conviction in that had not wavered. Scotland had lost its champion, and its hope for freedom.

"Of course I do." She bowed her head in acquiescence, tears shimmering in her eyes as everything that had been lost, and everything that might have been, came crashing down on her.

"Go then, lass, get your things. There isn't much time. The Lord of Lorn will be hunting us."

A hot lump seemed stuck in her throat, knowing this was goodbye. "Where will you go?" *What will you do?*

The haunted look returned to his eyes. "We'll make for the coast. I have friends in the west. We'll rebuild. Gather more troops and try again."

Neither of them believed it. Robert Bruce's cause was lost. He'd be lucky to make it out of Scotland with his life.

The tears began to fall. "Goodbye, Robert."

He pulled her into his arms and hugged her hard. "Goodbye, brat." Despite the circumstances, she smiled through her tears at the memories of what he'd called her when they were young. "Take care of my wife." He hesitated. "This has been difficult for her. Elizabeth isn't used to hardship. She doesn't have your fighting spirit." He drew back and gave her one last look. "I'm sorry, Bella. I never meant . . ."

His voice dropped off.

"You've nothing to apologize for. I've done nothing that I wouldn't do again today. You are The Lion."

The symbol of Scotland's kingship. And despite all that had happened and the uncertain fate that awaited them all, she meant it.

She watched Robert walk away, and with a sigh turned back to the woods. She could only pray the king knew what he was doing.

She glanced up and startled, finding herself staring right into the eyes of the brigand himself. Her heart jolted. She couldn't look away, caught—trapped—by the force of the connection. She'd forgotten how intense his eyes were. They bored into her, hot and penetrating.

She flushed, awareness rippling across her skin like wildfire. To her disappointment, she realized her reaction to him hadn't changed. If anything it had grown stronger.

But it wasn't just her reaction that caused her pulse to flutter and race. One look in his eyes and she knew he'd heard her.

He was furious. And something else. Something raw and primal flashed in his eyes. Something that made her want to turn and run.

But she'd learned long ago to never show weakness. Controlling her emotions was how she'd survived her marriage. Stoic submission and indifference, not tears and fear. A man could control her body but not her will.

She lifted her chin and forced herself to walk toward him, giving no hint of the furious pounding of her heart. Their eyes held in a silent duel.

"Countess," he said with a nod of the head, an unmistakable note of mockery in his voice.

She pretended that it didn't grate. Instead, she lifted a single brow. "I'm surprised you are still around."

He smiled, but she sensed that her comment had bothered him more than he wanted to let on. "Just waiting for a better offer."

She knew he was trying to get to her, but it didn't prevent her mouth from tightening. Her attempt to combat his anger with disdain wasn't working. Lachlan MacRuairi was nothing like Buchan. There wasn't a weak bone in his body. It would take more than a few words and a cold look to defy him. But she wouldn't let him intimidate her. Her eyes skidded over him. "How much is a hired sword worth these days?"

He didn't say anything for a minute. But he held her gaze. "More than you could pay."

There was an edge to his voice that she didn't understand. But it made her feel as if she'd done something wrong. As if she'd pricked beneath the seemingly impenetrable surface of mockery and struck emotion. As if, like her, he was good at masking his emotions. She just hadn't thought he had any.

But as he turned on his heel and strode away, she had to wonder why a man who didn't care about anything was so angry.

Lachlan stormed into the tent he shared with a few of the men, ignored Gordon, and began stuffing his belongings into the leather bag he attached to his saddle.

He refused to acknowledge the burning in his chest, and the fierceness of the emotions surging through his blood. He didn't have time for this shite.

Like it or not, he was going to lead this party. He needed to focus on getting the job done. The sooner this was all over, the sooner he could return to his kinsmen in the west, and the sooner his body would stop aching for *her*.

But he couldn't shake the image of what he'd seen.

He jammed his hand deeper into the bag just thinking about it. When he'd come out of the temporary stables and seen Bella and Bruce standing there, the scene—the *intimacy* of the scene—hit him like a fist in the gut.

Her words had annoyed him, but it was her method of persuasion that sent his blood raging. Bella and Bruce had been standing as close as lovers. Her breasts, big and lush enough to tempt a monk, were grazing the king's chest. And the way she touched his arm, tilted her head back, and pleaded with that soft, beseeching mouth made a man think of one thing.

God knew he couldn't think of anything else since that day in the forest. The memory of her nakedness still tortured him. Apparently, four months in The Isles hadn't dulled his lust for her. If the jealousy raging through him was any indication, it had only gotten worse.

*Robert.* The king's given name had slid so easily from her tongue. The way a lover's would.

Could the rumors be true?

He hadn't wanted to believe it. Though he wouldn't put it past Bruce—the king had more than his fair share of bastards—he'd thought she was different. He'd actually come to admire her, which for him was a rarity. But if what he'd just seen was any indication, Buchan's attempt to set aside his wife as an adulteress, and his claim that she'd risked so much to crown Bruce because she was his lover, might have some truth.

With Scotland under interdict, a dispensation from the pope was impossible. But Buchan had set her aside anyway. A divorce *a mensa et thoro,* of bed and board, enabled the couple to live separate lives but not remarry. Annulment was the only way to do that. If grounds could be found, however, it would make their daughter a bastard.

Was it true? Perhaps that explained why she'd done it. Why she'd risked so much to crown Bruce.

Lachlan shoved the extra plaid that he used as his bedroll into the bag so hard it rattled the tent.

"What in Hades is the matter with you, Viper?"

Lachlan glanced around, making sure no one else was near before responding. "Nothing," he snapped. "Have care, Gordon, what you say. This isn't one of our typical missions."

When Bruce had given them war names at the private ceremony after the second coronation, he'd done so in a bid to keep their identities as members of the Highland Guard secret. On Highland Guard missions they used war names, but otherwise they were to blend into the army as regular soldiers. Officially the Guard didn't even exist.

As the mystery of the secret band of warriors grew, Lachlan knew it was going to be difficult but imperative to keep their identities hidden. Not only did the secrecy add to the mystique of the group, but it also made them harder to kill. War names would help.

He'd been surprised when Bruce had named him Viper, but as there was more truth in the name than jest he could hardly object. Originally an insult coined by Tor MacLeod for Lachlan's venomous disposition, the name was actually quite apropos. Like a snake, he was slippery when evading capture and had a silent, deadly strike. He'd been recruited for his ability to get in and out without being seen, which was useful for extracting people and information.

His Norse ancestors had names like "Eric Bloodaxe" and "Thorfinn Skull-Splitter," so he supposed Viper wasn't so bad.

Unfortunately, his warning hadn't distracted Gordon. "I don't understand. I thought you hated taking orders from MacLeod and would welcome the chance to be in charge."

Gordon was right. He didn't like taking orders from anyone—especially MacLeod. There were few men that were a match for Lachlan on the battlefield, but the leader of the Highland Guard was one of them. Still, not wanting to take orders didn't mean he wanted the responsibility of the king's women.

The countess thought he'd shirked his duty in refusing to lead his clansmen. She was right. After forty-four of his men had followed him into a death trap, because he'd been foolish enough to trust his wife, he'd abdicated the duties of chieftain to his younger brother.

He'd been so crazed with lust that he hadn't seen the warning that his young wife was tiring of him. Spoiled and too beautiful for her own good, Juliana regretted her impulsivity in marrying him—a chieftain, but a bastard without the lands to go along with the title. When she found a more lucrative suitor, she'd convinced her brother, John of Lorn, that MacRuairi intended to betray him. Instead of a surprise raid on a small band of MacDonalds, Lachlan and his men had found over a hundred English soldiers waiting for them at the bay of Kentra.

The MacDonalds, his enemies and kinsmen, had found him with a spear through his shoulder, left for dead. He'd been the only damned survivor. Men—friends—he'd known his entire life, who'd trusted him, had been slaughtered like pigs before his eyes. That he'd survived at all had been a miracle. Or a curse, depending on your perspective.

For reasons that today he still didn't understand, his cousin Angus Og, the younger brother of the MacDonald chief, had helped him escape from a MacDonald prison. But when Lachlan returned from the dead to find his wife betrothed to another man and removed to her brother's castle at Dunstaffnage, he found himself exchanging one prison for another. Angus Og had warned him, but he hadn't wanted to listen. Lachlan had been declared a traitor, his holdings and wealth forfeit, becoming a convenient scapegrace for Lorn, who was trying to make peace with the English and needed someone to blame for the recent spate of attacks against the king's men.

Disgraced, having been declared a rebel, and under suspicion of murdering his now dead wife, Lachlan knew it would be better for everyone—his family, his clan, and himself—if he left. So he'd sailed to Ireland, making his way as a gallowglass mercenary for anyone willing to pay his price.

His shoulders stiffened. Just because he didn't want to lead the party didn't mean he wanted to hear Bella MacDuff pleading for the same thing. *"I'm surprised you're still around."*

Her disdain pricked. She didn't know him, damn it. She *thought* she knew him because of his reputation, but just because he took money to fight didn't make him disloyal. It made him practical. Cynical perhaps, but also honest.

When he agreed to do something he did it. Lachlan might

not have wanted to lead the ladies' party, but that didn't mean he didn't intend to get the job done.

God damn it, why did what she thought even matter?

"I'm needed more out west," he said to Gordon. "God knows what kind of trouble MacSorley is going to get in without me watching over him."

Gordon laughed, though Lachlan hadn't meant it as a joke. Erik MacSorley was the best seafarer in a kingdom of seafarers, and he liked to prove it whatever chance he got. As a result, he was always in trouble.

"Hmm. I thought it might have something to do with the countess."

Lachlan stopped what he was doing long enough to level a blank stare on Gordon. "Why the hell would you think that?"

If his voice held the hint of a warning, Gordon didn't pay it any mind. Lachlan knew he was treading dangerous ground. Gordon was beginning to think himself a friend. But Lachlan didn't have any friends. Not anymore.

"I couldn't help noticing that you didn't part on the best of terms last time. You seemed a little . . . edgy."

The smile on Gordon's face pricked him more than it should. "A situation I remedied soon enough," he lied. "One pair of velvety thighs is as good as another."

Gordon shook his head. "You have a real gift for the poetic, MacRuairi. If I ever need a bard, I know who to come to."

Before Gordon could ask any more questions about the countess, Lachlan ordered him to gather everyone and meet by the shieling. The king had decided to let the ladies take the few remaining horses. Bruce and the handful of men who would accompany him were taking to the heather and mountains, where the horses would only slow them down.

Lachlan followed Gordon a few minutes later. His anger had cooled, though not completely abated. He was more upset at himself than anything else. He should have more control.

If his reaction after the attack in the forest hadn't warned him, this should. The sight of her naked . . . the vision had been haunting him for four damned months. Christ, his body hardened just thinking about it. It had taken everything he had to not react. To not let his eyes gorge on every inch of that creamy naked flesh. One glance had been enough to nearly push him over the edge.

God, those breasts . . . sinfully big, perfectly round, and tipped with tight pink nipples. His mouth watered just thinking about them.

Bella MacDuff had been built for men's fantasies. He'd wanted her more than he'd ever wanted a woman in his life. Instinctively, he knew that after years of self-control, he'd met the woman who could break him.

He'd been furious. At himself. At her. So he'd lashed out. Not just with lust, but also, he knew, with something equally unsettling: fear. Seeing her vulnerable in that bastard's arms had chilled his blood.

And now he was jealous, for Christ's sake. What the hell was happening to him? He knew better than to fall prey to that weakness. Jealousy fueled by lust had wreaked enough havoc in his life. The last time people had counted on him he'd let his emotions distract him. His men had lost their lives because of it, and he'd lost everything. Now, when he was so close to getting some of it back, there was no way in hell he was going to travel down that path again. He'd worked too hard to risk it.

He weighed the sack of gold at his waist. Bruce had kept his promise so far, and Lachlan intended to keep his. The first chance he had, this gold would be on its way to the Isles. One more payment on a debt he hoped to pay in full in two and half years' time.

What was it about Bella MacDuff that got to him? Her bold tongue? Her harlot's body? He didn't know. But since

he couldn't very well cover her with a sack for the next
God-knows-how-long (no matter how much he was
tempted), he'd do his best to avoid her.

He suspected he was going to be too damned busy getting the women to safety to worry about one lass no matter
how distracting, anyway.

A suspicion that was confirmed a few minutes later when
he got his first glimpse of his new charges.

*Ah, hell.*

The man known as the most feared mercenary in the
Western Isles, meaner than a snake and just as deadly,
who'd never backed down from a fight no matter how bad
the odds, wanted to walk—nay, run—away.

He'd become a hired sword just to avoid this kind of
situation. The king asked too much. No debt, no land, no
amount of coin was worth this.

One, two, three . . . *three* children, damn it! And more
women than he wanted to count.

*Jesus.* He felt ill. He didn't need this. How the hell was he
going to get them a hundred miles across some of the most
difficult terrain in Scotland to safety with half the English
army hunting them?

Almost as if she knew what he was thinking, he met the
bold, blue-eyed gaze of Bella MacDuff. The hint of challenge there was enough to spur him to action. He had a job
to do, damn it, and he'd do it.

But the weight of responsibility sat heavy on his shoulders. He'd had enough death on his watch.

He quickly organized the men, giving them their instructions for the first part of the journey, but it took longer to
sort out the horses than it should have, as it turned out a
number of the ladies had limited riding experience.

He, in turn, had limited experience commanding a group
of women. Hardened warriors didn't have tender feelings,
and they sure as hell didn't look like they were about to
burst into tears when you snapped an order or two.

When one of the ladies balked at getting on the big war horse with MacKay, his frustration nearly got the better of him. He was half a second away from tossing her on the horse himself—or telling her she could wait for the English to arrive to escort her if she didn't get on the damned horse—when he found relief from an unexpected source.

The countess put her hand on his arm. He stilled, a fierce swell rising inside him. The gentle touch had an instant calming affect. She looked up at him, and for a moment he was lost in a sea of blue.

*Beautiful,* he thought. With lashes as long and feathery as the wing tips of a raven.

"Perhaps I might be of some help?"

He'd forgotten how husky her voice was. How it spread over his skin and seeped into his bones.

When she looked at him like that—with kindness and understanding—it felt as though his chest had suddenly grown too tight. The unfamiliar reaction rattled him. Lachlan had survived this long by an acute sense of danger, and right now every instinct flared with warning.

Hell, he liked it better when all he could think about was swivving her.

Not wanting her to guess the force of his reaction to her, he managed to nod, more grateful for her help than he wanted to admit.

After some encouraging words from the countess, the woman was on the horse with MacKay a few moments later. As she seemed to have a good idea of the relative riding strengths of the rest of the ladies, he welcomed her suggestions as to the other pairings, and in less time than he would have thought possible they were on their way.

One queen, one princess, two countesses, five lady attendants, a young sister to a king, two earls—one only four years old—and a young knight anxious to prove himself.

Five members of the Highland Guard were all that stood

between them and the army of the most powerful and vengeful king in Christendom.

Lachlan gave no acknowledgment of the sense of doom that came over him, but it followed them like a dark, maleficent shadow into the forests and hills of Atholl.

# Five

❧

Bella didn't know how much more of this she could take. Three days of evading the English, while trying to keep more than half their party from falling apart in a panic, had taken its toll. She'd been stretched to the breaking point.

She told herself it was the ever-present fear of what would happen to them if they were captured, the pressure of keeping everyone's spirits up—especially the children's—and the bone-weary exhaustion of riding all day and being too scared to sleep well at night.

Her frayed emotions had nothing to do with the man who led them.

"I'm tired," Lady Mary Bruce said.

Bella's heart squeezed as she gazed at the girl riding beside her. Every time she looked at Mary she thought of her daughter. The girls were so close in age, even if they were nothing alike in temperament or appearance. Joan was as quiet and reserved as Mary was bold and outspoken, and although both girls were dark in coloring, Mary, at a year older, had already developed a woman's body. The constant reminder of her daughter caused her pain, but she also felt a fierce protectiveness toward Robert's youngest sister.

"I know, sweetheart, I know." They were all tired. But they had to keep pushing toward Kildrummy. When they reached the castle they would be safe. She hoped. "Do you wish to ride with Magnus for a while?"

Bella, Queen Elizabeth, Robert's sister Christina, and the queen's lady-in-waiting were the only four women who'd been given mounts of their own. The other women and the children were being shuffled around, at times riding on their own, at others riding with one of the men.

After so many hours on the road, certain preferences in riding companions had developed. The four-year-old Earl of Mar, Christina Bruce's son with her first husband, had taken to riding with her new brother-in-law, Sir Alexander Seton. Christina's second husband, Christopher, had been missing since Methven, and the fear of what had happened to him hung like a dark cloud over them all. He was one of the greatest knights in Christendom.

Robert's ten-year-old daughter Marjory by his first wife had been taken under the protection of one of the most intimidating-looking warriors Bella had ever seen. Robert Boyd hailed from the Scottish Marches, and she doubted there was a man on either side of the borders more formidably built. If sheer brute strength counted for anything, the princess was in the best hands. Like Sir Alex, Boyd's brother was also missing and feared dead.

Mary rode with Magnus or, at times, Lachlan—who seemed willing to share a horse with everyone except Bella. Not that she noticed.

Mary shook her head. "I'm fine. For now." Bella knew who she was waiting for. She feared Mary had developed a young girl's *tendre* for their disreputable leader. Big, anxious dark eyes looked up at her. Her voice came out in a near whisper. "Do you think something happened to them?"

Bella shook her head vehemently. "No," she said firmly,

hearing the fear in the girl's voice that mirrored her own. "No."

*But where were they?* They'd been gone so long. *Too* long. Lachlan had ridden out with Sir James Douglas and William Gordon after they broke their fast to scout for enemy soldiers or other war parties. It wasn't just the English after them; their own countrymen were hunting them. The men were constantly taking turns scouting, but they'd never been gone for so long.

"Shouldn't they be back by now?"

Bella heard her own thoughts echoed in her cousin's voice. Though Margaret was riding behind them—the narrow mountain pass barely accommodated two—she was close enough to have heard Mary's question. Her cousin, too, looked worried. And also, Bella thought with a touch of uncharitable resentment, very fragile and scared.

It was exactly how Bella felt, though she could never show it. The other women and children needed someone to be strong, and that someone had turned out to be her. They were looking to her, and she would do whatever she had to do to keep them from falling apart, even . . . *lie.* "I'm sure they'll return soon," she assured her cousin. "The captain said they would be gone most of the day."

Mary gave her a look that suggested she was not as believing as her cousin, but neither of them pointed out the day was quickly fading. That it was the heart of summer was one of the only positives about their bleak situation. Unlike her last journey, there was little rain, and the nights in the mountains were cold but not unbearable.

The sound of approaching hooves forestalled any more conversation. For a moment she wasn't sure whether it was friend or foe. Her heart drummed in her frozen body. The remaining warriors fanned out in front of them to provide a barrier. But with only four of them, Bella knew their journey could well be at an end.

*Dear God, what will become of us?*

When three men rounded the bend ahead of them, Bella's eyes immediately landed on the one who rode in front. She closed her eyes, relief crashing over her.

The intensity of her emotions proved just how much she'd come to rely on him. No one was more surprised than she. Lachlan had gotten them this far with more skill and determination than she'd thought possible.

For a man who shirked his duty as chieftain to his clan, he was a surprisingly competent leader. Not just competent, she admitted, strong. The other men might not like him very much—except for William—but they followed his orders without question. He might be cynical and opportunistic, but he was also clear-headed, confident, and efficient. He'd led them through seemingly impassable terrain and had managed thus far to evade the countless parties who pursued them.

He'd kept them safe.

But as much as she'd come to rely on him, she knew that he'd come to rely on her as well—which she suspected was a rarity. They were alike in that regard, she supposed.

As decisive and efficient as he was at managing the men, he had little experience directing women and children. Sensing his frustration, she'd taken pity on him the first day, and in the intervening days they'd formed a silent partnership born of necessity—he took charge of their safety and she took charge of their spirits.

She didn't care if that was the only reason he talked to her. But telling herself that didn't make her believe it. She was drawn to him, whether she wanted to be or not.

She blanched as the men drew closer. Dirty and disheveled, covered with dust and dark red stains that could only be blood, they were peppered with cuts and bruises of varying degrees of severity. Thankfully, however, none of the injuries looked serious.

"What the hell happened?" Robert—or Robbie, as the men called him—Boyd asked, before anyone else could.

"An ambush," MacRuairi said grimly. He waited for the frightened cries and gasps from the ladies to fade before he explained. "They were lying in wait in the pass a few miles ahead."

*Were,* she noted.

"How many?" MacKay said.

Lachlan shrugged, but Douglas answered proudly. "A score. Maybe a few more."

Bella's heart rose to her throat. Good God! They should have been killed.

"They're taken care of?" Boyd asked.

"Aye," Douglas said. "I killed five myself." The young knight pointed to Atholl. "The earl here took down almost as many."

Bella could guess who killed the rest.

"Who were they?" Magnus asked.

"Comyn's men." Lachlan glanced at Bella, almost as if to make sure the news that her husband's men were looking for her did not distress her. "Someone will eventually come looking for them. We'll have to take a different road."

Bella bit back her groan, knowing that couldn't be good. The "roads" through the mountains were scarce, and anything off the main one was sure to be rough.

Rough turned out to be an understatement. By the time MacRuairi gave the signal to stop for the night, they were all ready to collapse.

Bella drew her horse to a halt and waited to be helped down. Like Bella, Margaret had been riding alone and was waiting as well. Unlike Bella, however, she didn't have to wait long.

Bella glanced over just in time to see Lachlan reach up and slide his hands around her cousin's waist to help her down. It turned out the brigand could be quite solicitous— to everyone but her, that is.

When he looked at her cousin, there was almost a hint of reverence in the brigand's gaze. It was nothing like the hot, lusty way he looked at her. As if he were seeing her naked all over again.

Her chest pinched. She quickly looked away. But the hurt wasn't so easily dismissed.

Just once she wished a man could look at her like that.

It wasn't Margaret's fault. Her cousin was as sweet and innocent as a postulate. MacRuairi's reverence was deserved.

Bella was neither of those things.

Magnus helped her down after he attended to Lady Mary, whose exhaustion had convinced her to ride with him. But it hadn't deterred the girl's interest in their leader. She seemed even less pleased by his solicitousness toward her cousin than Bella.

"Your cousin is very sweet."

Bella almost smiled. She doubted Mary realized she was frowning. "Yes, she is," Bella agreed.

Mary looked as if she were trying to work out something in her mind. "Do you think what they say about him is true?"

The spark of excitement in her eyes made Bella nervous. She knew some women found dangerous men irresistibly attractive, their naughtiness the very heart of their appeal.

Who would be so silly and foolish? she thought glumly.

She thought about how best to answer her, not wanting to pique the girl's curiosity. Though she suspected from her own example that it would prove impossible. Men like MacRuairi made women curious. They made a woman want to dig down deep and find the kernel of good amongst all the bad, even knowing very well it was probably all rotten.

It was intrigue and curiosity at work, nothing more—at least that's what she told herself.

"I suspect some of it is true and some exaggerated," she hedged.

Mary's gaze flickered to him and back. "Do you think he killed his wife?"

Bella quickly covered her shock and gave the girl a stern look. "You shouldn't repeat such things. Of course it's not true." She conveniently ignored that she'd wondered the same thing. "Do you think your brother would put a man who'd killed his wife in charge of his family?"

Mary had the good grace to blush, but the girl was not easily cowed. "I didn't make it up. I'm only repeating what I heard."

Bella raised a brow. "How do you think he would feel if he heard you repeat such a thing?"

Actually she doubted he would care, but Mary didn't know that, and importing the lesson was what mattered.

Mary's eyes widened. "You won't tell him?"

Bella pretended to think about it. Her mouth quirked, trying not to laugh at the girl's horrified expression. "I won't if you promise to go to sleep right after the evening meal tonight. No more listening through the tent to the men's conversation."

Rather than be embarrassed, Mary only giggled. "I find them very . . . instructive."

Bella tried not to laugh. No doubt *very* instructive. "Promise?"

Mary nodded. "I'm so tired tonight, I doubt I could stay up if I wanted to."

Bella knew exactly how she felt. She couldn't wait to collapse on her makeshift pallet of animal skins and thick woolen blankets. Tonight, she might even get some sleep.

Lachlan sat alone in the dark, listening to the sounds of the forest. It was the dead of night; two, perhaps three hours after midnight. It was his favorite time of day. Everyone else was sleeping.

Usually the sounds calmed him, but nothing could ease the restlessness teeming within him tonight. He'd volunteered for the watch, knowing he wouldn't be able to sleep. Not with the battle lust still coursing through him.

His mind went to one of the three tents behind him. Unfortunately, that wasn't the only kind of lust coursing through him.

He got up angrily from the log he was sitting on and started to patrol the perimeter. He needed to move.

But distracting himself with duties, with a cold loch—hell, even with other women—wasn't working, damn it.

Take her cousin, for example. Margaret MacDuff was sweet, innocent, and uncomplicated. The type of woman who would never make demands and never give him any trouble.

Taking her to bed was the farthest thing from his mind when he looked at her. Her fair features were serene and angelic, not tilted with temptation. His blood didn't heat, his muscles didn't tense, his temper didn't flare, and his senses didn't flood with the scent of whatever damned floral soap she washed with that morning. Who in Hades knew he could discern lavender from roses?

Margaret could talk to MacKay and Gordon all day long and he wouldn't give a shite. She did nothing to him. He could think rationally, breathe evenly, and stand right up next to her without hardening like a squire with his first maid.

With a woman like Margaret, he would never get angry, and sure as hell never get jealous.

Compared to her proud, spirited cousin, who never seemed to miss the opportunity to challenge him, Margaret was sweet, agreeable, and deferential.

And bland.

And passionless.

And timid as a kitten.

He'd be scared to touch her, let alone do all the wicked things he wanted to do to the countess.

Margaret would never have the courage to follow her

convictions (even if they were naive), to do what she believed to be her duty under threat of treason. She would never have the strength to rally a terrified group of women and children under conditions that would make even hardened soldiers despair.

Lachlan muttered an oath as he pushed through the trees.

As much as he wanted to blame his restlessness on unspent lust, he knew it was more than that. And *that* was what truly bothered him.

Christ, he couldn't wait to get back to the Isles. He was an islander; he could be on land for only so long before he started to go crazed. And crazed was the only explanation for why he was even thinking about her. Thinking about any woman outside of the bedchamber was a mistake.

With that in mind, he pushed aside thoughts of anything but the task before him. He circled the camp, checking to make sure nothing was out of the ordinary, before returning to his post in the trees a few dozen yards from where they'd set up camp for the night.

He picked a stem of thyme to chew on, and was settling back against a tree when he heard a sound.

He snapped into battle mode, tossing the stem away. His senses sharpened, every muscle tensed with readiness. His gaze shot toward the loch, in the direction he'd heard the rustle. He peered into the darkness, but not even his unusually keen vision at night could penetrate the thick forest.

He moved forward slowly. Silently. Keeping to the trees, sneaking up on the enemy with the stealth of a predator and with extreme caution. The loch was banked by a steep hillside, rousing memories of the earlier ambush.

As he drew closer, he heard the sound of whispers and frowned. The voices were soft, but talking at all during an attack was foolish. The sounds were also coming from loch level and not the hillside, where an ambush would be more likely.

He caught a glimpse of white in the black shadows ahead of him. Eyes honed, he made out two figures.

*Ah, hell.* Not an attack at all. It was two of the women. His mouth flattened. One of whom was the countess.

The flare of anger replaced the flare of battle. God's blood, didn't they know it was dangerous out here at night?

"I couldn't wait," he heard the smaller figure murmur. It was Bruce's young sister Mary, unless he was mistaken. "I had to go."

The countess had her hands on her hips as if she didn't believe her. "You should have woken me. It's dangerous to wander away from the camp at night alone."

Her tone made him think of his mother. Something he rarely did.

They started to move back from the edge of the loch when they stopped, alerted by a sound coming from the steep hillside above them.

Lachlan's stomach dropped. He shouted a warning, but it was too late.

Their presence had startled an animal—probably a deer—and when it jumped away, it caused a small rock slide. Unfortunately, one of the rocks was the size of a pig's bladder and it pitched over the cliffside right toward Mary Bruce.

The girl didn't realize the danger.

But the countess did. Without hesitating, she lurched toward the girl and pushed Mary out of the way just as the stone crashed to the ground behind her.

Lachlan moved as fast as he ever had, but he couldn't catch her in time. She flew forward, stumbling, and hit the ground with a blood-chilling thump.

He was at her side a split-second later. Gently, he lifted her shoulders from the ground to turn her around. "Christ, Bella, are you all right?"

He didn't recognize his voice. It sounded . . . thick. Gruff. *Concerned.*

She blinked up at him, temporarily dazed. "I-I think so."

Relief rushed through him in a hot wave.

Mary knelt on the other side of her, her eyes as big and round as two pieces of silver. "I didn't see it coming. I didn't mean for anything to happen."

Lachlan's jaw hardened. He was about to give the lass a severe tongue lashing, but Bella stopped him with a soft press on his arm.

How the hell did she do that?

"I'm fine," the countess said to the girl, trying to calm her. She sat up and started to brush the dirt off her clothes, but then winced. She turned her palms over just enough for him to see the dirt and rocks embedded in the tender skin. Keeping her hands hidden from the girl, she smiled. "Just a few scrapes, that's all."

To prove it, she stood up. With his help. He couldn't seem to let her go. He kept his hands on her upper arms as she steadied herself. Thus, he felt her stiffen and shift her weight back to her left side.

"I'm fine," she repeated, silently begging him not to say anything.

He frowned. God knows, he didn't know anything about children, but Mary Bruce seemed old enough to be told that her nighttime escapade had resulted in what he suspected was a twisted ankle, but which could have been a whole hell of a lot worse.

The countess walked over to the loch with what he assumed was considerable pain, smiling the whole time. "I'm going to clean up a little. Could you see that Mary gets back to the tent?"

The girl looked torn, looking back and forth between them. It was clear she wanted to stay, but it was equally clear she wanted to go with him. His eyes narrowed, wondering what the chit was up to.

"I'll wait," the girl decided.

Bella shook her head. "You need to get your rest. I won't be long."

"The countess is right," Lachlan said. "We have a long day tomorrow. I'll see that the countess makes it back all right."

Bella's eyes widened. "That's not—"

"I insist," he said, cutting her off in a voice that dared her to challenge him. She wasn't getting rid of him that easily. Not until he took a look at that ankle.

"Thank you, my lady," the girl said, looking like she was about to cry. "Thank you for what you did."

The countess had saved her, heedless to the danger to herself. It didn't surprise him.

"It was no more than anyone would do," she said, as if she actually believed it. But she was wrong. His wife would never have done something like that. "Get some rest, sweetheart," she said with a kind of gentleness that made his chest tug strangely. "I'll see you in the morning."

If he noticed Mary's furtive looks at him under her lashes as they walked back, he pretended not to. It didn't take him long to realize why she wanted to be alone with him. Christ, this was all he needed: to be dodging the attentions of a girl young enough to be his daughter. He'd be three-and-thirty on his next saint's day.

Why had he signed up for this? He had to keep reminding himself: two more years and his debts would be paid. Two more years and he'd have the independence and solitude he craved.

By the time he'd returned Mary to her tent and roused Gordon to keep watch, Lachlan was reconsidering his eagerness to be rid of the chit. He knew the countess didn't want the lass to see her injuries, but being alone with Bella MacDuff wasn't a good idea.

He should have sent Gordon.

But he didn't want to send Gordon, damn it.

He stomped through the trees, making his way back to

the loch, almost hoping someone would leap out and attack him. He could use a good fight.

He was acting like an idiot. He wanted her. So what? He'd wanted a lot of women in his life. There was nothing special about—

He stopped mid-step as the edge of the loch came into view.

His mouth went dry. Everything went dry. It felt as if his insides had drained in a rush of heat to the floor. *Not again*.

She was sitting at the edge of the loch on a rock with her gown raised to her knees to dip her hurt ankle in the cold water. Smart, but he wasn't thinking about that right now. All he could think about was the creamy perfection of two very shapely legs. Every inch of that smooth, satiny skin was emblazoned in his memory.

*Damn it*. He marched forward with determination and a very clenched jaw. He could do this.

If it was any consolation—which it wasn't—she didn't look very comfortable either. Nor was it any consolation to know that he wasn't the only one feeling this tension. She was attracted to him, though clearly the thought of being attracted to a notorious bastard who lived by the sword didn't sit well with her. He was everything she disdained. A mercenary who didn't believe in anything to her fiercely loyal patriot.

"Is Mary all right?"

"The child is fine." He knelt beside her. "How is your ankle?"

"A little sore."

He arched a brow. "A little?" She stared at him defiantly. "Is it broken?"

She bit her lip. *Jesus*. Could she make this any harder on him? "I don't think so."

"Let me see."

She hesitated, but his curt, businesslike tone must have

convinced her. She lifted her foot out of the water and held it up for him to examine.

His teeth were clenched so tightly he was surprised he didn't hear cracking. He steeled himself, but nothing could have prepared him for the smooth, velvety softness of her skin under his palms. It took everything he had not to slide his hand up the long length of her leg. And then do the same thing with his mouth. Just knowing how close he was to that sweet little juncture between her thighs made every inch of his body hot and hard.

She quivered at his touch. The knowledge that she was not unaffected was almost more than he could take. *Don't look at her.* If he saw anything resembling desire, he'd do something foolish.

Sweat gathered at his brow. Every muscle in his body flexed with restraint. The flames of desire licked and snapped around him, threatening to incinerate the last threads of control.

*Focus. She's hurt, damn it.* He needed to be careful. Bella MacDuff was dangerous. He had a job to do and couldn't afford any distractions, not if they were going to make it through this alive. They had two countries chasing them.

He held her foot in his hand, steadying himself. For as strong as she appeared on the outside, her bones were as fine and delicate as a bird's. He'd never seen such a dainty foot in his life. Not much bigger than his hand, the tiny toes, the high arch, and the thin, albeit slightly swollen ankle seemed to belong to a fairy.

*She's hurt,* he reminded himself. But he was touching her this time, not just looking. His blood pounded. Slowly, he slid his hand up around her ankle, pressing gently on the swollen skin, pleased when it didn't appear to cause her too much pain. He rotated her foot a little just to make sure, but she was right: It wasn't broken. Not that it would be any less painful to walk on for the next few days.

She wouldn't be able to ride on her own. Someone would

have to ride with her. His mouth thinned, not knowing why the idea didn't sit well with him.

He lowered her leg carefully back into the water and removed his hands, feeling as if he'd just survived an ordeal. Hell, he'd rather walk across hot coals than go through that again.

He stood up and ventured a glance in her direction, telling himself it was too dark to see a soft flush on her cheeks. "You'll need to wrap it when you get back to camp. If you don't know how, I can show you."

"I can do it," she said quickly.

Clearly she was no more eager for him to have his hands on her than he was. He bit back the flash of anger. "How are your hands?"

She held them out, palms up. "Not too bad."

They were scratched and scraped raw. The lady had the understatement of a Highlander.

"MacKay has some salve. Put it on, and try to keep them covered with cloth or gloves."

She nodded, and as she did he caught a glimpse of something under her chin. He reached out and cradled her jaw between two of his fingers, tilting her face up. He swore. "Your chin is scraped."

Instinctively, she reached for it and winced when her fingers came into contact with the raw skin. The admiration he felt for her was almost as annoying as his lust. Almost.

Bending down, he dunked the edge of his plaid in the water, getting it good and wet.

"You don't need to do that," she said hurriedly.

He ignored her protest, and proceeded to dab the sopping cloth on the underside of her chin to clear away the dirt.

He was close to her, very close. Close enough to make her nervous. Close enough to smell the subtle scent of her skin. Roses today, damn it.

He could hear her breath turn shallow. He looked into her eyes, seeing the confusion.

But then he made a mistake. He looked down, his gaze catching on a rivulet of water as it made its way past her throat to the open collar of her chemise. Her now—thanks to his sopping plaid—very wet chemise that clung to two incredible breasts.

His mouth went dry. Nay, watered. His memories hadn't done her justice. Perfectly round, big and lush, the nipples were peaked like two tiny berries waiting to be sucked.

Lust hit him hard. An entirely different kind of lust. It was hot and visceral, claiming every inch of his body. His muscles shook with restraint.

She gasped, quickly covering herself with the edge of her mantle. "Don't," she cried. "Don't look at me like that."

Something in her voice penetrated the haze of desire. He lifted his gaze back to hers.

"What are you going to do now, rip off my clothes like I'm nothing but a piece of flesh to serve men's pleasure?" Her voice broke in a dry sob. "Throw me down on the ground and tell me that I asked for it? That I deserved it?" She cupped her breasts and held them up to him defiantly. "That this is all I'm good for. That because I look like a whore, I must be a whore."

He swore softly. Not just because her words shamed him—which, surprisingly, they did—but because of what she was revealing. Suddenly, it all fell into place. He understood the wariness and at times almost hurt reaction to his desire.

God's blood, what had Buchan done to her? If the bastard were before him right now, he'd kill him.

His fists tightened at his side. "Tell me," he said. "Tell me what he did to you."

She gave a harsh laugh. "You want all the salacious details?" Her eyes narrowed, and then grew heavy-lidded as her face transformed into the exaggerated mask of a wanton. Her voice grew soft and husky. "Do you want to know exactly how he taught me to pleasure him?" Her eyes slid down his body, resting on the tightening bulge between his legs that didn't know how wrong it was to respond. Her tongue slid with feline calculation over her bottom lip. She leaned forward, looking up at him from under her long lashes. "Should I show you, Lachlan? Give you a demonstration of my skill?"

"Stop it." He grabbed her, angry at his reaction as much as he was at her for acting like this. "That's not what I meant."

The mask slid from her face, replaced by the hurt anger that had been there before. "What, then? Do you want to know how he forced me to do my wifely duty from the time I was fifteen? *Fifteen*, Lachlan. Not much older than Mary and Marjory." He grimaced with disgust. She took note of his reaction and dug her sword in deeper. "But it wasn't enough that I submitted to him, that I became more whore than wife; I was supposed to enjoy it, and when I didn't he tried to force that, too. Can you imagine what it's like to be so utterly powerless? To have your every action controlled?" Aye, he could. "To be forced to do something and then be punished with accusation and suspicion for not enjoying it? Because surely if I was not getting pleasure from him, I must be finding it somewhere else. With a mouth and body like this, what else is there?"

Lachlan was shamed to realize he'd jumped to similar conclusions. Was he wrong about what he'd seen with Bruce?

"Not all men are like that," he said quietly.

She made a harsh scoffing sound that was almost a cry. "I see the way you look at me. Do you deny that you want me?"

He gave her a hard look. "Nay, I won't deny it. You're a beautiful woman. But I'd never force a woman to do anything she didn't want to do."

As bad as it had been with Juliana in the end, the idea of bullying her or using his physical strength to control her had never occurred to him. Only a weak man would try to dominate someone he had a duty to protect.

"You expect me to believe that? With all the fighting you've done? It's common for men to take their 'spoils' of war."

"Among some men perhaps, but not me. Despite what you might think, I do have some principles. There are some lines not even I will cross." He held her gaze so she would see the truth. "An unwilling woman is one of them."

Her, he meant, her. He wouldn't touch her because he thought her unwilling.

Of course she was unwilling. His touch had momentarily confused her, that's all.

Bella had never felt anything like it. The gentle caress of his hands and fingers on her leg had flooded her with a myriad of unfamiliar sensations. *Wicked* sensations. *Delicious* sensations.

Her skin had prickled with sensitivity. She'd been achingly aware of each point of contact, of the warmth of his fingers, of the hard scrape of his calluses across her skin, as he explored her ankle. She'd held her breath when his hand skimmed over her calf and for a moment, she'd thought—God, even hoped—that it would inch higher.

Heat radiated to every corner of her body, concentrating in a warm twitchiness between her legs. Desire. It was desire. She'd thought herself incapable of responding to a man's touch. She was wrong.

Lachlan had been touching her so tenderly that for a moment she'd thought he might be different. That maybe this strange connection between them meant something. That maybe, just maybe, he might actually care for her.

Which made the look in his eyes when he'd glanced down at her wet chemise all the more cruel. He saw her breasts and not the woman. No man had ever looked beyond. Just once, she wished a man could look at *her*.

All he offered was the very thing she'd just escaped. She would never go through that again.

Now she just felt foolish. One soft touch and she dissolved into a pathetic, lovesick schoolgirl. Was she so desperate for someone to care for her that she'd find emotion in a touch?

She'd overreacted because he'd made her feel something different, and in doing so revealed far more than she wanted to. She'd never told anyone what she'd just told him. Not even her mother, though Bella suspected she had guessed.

"If you are ready," he said, "I can carry you back."

Her eyes widened with alarm. *Good god, no!* "That isn't necessary," she said hastily.

The slightly bored, slightly mocking expression that she found so confoundingly impenetrable had returned to his face, but the muscle ticking below his jaw made her think the vehemence of her reaction had bothered him. "I think I can control myself for a few minutes, Countess."

"It's not that." She flushed, realizing her reticence had offended him. Was she to believe that a hired sword, a man who made no qualms about selling himself to the highest bidder, would balk at forcing a woman? Surprisingly, she did. "I believe you."

It was the willingness part that worried her.

His eyes held hers for a moment, and he nodded. Before she could find a reason to object further, he scooped her off the rock, cradling her in his arms like a child.

She gasped in surprise, instinctively looping her arms around his neck to keep from falling. But he was in no danger of dropping her. She might have been a bairn for all the effort it took him to carry her.

It might have had something to do with the size of the muscles in his arms and the steely shield of his chest. She'd noticed his strength before, of course. He was so power-fully built and tall it was hard not to. But being confronted with the flexed proof wrapped around her was a different kind of noticing.

She hadn't expected him to be so warm. His heat en-gulfed her, making her feel a little funny. All warm and melty.

She turned her head, resting one cheek against his shoul-der, not wanting him to see the effect he had on her. She breathed in his warm, masculine scent, thinking it strange again that a brigand could smell so good. He must bathe more than any man she'd ever met. Apparently, he had a strange liking for cold rivers.

Unwittingly, she relaxed. He carried her in silence for a moment, navigating easily through the darkened forest. She peeked up at him from under her lashes. He hadn't shaved in a few days and his jaw was shadowed with dark stubble. It made him look even more dangerous. Except for his lashes. She'd never noticed how long they were. It was strange to find a hint of softness on the otherwise hard fa-cade. She could see that tic again, and there were tiny lines around his mouth. Maybe it was more difficult to carry her than she'd realized?

She frowned, noticing something else. There were a few fresh cuts and bruises on his face, but nothing as deep as the cut across his cheek. Unconsciously, she reached up to trace it with her finger. She thought she felt him tense, but it was gone before she could be sure. "That must have hurt."

He shrugged as if it didn't matter.

"How did it happen?"

She didn't think he was going to answer her, but he fi-nally said, "I turned my back on someone with a dagger."

There was something more to the story, but it was clear he wasn't going to tell her. "Did you get it while you were imprisoned?"

There was no mistaking the tensing of his muscles this time. He tried to erase his reaction with a sardonic lift of his brow, but he was holding her too close: she'd felt it. "I wasn't aware you knew so much of my history, Countess."

She tried not to flush under the accusation in his gaze. "It's hardly a secret."

"Is that right? And what do you know about it?"

His words were cool, but she sensed the emotions simmering under the surface. Suddenly she knew exactly how Mary had felt when she'd confronted her about spreading rumors: guilty and defensive. "That you betrayed your brother-in-law, John MacDougall, Lord of Lorn, in battle, and that he caught you and had you imprisoned."

"That's what they say?" He laughed, but the sound was harsh and without humor.

"Do you deny it?" She realized how badly she wanted him to.

Without her realizing it, they'd reached the tent. He set her down carefully. "If you want to know something, ask me. But you shouldn't believe everything you hear, Countess."

The subtle taunt in his voice pricked. Did nothing matter to him? "You mean things like did you kill your wife?"

He stilled. Something raw flashed in his eyes, and she immediately wished her question back.

"Nay," he said evenly. "That's true."

She sucked in a sharp breath. He'd shocked her, as was obviously his intent, but she sensed there was something he wasn't saying.

Before she could question him further, he gave her a slight mocking bow. "Good night, Countess. Get some rest. We have a long day tomorrow."

And with that, he turned and walked away, disappearing into the shadows.

# Six

❧

Lachlan had never been so glad to see battlements in his life.

The distinctive shield-shaped curtain wall of Kildrummy Castle rose out of the mountainous landscape like the warrior's paradise of Valhalla.

With its ashlar stone walls and six massive towers, Kildrummy had been built by the Earls of Mar not only as a defensive stronghold, but also as a magnificent testament to the wealth of the earldom.

It wasn't because the castle was considered one of the finest in Scotland that Lachlan was happy to see it. Nay, he was glad to see it because the last two days of riding had been torture.

Of his own damned making. What the hell had he been thinking?

God's blood, even through the thick leather of his *cotun* he could feel her softness burning against him. Every shape and curve of her back seemed imprinted on his. And that bottom. He groaned. Two days of having that soft, round bottom nestled against his groin was more than any man could be expected to bear.

He couldn't even breathe without being aware of her—

the air around her seemed infused with the faint scent of roses.

She shifted against him, giving a contented little sigh in her sleep as she snuggled her back deeper into his chest, her silky-soft, downy head tucked under his chin.

She forgot to be wary of him when she slept. He liked it. Too damned much. His arms drew tighter around her. To keep her steady in the saddle, of course.

He should have let her ride with one of the other men. But when they'd stood by the horses the morning after her accident, deciding whom she should ride with, he'd found himself ordering her to ride with him.

It wasn't because she'd wanted to ride with MacKay, damn it. And it sure as hell wasn't because he couldn't stand the thought of another man touching her. He just didn't want to be dodging the girlish flirtations of Mary Bruce all day. Besides, her ankle was tender and one of the other men might forget she was injured.

But if he'd known how hard it would be to have his arm wrapped around her waist for hours, while her incredible breasts—the size and shape of which had been burned on his memory—bounced against it, he might have reconsidered.

He glanced down. His chest swelled with an unfamiliar emotion, and he quickly looked back to the road in front of him. God damn it, did she have to look so sweet? With her cheek resting against his chest, wispy little tendrils of white-blond hair curling at her temples, her long, dark lashes curling against her creamy skin, and her bold features soft in repose, the proud countess looked almost vulnerable.

This swell—whatever it was—in his chest bothered him. It made him feel—damn it—protective.

A feeling that thankfully went away as soon as she woke up and turned those flashing eyes on him.

But he didn't like this at all. His control was faltering. He couldn't think straight around her, which was dangerous for all of them. He needed to do something. Clearly, fighting this maddening desire for her wasn't working.

It had been too long. He needed to find a way to take the edge off.

Almost as if she knew what he was thinking, she stirred. He knew she was awake when he felt her back stiffen and pull away from him. He clenched his jaw. Not that it bothered him.

Suddenly, she sat up even straighter. "We made it?"

She glanced up at him, and he could see that the relief in her eyes matched the excitement in her voice.

"Aye," he answered, trying not to notice how close her mouth was to his.

Her eyes filled with something else. Gratitude, he realized, when she said, "Thank you."

He felt that uncomfortable swelling again in his chest and turned sharply away. "Don't thank me yet."

"What do you mean?"

"The English will not give up so easily. Even now they could be marching toward us."

He almost regretted his forthrightness when he felt a shiver shudder through her. But hiding the truth from her wouldn't help keep her safe. She needed to know exactly what they were up against: the most powerful, wily, and vengeful king in Christendom, who was out for blood.

Bella MacDuff had made a powerful enemy when she'd placed a crown on Bruce's head. He hoped to hell it was worth it.

Though the light was fading with the dusk, he could still make out the play of fear and worry on her stubborn features. "But we shall have at least some reprieve. They will not find us right away. You said they did not follow us?"

He shook his head. "Not from what we could tell." Hopefully, the English wouldn't realize the ladies had separated from the rest of the army. What was left of it, anyway.

"It's Rob—the king—they want. They'll follow him west."

This time he didn't tell her what he thought. It wasn't just the king Edward would pursue with a vengeance. If they discovered the ladies missing, they would come after them as well. Moreover, Kildrummy Castle, with its strategic location at the juncture of the roads leading north into Buchan and Atholl, was a valuable prize even without the queen and Bella.

She took his silence as agreement and relaxed against him slightly as they navigated the path leading up to Kildrummy. The castle sat on a rise, surrounded by a wide ditch in the front and a steep riverbank in the back—natural defenses made nearly impenetrable by the strength of the castle itself. High, thick stone walls were topped with numerous towers to defend against any encroachers who attempted to cross the ditch. The massive donjon known as the Snow Tower was seven stories high, with walls in places eighteen feet thick.

Lachlan knew something was wrong even before they crossed the narrow bridge to the two gatehouse towers that guarded the main entry to the castle. Though it was dusk, it was still light enough for villagers to be milling about. But the place was deserted.

He could almost feel the tension in the air. If Gordon hadn't ridden ahead to warn Nigel Bruce of their arrival, he suspected they would have found the portcullis down, the gates barred, and the arrow slits in the towers filled with archers.

He tried to keep his wariness from the countess, not wanting to wipe the relieved smile from her face as they passed under the gate.

But his instincts were validated the moment they rode into the courtyard. His eyes found Gordon's in the subdued crowd that had gathered to welcome them. The other man shook his head.

*Damn.*

Lachlan quickly dismounted and helped Bella down, taking care for her ankle, though it seemed to have healed.

After Nigel Bruce greeted his sister-in-law, his sisters, his niece and nephew, and Bella, the young knight turned to him and extended his hand. "MacRuairi."

Lachlan returned the firm grasp of forearm to forearm. Much like Gordon and MacSorley, Nigel Bruce was a hard man not to like. Bruce's favorite brother had wit, charm, and the kind of even-keeled temperament that people gravitated toward. He'd impressed Lachlan on the battlefield as well, fighting with a ferocity not typically seen in his noble counterparts.

"I'm glad to see you," the young knight said, "but I fear it will not be for long."

Though he spoke in a low voice, Bella had heard him. The momentary relief Lachlan had glimpsed when they'd entered the castle gates was gone. "What is it?" she asked.

Nigel gave her a somber smile. "Come," he said, taking her hand. "You must be hungry and exhausted. You can eat and sit in comfort by the fire in the Great Hall while I tell you what is happening."

But Lachlan already knew what young Bruce was going to say: The English were coming.

Bella listened to Robert's younger brother with a growing pit in the bottom of her stomach. The safe sanctuary she'd hoped to find at Kildrummy had proved a cruel mirage. A nightmare from which she could not wake. How much more of this could she take? The constant danger. Living on the run. When would it ever end?

"The Prince of Wales landed in Aberdeen the day before yesterday," Nigel said. "Even hauling their siege engines, it won't take them longer than a few days to cover less than forty miles. When the scouts return we will know for sure, but I expect they will camp near Alford tonight and be outside our gates before the sun has set tomorrow night."

Only Bella, Christina Bruce, and the queen had remained on the dais after the meal to hear the men discuss their plans, and the three women exchanged distraught glances.

"We'll leave for the coast in the morning for the journey to Norway," Lachlan said.

Bella bit back a cry. Norway! It was so far away.

Nigel shook his head. "You can't go by ship. At least not from here. They're expecting my brother to escape by sea, and Edward has his fleet patrolling the east coast from the Knuckle of Buchan to Berwick." He cut off MacRuairi's protest. "I know what you Islanders can do in a galley, but you will have women and children to man your ship, not seasoned warriors. I can't spare many men. We'll need all the soldiers we can get to hold the castle for my brother. It's safer to travel by land, at least until you've reached the Firth. Once you've past Buchan you can secure a galley."

Bella couldn't stand silent any longer. "But why must we leave at all? Why can't we just stay here with you?"

Lachlan pinned her with his gaze. She saw the hint of compassion in his eyes and knew he saw too much. He'd guessed her reason for not wanting to flee to Norway. The separation the past few months from Joan had been hard enough. But leaving Scotland . . .

"It will only be for a little while," he said quietly.

Tears sprang to her eyes. This time they both knew he lied. "But this castle is one of the strongest in Scotland. Built to withstand even Edward's Warwolf," she said, referring to the King of England's infamous trebuchet. "Surely it is safer to stay behind these walls than to be hunted across the countryside?"

Nigel might not know the source, but he'd sensed her distress. "Have you ever been through a siege, my lady?" She shook her head, and he continued. "You would not wish to. I need to hold the castle for my brother's return. It could take months."

Bella swallowed. *Or longer.*

"My orders were to take you to Norway if the English drew too close," Lachlan said.

Her fists clenched. Every bone in her body recoiled at the idea of leaving the castle. At leaving Scotland. At leaving her daughter—again.

The queen put her hand on hers. "It's what Robert wished," she said gently.

Bella held the other woman's gaze for a moment, seeing her own fear reflected there, and nodded.

*Forgive me, Joan. I swear it will not be much longer.* The distance might be greater, but her goal would never change: to have her daughter back in her arms as soon as possible.

She felt Lachlan's eyes on her again and when she turned, was surprised to see the flash of anger before he shifted his gaze back to Nigel.

What had she done now?

"We do have an advantage," Lachlan said.

"What advantage can we possible have?" Christina Bruce asked.

"Nigel said there are spies and roving war parties all over the area, and that they probably have marked our arrival. If we can get out of the castle without being seen, they will think we are still inside and won't be hunting us."

"But how can we leave without being seen?" the queen asked.

Lachlan turned to Nigel. "Is there still a passage to the well-house on the other side of the riverbank through the old cistern chamber?"

Nigel lifted a brow. "You know about that? Aye, it still exists. The well dried up years ago and 'tis no longer needed since the new one was dug at the base of the Snow Tower.

The passage hasn't been used in some time; I would not vouch for its state of repair."

Lachlan explained his plan. They would leave from the postern gate before dawn and enter the sunken stepped passageway that descended the steep wall of the riverbank to the cistern chamber and emerged on the other side in a tunnel to the abandoned well-house. They would disguise themselves with dark cloaks over plain clothing, and travel on foot until horses could be procured.

"You will not be able to take much," he said.

None of the women said anything. They didn't have much left. Most of their belongings had been left behind after Methven.

"But it must be over sixty miles to Moray," Christina Bruce cried. "My son will never be able to walk that far."

"We'll find horses as soon as we can. Until then we'll take turns carrying the young earl," Lachlan said.

He had a plan for everything, Bella thought glumly, wishing a reason could be found not to go.

Out of the corner of her eye she caught a movement. A man of about forty years with enormous arms—rivaling those of Robbie Boyd—passed by the table with a sack of grain on each broad shoulder. Another man soon followed. And then another.

She waited until the men had finished discussing their plans before asking Nigel, "What are they doing?"

"The blacksmith and his sons are helping to move the grain into the Great Hall for the siege."

Her eyes widened with understanding. The Great Hall was built of stone and wouldn't burn as easily if fire were pitched over the walls.

The gravity of what had befallen them knotted in her chest.

Bella lingered at the table after many of the others had left to start preparations. Her cousin and a few of the other ladies had returned from putting the children to sleep, and

Lachlan had gone over to inform them of the plan. She could see from their pale faces that the news was not being received well. They were all exhausted and scared.

He seemed to be trying to ease their worries. How gallant of him, she thought with a pinch in her chest. A pinch that grew worse when she saw him lead them out of the Hall. She watched them go, not knowing why she suddenly felt so forgotten.

"He's not interested in them, you know."

Bella turned to find William beside her. She hadn't even heard him approach. Her cheeks flushed. "Who?"

He smiled at her attempt to feign ignorance. "MacRuairi. He's relaxed around those women because they're safe."

*And I'm not?*

William laughed, guessing her thoughts. "Exactly. He avoids you on purpose."

Embarrassed, she tried to dissuade him, not wanting him to get the wrong idea. "It doesn't make any difference to me. He's hardly the sort of man a lady would be interested in."

Something she needed to remember.

Though it was the truth, Bella felt a pang of conscience in saying it. She sounded priggish. But a bastard, a heartless mercenary, a disreputable scourge, wasn't an appropriate suitor for ladies of their ilk. Even if he wasn't as wholly unredeemable as she'd initially thought.

William frowned. "Don't judge him too harshly. MacRuairi's had a rough time of it."

The dangerous spark of curiosity rekindled. "What do you mean?"

The young warrior shrugged. "Ask him. He'll tell you."

She hid her disappointment with indifference. "No matter. It's not important." Not wanting William to get the wrong impression, she changed the subject. "Will you be going with us?"

"Aye." He gave her a sympathetic smile. "Norway isn't

all that far, my lady. It's faster to get to Norway by ship from the Isles than it is to get to Edinburgh. If your daughter needs you, you can reach her. She'll know you had no choice."

Bella smiled, a fresh wave of tears brimming in her eyes. He was a kind man. "I know, but thank you for saying it. At least Joan knows that I did not intend to leave her. I can take solace in that. I'm grateful to Robert for thinking to take word to her."

Gordon's brows drew together. "Bruce didn't have anything to do with it."

"But he told me a messenger had gotten word to Joan."

"Aye, but the king didn't order it."

"Then, who . . . ?" Her voice slowed to a stop. Her gaze snapped to William's in silent question.

He pushed back from the table and cast a glance toward the opposite end of the dais. "Who do you think?"

Bella was stunned, following the direction of his gaze. Lachlan had returned to the Hall and stood talking to Nigel. Had he been the one to take the message to Joan? But why, why would he do that?

It was kind and thoughtful. Two words that didn't usually come to mind when she thought of him.

Had she misjudged him? Was he not the opportunistic brigand, loyal only to his purse, that she first thought? Was he not immune to what was going on around him? Did he care more than he let on?

Did he care for . . . *her*?

It shocked her how much she wanted it to be true.

Barely had the question formed when Nigel withdrew a small leather bag from the sporran at his waist and handed it to Lachlan, who quickly tucked it in his *cotun*.

It was like a slap in the face. There was no noble purpose hiding under his mercenary facade. He'd never pretended differently; why should she try to make him into something he wasn't? She knew why: to find an excuse for this illogical attraction to him.

Feeling foolish and not a little angry with herself, Bella left the Hall. If she was walking a little fast, it was because there was so much to do before they left. She wasn't fleeing. And if her eyes were blinking a little too rapidly, it was because they were burning from the dry air of the peat fires.

What the hell was wrong with her? Why had she fled the Hall as if the devil were nipping at her heels?

Lachlan followed her out the door and into the courtyard. "Countess!"

He knew she heard him when she flinched, but she didn't stop. He caught up to her and grabbed her arm. "Damn it, what's the matter with you?"

In the torchlight, her eyes shimmered. "Nothing." She tried to jerk away. "Let go of me."

He dropped her arm, surprised by the coldness of her voice.

"Was there something you wanted?" she said tonelessly, not looking at him.

He frowned, confused. "You should be more careful with your ankle. You were walking too hard and too fast."

Hell, he sounded like a nursemaid. The lass was making him daft.

"I'll keep that in mind."

"Damn it, Bella. What's the matter? Why are you so angry? Is it about Norway? We can't stay here. Surely you see that? It's the king's orders," he reminded her. It hadn't escaped his notice what had persuaded her before. *"It's what Robert wishes,"* the queen had said. It was clear Bruce held great power over her. The question that kept grating on him was why.

"And how much is our safety worth?"

He jerked back at the scorn in her tone. "What are you talking about?"

"I saw Nigel give you the bag of coin. I don't know why it surprises me. You would probably sell your mother if the price was high enough."

He stilled; every muscle in his body went hard. Slowly, he forced himself to relax. A smile curled his mouth. "She wouldn't have been worth much."

Bella gasped in shock. "How can you say something so horrible?"

He shrugged indifferently. "It's the truth."

She studied him in silence for a moment. He knew she'd sensed there was more to the story when she asked, "Who was she?"

"A Welsh princess my father caught sight of on one of his raids and decided to take, in keeping with my Norse ancestors' penchant to take thralls." He didn't waste time on bitterness. The past was the past; it couldn't be changed.

"What happened to her?"

He held her gaze, deciding to tell her the truth. No matter how ugly. "She killed herself after my youngest brother was born rather than bear more bastards."

The petite, beautiful woman who'd once been a princess had hated the sight of them. Servants had raised him and his brothers.

She put her hand on his arm. "I'm sorry."

He was long past the point of compassion, but he accepted the gesture with a nod.

A sharp bark of laughter rose in his throat. "She won in the end, though." The countess's brows furrowed together over her nose. He answered the silent question. "She died cursing my father, and her curses came true."

She hesitated. "What did she say?"

"She vowed that he would have no more sons. He didn't. Leaving one of the most ancient kingdoms in the Western Isles without a legitimate male heir."

"Your sister might have inherited the land, but you could still have been chieftain." He didn't say anything. "Why have you turned your back on your clan?"

*They were better off.* He smiled, unable to resist. "It's more lucrative escorting countesses."

Her mouth tightened a little, but his words didn't prick as much as he intended.

It shouldn't bother him that she'd jumped to the conclusion she had about the money. Usually it was warranted. He wasn't ashamed of what he did. And he sure as hell didn't explain his motives to anyone. But her scorn bothered him, damn it. For the first time in a long time, someone's opinion mattered.

And he sure as hell didn't like it.

"Did you take a message to my daughter?"

The quick change of subject disarmed him. It took him an instant too long to respond. "What are you talking about?"

His annoyance didn't put her off. He must be losing his touch.

"Someone took a message to my daughter. Was it you?"

He held her gaze in the moonlight, looking for something he didn't expect to find. "Does it matter?"

She didn't answer right away. "I think it does."

Lachlan felt himself pulled by the strange emotion he saw in her eyes. Curiosity. Attraction. And most dangerous and tempting of all: possibility.

He could almost believe she meant it.

His gaze dropped to her mouth. He leaned closer. Her lips parted instinctively at his movement. He smothered an oath. Knowledge surged inside him, hot, primitive, and raw. He could kiss her. And God, he wanted to! Wanted it so badly it scared him. Christ, he could almost taste her on his lips.

He'd been careful to hide his desire after that night by the loch, but it was still there, simmering just under the surface. And he felt it now. Felt it rise up and grab him in its steely grip, trying to drag him under.

His hand reached out. Slowly. Carefully. As if she were the most delicate piece of porcelain, his finger grazed the side of her cheek.

His heart jammed in his chest. *Jesus!* He groaned. So damned soft. As smooth and velvety as a bairn. His big, battle-scarred hand looked ridiculous against something so fine.

He tipped her chin, feeling himself falling, lured by the promise in her eyes. His mouth lowered . . .

He caught himself at the last moment.

He dropped his hand. What the hell was wrong with him? He didn't like this feeling at all. It almost felt like—Jesus—*tenderness*. But only a fool would let himself believe there could ever be more between them. He was a bastard. A man stripped of his lands and reputation. A brigand. He wasn't ashamed, but he was also a realist.

She was curious, that was all. Intrigued by what she perceived as an inconsistency in his character. She thought she saw something in him worth saving. But it was all black.

He didn't want to confuse either of them.

"Nay," he lied smoothly. "I didn't have anything to do with it."

He saw a flicker of hurt in her gaze but forced himself to ignore it.

Taking a step back, he gave her a curt nod. "Good night, my lady. Have more care as you are walking. You will need all your strength over the next few days."

He walked away, pretending not to notice that she watched him the entire time.

*He's lying.* Bella didn't know how she knew, but she did. Lachlan had taken the message to her daughter.

Why didn't he want her to know? Was it the same reason he hadn't kissed her? Was it the same reason he tried to scare her off by telling her he'd killed his wife? She knew there was more to the story than he'd let on.

She would have pushed him away, of course. She was almost certain. Sanity would have prevailed before his mouth touched hers. She would have seen past the nearly overwhelming desire of how wrong it was to give in to the strange current drawing them together.

Her husband had set her aside, but his accusations had been pounded into her for too many years to forget. Lachlan could never be her husband; all he could be was something illicit. Letting him touch her would make her exactly what Buchan had always accused her of being.

She was glad he'd rejected her. Glad he'd realized the mistake before she had. Glad he'd cured her of any illusions.

If she'd seen some glimmer of kindness inside him, she was mistaken.

If her heart had gone out to him when he told her about his mother, he didn't want or need her sympathy.

He'd imparted the tale as if he'd been talking about someone else. Dry. Unemotional. Factual. It was as if he were giving a report to one of his commanders.

The events of his childhood no longer mattered to him. *Nothing* mattered to him. It was best that she remembered it. Even if at times he made her want to forget.

She inhaled deeply, forcing an uneven breath through her tight chest. The hurt would go away.

But it didn't. All through the painfully short night it burned, and then in the cruel, dark hours before dawn she was forced to confront him again. When his gaze slid over her in the small crowd of travelers that had gathered in the courtyard, she felt a fresh wave of it.

His indifference stung like a slap, bringing her harshly back to reality. He was the man charged with leading them—*all* of them—to safety. That should be her first and only concern.

Funny that she accepted his leadership so easily when not a week ago, she'd rebelled so strongly against it. But brigand or not, Robert had been right. If anyone could get them to safety, he could.

She trusted him with her life, if she could trust him with nothing else.

"Keep your hoods over your heads," Lachlan said. "We want to blend into the night as much as we can."

The rough and scratchy, dark brown wool cloaks would be hard to see in the darkness. The group would be visible only for a moment as they left the postern gate before descending into the cistern chamber, but it was better not to take any chances.

"Are you ready?" he asked, his eyes scanning the women and children before him.

After a moment of hesitation they nodded.

The next sound she heard was of the gate being opened—slowly and as quietly as possible. Her heart fluttered wildly. She gazed at the pale, anxious faces around her and knew she was not the only one to feel fear.

The group was much the same as the one that had arrived the night before: the queen, Robert's daughter Marjory, Mary Bruce, Christina Bruce and her young son the earl, Margaret and the other lady attendants, Atholl, Magnus, William, two other men-at-arms she did not know, and, of course, Lachlan.

Of their previous companions, Sir James Douglas had been dispatched earlier with a message for the king—if he could be found—and Robbie Boyd and Alex Seton had remained with Nigel to defend the castle.

When the gate was open, Lachlan did a quick check outside and then began to usher them through. Magnus went first, leading the group outside in a long snake. The young earl started to talk, but his mother Christina quickly shushed him.

"Your turn, Countess."

Bella looked around, realizing she was the last one. She nodded and treaded down the steps of the postern gate. She couldn't hear Lachlan behind her—he walked as soundlessly as a ghost—but she knew he was there.

To take advantage of its natural defenses, the curtain wall had been built to the edge of the steep, rocky riverbank that the locals called the back den. A steep sunken stairwell had been carved into the rock to connect the castle to the old cistern chamber and the well-house on the other side of the crevice. They had to walk only a few feet outside the castle before they came to the entrance, covered with a piece of now-rotting wood and obscured by years of disuse.

Magnus had lifted the wood and cleared the growth enough to enable them to squeeze through the opening. William led them down the narrow stairwell built into the side of the cliff.

It was a little bit like descending into a black hole. Thankfully, she could see the soft glow of the torches in the tunnel ahead.

She took her first step inside, and the cool smell of musk and damp earth hit her. She hesitated and instinctively turned behind her.

The last glint of moonlight caught Lachlan's face in its ghostly glow.

She'd expected a nod of encouragement, an impatient gesture, something. What she didn't expect was to see his face tight with pain, his teeth clenched so hard his mouth had turned white, and his eyes flash with what she could only think was panic.

But the look was gone in an instant, and then his face was shadowed in the darkness. "It's all right," he said softly. "Just go slow. I'll light a torch in a minute."

But it was difficult to see, even with the torches, and it took them a long time to wind their way down before they entered the vaulted cistern chamber.

William swore.

"What is it?" Lachlan asked.

"There's a gate to the tunnel to the well-house. It's locked."

"Let me see." Lachlan crossed the room, removing something from his sporran. Bella drew closer, trying to see what it was. It looked like a nail. He seemed to slip it inside the opening and move it around, and a moment later he pulled the lock open.

"I must not have pulled it hard enough," William said dryly.

"How'd he do that?" Mary whispered at her side.

Bella frowned. "I don't know."

Once opened, they passed through the gate into a tunnel. When they came to another staircase, they had to wait a few minutes while a few of the men climbed into the well-house to make sure no one was about.

As soundlessly as seventeen people could manage, they emerged from the darkness of a tunnel first into a wooden well-house thick with spiderwebs and debris, and then into the fresh cusp of dawn air.

"I can't find my horsey," a small voice whinged softly. "I d-dropped it." From the way the little earl's voice wobbled, Bella knew that the lad was close to tears.

Christina Bruce knelt beside her son, trying to calm and quiet him at the same time. "Did you leave it at the castle?" she asked.

He shook his head, tears filling his little eyes. "I had it in my sporran."

"Did you take it out?"

He nodded. "In the scary room."

Christina smoothed the tears that had started to stream down his cheek with her finger. "Then it's probably lost, my love. We'll get you a new one when we get to Norway."

The little boy shook his head, sobbing harder now. "Father made it for me."

Christina looked up at her and Bella felt her throat constrict with a hot ball of tears. The child had lost his father only a year ago. And the man who'd replaced him was missing. War had cost this little boy so much.

"I'm sorry, love," Christina said.

Lachlan had come up beside them. He looked down at the boy. "What's the matter?"

Bella explained. William was standing near the door to the well-house and must have overheard. Before Lachlan could stop him, he said, "I'll get it. I have to block the opening anyway. Go ahead, I'll catch up."

Lachlan's mouth fell in a flat line, but he didn't argue.

With Magnus and one of the other men-at-arms leading, they headed away from the well-house into the dense woodlands that surrounded it. A few minutes later she heard the dull sound of a boom.

Her gaze shot to Lachlan's "What was that?"

"Nothing to worry about. Gordon is just making sure no one can use the tunnel to get close to the castle. It should have been destroyed years ago."

But no sooner had the words left his mouth than a loud crash came from behind them, followed by the unmistakable scent of smoke in the air.

Lachlan swore.

She turned around just in time to see the well-house explode in flames.

# Seven

❧

Bella's heart lurched as she stared at the inferno. Dear God, William was trapped inside!

She heard the cries of the others as they realized the same thing.

Lachlan pulled one of his swords from his back and turned to MacKay. "Get the women and children back. Someone might have heard."

His voice was calm. Steady. Controlled.

MacKay nodded soberly and started barking orders to the other men, trying to make order out of the chaos.

All of a sudden Bella realized what Lachlan meant to do. Her eyes widened with horror. She grabbed his arm to stop him. "You can't go in there. It's too late. You'll never be able to reach him."

The old wooden well-house was engulfed in flames, burning like tinder.

Lachlan refused to see reason. His eyes blazed with a strange intensity. "I have to try, damn it. I'm not leaving him."

Before she could protest again, he broke away and raced toward the well-house. Wrapping his plaid around his face, he kicked down the burning door and raced into the flames, using his sword to defend against the falling timbers.

"No!" Bella heard a bloodcurdling scream tear through the forest. The stab of pain was so overwhelming she didn't realize right away that the scream was hers.

She lunged forward, but someone grabbed her from behind. Magnus. "You can't go in there. You'll only get yourself killed. They need you, my lady."

Magnus's plea broke through the haze of horror and shock. They needed her, and there was nothing she could do for Lachlan or William. Numbly, she nodded as tears gushed in hot waves from her stinging eyes and allowed Magnus to pull her back. Pull her away from the flames as her heart twisted with pain.

Oh God, why had he done it? Going into that burning building was suicide. Lachlan was supposed to be selfish. A man who fought only for his purse. He didn't care about anyone else. Why couldn't he act true to character just this one time?

They needed him. His duty was to stay and protect them, not be a hero.

Losing one man was bad enough, but two . . .

*Losing him.*

A loud crash sounded behind her. Her gaze jerked around, and she blinked in disbelief. Lachlan burst through what remained of the well-house door, dragging another man behind him. It didn't seem real. *He* didn't seem real. How could he have survived that? He should be dead. They both should be dead.

"Magnus?" she asked hesitantly, seeking confirmation.

"He has him, my lady," the big Highlander said with a grin. "He has him."

She closed her eyes, giving a silent prayer of thanks, as emotion strangled in her throat.

She followed Magnus, who'd gone to Lachlan's assistance, relieving him of William and helping to drag him away from the flames. Lachlan was bent over coughing, fighting to get air back into his lungs, but William wasn't moving.

She knelt beside the unconscious warrior. William's hair was singed and his face was black with smoke and soot. She couldn't tell whether he was breathing. "What can I do?"

Lachlan's gaze shot to hers. "What the hell are you doing here? I told you to get back."

Her heart hitched. His voice was raspy from the smoke, his face was nearly as black as William's, and his eyes burned into her with an intensity that she didn't recognize. But none of that mattered. He was alive.

"Are you all right?" Bella couldn't hide the fear in her voice; it simmered too close to the surface.

Some of his anger seemed to dissipate. Their eyes held and for a moment it felt as though the rest of the world had fallen away. She didn't understand it, but the connection she felt to this man was at a primal level unlike any she'd ever experienced before. He cared for her. He had to.

"Aye," he said softly. "I'm fine." Seeming to catch himself, he turned to Magnus, who was still examining the unconscious William. "How is he?"

"His pulse is slow and his breathing is shallow. I don't know—"

Suddenly, William's chest started to rumble. He wheezed in a staggered breath of air, and then exploded in a fit of coughing that racked his entire body. He rolled to the side, curling into a ball, and coughed until Bella thought his lungs would give out.

She glanced up and caught Lachlan's eye, beaming a relieved smile at him. She was surprised when his mouth curved in a wide smile in return.

She sucked in her breath. Her heart slammed against her ribs. The transformation was stunning. Gone was the heartless, dangerous mercenary, replaced by an almost boyishly handsome man who could steal her heart if she let him. The realization jarred her.

"How is he?"

Bella turned to find Queen Elizabeth by her side. She'd been so caught up in the moment, she hadn't noticed that the women had circled around them.

"I don't know," Bella answered.

William must have heard the queen's question through his violent coughing spasms. "I'll b-be fine." His voice sounded worse than Lachlan's.

He tried to sit up, and Magnus helped him. "Take it easy. You took in a lot of smoke."

"I would have taken in a lot more." William looked to Lachlan. "Thank you. I owe you my life."

Lachlan shrugged off his gratitude. "How are your hands?"

William held them up, examining the singed leather of his gauntlets. "Minor burns," he said. "I've had worse."

"What the hell happened?" Lachlan asked.

"I must have used too much powder. The entire building collapsed, and I was hit in the head with a beam."

Suddenly, William reached into his *cotun* and smiled. Pulling out a carved wooden horse, he handed it to the young earl. "I did manage to retrieve this, though."

The little boy beamed with pleasure. "You found it!"

"Aye," William said. "I hope you will not lose it again."

Wide-eyed, the lad shook his head. "I won't. Thank you, Sir William." He turned to Lachlan. "And you, Sir Lachlan."

The lad looked so solemn, none of them had the heart to correct him. They weren't knights.

But they weren't regular soldiers, either. Bella's brows furrowed, looking back and forth between Lachlan, MacKay, and Gordon. None of them were. Which begged the question, just what were they?

There was something between these three men. Some

kind of bond strong enough to send Lachlan into a burning building after one of them.

Magnus helped William to his feet, and Bella turned to find Lachlan extending his hand toward her. She slid her fingers into his, feeling the unmistakable rush of warmth at the contact. Her gaze found his.

He must have felt it, too, because his mouth was set in a grim line as he helped her to her feet.

"Ready the women," he said, looking away. "We need to go quickly. If anyone is nearby they will come to investigate."

He turned to leave, but she stopped him with a hand on his arm. He stilled at her touch; she could feel the rigid muscles flexing under her fingertips.

"Why did you do it?" she asked. "Why did you go after him? You could have died."

He looked down at her, and Bella felt her chest squeeze. A corner of his mouth lifted in a wry smile. "You won't get rid of me so easily, Countess. I'm not so easy to kill."

She suspected he was very hard to kill, but he was evading her question. "Why are you really here? Why are you fighting for Bruce?"

His gaze held hers, piercing. "I already told you why."

"Aye, money and land, but I think there is more to it. What is between you and William and Magnus? And Boyd and Seton, for that matter?" His expression didn't flicker, but she sensed a steel curtain go down. "Who are those men to you?"

His eyes were hard and his voice flat. "Warriors under my temporary command." He pulled his arm away from her grip and started to move toward the other men. "Do not invent noble purposes for my actions, my lady. You will only be disappointed."

"You make it difficult to trust you."

He gave her a long look. "Trusting me is the last thing you should do."

He walked away, his none-too-subtle warning ringing in her ears. She sensed he spoke the truth, but she also knew it was more complicated than that.

Something had changed. She could no longer see him as the mean, opportunistic brigand, working completely for his own ends. Selfish men didn't race into burning buildings to rescue a man who should have been dead. A heartless man wouldn't have taken it upon himself to take a message to her daughter.

There was good in him, whether he wanted to admit it or not. He wanted everyone to think that he was mean and heartless, a hardened mercenary who didn't care about anything, but it was only a mask. Beneath the mask of mockery and indifference, she sensed the pain and restless energy teeming inside him, ready to explode.

Something deep inside her made her want to trust him—despite what he said. And if her reaction to the thought of his death was any indication, she was no longer indifferent. Sometime in the past few months, Lachlan MacRuairi, the scourge of the West, had come to matter to her. Matter to her quite a lot. And no matter what he wanted her to think, she knew he was not indifferent to her.

He wasn't noble, damn it. And Lachlan didn't need the countess looking at him as if he were.

He didn't leave men behind; it was as simple as that. He wasn't going to let William die, not if he could do something to prevent it.

If the face of his foster brother had flashed before his eyes, he'd pushed it aside. He'd done everything then, too, but it hadn't been enough. This time it had.

But if the countess's newfound belief in his nobility had made him uneasy, he didn't have time to think about it. After securing horses—which hadn't been easy in the war-torn area—they were on the move. And moving is exactly what they did for the next two days. The women and children doubled up on the horses, while the men kept pace beside them. Sometimes at a fast march, more often at a slow run.

He drove them relentlessly, mercilessly, stopping only for brief periods to rest. The men slept for a few hours at a time; the women took turns sleeping in the saddle.

On the third day it started to rain. A nonstop heavy rain with swirling wind that lashed and flailed like a whip, sapping their strength and demoralizing their spirits. As they neared the Moray coast that night, he sent Gordon ahead to scout. He returned with bad news. Not only were the rough seas too perilous to attempt a journey, galleys patrolled the coastline.

They had to go farther north.

Waiting for the weather to break, Lachlan drove them on. He couldn't escape the feeling that their enemies were closing in on them. The ships in Moray had bothered him. It was almost as if their enemies knew where they were headed.

At dusk the following day, they stopped to water the horses just outside of Tain. He was bent over a crude map with MacKay and Gordon discussing their route. He wanted to get out of the area quickly. They were in Ross, and to say that he and the earl weren't friendly was to put it mildly. Ross was every bit as much a threat as the English hunting them.

"We'll take the road north into Sutherland." He indicated the route on the map. "And then into Caithness. Hopefully by the time we reach Wick, the weather will have calmed enough to make the crossing to Orkney."

It was MacKay country. Saint would be able to get them through it.

He sensed her presence before she spoke. His skin prickled with awareness, every nerve ending flaring to life.

"We can't go any farther tonight; we need to rest."

He turned slowly to face her. "Not yet."

An angry flush rose to her cheeks. "We have to. The children can't go on like this, and some of the women are so weak they are about ready to fall off their horses. We are soaked to the bone, hungry, and need to sleep for longer than a few hours."

Lachlan's mouth fell in a hard, unrelenting line. "It can't be helped. You can sleep on the galley when we reach Wick."

"They won't make it to the galley. Not at this pace." Her eyes bored into his. "Why are you doing this? Why are you pushing us so hard?"

He didn't want to alarm her unnecessarily. All he had was a bad feeling. "We won't be safe until we reach Norway."

"Please, Lachlan." The sound of his name on her tongue made something in this chest tighten. "Just look at them. They can't go on."

He did what he'd purposefully avoided. His gaze scanned the once fine ladies who now looked as scraggly as beggar women collapsed against the trees or rocks for support. The young earl was curled up in a ball in his mother's lap, Mary Bruce lay with her cheek resting against a moss-covered log asleep, and Marjory, the young princess, was asleep in the queen's arms.

"There's sanctuary in Tain," she said. "We could take shelter at St. Duthac's Chapel for the night."

She'd obviously thought about this. She was right; King Malcolm had granted Tain the status of sanctuary by charter over two hundred years ago. By law and tradition, it was a place where fugitives could take refuge.

His mouth fell in a hard line. He knew he'd pushed them as far as he could. "Very well. We'll stay the night in Tain." He looked up to the sky; the rain had turned into a fine mist. "If the weather breaks, we can try to secure a galley from there."

Even before they reached the church, Lachlan regretted

going against his instincts and acceding to the countess's demands. What the hell was happening to him? Once again he was letting a woman control his actions.

He couldn't let her get to him like this. This fierce attraction, this . . . whatever it was that was making him feel like this, had to end. He wouldn't let a woman hold that kind of power over him again. All his men had been killed because his cock was hard for a woman. The same weakness was biting him in the arse again.

But Bella was nothing like his wife . . . was she?

He couldn't get that image of her and Bruce out of his mind. It gnawed at him, festering, like a sore under his skin.

He was in a foul temper by the time they reached the old chapel nestled on a rise overlooking the sea. No more than thirty by twenty feet, the stone building with a vaulted wood roof held a few benches, a stone altar, and little else. Fortunately, as it was late, it was also deserted. The priest probably slept in the nearby rectory.

He made sure the women were settled before heading out to scout the area to ensure they hadn't been followed. Since the rain had stopped, he would also look for a galley. The sooner they were on the way, the better.

He'd just closed the wooden door behind him when Bella turned the corner, nearly running into him.

"Where are you going?" she asked. Her eyes raked his face. "Is something wrong? You seem angry."

He doubted she realized she'd taken a step toward him, but he did. Every muscle in his body pulled taut as her soft scent rose to play havoc with his senses—and his sense.

"To look around and see about finding a galley," he said in a tight, clipped voice.

He wondered if she knew how much effort it took not to touch her. Not to push her up against the door and give in to the maelstrom raging inside him. Maybe then he would rid himself of this ache of need that seemed to be consuming him. She'd shredded years of control to ribbons. He didn't want to feel like this, damn it.

He gritted his teeth. *Get the job done.* But he didn't know how much more of this he could take.

She had her head tilted back to look up at him, and he could see the mark of sadness in her eyes. "Must we leave Scotland? Is there no place else we can hide?"

He knew she was tired. That she wasn't thinking rationally. That the thought of leaving her daughter was tearing her apart. But he felt the anger flare inside him.

He'd warned her what she risked, but she hadn't wanted to listen to him. Part of her still didn't realize the magnitude of what she'd done. Whether in Norway or in Scotland, the truth was the same. "Don't you understand, Countess?"

His darkly mocking tone caused her to draw back a little. "Understand what?"

"Your daughter was lost to you the moment you put the crown on Bruce's head. Buchan will never let you take the lass. For all you know, he's probably already hidden her away in England."

She gasped, but he forced himself not to react to the stricken look on her face.

"Why are you saying this? Why are you being so cruel?"

"Because it's the truth, whether you want to see it or not."

"You're wrong. I will *never* stop fighting to get my daughter back. I'll find a way. When Robert—"

The mention of the king's name made something inside him snap. He grabbed her by the arm, wanting to shake her as badly as he wanted to pull her up against him. "Robert?" he scoffed. "Bruce is done, Bella. He'll be lucky to make it out of the country alive." He hated himself for asking the question, knowing the weak emotion that was driving it. "Why did you do it? Why did you risk so much?"

Her eyes scanned his face; it was clear she didn't understand the intensity behind his question. "Because I believe in him, and things you believe in are worth fighting for." She waited, hoping for him to say something—probably to agree with her—and seemed disappointed when he didn't. "I couldn't stand by and do nothing when I had a chance to help. Robert is Scotland's best chance for freedom. He sees what the men who came before him did not: that to win we must not only defeat the English on the battlefield, we must also not defeat ourselves. He will do whatever it takes to unify Scotland behind him, even if it means forgiving old enemies. And you're wrong. He isn't done. Done is how legends are born."

Her endless idealism where Bruce was concerned only fueled his suspicions. "And that's the only reason?"

Her eyes narrowed. "What other reason could there be?"

He didn't say anything, but merely held her gaze.

Suddenly, shock transformed her features. Her eyes widened and her lips parted with a harsh gasp.

If he was in his right mind, he would have understood the flicker of pain in her eyes, would have realized that his accusation had hurt her. That he'd hit a nerve and found another vulnerability beneath the proud mask. And if he could think about anything other than crushing her mouth to his, he would have seen that he was wrong. That once again jealousy had made him act like an arse.

But he wasn't in his right mind. He was consumed by feelings he didn't understand. Anger, jealousy, lust, and something he rejected with every fiber of his being.

All he could think about was pulling her against him, covering her mouth with his, and kissing her until she stopped making him feel this way. Until she denied the unspoken accusations. But one look in her eye told him she wasn't going to do that.

If he'd stabbed her with a knife, the wound would have been no less painful. Bella couldn't believe it. Were all men the same? He was no better than her husband, jealous and suspicious, believing that large breasts and a wide mouth left her without honor.

Lachlan thought she was doing all this because she was carrying on some illicit liaison with Robert. How could he think such a thing? How could he believe the rumors?

He didn't know her at all. She couldn't believe she'd let herself be deceived into thinking he was different, that he might actually care for her, if only for a moment.

If he thought her a whore, she would not disabuse him of the idea. She lifted her chin defiantly and met his angry gaze with a gleam of pure wickedness. She tossed her shoulders back and stuck out her chest to better vantage.

He made a sharp sound and his face went white.

A deep feminine instinct rose inside her. She slid her tongue across her bottom lip, as if she were a hungry spider waiting to trap her next meal. Her eyes slitted and her voice deepened seductively. "What do you think?"

She realized her mistake right away. Or maybe she'd known what would happen all along and wanted it to happen. She wanted to have even more of a reason to hate him. Lachlan MacRuairi was not a man to provoke.

He pulled her into his arms. Pulled her against the powerful chest that she'd noticed far more times than was proper.

She gasped as her body came into contact with his. He was so hard. His chest was like a wall of granite. It should be uncomfortable—intimidating—but it wasn't. The visceral awareness of his strength made her feel safe and protected.

As he lowered his head, her heart seemed to stop, pausing in that terrifying, agonizing moment that she'd both dreaded and craved. Finally, he covered her mouth with his.

She felt his groan all the way to her toes. The primitive,

masculine sound poured through her veins like molten lava.

The first taste of him was like a shock. Her heart slammed against her ribs. Sensation exploded inside her. His lips were so soft and warm, his taste sublime. Like a dark, rich wine mulled with cloves.

She felt infused with it. Infused with him. As if one touch—one taste—could mark her forever.

His mouth moved over hers deftly, passionately, demanding a response.

She should push him away. This was wrong. It wasn't supposed to be like this. Usually she didn't feel anything. Except this time she did. She felt her body flush, her pulse race, and her senses fire with unfamiliar yearnings.

Bella didn't understand what was happening to her. She felt so warm, her body so heavy. And there was an insistent knot coiling low in her belly.

She waited for her body to stiffen. For the vague feeling of revulsion to come over her as his mouth accosted hers.

But it didn't happen. For a brigand who took what he wanted, there was nothing forceful about Lachlan's kiss. His passion was warm and enticing, not cold and cruel. It was not an assault or mauling but a dark seduction.

Lachlan made her want to wind her arms around his neck and pull her body closer. To melt against him. To mold her soft curves to every hard inch of him.

Lachlan made her want to yield. To open her mouth and give freely of what her husband had tried to take.

Lachlan made her . . . *want*.

God help her, she wanted him. Desperately. Like she'd never wanted anyone before. She'd thought herself incapable of desire. Every bit as cold to passion as her husband accused. But she felt it now. Felt it awaken in a tingling rush of heat and pleasure.

She sank against him, savoring the wicked sensation of

her breasts crushing against his chest. And then with a sigh, she opened her mouth.

Lachlan let out a growl of satisfaction when he felt her yield. He'd wanted to punish her for making him lose control. For giving in to the lust that he'd sworn to avoid. He was mad. Angry. Pushed to the edge. But his anger dissolved the moment he touched his lips to hers. A wave of something soft and powerful crashed over him. Tenderness, damn it. He could never hurt her. He'd told her he would never use force, and he meant it.

God, she was sweet. Sweeter even than he'd imagined. He couldn't have pulled away if he wanted to.

He half—more than half—expected her to push him away. But her tentative, innocent response nearly undid him.

The sensation of her soft, sensual lips opening under his drove him wild. He slid his tongue into her mouth, kissing her deeper, harder, claiming every inch that she was willing to give.

She was kissing him back, her sweet little cries urging him on. He could feel her press against him. Feel the desire building inside her. Feel the increasing urgency of her kiss.

His tongue circled hers. Slowly at first, then faster, as the sensations swirling between them built.

He'd been waiting so long for this, he couldn't take it slow.

Heat surged through his veins. His skin was hot. Tight. Too small for his body. His muscles flexed, straining against the sensations. His cock lengthened and hardened against her.

He could feel every one of those lush, soft curves against him, but still it wasn't enough. Closer. He had to get closer.

He plunged his fingers through the soft silk of her hair, cushioning her head as he leaned her up against the door, bending her deeper into him.

*There. Oh, Jesus, right there.* A wave of heat nearly dragged him under.

His body melded to hers, his cock wedged in that soft place between her legs. The urge to thrust taunted.

It felt too good. Too right. He could almost feel what it would be like to slide into her. How he could cup her bottom with his hands and lift her against him, wrap her legs around his waist and push into that soft, wet glove of her heat.

He'd rip open her bodice so he could feel the hard points of her breasts raking against his skin. Her skin would be flushed, hot, the scent of roses even stronger.

He could feel the frantic beat of her heart as he brought her mouth more fully against his and gave over to the passion long denied unfurling inside him.

Bella was lost in a haze of desire unlike anything she'd ever imagined. His kiss grew more insistent. Each carnal slide of his tongue against hers licked the flames a little hotter.

She could feel his hardness between her legs, and it flooded her with even more intense yearnings. He moved against her. A slow grind of the hips that sent a flutter of awareness shooting up her spine. She wanted to feel him inside her. Wanted to feel him moving—

*Dear God!*

The wickedness of her thoughts brought her harshly back to reality. What was she doing? How could she have succumbed so easily, so completely? What was wrong with her?

A flush of shame replaced the heat of passion. After years of suspicion and irrational jealousy, she'd finally made her husband's accusations come true.

She pushed him away. "Stop!"

He pulled back, his eyes dark with desire. With lust. Seeing what she feared so badly made her lash out. She slapped his face. "How dare you touch me like that!"

She didn't know who was more shocked by the violence

of her reaction. His face turned back to her slowly, and she cringed seeing the imprint of her palm.

"Are you offended that I touched you, Countess, or just mad that you enjoyed it?"

The truth of his accusation stung. Tears swelled in the back of her throat. "What do you want from me?"

A slow, lazy smile curled his mouth but never reached the hardness in his eyes. "What are you offering?"

The mocking brigand was back. The man who didn't care about anything. How could she have thought differently? "It's always about money to you, is that it?"

His gaze, an even more piercing green than usual, raked over her in a way that made her feel dirty. "I wasn't talking about money." She gasped. "Countess, if I wanted money from you, I'd take you to Edward myself."

"I'm surprised you haven't, since gold is all that matters to you. Didn't you tell me yourself that Robert is done? Seems like you picked the wrong side this time. What will happen to all that coin you've been promised?"

"You have me all figured out, don't you, Countess?" He held her gaze, and something in his eyes made her wish her taunts back. "You make a good point. One I'll have to consider. It's always good to weigh your options." He gave her an exaggerated bow. "Now, if you'll excuse me, I have more important matters to attend to."

Bella almost called him back. She knew she'd been unfair. That the shame of dissolving in his arms had made her lash out at him. It wasn't his fault she hadn't pushed him away the way she should have.

But she didn't. Calling him back wouldn't change anything. Even if they made it out of this alive, what kind of future could they have? She was the set-aside wife of another man. Nothing good could ever happen between them. These feelings—the intensity of emotion pouring through her—scared her. She feared what they might make her do. It was better this way. She had to make sure something like that never happened again.

Now that she'd tasted passion, she wished she never had.

She joined the others in the chapel and tried to sleep. But she kept one ear pinned to the door, hoping to hear him come back.

He never did.

Just after dawn, she stirred at the sound of a door closing. It was Magnus again. He'd come in and out a few times, during the night, probably checking on the men keeping watch outside. She could hear him whispering to William, "He should be back by now."

She quickly got up and hustled over to them. "Is something wrong?"

"I don't know," Magnus said honestly. "But we should gather the rest of the women and get ready to go."

By the time she did, it was too late.

"You can't do this!" The frantic voice of the priest was the first hint of what was to come. Through one of the arched windows they could see the old man standing a few feet before the church door, arms wide, trying to block the entrance.

But the soldiers paid him no heed. The Earl of Ross and at least a hundred of his guardsmen had surrounded the church.

Dear God in heaven, they'd been discovered! She couldn't believe it. It wasn't just the shock of discovery, but also the egregiousness of what she was seeing that made her blink with disbelief: Ross was breaking the sanctuary of the church.

She heard Magnus swear. He and William exchanged looks. She knew they wanted to fight. William shook his head. They were outnumbered, even for men of their skill.

"Someone could get hurt," William said.

Magnus nodded, his expression as grim as she'd ever seen it.

The men would be the first to be punished, imprisoned, or executed without trial. "Go," she said. "Save yourselves. Nothing you can do will help us now."

Both men looked outraged by her suggestion. "Our duty is to protect you, my lady," Magnus said. "As long as there is breath in my body, I will do so."

While Magnus went out to negotiate their surrender with the treacherous Earl of Ross, Bella tried to calm the rising panic of the other women. But there was nothing she could say. After over a month of hiding, of running for their lives, it was over. Ross would take them to Edward, and they would be at the English king's mercy.

Thank God, Lachlan wasn't here. It was fortunate indeed that he'd managed to escape their fate.

But where was he? Could he be watching? Part of her feared that he might do something rash to try to rescue them. The other part actually believed he could. If there was one thing she'd learned about Lachlan MacRuairi, it was that he would do whatever it took to get the mission done. He'd rushed into a burning building without thinking to save one man; what would he do with all of them?

When she'd stepped out of St. Duthac's Chapel into the crisp morning sunshine to surrender to the Earl of Ross, she couldn't help scanning the countryside, half-expecting him to race out of the trees.

The earl must have been watching her. Ross was similar in age and expression to Buchan—and just as stern and proud. He'd spent six years in Edward's prisons after his capture at Dunbar; never would she have thought him capable of this travesty. "Looking for someone, Countess?"

She tried not to show her surprise, but her heart immediately started to pound. Ross knew about Lachlan, which meant . . . *Oh God, what had happened to him?*

Ross's smile was smug. "I must admit I thought Bruce had better sense than to put an opportunistic scourge like that bastard MacRuairi in charge of you. The man can't be trusted. He's stolen rents for me for years. More than even the capture of Bruce's ladies can repay."

Bella rejected what he was saying, ignoring that her initial characterization of Lachlan had been much the same.

Despite what she'd accused him of, the thought that Lachlan might have betrayed them hadn't occurred to her. Should it have? But at the mention of "repay," a vague uneasiness settled in. "Where is he? What have you done with him?"

Her voice must have given something away. Ross lifted a brow speculatively. "The bastard is hardly worthy of your concern, Countess. He's the one you have to thank for leading us to you. He won't be any help to you now. But don't you worry, Lachlan MacRuairi will get exactly what he has coming to him. All his debts will be paid."

Bella's stomach knifed. *Leading us to you* . . .

*No, he wouldn't.* She couldn't believe him capable of such treachery. To sell them to Ross, knowing what would befall them.

*"Don't trust me . . ."* His warning came back to her.

Ross walked away, ordering his men to put them in a cart to take them to Auldern Castle.

William must have seen the horror in her expression. He came up beside her before she was roughly shoved into the cart. "There has to be a mistake, my lady. The captain wouldn't—"

His voice stopped as disbelief filled his eyes. Bella turned in the direction of his stare, and gasped. Her heart seemed to shrivel in her chest. All hope that she'd been wrong died.

Lachlan stood at the base of the hill, surrounded by a handful of Ross's men. He was staring at her. When their eyes met, there was no mistaking what she saw: guilt.

Her chest burned with emptiness, as if a big, hot stake had hallowed it out. She'd trusted him. She'd thought . . .

She turned away. Of all the disappointments in her life— her father, her husband—none had cut this deeply. By now she should have known better. She was no longer a fifteen-year-old bride or a little girl begging for crumbs of her father's attention.

Lachlan had shown her the kind of man he was—he'd told her not to trust him—but she'd invented romantic fantasies, making herself believe there was something more to him. She'd actually convinced herself he cared for her. But all he'd wanted was what was between her thighs, and once she'd denied him that . . .

God, it shouldn't hurt this badly.

"Chane—" Gordon tried to yell something as the cart was pulling away, but one of Ross's men pushed him to the ground.

Changed? Was that what he was trying to say? Bella realized it no longer mattered. What difference did it make, when they'd been caught?

Mary Bruce cried on her shoulder as the cart bumped along the road to Auldern, and Bella tried to soothe her.

The girl who reminded her so much of her daughter looked up at her with terrified, tear-filled eyes. "What will become of us, my lady?"

"I don't know, my love. I suspect some time in the tower. It won't be so bad. Some of the rooms I hear are quite nice."

Neither of them could have imagined just how wrong she would be.

# Eight

*Dunstaffnage Castle, Lorn, October 10, 1308*

This was it—the information Lachlan had been waiting for. The king wasn't going to put him off again. For over two years Lachlan had been forced to bide his time. No more. He was going after Bella and no one was going to stop him. Not Bruce, not MacLeod—hell, not the entire blasted English army.

The sounds of revelry that followed him into the solar were proof enough the time had come. It wasn't just the wedding of Arthur Campbell and Anna MacDougall that they celebrated, but also the capitulation of Ross—the last of Scotland's great magnates to hold out against King Robert. The bastard who'd turned Bella and the other women over to Edward had made his peace.

From the jaws of almost certain defeat, Bruce had risen again like a phoenix from the ashes, first defeating the English, and then the powerful Scottish nobles who'd stood against him. Bella had been right: Bruce's near miraculous comeback was the way legends were made. Her faith in the king had not been misplaced.

It was they who'd failed her. Bruce. Himself. Everyone.

But no longer. With MacDougall and Ross tamed, there were no more excuses. No more enemies to defeat before he could go after her again.

Lachlan paced the small room with all the calm of a caged lion while he waited, trying to tamp down the excitement coursing through him. God knew there'd been too many disappointments in the past. Bad intelligence. Rumors of release. Negotiations that went nowhere. And even a failed rescue attempt.

He'd been so damned close. But one guard had managed to raise the alarm before Lachlan had gotten halfway up the tower where Edward's barbarous prison cage hung. He and the other members of the Highland Guard who'd accompanied him had barely escaped with their lives.

Seeing her in that abomination was something that would haunt him the rest of his life. She'd seemed so thin and pale. Her big, round eyes dominated her face, as she stared into the distance with a look of desolation that cut to the bone. He'd never felt so damned helpless in his life. Seeing her and not being able to reach her had driven him half-mad.

He'd taken some comfort that she'd been released from the cage not long afterward, but the failure ate at him.

But not this time. He wouldn't fail again.

A few minutes passed before he heard the door open. The king entered, followed by Tor MacLeod, the captain of the Highland Guard—or Chief, as his war name proclaimed him. Neither man appeared pleased to have been pulled away from the wedding festivities.

The king sat down in the thronelike chair recently occupied by John MacDougall, Lord of Lorn, and gave him a hard look. "I assume since this couldn't wait the few hours until morning it must be about the countess?"

Lachlan stared across the table at the man who'd spoken so calmly. But like him, Lachlan knew that Robert the

Bruce, King of Scotland, was anything but calm. These past two years since the women had been taken in Tain had been almost as hard on Bruce as they'd been on Lachlan. Almost. But not quite.

Bruce wasn't the one responsible for their capture.

"She's to be moved—Mary as well."

The king sat forward; clearly Lachlan had surprised him. "And how did you learn of this?"

Lachlan shrugged. "I have my sources."

Bruce's eyes narrowed. "Bribing spies? Damn it, Viper, why was I not told of this? Is that where all the money I pay you is going?"

Lachlan's mouth fell in a hard line. He didn't explain himself—even to a king.

MacLeod stepped in to defuse the tension. "Where are they to be moved?"

Lachlan shook his head. "I don't know. It doesn't matter. This is the opportunity we've been waiting for. With Bella leaving the castle, there won't be a better time for a rescue."

The king and MacLeod exchanged a glance, but neither man disagreed.

"I'm not surprised that they've decided to do something about Bella," Bruce said after a moment. "With Buchan dead and no longer calling for her head, De Monthermer was able to persuade the new English king to release her from the cage, but since then no one knows what to do with her. No one wants her around. She's a black mark on the first Edward and on England, and too powerful a symbol of the rebellion to simply let go free. They want her to disappear. My guess would be a convent or a castle in a remote part of England. But that doesn't explain why they're moving Mary."

No one had an answer.

"When is this supposed to happen?" MacLeod asked. The captain of the Highland Guard and at one time one of

Lachlan's fiercest enemies would want to know every detail.

"My source says in a few days. They are making preparations now. For obvious reasons, they are keeping it very quiet."

"How can we be sure your source is telling the truth?" the king asked. "What if it's a trap?"

Lachlan's mouth thinned. "That's a risk I'm willing to take. I'm leaving tonight."

He looked at both men, daring either one of them to argue with him.

The silence dragged on. Lachlan sensed he wasn't going to like what was coming next. He was right.

"Are you sure that's a good idea?" Bruce asked. "Perhaps it would be best if you let MacLeod—"

Lachlan leaned forward. "There is no way in hell I'm not going."

The king pretended not to notice the threat, but MacLeod frowned. "Have care, Viper," he said. "You aren't exactly rational about this."

That was putting it mildly. Hell, *obsessed* was putting it mildly. From the moment he'd seen her loaded into that cart, knowing he was responsible, Lachlan had vowed to see Bella freed.

When he'd learned of the fate that had befallen her, he'd been half-crazed with the need to get her out. But delays, war, and a failed attempt had stood in his way. Now, thanks to this new information, he had another chance. There was no way in hell he wasn't going. This was *his* mission.

"The king has good reason for caution," MacLeod added.

"Indeed I do," Bruce said. "Thanks to John of Lorn, your identity as one of the members of my 'secret' army has just been revealed. You are one of the most wanted men in Scotland right now. If you are captured, the English will torture you until you reveal the names of the others. With three hundred marks on your head, everyone will be hunting you. You need to stay hidden for a while. Perhaps visit that isle you will soon be calling home."

Lachlan's glare was mutinous. The king wouldn't distract him with talk of his reward. Lachlan's three years of agreed-upon service was all but fulfilled. The land and coin he'd been promised would be his when Bruce held his first council. His debts would finally be paid, and he'd have the solitude and peace he craved. It was almost done. But he had one final mission to complete before he could leave.

"I've been tortured before," he said flatly. "Nothing they do to me will force me to reveal the names of my fellow guardsmen. Just like nothing will stop me from doing this." He held the king's gaze. "I *have* to do this."

The king studied him silently for a moment before turning to MacLeod. The fierce Island Chief shrugged. "I didn't think he'd see reason."

"Neither did I," the king said with a sigh of resignation. He turned back to Lachlan and gave him a black scowl. "You'd better be careful."

The king didn't need to tell him that. He had no desire to ever be locked up in another pit prison. Dark holes held no fond memories for him. He repressed the reflexive shudder. To free her he would risk it. He would risk just about anything. "Who can I take?"

The king and MacLeod conferred privately for a moment before MacLeod answered. "Raider, Dragon, Hunter, and Striker."

Lachlan muttered an oath. He'd be glad for Lamont's tracking skills and MacLean's gift with strategy, but he'd be spending half his time trying to prevent Boyd and Seton from killing one another. "What about Saint and Templar?" he asked, referring to MacKay and Gordon.

"They're coming with me, Hawk, and Arrow," MacLeod said. "If they're both being moved, we're going to try to free Mary as well."

Lachlan nodded grimly. Like Bella, young Mary Bruce had been hung from a cage—hers was located at Roxburgh Castle.

The first Edward also had originally wanted to hang Bruce's daughter Marjory from a cage at the Tower of London, but she'd been given a reprieve. Like her Aunt Christina, Marjory had been sent to a nunnery instead.

The queen, probably due to her powerful father, Edward's close cohort the Earl of Ulster, had been placed under house arrest in Burstwick. The young Earl of Mar had been sent to the English court to be raised. The Earl of Atholl, however, had not been so fortunate. He'd been sent to the gallows.

MacKay and Gordon had been mistaken for ordinary men-at-arms. They'd been imprisoned at Urquhart for a few months, but Lachlan and other members of the Highland Guard had managed to free them.

"And the other women?"

Bruce's face was somber. "We've heard from my old friend Lamberton, the Bishop of St. Andrews—freed from prison but still confined in England—that my wife, daughter, and sister Christina are being treated well. They are still too far south and too well guarded to attempt anything. But when the moment is right, I will lead the damned rescue party myself."

Lachlan nodded. Though he wished all the women could be freed, it was Bella and young Mary whose harsh treatment had made them the first to rescue.

With his team in place, Lachlan didn't waste any time. Before the cock had crowed, he and the other guardsmen were riding hard for Berwick.

Bella stood gazing out the small window in her tower room, watching the people bustling around the courtyard below as they went about their duties and activities for the day. After more than two years, the faces were familiar to her. There was Harry the young stable lad, fetching water for the horses, and Annie, the young girl from the village who seemed to look for any excuse to linger near Will, the green-and-gold-liveried man-at-arms who excelled with a bow.

Those weren't really their names, of course. But with nothing but needlework to pass the time, she'd made up names and stories for the villagers and occupants of the castle. At times it could be quite entertaining, almost like watching a play. But most importantly, it was a way to relieve the monotony that had proved her most dogged enemy—inside the cage or out.

She stood here most of the day. The window was small, but there were no bars to obstruct the view. Sometimes, for a fraction of an instant, she could forget the small room behind her. Forget the smothering sense of confinement that lingered since her release from the cage three months ago—ninety-seven days, to be exact.

But she was careful not to look up. She never looked up.

She knew the location of her chamber wasn't an accident. They'd placed her in a tower room opposite the cage. It was just another way to torment and manipulate her, to not let her forget what they could do to her.

As if she could ever forget. She didn't need a view to remind her of the hell of her imprisonment. She carried the memories with her every day.

How she'd gotten through it she didn't know. Her daughter. Her pride. An obstinate refusal to let them win. Somehow she'd managed. She'd learned to ignore that people were always watching her. That she never had a moment of privacy. The pitying glances. The bars. She'd combated the sense of confinement by walking in place and stretching her limbs every morning. Alleviated her boredom by making up stories about the people in the yard.

The one thing she could not control was the cold. She shivered reflexively. This small, damp, soulless room seemed like a sultry haven by comparison.

She'd walked out of that cage thinner, weaker, and sadder, but with her back straight and her chin up.

She'd gotten through it once, but she didn't think she could do it again. It wasn't until she'd been released that the horror caught up to her. But each day she was getting stronger and feeling more like her old self.

Suddenly, the door slammed open. She stiffened, knowing exactly who it was. Other than the boredom, the one constant throughout her long ordeal was Sir Simon. Her personal tormentor.

She turned, knowing that if she ignored him it would be worse.

His eyes narrowed, as if he were trying to find something wrong with what she was doing. "You spend a lot of time looking out that window."

Panic rose up her throat. The window was the one thing keeping her from going mad. If he guessed how important it was to her . . .

Bella felt her mouth go dry. She moistened her lips with a quick flick of her tongue, but immediately regretted the action when she saw how Simon's eyes flared. After two years, she knew better than to draw attention to any part of her body—especially her mouth—but her nervousness betrayed her. "I was merely hungry and wondered at the time. Did you bring my meal?"

"I'm not your blasted servant," he said angrily, as she knew he would. Distracting him with anger was the best way to steer him from the scent of her weakness.

She lifted a haughty brow, knowing she was playing with fire. "Then what did you want?"

His fists clenched, as did his jaw. "You're leaving."

Her mouth dropped open. She was so stunned, for a moment she forgot to control her reaction. She tried to tamp down the reflexive burst of hope. She couldn't have heard him right. "Leaving?" she echoed.

"Aye." He was watching her, toying with her, knowing exactly the effect his words would have.

She sat down on a stool and picked up her mending as if he hadn't spoken, forcing her trembling fingers to work the needle through the linen tunic. She spoke with as little care as she could manage. "Where am I to go?"

Was the war over? Had her freedom been negotiated? Could she finally be going home?

"A convent."

The twinge of disappointment was minor. If she wasn't going home, a convent was certainly preferable to an armed fortress like Berwick. A convent would give her hope of escape.

But Simon had known the direction her thoughts would take and had only sought to torment her. He smiled before adding, "There's a Carmelite convent of nuns on the out-skirts of Berwick. You are to be sent there, where you will immediately take your vows."

*Vows? Good God!* Every instinct rose in immediate re-bellion. She wanted to shout out her refusal, to cringe at the mere suggestion. Vows were a prison she could never escape. Once taken, there would be no going back. She'd be locked away forever. The solitude . . . the monotony . . . the confinement would never end. Oh God, she should have guessed there would be some cruel twist.

But the years of controlling her emotions with Buchan had served her well during her imprisonment at Berwick. Her expression betrayed none of her horror.

Still, he knew. "It should make you happy," he taunted. His dark eyes ran over her shapeless woolen gown. The fine gown she'd been imprisoned in was long gone, re-placed by plain, serviceable cast-offs from the castle ser-vants. The roughly spun wool was thick and scratchy, but that didn't matter. It was *warm*. "You've been acting like a nun for years," he sneered with a crude glance between her legs. Her thighs tightened instinctively. "Now you can be one."

She heard the bitter reproach in his voice. How much easier it would have been had she just given in to his demands! Let him use her body as Buchan had done for years. She might have had more coal for the brazier, more blankets for her crude pallet, better food, a host of small luxuries to make her imprisonment if not comfortable, at least bearable.

But she couldn't do it. It wasn't just because every little thing about his person revolted her. The brown stains on his teeth. The white flakes in his greasy dark hair. The layer of sweat that made his face shine like the skin of a fish. Nay, submitting to him would be something she could never excuse. With her husband, she'd had a duty. With Lachlan, she'd foolishly believed there was something special between them. But with Simon, she would be selling herself. And she'd be damned if she'd give proof to the rumors. First about Robert, and then after her capture, thanks to Ross no doubt, about Lachlan.

She did not care that people called her a whore, but she would not make herself one.

So she'd endured cold, hunger, and two years of endless tormenting. Twice he'd gone too far and nearly killed her. Once the rotting food he'd given her had sickened her. Another time he'd punished her defiance by taking away her blankets on a night of cold and rain; she'd nearly frozen to death.

Like her former husband, Simon wanted to see her react. He looked for ways to break her. Many times over the past two years she'd wanted to give in. But one thing had kept her going: her daughter. She had to get through this for Joan.

"I hear the rooms are small and windowless," he said snidely. She repressed a shiver. Though she'd hid her fear well, still he'd guessed it. "But you're used to that, aren't you, Countess?" He emphasized the last, then slapped his forehead with exaggerated affect. "Oh, that's right. With Buchan dead, King Edward, the second by that name, has decided that you are no longer a countess."

She held his gaze and smiled. "Aye, now I am merely the daughter and sister to the most ancient and powerful of all Scottish earldoms."

Simon's face turned florid. She might have been set aside by her husband, and her title stripped by a king, but she was still descended from Scotland's most noble blood, and as such, far above a coarse brute like him.

When Margaret, her only source of outside events, had brought her news a few months back of her husband's death, Bella had felt nothing. Not happiness that the man who'd fought for her death for two years had met his own, or even relief from the knowledge that she would never have to see him again. Her only thought was for her daughter. Joan was alone now. What would happen to her?

Buchan's death had made her even more determined to get out of this nightmare and return to her daughter. Something she would never be able to do if she took her vows.

Simon crossed the small chamber in three strides. He tore the embroidery from her hands and harshly jerked her body up against him.

She hung there like a poppet of rags. Having grown used to such treatment, she didn't resist or feel any fear. Simon was a mean, foul-tempered bully who would touch her and manhandle her whenever he got the chance, but the worst he dared was crude gropings and a few bruises.

He'd wanted to rape her—more times than she could count—but despite the barbarous treatment done to her by England's kings, they apparently had not forsaken every last bond of civility. Her status protected her, and she never let him forget it.

His face drew so near, she could see every black-dotted pore on his ill-shapen nose. Used to his stench, rather than cringe, the staleness of his breath beating down on her merely caused her nose to wrinkle.

"You're nothing but a haughty, worthless whore. For years you've been flaunting your wares, trying to tempt me from my duty. But look at you: a pale, skinny crow. I'll be glad to be rid of you." He gave her a violent shake. "But you'd better dull that sharp tongue of yours. The nuns will not be as tolerant as I am of your sinful pride."

If she could summon the effort, she would laugh. *She* tempt *him*? He, tolerant? No doubt the buffoon actually believed it. But his words pricked the small streak of vanity she had left. Had the years of imprisonment taken as much of a toll on the outside as they had on the inside? Bella hadn't seen her reflection in a looking glass in over two years.

But what would it matter in a convent?

She didn't respond, merely meeting his anger with a mute, emotionless stare. He hated when she did that. And heaven help her, no matter how bad it got, something inside her couldn't resist defying him.

It was the same flaw that had reared its ugly head with her husband.

He tossed her aside with an oath. "Be ready to leave in the morning. The constable will be here himself to see you gone."

She picked up her mending as if the entire unpleasant episode had never happened. "I will go to the convent," she said quietly. "But no one can force me to take the veil."

Bella kept her eyes on the needle, poking in and out of the cloth. For a moment she thought he hadn't heard her. But a surreptitious glance out from under her lashes told her he had. A shiver of trepidation ran down her spine. He was smiling.

Her heart pounded, knowing what was coming. The English held the one weapon that would always defeat her.

"That's too bad," he said. Despite the idleness of his tone, Bella sensed the shift in power. Her victories were always short-lived. "I believe Sir John was reconsidering your request."

Her heart stilled. She tried not to react, but his words tortured her with hope. "The constable has agreed to let me see my daughter?"

Allowing her jailors to know of her desperation to see her daughter had been her biggest mistake. They controlled her behavior by dangling the promise of contact with Joan before her, as if she were a hare with a tasty carrot hanging above its nose.

"Your daughter has no wish to see you."

She stiffened. Sir John had told her Joan had cut her off years ago, denying all connection with the "Scottish rebel." Bella lifted her chin. "I refuse to believe that."

He shrugged his wide shoulders, the slouch of which had always reminded her of an ape. "Too bad, with her being so close."

"Close?" she said hoarsely, her heart in her throat.

He smiled like the sadistic monster he was. "Aye, didn't you know? The gel is at Roxburgh for her cousin's wedding."

Her heat stopped.

Roxburgh. Only a day's ride away. Dear God, so close! Bella had assumed Joan was still residing in Buchan's lands in Leicestershire with her uncle William, until the matter of her wardship had been settled. The knowledge that her daughter was so close ate at her facade of control like acid.

Simon was watching her carefully, knowing exactly what his words had done to her. "I suppose it doesn't matter, though, since you aren't interested in Sir John's proposal."

He turned to leave.

She clenched her fists, trying to resist, knowing it was all a game, but powerless to do so. If there was any chance . . . "What is it? What does the constable propose?"

With Sir John de Seagrave having been made Guardian of Scotland, Sir John Spark had replaced him as constable of Berwick.

He smiled smugly. The brute was enjoying this. "Sir John will permit you to write the lass and will ensure that you receive a response. *If* your daughter wishes to continue the correspondence, you will be permitted to do so as long as the nuns are given no cause for complaint. Once you have taken your vows, the girl will be permitted to visit you as often as she likes."

Bella couldn't breathe. Was it possible? Would she finally be permitted contact with her daughter? Or was this one more trick to keep her compliant?

"Why should I believe you? The constable has made promises before."

Once she'd been released from the cage, they'd used the prospect of a reunion with her daughter to keep her in line. But whenever she got close, they always found a small infraction to delay it.

"You aren't in any position to make demands. You are a rebel. A traitor. Consider yourself lucky that you are not still hanging from the tower cage. I told Sir John he is too soft with you, and this is how you reward him? You will take the veil, my lady," he sneered, "or you won't be the only one to suffer the consequences."

She knew he was only trying to scare her, but it was working. After the unsuccessful attempt by some of Robert's men to free her from her cage, her captors had none-too-subtly warned her that Joan would be the one to suffer if she were to escape.

His smile taunted malevolently. "I hate to think of the harm that could befall a young girl, without anyone to protect her. There's a powerful fever spreading through England right now. You know how easy it is to catch a chill."

Bella's blood went cold. The beat of her heart seemed to pound in her ears. "You would threaten a young girl? My daughter is the sole heir of the Earl of Buchan—a loyal subject to your king. Would he let the blood of an innocent child stain his hands to punish one insignificant woman?"

"Insignificant?" he snorted. "You've caused the king almost as many problems as King Hood. Do you know that the Governor of Berwick had to make a law against the wearing of a pink rose? I should have crushed it under my heel, just as the king will do to all your rebel friends." His eyes narrowed. "And no one's threatening anyone, I'm merely making an observation. You wouldn't want the girl to be blamed anymore for her mother's actions, would you? The king wants you to be a nun, and if I were you I'd bow my head and find a little meekness to tame that wicked pride of yours."

He slammed the door behind him. She heard the bar clang into place, and then the click of the lock.

Both precautions were unnecessary. They knew as well as she did that she wouldn't do anything to jeopardize the person who mattered to her most in the world. Her fate had been sealed the moment he'd entered the room, her defiance illusory. As long as Edward of England had Joan, he controlled Bella.

A tear slid from the corner of her eye, burning a path down her cheek. *A nun*. The rest of her life confined in a convent. She didn't want . . .

*No*. She wiped the tears from her eyes. It didn't matter what she wanted. She would do whatever she could to keep her daughter safe.

# Nine

Sneaking into an enemy fortress wasn't the wisest course of action for any of Bruce's men, but for the most hunted man in Scotland it bordered on foolhardy. If Lachlan was caught or anyone recognized him, he knew from experience exactly what would happen to him. Knowing he could withstand the most brutal torture sure as hell didn't mean he wanted to go through it again (although the current contraption he was wearing just about qualified), but an opportunity had presented itself, and Lachlan decided not to waste it. They had a much better chance of success if the countess was prepared and ready when the attack came. Besides, what was the chance of anyone recognizing him?

He pulled the cowl farther over his head, following the castle guardsman up the stairs. The young English soldier had turned to look at him more than once, but the deep hood hid Lachlan's features and his downcast head did not invite conversation.

If Lachlan hadn't already been guaranteed an eternity burning in hell's fires, this was sure to do it. He was the last man in the world who should be wearing a churchman's robes. God knew how many sins he was committing just by putting the bloody thing on. It itched like hell. Who needed a hair shirt with wool like this?

He'd wanted to leave his armor and clothes on underneath, but Boyd and MacLean had insisted they could be seen. The bastards probably just wanted to see him suffer. All four of his fellow guardsmen had howled with laughter as soon as he'd put the damned thing on. Even Seton, who'd borne a hefty percentage of Lachlan's barbs over the past few years—the young knight was an easy target—had snapped out of his brooding long enough to get in a few jibes.

Lachlan had let them have their fun, but he'd drawn the line when they'd tried to shave his head. He'd taken to wearing his hair short like the other members of the Highland Guard, but he didn't need a damned bald spot at the top of his head. Just his luck, the priest was also a monk.

It seemed as if he and the young soldier climbed forever, but five stories later they finally reached the top floor of the tower. The man leading him nodded a greeting to the guard at the door. "The priest," he said, "to see the lady."

The other man frowned. Lachlan didn't like the look of him. He was bigger, older, and shrewder than the soldier who'd led him to the tower. Though Lachlan had a small dirk strapped to his leg under the blasted robe, he didn't want to use it. Dead bodies were a sure way to put them on alert.

"Sir Simon didn't tell me there'd be any visitors today," the guardsman said. "Only the lady's attendant."

Lachlan affected his most pious and subservient pose, slouching to hide some of his height. But unfamiliar as he was with either piety or subservience, he feared he did a piss-poor job of it. He slid the parchment from his robe and handed it to the guardsman. "My instructions," he said with as much meekness as he could muster.

The guard's frown deepened at the deep sound of his voice that no amount of feigned humility could hide. The guard peered into the dark shadow of his hood but took the missive.

Lachlan kept his gaze down on his hands folded at his waist as the guard scanned the contents. *Damn.* He quickly stuffed them in the folds of his robe, hoping to hell the men didn't notice the battle scars and heavy calluses that covered his palms and fingers. He'd be hard-pressed to explain how a priest had come to have the hands of a warrior.

Sneaking around in the shadows was a hell of a lot easier than this. But he would never have made it past all these guards without leaving at least a few bodies behind. Intercepting the young priest in the forest beyond the gates of the castle had seemed a stroke of divine intervention, but now Lachlan was beginning to wonder. He had a bad feeling about this.

After what seemed an eternity, the guard folded the missive and handed it back to him. "You're to hear the lady's confession?"

Lachlan nodded. Seeing the man's continued scrutiny, he explained. "I'm to make sure the lady is ready to leave on the morrow. Body as well as soul," he said humbly.

The man held his eyes on him a moment longer, then grunted what Lachlan assumed was acquiescence when he removed the keys at his waist and began to unlock the door. "Ned here will wait to escort you down when you are done. It shouldn't take long. The lady is monitored too closely to get in any mischief; she hasn't seen anyone other than her attendant and my captain in months."

Lachlan debated moving his hand in the sign of the cross and saying "bless you my son." Though the situation seemed to warrant something priestly, he didn't want to overdo it. His disguise was perilously thin already.

As the guard started to open the door, Lachlan studied the crude leather tips of the too-small shoes he'd borrowed along with the robe, which he'd be almost as glad to give back to the priest when he woke from his drunken sleep as the robe. Lachlan didn't want the men to see his face, fearing they'd sense the excitement coursing through him. Excitement that was too palpable to hide.

This was it. The moment he'd been waiting for. The culmination of more than two years of agonizing delays, waiting until he could free Bella from the hell that he'd foisted upon her.

Unwittingly perhaps, but it was his fault all the same. He'd let it happen again. Instead of leading his men into a trap, he'd led Ross's men to the women.

He'd been distracted. Angry. Trying to calm the violent, unfamiliar emotions twisting inside him and cool his heated blood, his body teeming with the aftereffects of a kiss that had stripped every last vestige of his control. Christ, he'd been moments away from taking her right there against the chapel door.

She'd had every right to stop him. To slap him. But that didn't lessen the sting of her rejection. What was it about her that brought out the blackest part of him? That made him want to lash back when she taunted him?

He'd been so caught up in what had happened with Bella that he'd missed the threat. Because of his desire for a woman, he'd failed his duty, and those he'd been charged to protect had been captured. He knew that Bella thought he'd betrayed them. He hadn't, but it was his fault all the same.

The door opened.

He'd steeled himself, but nothing could have prepared him for the fist of emotion that hit him in the gut as his eyes fell on her for the first time in over two years.

His knees nearly buckled before he caught himself. Christ, he'd taken sword blows across the chest that had packed less of a wallop.

She stood with her back to him at the far end of the small chamber, silhouetted against the window in the fading daylight. She'd loomed so large in his memory, it was a shock to see how small she was in reality. Her back was slim, her shoulders as narrow as a child's. She was much more delicate than he remembered.

She tilted her head toward the door but didn't turn around, nor did she speak. The cool hauteur of that gesture released something inside him that he didn't know he'd been holding. *Fear,* he realized. A deep-seated fear that they might have broken the spirit and fierce pride that had at times infuriated him, but that had made her different from any other woman he'd ever known.

"A priest, my lady," the guard said. He waited for her nod, and then closed the door.

They were alone.

After so many months, he was so close he could almost reach out and touch her. Though he could practically span the small room with his arms, she seemed so far away. The forlorn look in her eye cut him to the bone.

She glanced in his direction. "The constable has sent a priest? He must fear for my soul to warrant such consideration the eve before I am to enter a nunnery."

A nunnery? So that's what they intended. But from her tone he suspected there was more.

Knowing the guard could well be listening and unsure of how she would react to seeing him, Lachlan crossed the room in two quick strides, slid his hand over her mouth, and pulled her against him so she couldn't move. He suspected she'd like it this time as much as the first time they'd met.

Shock nearly made him release her the instant he touched her. *God's blood!* His memory hadn't been faulty at all. What the hell had they done to her? There was nothing to her. She was so slim and slight as to be almost frail. The soft, lush curves that had so torturously haunted him had all but disappeared. Only the weight of her breasts on his arms felt familiar.

By all that was holy, someone would pay for this.

But touching her had been a mistake. His body hummed with other memories that apparently hadn't died.

He wasn't alone in his shock. Bella froze at his unexpected movement. But then he heard her gasp. Her gaze shot toward his face, hidden in the shadows of his hood.

Two big blue eyes dominated her pale face, made more pronounced by the dark shadows underneath and the deep hollows below her high cheekbones. A hand fisted against his chest. Gaunt and fragile, she seemed a ghostly shadow of the woman he remembered. She was still beautiful, but the once bold and sensual beauty was now ethereal and achingly delicate.

Even before he lifted the hood from his head, every inch of her body—what was left of her—turned as cold and stiff as a slab of ice.

Her eyes bored into his, shooting him with daggers of pure hatred.

Time, apparently, hadn't dulled her feelings for him.

He deserved it—had expected it, even—but damn it, one foolish part of him had hoped she might not have believed the worst of him.

"The guard," he whispered. "Have care. I think he's listening." Her eyes flared mutinously. He cursed silently, knowing the moment he took his hand off her mouth, she was going to let out a bellow that would bring the entire English garrison down on him.

She might appear fragile, but she still had fight. He was more relieved than he wanted to admit. They hadn't broken her. He'd hoped for as much but didn't know what to expect after what she'd been through. He, better than anyone, knew the toll suffering could take.

"Damn it, Bella, I'm here to help you. Give me a chance to explain before you do anything rash." He peered into her glaring eyes. "Please."

Her gaze narrowed as if the plea were some kind of trick. He didn't blame her. His plea surprised him. *Please?* The word had fallen so casually from his mouth, yet he could count on one hand the times he'd ever used it. He'd been tortured for nearly a week before Lorn's men had managed to wrest that word from him.

For a moment he'd didn't think she would relent, but just when he was trying to figure out what the hell he was going to do, she nodded.

He let her go.

She stood where he'd released her, staring at him with an intensity that made him step back and give her a little space. He didn't want to give her any excuse to change her mind.

She lifted her chin, and for a moment she looked like the Bella of his memories, not the delicate creature who stood before him now. "A priest?" she scoffed. "I'm surprised you did not burst into flames. Was my punishment not enough? Did you come to finish me off?"

Knowing he deserved her scorn didn't prevent the prick of his temper. She might look like a fragile piece of porcelain, but some things hadn't changed. She was still as stubborn and proud as he remembered, and still possessed the unique ability to get under his skin. "The king sent me," he said.

She made a harsh sound in her throat. "Which king has bought your sword this month?"

He clenched his jaw, reminding himself to be patient. "My loyalty is to the Bruce," he said solemnly. "As it's been for the past three years."

Outrage flashed in her deep-blue eyes. "You expect me to believe that? Were you fighting for Robert when you betrayed us to Ross?"

He was glad to see the rush of healthy color to her pale cheeks, but her voice had risen with emotion as well. He held his finger to his mouth to remind her of the guard. "I didn't betray you." He cut her off before she could argue. "I know what it looked like, damn it, but I didn't tell Ross where to find you. I was angry after I left you at the chapel. I wasn't being careful, and one of his men caught sight of me down by the docks, trying to arrange a *birlinn*. They followed me to the edge of the church lands and surrounded me before I could warn you. It might have been my fault, but I didn't betray you."

She didn't look as though she believed a word he said. Hard blue eyes bit into him. "That's quite a coincidence. They just happened to see you, recognize you, and guess that you would lead them to us?"

"There was nothing coincidental about it at all. They were waiting for us." From the flicker in her eyes, he knew he'd managed to surprise her. "We were betrayed, but not by me."

"Then by whom? As I recall, you were the only one not in chains."

He ignored the jibe. He had been in chains; she hadn't seen them from where she stood. "Do you remember the blacksmith and his sons bringing grain into the Great Hall at Kildrummy the night before we left?" She gave an impatient nod. "He overheard our plans and sold them to the English. They knew we were headed north. The blacksmith was the one to light the fire to the grain in the Hall a few days later that forced Nigel to surrender."

He saw the flash of pain on her face and knew she'd learned of the fate that had befallen the men at Kildrummy. After the castle surrendered, most of the garrison had been put to the sword. Nigel Bruce had been brought to this very castle at Berwick, where he'd been hanged and beheaded. He hoped to hell she hadn't been forced to witness it.

But the treacherous blacksmith Osborn had received his just reward. The gold he'd been promised had been melted down and poured down his throat by the very English soldiers he'd betrayed his countrymen to help.

"That's a nice story, but I *saw* you with Ross. He told me that you owed him a debt and that we were payment." Her voice shook. "How could you, Lachlan? I know you cared nothing for me, but what about the others? What about the children?" Her voice broke, and the sound tore at something deep and impenetrable inside him. "Do you know what they did to Mary?"

Her words flayed; he felt as if layer upon layer of skin were being stripped away. Every day for two years he'd thought of nothing else. She couldn't blame him any more than he blamed himself. But although he accepted his responsibility for what had happened, he hadn't betrayed her. "*I* was the payment of debt, Bella, not you. Ross meant to kill me, and would have done so had I not escaped. Gordon told me what Ross said, and what you thought, but I was in chains. He tried to tell you as you were being taken away."

A soft cry escaped from her lips. "William is alive?"

"Aye, as is MacKay. They were imprisoned, but we were able to free them before they were killed."

"We?"

He shrugged carelessly to cover the slip. "A few of Bruce's guardsmen." He left it at that. She knew nothing of the Highland Guard, and he intended to keep it that way. Even were he inclined to break his vow of secrecy— which he wasn't—her life was in enough danger as it was. Knowledge like that could get her tortured. A fact of which he was well aware.

For a moment, the hint of a smile softened her expression. "I'm glad," she said. "Margaret was unable to find out anything, and I thought . . ." Her voice dropped off as she turned to stare back out the window into the sunset.

She thought Gordon and MacKay had suffered a similar fate to those of the Earl of Atholl and Nigel Bruce.

She drew a deep breath, as if trying to get herself under control. When she turned back to him, her face was expressionless. "Very well, you've said your peace, now leave."

A sound at the door drew his attention. Probably the guard wondering what was taking so long. "Damn it,

Bella, we don't have much time. I swear I'll explain everything to you when I get you out of here."

She drew back as if scalded. "I'm not going anywhere with you."

Thinking that she still didn't believe him, he pulled the ring off his finger and handed it to her. He'd hoped to be able to convince her on his own but hadn't wanted to take any chances. "Here," he said. "Proof that the king has sent me. He said you would recognize it."

She handed it back to him with barely a glance. "I care not how much Robert is paying you to rescue me, or whether you are speaking the truth. I have no wish to be rescued by you or anyone else."

Lachlan couldn't believe it. Two hellish years fighting to get here, and she didn't want to leave? Was this some kind of bad joke?

He took an intimidating step closer.

She stood her ground, staring up at him with those big blue eyes flashing their challenge. Blood pounded in his ears. The temper he'd been struggling to hold flared. His hands itched to circle her arms and shake some bloody sense into her.

If he thought he could do so without kissing her, he might do just that. But he didn't trust himself to touch her. Not the way he was feeling right now. He was too raw, too frustrated, and too damned aware of her. He was trying to be patient and gentle, but while he might be dressed like a priest, he sure as hell wasn't a saint.

Pushed to the end of his rope, he leaned even closer. He admitted he took too much pleasure in the little hitch of breath and widening of her eyes. She might hate him, but she still was aware of him. He reached out his hand, when suddenly the door behind them opened.

Bella was grateful for the interruption when it came. Being alone with Lachlan MacRuairi had never been easy, and what he'd just told her had left her feeling as if she'd just taken her first steps on land after being at sea for years.

She'd never thought to see him again. She'd put him behind her. Hardly thought of him at all. She bit her lip. At least not as much as she used to. The sharp twinge in her chest had dulled to a pang. He'd become one more regret of an unpleasant past she had no wish to remember.

But part of her had always wondered what she would do if she ever saw him again. Would she stick a dagger in his back as he'd done to her? Curse him to the devil who spawned him? Hit him? Cry? Fall to her knees and beg him to tell her why?

She hadn't expected the hurt, the knife of pain that stabbed through her chest at the first sight of him, or the rush of churning emotions that swirled inside her, making her feel as if she were going to be ill.

Then, for one treacherous heartbeat, she'd felt something else. She'd looked into the face that had only grown harder, meaner, and even more sinfully handsome over the years, and felt a tug of longing so strong it stole her breath.

He'd cut his hair, she realized, but everything else was painfully familiar. She'd gazed upon that strong jaw, those eerily bright green eyes, the dangerously sensual mouth, and remembered exactly how it had felt on hers. How he could make her weak with pleasure and desperate for more.

She hated him for reminding her. For confusing her. For making her want to believe him. In her weaker moments, part of her had wondered if she'd been wrong. Maybe he hadn't betrayed her. Robert's ring seemed some proof that he might be telling the truth.

Why did he have to come now? For two years she'd prayed for someone to release her from her cruel prison. But even if she believed his story, even if she would dare to risk putting her life in his hands once more, she couldn't go. Not while there was a threat to her daughter.

Shame coursed through her as tears welled in her eyes. She'd be damned if she'd let him see her cry. Damned if she'd let him see her torment and know how desperately she longed for escape. She wouldn't let him see how close she was to falling apart.

Struggling for composure, Bella was relieved when the door opened and Margaret entered the room. It gave her the moment she needed to collect herself.

She forced a deep breath through her lungs, exhaling slowly to calm the emotions fluttering too close to the surface. For a moment she'd actually thought he meant to kiss her. But she'd never been much good at reading him, and after two years' separation he was a virtual stranger to her.

Except he wasn't.

The guard stood behind Margaret as her cousin entered the room. "Are you finished?"

Lachlan answered before she could. "Almost. Just a few more minutes."

Bella felt the ridiculous urge to laugh at his affected tone. Was that supposed to be priestly? He didn't have a pious bone in his body. Even with the hood thrown back over his head, and his attempt to slouch and appear unthreatening, Lachlan MacRuairi looked every inch the battle-hard brute. A man of undeniable and daunting physicality. Perversely, it was one of the things that had attracted her.

Margaret stopped in her tracks. "I'm sorry. I did not mean to interrupt. I can wait—"

"Nay!" Bella said, not giving Lachlan the opportunity to agree. She didn't want to be alone with him. "As the good father said, we are almost done."

Margaret looked back and forth between her and the "priest," a puzzled frown wrinkling her brow. "All right."

Bella feared the guard had noticed her jumpiness. He gave her a hard look. She forced a serene expression and met his gaze unflinchingly until he closed the door.

Lachlan tossed his hood back angrily. "What the hell do you think—"

Margaret's gasp stopped him.

He cursed under his breath, shooting Bella a glare as if it were somehow her fault he'd forgotten, and then turned to her cousin. "Lady Margaret," he whispered with a short nod. "I'm sorry to startle you. I've come to get your cousin out of here, only it seems she's refusing to go."

Margaret turned her surprise to Bella. "What's this, Bella? Of course you must go. If there is a chance to be free—"

Bella shook her head. "I can't."

Margaret looked to Lachlan as if she hadn't spoken. Bella owed her cousin so much. For two years she'd stood by her side, braving the horrible castle every day to attend her, keep her company, and bring her what news she could of the outside world. But Margaret's ready alliance with Lachlan—in the face of everything he'd done to them, or they thought he'd done to them—felt like a betrayal. "What is your plan?" Margaret asked him. "How can you sneak her out of the tower?"

"Not the tower," he said. "Tomorrow, on the road. You will be traveling with the countess?"

Margaret nodded, and Bella didn't bother to correct him about her title.

"Good," he said. "My men and I will attack your carriage, in the forest on the outskirts of town. I need you to be ready. Do not come out until it is over. I don't want either of you to be harmed."

Bella told herself not to listen. It would only make it harder. But her heartbeat quickened.

"What if something goes wrong?" Margaret said. "The constable will have us well guarded."

"You've nothing to fear, my lady. My men will take care of the soldiers. An entire army would not stand in our way."

Maybe not, but she would. "I'm not going," Bella said resolutely.

"But why not?" Margaret said, confused. "Do you wish to take the veil?"

"The veil?" Lachlan asked.

Margaret nodded. "They are forcing her to take the veil."

He swore.

Bella shook her head, scared that if she tried to speak, the tears closing her throat would break free.

"Then why not?" Margaret asked.

Lachlan's mouth thinned. "Your cousin doesn't trust me." He pulled Robert's ring out of the leather bag around his waist. "I brought proof that the king sent me, but it will not persuade her."

That wasn't the reason. But he was right: she didn't trust him.

Margaret turned the ring between her fingers and looked over to Bella. "This is the king's ring, cousin. Surely you remember it? What other reason could Lachlan have to be here? Surely it is worth the chance? You might not get another."

Bella's firmly set chin started to tremble. God, didn't she think she knew that? No force of will could keep the tears from misting her eyes. She could fight one of them, but not two. She fell to the chair, her legs suddenly too weak. "I can't," she said hoarsely.

Sensing her distress, Margaret rushed to her side. Taking her hand, she fell to her knees. "What is it?"

"Joan," she said softly, tears sliding down her cheeks. "They'll hurt Joan."

Briefly, she explained Simon's threats against her daughter and the enticement of contact if she agreed to take the veil.

She tried to ignore Lachlan, but she could feel his eyes on her. "Bastards," he muttered angrily.

She glanced up at him. Surprised by the sympathy in his gaze, she nodded. "Aye."

Margaret squeezed her hand. "Why didn't you tell me?"

Bella shrugged. "There was nothing you could do. I didn't want to worry you."

"We'll find a way to protect your daughter," Lachlan said. "No harm will come to her."

Ice ran down her spine. "I'll not risk it. What if you could not reach her in time? Look what they did to me. What they did to Mary. Do you think they will stop at harming another child?" She shook her head resolutely. "Nay, this will be for the best. My daughter has suffered enough. I will not see her harmed for my sake. It's a convent, not a prison. Perhaps I shall come to find peace with the nuns."

They both gaped at her. She lowered her eyes, unable to meet their gazes.

"Damn it, Bella, you aren't thinking straight. I swear to you the girl will be taken care of. I won't let anything happen to her."

She lifted her gaze to his. "I seem to recall you saying something similar to me before."

He flinched. She didn't think him capable of it, but apparently time had given him the vestiges of a conscience. His mouth fell in a tight white line. She could tell by the way his fists clenched and muscles flared that he was holding himself back. Clearly he wanted to say something—yell at her, probably—but he appeared determined to control himself.

Had the brigand learned some civility? Perhaps he'd changed more than she realized.

Margaret, who'd been pacing back and forth during the exchange, stopped. "I think I may have a solution."

Bella didn't allow herself to hope. She was cornered, with no way out.

"I will go in your place."

Bella's gaze shot to her cousin's. "No! Absolutely not! I won't let you sacrifice yourself for me."

Margaret smiled. "It's no sacrifice. It's what I have always wished. I was planning to enter the convent with you anyway. I shall simply take your place."

"Forever?" Bella asked. "For that is what this will be."

Margaret nodded. "I will not change my mind. This is what I want."

Bella tried to force her heartbeat to stop racing, telling herself it was impossible. "It won't work. We can't risk discovery."

"It will work," Margaret said. "We are of similar height and size." She looked to Lachlan for support. "And I think not too dissimilar in appearance?"

He looked back and forth between them as if he'd never considered it. Why did the fact that he'd never noticed the marked likeness between them make her feel worse? If she didn't compare to her cousin's ethereal beauty before, she certainly didn't now.

Bella hadn't missed the shock in his eyes when he'd first seen her. If she'd wondered what toll her imprisonment had taken on her, now she knew. She told herself it didn't matter. Beauty had never been important to her; indeed it had seemed more a curse. But the squeeze in her chest told her she was not without vanity.

"Nay, not too dissimilar. The countess's hair is a little lighter, and her eyes are blue whereas yours are green, but with a veil, and to people who do not know you . . ."

Margaret clapped her hands. "You see, it can work."

Bella gave Lachlan an angry look for encouraging her cousin, for encouraging them both. This was hard enough, and they were only making it harder.

But was it possible . . . ?

"We would have to change our plans a bit," Lachlan said, considering. "Arrange an accident on the road as opposed to a direct attack. We'll create a distraction and make the switch in the confusion." He gazed at Margaret. "You would have to find an excuse not to accompany Bella. But it could be done."

Oh, God. She felt the unmistakable rush of hope rising inside her. Could this actually work?

It could. She didn't know anyone at the convent. If they could make the switch without the constable's men knowing . . .

Her heart thumped wildly. Even if someone eventually discovered the truth, it would give her time to reach her daughter and get her to safety.

Joan was so close . . .

She tamped down the rising excitement and turned to Margaret to ask her again.

But Lachlan beat her to it. "Are you sure, lass? Are you certain you want to do this?"

A soft smile curved her cousin's mouth. "I've never been more certain of anything in my life." Margaret clasped Bella's hands in hers. "Taking the veil is my calling, dear cousin, now you can find yours."

Bella didn't miss the surreptitious glance her cousin stole toward Lachlan. But she was mistaken if she thought Bella harbored any thoughts in that direction.

She would put her fate in the brigand's hands one more time to be free, but she would never risk her heart. She'd had enough disappointments for a lifetime.

Sensing the battle had been won, Lachlan did not give her the chance to argue further. Tossing the hood back over his head, he went to the door and gave it a sound thump.

"Be ready," he said.

The door opened, and a moment later he was gone.

She stood by the window, her heart thumping erratically for what seemed forever. Finally, she saw the cloaked figure emerge from the tower and cross the courtyard to the gate. Only when he'd safely passed through did she exhale.

It was the chance to escape that made her worry, not fear for him. Lachlan MacRuairi always managed to land on his feet. Even if those around him did not.

# Ten

❧

This wasn't going to work. How were they going to distract the guards long enough to make the switch?

Bella sat on a bench in the carriage that was transporting her from Berwick Castle to the convent, fighting to keep her seat as the rickety contraption—which had definitely seen better days—bumped along the progressively rougher and more uneven roads.

A simple construction of a wooden base and arched roof covered with leather, the carriage was open at both ends, providing Bella a view in front of her and behind but not to the side.

She'd been spared the humiliation of manacles, despite the fact that there was no door to lock. If the threats against her daughter weren't enough to deter thoughts of escape, the twenty or so armed soldiers accompanying her should suffice.

As the royal burgh of Berwick-upon-Tweed gave way to countryside, Bella's tunneled glances outside grew more frequent and the beat of her heart more frantic.

It was nearly dawn now. The convent couldn't be much farther. Had something gone wrong? Perhaps they weren't expecting her to be moved so early? It was still dark when she'd left the castle. Or perhaps her cousin had changed her mind?

The pit in her stomach grew to despair. She'd been resigned to her fate. Accepted it. Allowing herself to hope—nay, to believe—she would have freedom, only to have it taken away again, was too much to be borne. She should never have listened to him, never should have agreed. But Lachlan had seemed so sure, so certain that this would work. Desperately she'd clung to any thread of hope, no matter how thin.

Had she learned nothing from their disastrous journey north two years ago? How could she have allowed herself to believe him even for a moment—

The carriage came to a sudden, jerking halt. Her white-knuckled grip on the edge of the bench was the only thing that kept her from pitching off her seat.

Voices rang out. Her heart hammered, knowing this must be it.

She waited a few moments before scooting to the back opening of the cart. She spoke to the closest man. "Is something wrong? Why did we stop?" She was grateful for the dark veil that hid her face, fearing that he would see her excitement.

He must have mistaken the breathlessness in her voice for fear. "Overturned cart up ahead," he replied. "Nothing for you to worry about. We should be on our way in a few minutes." He gestured with a nod of his steel-helmed head. "Some of the men have gone to help."

Bella nodded and tried to act calm. She wished she knew Lachlan's plan, and whether there was anything she could do to help. From what she could tell, there were at least six of the castle guardsmen still surrounding her carriage.

Five more minutes passed, though it seemed to her interminably longer as she waited on the edge of her seat for what might happen next.

She turned at the sound of a voice. From his heavily

Scots-accented English, she knew he wasn't one of the soldiers.

"You aren't safe here," the newcomer said to the soldiers. "Those ropes won't hold much longer. If those logs break free before we can get the cart upright, they're liable to roll into your horses and your carriage."

Bella stuck her head out the opening. "What seems to be the problem?"

The man, who from his rough clothing and large, muscular frame appeared to be a laborer, acted surprised to see a woman. He bowed deferentially, his manner instantly more anxious. "I'm sorry to disturb you, m'lady. There's been an accident. The cart carrying our load of logs overturned on the hill above. You should get out of the carriage while your men move it out of the path of the logs."

"The lady is fine where she is," one of Sir John's soldiers said. "Turn the carriage around," he shouted to the driver.

The carriage moved forward a few feet, rocking slightly as the driver attempted to turn the horses. Then it came to another sudden stop. "Not enough room," the driver said. "The road is too narrow right here. If one of the wheels gets stuck in the muddy ditch to either side there will be no moving her. I need to back up—"

A loud shout of warning came from the road ahead of them.

"Watch out!" the newcomer shouted to the frozen soldiers, meeting her gaze with a knowing look. "Out of the way. The ropes have snapped."

Bella didn't wait to see whether one of the soldiers came for her. She jumped out the back opening of the carriage and ran toward the stranger, who she knew must be one of Lachlan's men.

She heard a cacophony of sound. The crash of wood and rock as the logs barreled toward them. The terrified neighs and whinnies of the horses. The shouts of soldiers.

In the chaos, Lachlan's man pulled her to safety behind a

tree. No sooner had her feet touched the ground than she was spun around and handed to another man.

This one she recognized. She didn't need to look at his face. It horrified her to realize that she knew him by touch alone. By the way the air shifted, her stomach fluttered, and every nerve ending stood on end.

God help her for a fool.

Suddenly, her cousin appeared next to her, slipping into the place Bella had just vacated by the tree. Their eyes met from behind the mirroring black veils.

"Take care, cousin," Margaret said softly.

Tears sprang to her eyes. "Thank you," Bella whispered, but Lachlan was already dragging her away.

They traveled a few dozen feet before he pulled her into a dense patch of shrubbery.

He held her pinned to his side, tucked under the protective shield of his chest and arms. She couldn't help herself from leaning into him, savoring—absorbing—his warmth and strength. It had been so long since she'd felt safe. And tucked up against him, his big arm wrapped tightly around her, it was so easy to allow herself a moment of weakness, so easy to forget all that had happened, so easy to believe that she could rely on him. She felt safe and protected for the first time since—

Since the last time he'd held her.

She'd forgotten how strong he was. Forgotten how it felt to have layer upon layer of steel-hard muscle pressed against her. Her heart did a funny little stutter as feminine awareness, long dormant, flared to life. It poured through her veins in a hot molten rush that no force of will could deny. Her breath fell in uneven gasps that she hoped he mistook for exertion.

Her body's betrayal bothered her. With all that had passed between them, she shouldn't be feeling like this. She didn't want to feel anything for him. The death of her husband hadn't changed anything. Lachlan MacRuairi was as wrong for her today as he had been two years ago.

But she couldn't force herself to pull away.

"Let's see if it worked," he said softly in her ear.

Bella ignored the shiver that ran down her spine and tried to focus on what was happening ahead of them.

The soldiers had recovered quickly. They surrounded Lachlan's man and immediately relieved him of Margaret. There seemed to be a tense moment of discussion before Margaret said something to one of the soldiers. A moment later, the big man walked away.

Freed of its heavy load, the overturned cart was righted. The logs that had crashed down the hill on a perilous collision course with their party were cleared from the road. Margaret was loaded back into the carriage, which fortunately along with the horses had escaped the onslaught of logs, and not twenty minutes later the party was once again on its way to the convent.

Bella waited for them to pass out of sight before she spoke. "Do you think she'll be all right?"

Lachlan pulled her to her feet, and then turned her to face him. "I think she'll be more than all right, I think she'll be happy. It was your cousin's wish to do this, Bella. You've nothing to feel guilty about." She didn't like how easily he'd read her thoughts. He didn't know her. The connection between them—had it ever existed—had been severed long ago. "You can't be completely surprised by her decision?"

Bella held his gaze, the striking green eyes that seemed even sharper and more intense than she remembered. Everything about him was more striking than she remembered. His darkly handsome face, his height, his broad, heavily muscled chest and arms.

God, why did it have to be him? Couldn't Robert have sent someone else for her?

Two years of imprisonment had taken more from her

than she wanted to admit, and Lachlan made her feel weak even when she was strong.

She forced herself to consider his question—not the hard, stubbled lines of his jaw or the sensual curve of his sinful mouth. He was right; she wasn't surprised. If anyone was destined for a convent, it was Margaret. "I can't stop thinking that someone will find out."

"Two of my men will stay behind to watch the convent for a few days to make sure nothing happens." His grip tightened around her upper arms, forcing her to heed his words. "You're free, Bella. You aren't going back there."

The fierceness in his voice touched something inside her. She blinked up at him. It took a moment for his words to penetrate. *Free.* Dear God, she was free! For so long she'd dreamed of this moment; now that it was actually here it didn't seem real. Or maybe she wouldn't let it seem real. Maybe she was scared that something might happen to force her back. Lachlan's words had been aimed right at that fear. How was it that he seemed to understand her feelings before she did?

*Because he's been there.* The jolt of realization reverberated through her. He'd been imprisoned, too. Their eyes held in shared understanding. She wanted to say something, but couldn't seem to find the words. "Thank you," she said softly.

It seemed ironic to be thanking him for rescuing her when she'd blamed him for putting her there for so long. Bella was not yet ready to absolve him of guilt in that regard, but he'd saved her from a lifetime of imprisonment, and for that alone, he deserved her thanks.

He gave her a terse nod, his uncomfortable expression making her think he saw the irony as well. "Come," he said, leading her deeper into the forest. "The others are waiting for us."

By "others" Bella assumed at least a dozen men, perhaps a score. She should have known better. They reached a small clearing in the trees beside a burn, where his men waited for them with horses. Her rescue party consisted of only five warriors, although admittedly they were an imposing-looking lot. Lachlan, the man who'd posed as a laborer, another man she didn't recognize, and two she did.

A broad smile spread across her face and she felt the first prickle of tears. The last time she'd seen them was at Kildrummy Castle. She'd assumed they'd suffered the same fate as Nigel Bruce. Being forced to watch Nigel's vicious execution was one of the lowest points of her captivity. The murder of that golden knight would haunt her forever.

She rushed forward, grasping their hands in hers. "Robbie! Sir Alex! It is so good to see you."

Robbie Boyd and Sir Alex Seton returned her smiles and greeting. Sir Alex spoke first. "It is good to see you as well, my lady."

Two years had wrought changes in the young knight. The fresh-faced handsome and gallant youth had been hardened by war and tragedy. Their fears about his brother Christopher's fate two years ago had been realized. Alex's famous brother—one of Bruce's closest companions—had been executed by the first King Edward not long after the battle of Methven. Christina Bruce, still imprisoned in a convent in England, had lost yet another husband.

Robbie Boyd looked the same. He was still the strongest-looking man she'd ever seen. Big as a mountain, every inch stacked with heavy muscle, the dark-haired warrior looked as if he could take on the entire English army and win.

"MacLean. Lamont," Lachlan said, introducing the final two men. "Lady Isabella MacDuff."

More Highlanders, she realized. Bruce seemed to have surrounded himself with them. Not surprising, she supposed. Highlanders were a big, fierce lot, and these two were no exception.

MacLean, the man who'd pulled her from the carriage, had the tough, grizzled look of a man who lived on the battlefield. Of similar height to Lachlan, but with a leaner build, his dark-blond hair fell in disheveled waves to a jaw that hadn't seen a razor in some time. But behind the scruffy beard, his eyes were sharp blue and his features surprisingly refined and chiseled.

The other man, Lamont, was also unusually tall and broad-shouldered (she'd begun to see a pattern amongst Robert's men), with short, dark hair, light eyes, and a relatively clean-shaven jaw.

MacLean had exchanged his laborer's clothing for the padded war coat and dark leather chausses worn by the other men. They all wore heavy, dark cloaks to cover the various weapons strapped to them. There was no coat of arms or other insignia to identify them, which was understandable as they were in enemy territory.

Bella greeted the men and thanked them for their help.

Lachlan went to one of the horses, retrieving something from one of the leather bags tied to the saddle.

"Here," he said, handing her a pile of wool. "Put these on. They aren't fancy, but they're clean." She took one look at the clothes and gaped at him in disbelief. "You want me to wear breeches?"

He shrugged as if it were nothing. "You will attract less notice as a lad—especially if we come across any soldiers. Make sure you tuck your hair well up in the cap."

She wanted to argue, but what he said sounded reasonable. Being dressed like a lad was a better disguise than a black veil.

"There's an old forester's cottage over there," he said, pointing through the trees behind her. "You can change and have something to eat. Try to get some rest while you can. We'll leave as soon as it is dark. With so many English around, we don't want to take any chances."

Bella looked at him in shock. She thought he'd understood. "I'm not going back to Scotland. Not yet."

The men looked at her in surprise. Except for Lachlan.

He knew exactly what she wanted to do. His piercing gaze held perfectly steady. Unflinching. Unmovable. Prepared to do battle. She didn't have to look into those ruthless eyes or glance at the wall of steely muscles to know that he wasn't a man accustomed to losing.

"No," he said in a voice that brokered no argument.

The terse, autocratic refusal—without explanation and without even considering what she had to say—stung. She was tired of letting men decide her fate. God knew, they'd done a horrendous job of it. She'd been waiting too long for this. She wasn't leaving until she saw her daughter. Not with her so close. Let him try to stop her.

The pride that had been both her bane and her savior flared to life. She tilted her chin, every inch the regal countess to his brutish brigand. He wasn't her husband; he had no authority over her. "I am not one of your men to order about."

Her attempt to put him in his place only served to harden his resolve. It was almost as if she could see the wall of steel going down around him. A wall that nothing she could say or do would penetrate.

"Wrong, *my lady*." She didn't miss the lilt of mockery in his gravelly voice. "The king put me in charge. It's my duty to get you to safety, and this time I damned well intend to see it finished. If you want to risk your life to see your daughter, do it on someone else's watch."

*See it finished.* Her heart stalled. It wasn't just the mission he was talking about. It was her. He wanted to be finished with her. It seemed he'd been trying to do that from the start.

She ignored the foolish pinch in her chest. She was just as eager to be rid of him.

Before she could argue further—the matter apparently decided—he turned and walked away.

Conscious of the eyes upon her, Bella bit back an angry

retort. Clutching the scandalous garments in her arms, she stomped off in the direction of the cottage.

But if Lachlan MacRuairi thought this was over, he was dead wrong.

He knew she wouldn't give up that easily. Less than an hour later, Lachlan was seated on a rock at the edge of the burn, having just finished a meal of dried beef and oatcakes washed down with ale, when he heard her come up behind him. He turned, prepared to do battle, but not prepared for the shock of seeing her dressed as a lad.

*Ah hell.* He was wrong about her not attracting attention. The soft leather breeches, although loose, still revealed far more of her than the heavy skirts of a lady's gown. He could see the soft curve of her hips, her long, slim legs, and the hint of her shapely calves. Nor could the loose shirt and padded leather doublet completely hide the generous swell of very feminine breasts. She'd left the cap behind in the cottage, and her blond hair hung damp and loose around her shoulders. Despite the mild day, she had also donned a plaid around her shoulders. She looked dainty, fresh, and undeniably feminine.

She stood facing him with her hands on her hips, a soft flush on her cheeks. When their eyes met, she lifted her chin. "Thank you." It wasn't what he expected her to say. She must have noticed his surprise and explained, "For the bath."

He shrugged. He remembered how good his first dunking had felt after escaping from the hell of that pit prison. He'd scrubbed the stench and muck from his skin until it had been raw. Ever since, he couldn't stand to be dirty. Hawk, one of the other members of the Highland Guard (who was also his cousin), loved to taunt him about it. MacRuairi didn't give a shite. He'd rather smell "pretty as a lass" than like a pig.

"The small tub was all we could find." A corner of his

mouth lifted. "I don't think the former occupant bathed much."

"It was divine. They let me have a bath whenever I wanted, but Simon wouldn't let them heat it."

"Simon?"

Her face shuttered. "My jailor," she explained hastily. Looking around, she asked, "Where are the rest of the men?"

"Lamont and MacLean have gone to watch the convent. Boyd and Seton will be back soon. They're scouting the area. This part of the forest is fairly quiet, but there's always a chance there could be hunters or poachers around." He gave her a hard look. "Did you eat something?"

"A little," she said. "You had enough food in there for an army."

He frowned. "You're too thin. You need to get your strength back."

She stiffened. "I know I am much changed, but gorging myself won't put me back to the way I used to be."

*Damn*, she'd taken his concern as a criticism. He stood up, forgetting how small she was until he towered over her. "Don't you think I know that? I've been there, Bella. I know some of what you are feeling." He scanned her face. "You're still breathtakingly beautiful, but I know the changes aren't always easy to see."

She looked startled. "You think I'm beautiful?"

Was she daft? He cupped her chin, tilting her face to his. "I think you are the most beautiful woman I've ever seen."

Her eyes widened, and it took everything he had not to lean down and kiss her. She was standing so close, the soft fragrance of her freshly washed skin and hair rose up to grab him. Entrance him. Make him forget why he was here: to get the job done. Being with her after thinking about her for so long was even harder than he'd thought it would be.

He dropped his hand. "Get some rest," he said gruffly. "We've a long journey ahead."

"I'm not going," she said quietly. "I meant what I said. I'm not leaving without seeing my daughter."

God's blood, did she always have to be so stubborn? He didn't want to argue with her. His mouth fell in a hard line. "And I meant what I said. My job is to get you to safety, and that's exactly what I intend to do." Seeing her mulish expression, he dragged his fingers through his hair. "Christ, Bella, try to see reason. Be patient. Your daughter is safe as long as the English believe you are in that convent. They don't know you escaped, but every minute you stay on English soil you put that at risk."

It put all of them at risk. He was antsy enough as it was. The price on his head made him a fat target—and he had too many enemies. Despite his nonchalance to Bruce, Lachlan couldn't wait to get the hell out of there.

"I've been patient for three years. My daughter is not twenty miles from here. *Twenty miles,*" she repeated. The soft plea in her voice tugged at him mercilessly. "It's the closest I've been to her since I left her at Balvenie. I can't leave without at least trying to contact her. With Buchan dead, she's all alone, Lachlan." Her voice caught. "I just need to make sure she's all right."

He didn't want to hear her fear, her desperation, damn it. He didn't want to look down, didn't want to look into her big, imploring blue eyes. He didn't want to remind himself that the specter of a husband no longer stood between them.

His jaw locked. He couldn't let himself be swayed. Going off without intelligence, without a plan, was a sure way to end up in another English prison. It was better to wait. Get Bella to safety, and then when the time was right, make plans to find her daughter. "I'm sorry. I can't. It's not part of my mission."

It was the wrong thing to say.

She lashed out in anger. "Is that all this is to you, Lachlan? Another mission? Another bag of silver to collect?" Scorn dripped from her voice. "I thought you might have changed. That after two years of fighting for Robert you might realize that there were things worth fighting for. But you're exactly the same. It's still all about the money."

Damned right it was all about the money! Free Bella. Get the job done. Collect his reward. Pay off his debts. Retire in peace. Follow nobody's orders but his own. That was all he wanted.

He stared down into her upturned face, seeing the beautiful features so achingly close, and felt a pull of desire too strong to resist. Nay, it wasn't all he wanted. He wanted *her*. Every bit as badly as he had before.

His fists clenched. His control pulled taut as a bowstring.

This was all her fault. She was confusing him. He didn't care, damn it. Not about Bruce. Not about the Highland Guard. And sure as hell not about her. No loyalties to get in the way. No loyalties to betray him.

He was a selfish bastard. A mercenary. Not much better than the pirate she'd first accused him of being.

He knew three emotions in his life when it came to women: disappointment, hatred, and lust. Not much to offer one of the most noble women in Scotland who'd become a hero.

Damn her for doing this to him.

"Three years," he corrected. It was three years ago he'd joined the other members of the Highland Guard on the Isle of Skye for training. "And of course it's about the money." A sneer turned his mouth. His eyes drifted down, sliding over her formfitting clothes in a hot caress. "So unless you can think of a way to pay me, this discussion is over."

She gasped, her eyes widening in shock. She drew her hand back to give him the slap he surely deserved. Before it fell across his face, he caught her wrist and twisted it down around her back, pinning her against him. Bodies locked, he stared down into her furious face—the face that had haunted him for two bloody years—and felt the battle seep out of him as he gave in to the demon of desire roaring inside him.

He'd been a fool to think he could control this.

His mouth fell on hers. Hot and hungry. Starved from two years of deprivation. Two years of wanting a woman who would never be his.

# Eleven

❧

Lachlan groaned at the contact. She tasted so good. Warm and sweet, with a faint hint of the wine he'd left for her.

She gasped, whether in shock or protest he didn't know. For one agonizing heartbeat she went stiff in his arms, and he thought she would push him away. But then he felt her soften, felt the shudder of desire tremble through her, and she melted into his embrace.

A rush of heat poured through him as his body flooded with desires long kept in check. He hardened. Throbbed. Blood pounded through every vein in his body.

He dug his fingers through the soft dampness of her hair, cupping the back of her head in his palm to bring her mouth even closer, bending her into him as he drank in every inch of her. Her soft scent floated around him in a haze of intoxicating fragrance. He couldn't seem to get enough. He wanted with a desperation he'd never known before.

When she opened her mouth, he nearly lost his mind. Blood roared in his head. Sliding in his tongue, he kissed her deeper. Claiming every inch of that sweet mouth and growling with pleasure when the first tentative strokes of her tongue met his. The innocence of her response nearly undid him.

This felt too good. He'd dreamed of this for too long.

He couldn't seem to calm the wicked sensations raging inside him. He wanted her too badly; his body had been too long denied.

His mouth moved over her jaw, down her neck, tasting every inch of velvety-soft skin. Christ, she was sweet. Ambrosia to a man who'd been starving for too long.

He cupped her bottom, bringing her more fully against the throbbing column of his manhood. He needed her closer, needed to feel her against him, needed the intimate pressure, the delicious friction of bodies grinding together. He rocked against her, nearly coming out of his skin when she moved against him.

She was pressing against him so intently, her sweet feminine mound rubbing against his cock, he didn't know how much longer he could take it. It felt so good. A tantalizing hint of what it would be like to be inside her. Thrusting in and out. Circling. Pounding. Finding that perfect rhythm. He could tell from the way she moved that they would be incredible together. That it would be like nothing else he'd ever experienced.

He sank against her, his cock wedged at her cleft. Perfect. Right there. He gave a little thrust. *Jesus!* Sweat beaded on his forehead from the exertion of restraint. He felt as if he were going to explode. Heat pulled in his groin, gathered at the base of his spine, tightening his buttocks.

He wanted to come. Wanted to scream out her name as he plunged deep inside her and possess every inch of her, claiming her in the most intimate of ways.

He was going faster now, any pretense at control long gone. His body was on fire. He heard the quickening of her breath and knew she felt it, too. The urgency, the need, that had descended over them both. There was nothing to come between them. No husband to stop her. She was free. She was his.

His lips trailed over the tender, sensitive skin of her throat. He nuzzled her with his nose, licked her with his tongue, devoured her with his mouth.

His hands slid up her tiny waist to cup her breasts. A bolt of pure lust shot through him, as the soft mounds of flesh spilled over his palms. He felt her nipples pressing against him like two hard pebbles. He couldn't stop himself. They were too incredible. Too lush. Too ripe to the touch. He needed to squeeze, to caress, to lift the perfect round globes of flesh in his hands and rub the taut bead of her nipples between his thumbs.

The soft sigh of pleasure that slipped from between her parted lips drove him wild. He had to taste her. To put his mouth on bare skin. Nothing could have denied him from putting his lips around those firm, succulent nipples and sucking. From circling them with his tongue and nibbling them with his teeth.

He was going to have her. Knowledge pounded through him. Finally, after two years of wanting her, she would be his.

He slid his mouth lower, moving toward the open neck of her shirt. Easing the fabric aside with his chin, he feasted his eyes on the pale, creamy white skin—

He stilled. Everything inside came to an abrupt stop—his breath, his racing heart, his surging passion.

His half-slitted gaze slowly came into focus.

Straightening, he pushed aside the fabric, tearing the neck opening of her shirt a little to get a better look. But there was no mistaking it. Dark, mottled bruises marred the creamy perfection of ivory skin around the inner curve of her right breast.

Fingerprints.

His heart started to beat again. Louder. Harder. Passion had been replaced by another primal urge—this one to kill.

She must have realized what had gotten his attention, because she pulled away with a gasp and gripped the open ends of her shirt back together to try to cover herself.

But he was having none of it. He grabbed her arm, forcing her to look at him. "Who did this to you?" His voice held the cold edge of one of the most feared and dangerous men in the Highlands. "Who hurt you?"

Bella was in another world. Transported to a place of feeling and sensation that she'd never been to before. The heat of his kiss. The pressure of his hands. The feel of his body against her. It was too much.

It felt too good.

She'd been alone for so long, and her body responded. She wasn't strong enough to fight. Imprisonment had taken more from her than she wanted to admit. She was weak. Needy. And he was strength.

But she knew it wasn't just the imprisonment that caused her to react with such need and hunger. It was Lachlan. He alone had the power to turn her into a mindless wanton.

She'd never responded to a man the way she did him. She hadn't understood it then, and she didn't understand it now.

The difference was she no longer cared.

So she gave over to the sensations. Let them consume her. Let him take her where he would. She hadn't felt anything for so long, and he made her feel alive again.

He'd flamed the passion, kissed her and touched her until she thought she had glimpsed a piece of paradise, only to bring her harshly back to earth. *Who hurt you?*

She gathered up the torn edges of her shirt, wishing her tattered pride was as easily managed.

"It's nothing," she said, trying to turn away. "It's none of your concern."

But he wouldn't let her. He grabbed her by the arm and turned her back to him. "I'm making it my concern."

The flatness of his tone didn't fool her. He was furious. Peeking up from under her lashes, she glimpsed the terrifying, slitted, green-eyed gaze of a mercenary. He looked every bit as mean and merciless as she remembered. The latent dangerousness that surrounded him was still there.

She hadn't realized Simon had left marks. He'd come to her chamber well before dawn this morning. Her imminent departure had forced all subtlety from his exhausted repertoire of attempts to coerce her into his bed. He'd promised to keep them from forcing her to take the veil if she would let him have her. When she refused, his "request" had become physical. He'd squeezed and twisted her breasts with his brutish hands, put his foul mouth on hers until she couldn't breathe, and attempted to wedge himself between her legs.

For a moment, she thought he wouldn't stop. That the threat of rape that had hung over her head like an axe would finally fall. But she'd stood there cold, letting him push her into the stone wall until she thought she would be crushed, and eventually, he'd let her go.

In the end it was only incrementally more horrible than the many previous instances she'd had to endure over the years. So why did it feel so much more so now with Lachlan to witness her shame?

She brushed the errant dampness from her eyes. She was a fool. What difference did it make?

"My jailor," she said. "Sir Simon Fitzhugh."

He stared at her intently, his cold, eerie gaze as hard as granite. "Did he force you?"

The emptiness of his voice sent a shiver down her spine. She shook her head, eyes glued to her feet. "Nay, my rank had some benefits." Her attempt at a wry smile wobbled. But it didn't matter. Lachlan would see through her bravado; she hated how easily he could read her. "There are some things even the English will not tolerate."

"But he wanted you?"

Bella didn't want to talk about this anymore. Didn't like the probing intensity of his questions, or, when she forced herself to look up at him, his gaze. "He was a brute who at times got a little rough. It's over, Lachlan. There is nothing you can do to fix it; it's in the past. I just want to forget about it."

It was the truth. Simon held no power over her any longer. Soon he would be one more bad memory.

If only Lachlan were as easy to forget. She could still feel the heat of his kiss on her swollen lips. Still feel his hands on her breasts, the frantic quivering between her legs, and the burn of his beard on his skin.

How did he manage to devastate her so quickly and completely? To make her feel weak and vulnerable?

"I'm sorry, Bella. So damned sorry for what you had to go through."

"Then take me to my daughter." She knew she was playing on his guilt, but didn't care.

He was quiet. Too quiet. His expression gave no hint of his thoughts.

She drew herself up, trying to push aside the memory of that devastating kiss and remember what was truly important. Putting aside her pride, she did what her captors had wanted her to do: she begged. "Please, Lachlan. Please, take me to Joan. I need to see my daughter."

His stony expression didn't move. Not one little flicker. Not one hint that her pleas might have some effect on him. That *she* might have some effect on him. He'd kissed her as though he couldn't live without her, but it made no difference.

He shook his head. "I'm sorry. It's too dangerous."

*Sorry?* Tears started to fall from her eyes. How could he stand there like that—after everything they'd been through—and deny her the one thing that mattered to her? The one thing she wanted more than anything else in the world.

At that moment she hated him. Hated him for his strength and her weakness. Hated him for kissing her and making her think . . .

What had she thought? That those foolish thoughts she'd harbored two years ago were true? That she actually meant something to him? That there was a reason other than a mission that he'd come for her?

She blinked up at him through the hot haze of tears. Stared at the handsome battle-scarred face, wanting something from him with all her soul, with every fiber of her being, but not knowing what—except that he could never give it. It seemed she always wanted something from a man who could not give it.

Suddenly, it became too much. The kiss. His refusal. The escape from the nightmare of her prison. All the emotions that she'd held in check, that pride had forbidden her from shedding, came pouring out in one torrential rush of tears.

Bella MacDuff had finally broken.

Lachlan swore. But the crude oath only made her cry harder.

She slid to her knees, holding her arms around her waist as if in pain, her shoulders wracking with shuddering sobs, tears pouring down her cheeks, and Lachlan had never felt so at a loss in his life.

He didn't know what the hell to do. He dragged his fingers through his hair, feeling as if the rats from John of Lorn's pit prison were crawling all over him again. The leather *cotun* he wore suddenly felt too tight. He couldn't breathe.

Jesus, he couldn't take this. He couldn't see her suffer like this. Each tear fell like acid on the steel of his resolve.

Not knowing what else to do, he bent down and awkwardly wrapped his arms around her. To his surprise she didn't push him away, but grabbed onto him like a lifeline. Her tiny fingers dug into his chest like kitten claws.

After a moment of panic when he realized he didn't know what the hell to do—he'd never tried to offer anyone comfort before—he found himself stroking her back, smoothing her hair, whispering soothing words, and eventually pleading—anything to make her stop. "Don't cry, Bella. Please, don't cry."

He hated seeing her so miserable, but damn, it felt good to hold her in his arms again. It had been too long. He remembered every time he'd touched her, every time he'd held her. The memories seemed burned into his brain. But memories couldn't replicate the silkiness of her hair or the delicate fragrance of her skin.

He savored the sensation of her tiny body pressed against him, her cheek pressed against his chest, her tiny fingers clutching him as if he were her only hope. For a moment, he could almost convince himself that she needed him. He knew he was taking far too much pleasure from it, but hell, he'd never been known for his sensitivity.

Eventually, the sobs ebbed, and she blinked up at him through the watery haze of tears. "If you won't help me, I'll go myself."

*Christ's bones!* So much for being needed. Even shattered, she still managed to be stubborn. He couldn't take this anymore. "Damn it, Bella, you're not going anywhere by yourself."

Her eyes searched his, and the hope shimmering in the sparkling blue depths tore at the last vestiges of his resolve. "Does that mean you'll take me?"

Could he offer her a compromise? He supposed there was a first time for everything. But he hoped to hell he didn't end up regretting this. He could manage one short— very short—detour.

"It's too dangerous to take you"—her face fell— "but . . ." She looked up at him again. "But I will see if I can get a message to her."

The look of abject joy on her face was almost harder to take than her tears. "Oh, Lachlan, thank you—"

He stopped her. "Don't thank me yet. I'm not making you any promises. And you must swear to do *exactly* as I say. I don't want you anywhere near danger. Where is she?"

"Roxburgh."

He lifted a brow. "Your daughter is at Roxburgh Castle?"

She nodded. "Aye, her cousin Alice Comyn is marrying Henry de Beaumont—he's just been appointed constable." She must have sensed the interest in his tone. She pulled away, wiping her eyes. "Does it matter?"

He shook his head. "Nay." But it might explain why Mary Bruce was being moved from her prison. He hoped MacLeod and his other Highland Guard brethren attempting to free Mary had found the same success he had. But unlike with Bella, they didn't know when Mary was supposed to be moved. He knew his fellow guardsmen could still be there and didn't want to interfere with their plans— nor would he say anything to Bella or anyone else that might compromise the mission. But at the same time, the wedding could provide a good distraction. There would be lots of people—and lots of celebrating.

"When is the wedding?" he asked.

She shook her head, eyeing him curiously. "I don't know." She stared up at him, big blue eyes dominating her pale, tear-stained face. He felt something inside him tug, and it was too high and too close to his heart to be lust. What the hell was she doing to him? "Did you mean it, Lachlan? You aren't saying this just to appease me. Will you really take me to Roxburgh?"

He nodded grimly. At most it would add a day to their journey, but he did not delude himself: Every minute they stayed in the borders—on the English or Scottish side— was a minute too long. If anyone recognized them . . . he'd better make damn sure they didn't.

Although Roxburgh was technically in Scotland, the English had garrisoned all the major strongholds in the Marches.

"We'll go," he said. "And I'll see what I can find out, but you aren't going anywhere near the castle. I mean it, Bella. Do you understand?"

The sternness in his voice fell on deaf ears. She nodded exuberantly and then tossed her arms around his neck, hugging him with all her strength.

Gratitude was a new experience for him, and if the swell in his chest meant anything, he suspected he could get used to it if he wasn't careful.

The smart thing to do would have been to extricate himself, step away, and return to his duties. But he'd never been smart when it came to Bella MacDuff. So he let his arms circle around her and savored the strange peace that came over him just from holding her.

It would be over soon enough.

# Twelve

❧

With the long journey ahead of them, Lachlan ordered Bella to get some rest as they waited for night to fall. A wait that seemed interminable. But finally, as the last rays of sunlight filtered through the trees, they were on their way.

As he'd promised, MacLean and Lamont had stayed behind in Berwick for another couple of days to watch the convent, leaving their party at four: him, Boyd, Seton, and Bella.

Traveling at night was fraught with risk and usually undertaken at a slow pace, but Boyd had been raised in the Marches and knew every inch of the terrain. With his skilled navigation, they kept a steady pace on the darkened road that ran along the banks of the River Tweed.

Every instinct urged him to push hard and get out of the area as quickly as possible, but Lachlan was conscious—too damned conscious for his peace of mind—of Bella. He knew he should be paying attention to the road, but more often than not, his eyes were on the slim back riding a few feet ahead of him, making sure she was all right.

Though her spirit seemed undiminished—he still couldn't believe she'd managed to get him to agree to this—her frailty worried him. The imprisonment would have taken a toll on her physical strength. When he'd been released from prison, he'd felt as weak as a kitten.

He frowned. Was it his imagination, or was she slumping more in the saddle with each passing mile?

Although it was a fairly warm autumn night, she had two plaids wrapped around her narrow shoulders. His mouth fell in a grim line, suspecting the cause. He'd been imprisoned before. He knew what it was like to be cold. The kind of cold where you never thought you'd be warm again. But his icy pit in the ground wasn't a cage high on a tower exposed to the elements. He couldn't imagine—

*Damn it.* He couldn't think about it. He'd go half-crazed if he thought about it.

She might look soft and feminine on the outside, but that fragile exterior hid a will of steel. He'd always admired her strength but had never realized its magnitude.

"Here," he said, unfastening the plaid he wore around his shoulders and passing it to her as they rode. "It's getting cold."

A small furrow appeared between her brows. "But you only have a *cotun*."

"I'm fine," he insisted. "Take it."

Her gaze met his in the moonlit darkness, but she didn't protest further, taking the plaid and wrapping it around her shoulders. He didn't miss the little sigh of contentment as she snuggled in its deep folds. She gave him a sidelong glance from under her lashes. "You gave this to me once before."

"Did I? I don't remember." One side of her mouth curved as if she knew he lied, and he decided to change the subject. "Are you holding up all right?"

"I'm fine," she said firmly, sitting up a little straighter in her saddle—trying to convince herself or him, he didn't know.

He held her gaze, wanting to say something more, but

not wanting to upset her with bad memories. Finally, he nodded. "Let me know if you need to rest."

She started to protest—stubbornly—but he cut her off with a sharp glance. Though it was dark, he swore he could see the soft pink of a flush rise to stain her cheeks before she nodded. "As you wish."

Suspecting that was about as much compliance as he would ever get from her, he left it at that.

They rode through the long hours of the night. Although they would take care to avoid contact with anyone and veer well off the road whenever they drew near a village, danger lurked around every bend.

He'd feel a whole hell of a lot better when they were back in the Highlands. But at this pace that might take some time.

His gaze slid back to Bella just in time to see her head roll forward and her body start to fall to the side.

*Damn it!* He yelled her name as he lurched his mount forward. She startled back awake with an upright jolt at the same time that his arm latched around her waist to catch her. Because it was easier—and his heart had taken enough of a strain tonight—he gave momentum a little help and pulled her right onto his lap.

She stiffened, cranking her ahead around to peer up at him in the darkness. "What are you doing?"

His mouth thinned. "What does it look like I'm doing? You're riding with me." He pulled her in tight against his chest. Only to make his point, of course—not because having her pressed against him was about the best damned feeling in the world.

Her eyes widened in the darkness. "That isn't necessary, I'm not a child—"

"Then don't act like one," he said bluntly. "You almost fell off your horse; you're so exhausted. Damn it, Bella, I told you to get some rest."

"I did," she protested. She slumped against him, defeated. "I tried. But I was too excited."

He wanted to stay angry—angry was safe—but he felt himself soften. "To see your daughter?"

She nodded, a radiant smile lighting her face. "It's been so long since I've seen her."

There wasn't anything accusing in her tone, but he felt a stab of guilt nonetheless. "I know."

As their eyes met in the darkness, a lifetime of memories passed between them. "I don't blame you," she said softly. "Not anymore. You were right. If I'd taken my daughter, she might have . . ."

Her voice was too thick to continue. But he knew what she was thinking. Her daughter might have suffered the same fate as she did—as young Mary Bruce had as well.

"What's she like?" he said, trying to distract her.

It worked. The smile was back on her face. "Smart. Quiet. Not shy, but reserved. She has her father's coloring but my eyes." Her mouth quirked, and she gave him a sly glance. "But I don't need to tell you that, since you've met her for yourself."

He knew she was referring to the message he'd taken the girl not long after her mother's departure—a message he'd denied taking. Obviously she hadn't believed him.

He didn't bother denying it a second time, but her faith in him after all that had happened surprised him. It caught him off guard. "She's a lovely girl."

*Just like her mother.*

Bella stared up at him as if she could read his mind. His chest tightened. Squeezed tight with an emotion that didn't belong to him. He'd forgotten this. Forgotten the intensity of the connection and how hard it was to resist her. He had to force his gaze from hers. "Get some rest, Bella," he said, as sternly as he could muster.

She seemed to want to say something more, but after a moment she nodded. It didn't take her long to fall asleep. A few minutes later, he felt her body slump into his and heard the soft, even sound of her breathing.

A wave of contentment came over him. He was glad to have her safe, that was all.

If he relished holding her just a little too much, he consoled himself that at least this way they could quicken the pace.

In fact, he might just have to ride with her the entire way back to the Highlands. For her safety as well as theirs, of course.

Bella sighed with contentment, burrowing deeper into the warm coverlet that smelled of leather and spice. She felt so safe and warm.

The eye that wasn't resting against the coverlet popped open. Her coverlet was of silk, not of leather, and it smelled of lavender, not spice. And she hadn't slept with a coverlet and been warm since . . .

She startled, but his arms tightened immediately around her. Lachlan. Sensing her disorientation, he soothed, "It's all right, Bella, you're safe."

Safe. A wave of relief flooded her, followed immediately by one of gratitude. She was out of prison. It wasn't a dream. *He* wasn't a dream.

She leaned her head back to look up at him. "You came for me." She hadn't been awake long enough to form her defenses, and the wonder and emotion rang clearly in her voice. "Not just this time but before also. The rescue. That was you."

Her heart stabbed at the memory. She remembered looking down into the darkness at the two men racing out of the tower after the explosion had woken her. One of the men had looked up. For a moment she'd *known,* but then she'd told herself it couldn't be. He'd betrayed her.

But now she knew differently. He hadn't knowingly betrayed her. She believed him. Part of her had always known.

His jaw tightened. A strange emotion crossed his face. If she didn't know him so well, she would think it was pain. "I vowed the moment I saw you being loaded in that cart that I would get you out. I just wish it could have been sooner."

"What happened that day?" He'd given her a brief explanation, but she wanted to hear it all.

He stiffened. She could see from the hardness of his jaw that the subject was a distasteful one. He looked angry, but she knew it was at himself, not her. "I told you most of it. I was angry and not paying as close attention to my surroundings as I should have been. One of Ross's men saw me near the docks while I was trying to arrange a *birlinn*. While I drowned my sorrows in a flagon of the local ale, he had time to warn Ross. They followed me from the alehouse, and once they realized where I was going they surrounded me. I put up a fight, but there were too many of them and the drink dulled my reactions. They knocked me out and put me in manacles. I regained consciousness right before you and the rest of the women walked out of the chapel."

"Chains," she said. "That's what William was trying to tell me. He saw the chains."

Lachlan nodded. "I tried to go after you. Even managed to slip out of one of my manacles before someone noticed. But Ross was watching me too closely. He had reason not to trust me. We'd had dealings before."

"You were imprisoned?"

"For a few months."

"But you managed to escape?"

He nodded. "But by that time you were already imprisoned, and I'd learned Bruce was on his way back to Scotland."

She frowned. "How did you learn that?"

"Bruce had a spy in the English camp. A man I knew. I also learned that Gordon and MacKay were being held at

Urquhart. I went south to get some help, caught up with Bruce and the rest of the Guard—"

He stopped. "The army," he corrected. His jaw clenched even tighter. "It took nearly a year longer for the king to solidify his position enough to risk a rescue. And then when we finally got there, we failed," he said bitterly, shaking his head. "God, we were so close. I was halfway up the tower with Seton, but a soldier had been using the garderobe and heard us go by. He raised the alarm. Gordon was forced to set off his explosion early. Seton and I barely made it out in time."

Part of her was glad she hadn't known how close they'd come. It would have made the disappointment all the more difficult to bear.

"I saw you." There was a strange hollowness in his voice that she didn't recognize.

The realization that he'd seen her at such a moment made her feel oddly vulnerable. "I thought I saw you, too."

Clearly, she'd shocked him. "You did?"

"When you exited the tower and looked up. Another man was pulling you."

He held her gaze. "Seton," he said flatly. "I didn't want to leave."

"Thank you," she said. "Thank you for coming for me twice."

His mouth fell in a hard line. "I would have come for you a thousand times." He looked away, as if he'd said too much.

"Why, Lachlan? Why was it so important to you?" She held her breath. It felt as though they were on some kind of precipice.

But he didn't leap. "I always finish the mission. No matter what it takes."

The mission. Finishing the job. Of course that was why he'd come. Not for her. He would have done so for anyone.

If her heart squeezed with disappointment, Bella quickly smothered it.

They rode in silence for a while. She was content to lean against him and let his warmth encompass her. The thought of being cold . . .

Some memories would be harder to forget than others.

The closer they drew to Roxburgh, the more her excitement grew, and the more she started to wonder whether she could rely on Lachlan to keep his word. She knew he wasn't happy about their detour to Roxburgh—that he regretted giving in to her—and she couldn't help but wonder whether he'd done so merely to appease her.

Could she trust him? Would he really attempt to take a message to her daughter, or was he only trying to placate her?

Clearly, he couldn't wait to get out of the Marches. Not that she blamed him. The borders were still under firm English control and were a dangerous place for Bruce's supporters. But she wondered whether something more was at work. She'd never seen him look so wary, even when they'd been hunted across Scotland after Methven and Dal Righ.

When she tried to question him about it, however, he told her that of course he was wary—it was bloody dangerous. They could leave anytime she came to her senses. She glared at him and didn't raise the subject again.

The full moon was still aglow in the inky sky as the first light of dawn appeared on the horizon. Wisps of mist curled off the river like dragon's breath. A shimmering blanket of dew glistened on the grassy banks. On their right, to the north, a dense forest of trees—their branches weighed down by lush leaves and moss like a druid's beard—hugged the side of the road, providing cover in their dark and wizened limbs should the need arise.

If danger didn't lurk behind every tree and bend in the road, Bella might have appreciated the lush, verdant beauty of the quiet countryside. Instead the forest seemed a sinister jungle of shadows, the river seemed a brewing cauldron, and the crisp dawn air felt eerily still.

But slowly the day opened up. The shadows faded, forced to reveal their secrets under the bright glare of daylight.

Trailing off the road into the trees, Lachlan led them up a small rise and came to a stop. She gasped. Opposite them, on the other side of a valley, lay Roxburgh Castle, spread out like a small city on a triangular knoll of land between the juncture of the River Tweed and the River Teviot. It was a vast fortress of walls, towers, and heavily guarded gates, the likes of which she'd never seen. The castle was reputed to be the strongest along the borders, but she'd never imagined *this*. Five, six, seven . . . she counted at least eight towers protecting the main fortress alone.

God in heaven, how could they hope to enter such a place unseen? And how could Lachlan possibly find her daughter?

Lachlan dismounted and conferred briefly with Robbie Boyd—Sir Alex had ridden ahead to see what he could find out from the villagers (his Yorkshire accent would draw less attention)—before turning to help her down. "We wait here until Dra"—he stopped himself—"Seton gets back."

She frowned, wondering what he'd been about to say, and nodded. But she hadn't realized how hard it would be, knowing her daughter was near and not being able to do anything about it. The castle—so close she could practically reach out and touch it—was the devil's own temptation.

Fortunately, they didn't have to wait long. She'd just finished breaking her fast with a few oatcakes and pieces of dried beef that Lachlan insisted she eat—God, he could be surly—when Sir Alex came riding through the trees. The dour expression on his face didn't alarm her; she'd grown used to discontent from the once gregarious young knight.

The war had changed him. As it had her. Death and suffering made the world seem a far crueler place.

Lachlan must have seen something she hadn't. "What is it?"

"The wedding was a few days ago," the knight said. The men seemed to take this as bad news, and she wondered if there was something they weren't telling her. "Many of the guests have left," he added.

*Left?* Bella's heart dropped. "My daughter?"

Sir Alex met her gaze, sympathy in his eyes. "I don't know, my lady."

"Did you see Lady Mary?" Lachlan asked.

Seton shook his head.

*Mary? Oh, dear God, no.* "What has happened to Mary?"

"Nothing," Lachlan said quickly, but the twinge of disappointment in his voice made her certain there was indeed something they were keeping from her.

Sir Alex looked at him intently. "There are rumors she was moved south a few weeks ago."

Boyd cursed, and Lachlan's expression turned grim. She looked back and forth between them. "What is it? What are you not telling me?"

The men exchanged looks. Boyd's shrug seemed to serve as some kind of affirmation, and Lachlan explained. "Yours was not the only escape that was planned."

She sucked in her breath. "You hoped to free Mary as well?"

Was that why he'd agreed to come? She'd thought he'd wanted to help her.

"Not us, but some of the king's other men. From the sound of it, they were too late."

Poor Mary! Bella's heart went out to the girl whose suffering had mirrored her own. It was hard to think of her friends still imprisoned while she had enjoyed freedom for . . . was it only a day? "But surely they will not give up?"

"Never," Lachlan said.

The adamancy in his voice proved oddly reassuring.

Suddenly a loud, grating sound drew their attention toward the castle. The portcullis was being raised. From their bird's-eye vantage, she had an excellent view of the main gate and inner close where, despite the hour, a crowd of people were milling about. Horses were being led out of the stables and a large number of soldiers had gathered.

"Someone must be getting ready to leave," Sir Alex said.

Bella spun on Lachlan, immediately panicked. "What if it's my daughter?"

He gave her a steadying look and spoke to her with exaggerated calmness. "There's no reason to think that. It could be anyone."

Bella clenched her fists. She didn't appreciate being treated as if she were unbalanced, or a delicate piece of porcelain that could shatter at any moment. Humored. Patronized. Didn't he understand how important this was to her? It was all she'd thought of for two years in prison. She couldn't come this close and take a chance. "But what if it is?" she insisted, not caring if she sounded stubborn. "We need to find out."

An angry spark appeared in Lachlan's eye. "*We* aren't finding out anything. *You* are staying right here. I'll go."

Her eyes widened. "You're going in the castle now?"

His gaze intensified. "How else did you think I would get a message to your daughter? I may as well go now, while there is a crowd. The sooner we can get the hell out of here." He said the last under his breath.

Bella bit her lip, feeling a prickle of unease. All of a sudden, the thought of him getting close to the castle didn't sit well with her. She didn't like the idea of Lachlan putting himself in danger for her.

*I don't want anything to happen to him.* The realization

didn't take her aback as much as it should. Without the anger and blame she'd used to block out her feelings for him, it was harder and harder to muster indifference.

"How will you get past the guards?" she asked.

"Let me worry about that." He was already giving instructions to the other two men while removing the arsenal of weapons he carried. He unstrapped the two baldrics that held the two swords he wore across his back, his bow, and the short-handled axe at his waist, which left him with only a pike.

"But . . ." Her voice dropped off. She couldn't turn her gaze from the formidable castle.

The motherly instinct to ensure her daughter was safe warred with another part of her. A part she couldn't identify but that proved surprisingly strong. A part that didn't want to let him go. That didn't want him to do something that might put him at risk. And there was no doubt that going into that castle would be extremely risky.

He seemed to sense her unease. "Trust me, Bella. I know what I'm doing. Just do as I say and don't move from this place until I get back."

He spoke with such authority, she felt herself nodding like one of his men.

"Do you have the letter?" he asked.

God, how could she have forgotten? She'd spent a large part of the previous day while they waited to leave composing it. She still wasn't sure she had it right. But she'd been careful to avoid any mention of her release from captivity. Lachlan didn't want to take any chances in case the letter fell into the wrong hands. Bella's safety and her daughter's depended on no one knowing she wasn't in that convent.

She removed the short missive from the leather bag at her waist—the lad's garments were proving surprisingly comfortable and convenient—and handed it to him.

He took it, and their eyes held for one long moment. Like

her, he seemed to want to say something but didn't know what.

She took a step toward him before she stopped herself. She had no right or cause to touch him, but the impulse was still there. The memory of his mouth on hers burned.

But then he turned, snapping the connection.

*Trust me.* The words echoed in her ears as she watched him scramble down the hill and disappear into the trees.

She'd done that before, and he'd left her daughter behind. As before, she felt the inexplicable urge to put her faith in him. Then it had proved a mistake. What was it about this man that made her want to trust him, when every indication was that she shouldn't?

Lachlan threaded his way through the crowd of villagers, doing his best to look like a common man-at-arms. He wasn't doing anything out of the ordinary; he'd blended in like this thousands of times. There was no reason to think anyone would notice him. But still he felt uneasy. Exposed. More so than ever before. The hair at the back of his neck was standing on end, for Christ's sake.

He didn't understand this strange apprehensiveness. He'd been in plenty of hair-raising situations with the Highland Guard over the last few years. Dangerous, seemingly impossible tasks under extreme conditions were exactly the type of missions for which the Highland Guard had been formed. They were the best of the best. Stronger, faster, better trained, and more experienced warriors who did the things that others feared. Hell, he never even thought about the danger. But the past two days he'd felt . . .

Realization dawned. Hell, he was bloody *nervous.*

It was an entirely new and unwelcome feeling. He was one of the most elite warriors in Christendom, and he was acting as jittery as a wet-behind-the-ears squire in his first battle.

His jaw tightened, knowing the cause. Bella. Her pres-

ence was the difference. She made him feel—blast it!—
*vulnerable.*

He was letting her get to him. Letting her get too close.
He never should have given in to her. He was angry at himself, but it was too late to do anything about it.

What was it about Bella MacDuff that made him lose his
resolve? That made him want to do anything to make her
happy?

Damn it, this mission wasn't going at all as he'd anticipated. Freeing her from prison was supposed to get her out
of his system. For two years he'd been telling himself that
when he got her out he'd stop thinking about her, stop
driving himself half-crazed with the memories of kissing
her. He'd told himself he'd only imagined the strange connection between them.

It was his failure to protect her that explained his infatuation with her, he'd told himself.

But he knew he was wrong. The connection was still
there. And he wanted her just as badly—perhaps even
more. Two years of built-up lust had taken its toll.

It had become painfully clear that ignoring his desire for
her—let alone trying to control it—wasn't going to work.

There was only one thing that was going to do that. He
should seduce her and be done with it. But damn it, after
what she'd been through, he couldn't do it.

It was a hell of a time for him to be plagued with a conscience.

Grimacing, he forced his mind back to the task at hand.
But he couldn't shake the feeling that he was walking
around with a giant target on his back.

With all the guests who had descended on Roxburgh for
the wedding, the village around the castle was a bustling
hub of activity. Tents had been erected in every open space
to house the extra servants and soldiers who had filled the
village far beyond its normal capacity.

Adding to the chaos, it was market day. Temporary stalls

had been erected in front of carts where the farmers had brought their goods to sell or barter. Vendors of livestock, fish, fruit, vegetables, grain, every kind of spice you could imagine, cloth, jewels, leather goods, and even a sword-maker cried out their wares.

It was just the kind of chaos and confusion Lachlan needed. His plan, if you could call it that, was to pose as a member of the bride's family's retinue. He'd had dealings with the Comyns before and figured his attempt to ferret out information on Bella's daughter wouldn't draw as much attention that way.

Of course, it was those very dealings with the Comyns that made being here so dangerous. He hoped to hell he wasn't unlucky enough to run into someone who would recognize him. He'd made a lot of enemies over the years— English and Scottish alike. At times like this, notoriety was damned inconvenient.

Avoiding the men, he focused on the women, striking up general conversations about the excitement of the wedding and sliding in what he hoped were innocuous questions where he could.

The comings and goings of the nobles at the castle were of great interest to the villagers—sightings of "Lord X" and "Lady Y" would be talked about for years—and he quickly learned the names of those who had already de-parted. Thankfully, none of the Comyns appeared to be among them. Hugh Despenser, one of the second King Edward's current favorites, was rumored to be leaving this morning and the villagers were eager to catch a glimpse of the illustrious nobleman.

Confident that Joan was still in the castle, he took his time to see what more he could find out. One of the women, a serving maid at the castle sent to purchase fresh vegeta-bles for the midday feast, provided his first bit of useful information about Bella's daughter, when she asked him whether he was serving one of the Comyn ladies staying in the constable's tower. It gave him a place to start searching.

But first he had to get in the castle.

His skill at getting in and out of places without being seen had earned him the war name of Viper. But it wasn't just a talent with locks and an ability to move stealthily through the shadows. It depended just as much on being able to read the situation and use it to his advantage. To see ways in and out that others didn't. Chaos, crowds, and diversions had opened as many gates as his blade.

He worked his way closer to the castle, waiting for the right opportunity. The level of scrutiny for those passing through the gate varied. In times of peace during daylight hours there was typically very little, and it was easy to pass to and from the village. But this was the Marches, a place that rarely saw peace, and he wasn't going to take any chances. To avoid questions, he needed to slip past the porter.

If Templar were here, it would be easy. Diversions were Gordon's forte. It was one of the reasons they worked so well together.

Lachlan was waiting for his opening when Despenser's large retinue started to ride out. He was forced to stand aside with a large group of onlookers and let them pass.

It took some time. Even if he hadn't known who it was, the lord's importance was evident by the size of his party. Lachlan counted at least a dozen heavily mounted knights in full armor and four times as many men-at-arms, most equipped with a horse and at least some mail.

After this imposing show of force came the lord himself, dressed in robes of velvet as fine as a king's and riding a magnificent stallion. Following Despenser were his household men and a handful of colorfully gowned and jeweled ladies, whom Lachlan assumed were family members.

Marching behind the ladies were another score of men-at-arms. And finally, bringing up the rear, came the carts laden with trunks of clothing and household plate, and servants on foot. Lachlan wouldn't have been surprised to see a menagerie of beasts in gilded cages.

It was an impressive sight. All in all, about a hundred people made their way down the road that led from the castle to the village. Throngs of villagers lined the road, watching as the great lord passed, and the party slowed to give them a better view. When Despenser's cavalcade reached the market, they slowed even further. A few of the ladies appeared to have been engaged by one of the more ardent salesmen.

Lachlan shook his head. The English and their bloody entourages. It took them forever to go anywhere. He'd go mad having to travel at such a snail's pace. The ability to move quickly was one of the reasons why he preferred to work alone.

He frowned, realizing that it had been some time since he'd done so. And hell, as much as he hated to admit it, he'd gotten kind of used to working with the other members of the Highland Guard, either in small groups, as in the current mission, or all together, as in the recent battle against John MacDougall, Lord of Lorn, at the Pass of Brander. Defeating Lorn, his former brother-in-law and the man who'd had him tortured for months in his pit prison hell—no matter that Juliana had lied to him, too—had been damned rewarding.

Seeing Lorn dead would have been even more rewarding, but Lachlan had agreed to Ranger's demand to let him live. Lachlan hadn't liked it but had gone along with it nonetheless. Something he'd found himself doing more than once with the other members of the Highland Guard.

He hadn't expected it, but over the past few years, his fellow guardsmen had earned his grudging respect. If it weren't for taking orders from MacLeod, he might almost be sorry to leave. But his agreed-upon service was complete. This was his last mission. As soon as he could collect his reward, he'd be gone.

There was no reason for him to stick around. He wasn't being paid to see this war to the end. Bruce had his crown for now—north of the Tay, at least. The inevitable battle with the English would come, but it wasn't his fight. He stayed out of politics.

But Bruce had made it interesting. He'd staged a comeback against nearly impossible odds. He still had a long way to go to victory, but he had a chance.

With Despenser's party stalled in the village, Lachlan was about to turn his attention back to the castle when a breeze caught the veil of one of the ladies, blowing it back in the wind like a streaming banner of crimson.

A chill ran down his back.

There was something about her profile, the assessing tilt of her head as she listened to the salesman who was holding a fistful of satin ribbons up to her hair, that was familiar to him. It reminded him of . . .

His stomach sank.

Bloody hell, it was Joan. He'd seen the girl only once—over two years ago. She'd been a child then. Now, she looked so much older than her fourteen years that he hadn't recognized her.

He'd almost missed her.

He didn't stop to question why she was leaving with Despenser; all that mattered was that she was leaving. He closed the distance between them as fast as he could without making it obvious. If he wanted to try to pass her Bella's note, his best chance was while the girl was talking to the merchant.

He looked around. If he could create a diversion . . .

His gaze fixed on the next stall, where a pig was tied to a farmer's cart. Perfect. He'd untie the pig and pretend to give chase, steering it toward Joan.

He looked up. Damn, he'd better hurry. Despenser had

apparently grown tired of waiting. He'd turned his horse around and come back to hurry the ladies.

Trying to determine his best course, Lachlan scanned the crowd around Joan just as he was about to untie the pig, when he noticed two people moving quickly through the crowd.

His blood froze in his veins. He swore, not wanting to believe it. But there was no mistake.

His fists clenched at his side. God's blood, he would kill them both.

Forgetting all about the pig, he darted through the crowd, trying to cut them off before disaster struck.

He didn't make it.

# Thirteen

Bella couldn't keep still. Anxiousness was eating away at her. Was Joan still in the castle? Was she all right? Would Lachlan be able to find her? What if he were caught?

As if the castle could answer her questions, she kept vigilant watch over the mighty stronghold after Lachlan left. If only they were a little closer. From her place on the hill, she could make out forms but not faces.

The side of the hill blocked the view to the village, so she had to wait for Lachlan to approach the gate. Even in the sea of leather war coats and brown wool cloaks, she was sure she would recognize him.

After over an hour passed and he still hadn't appeared, however, she began to wonder whether she'd missed him.

Or maybe . . .

No, he wouldn't lie to her again. Not about this. He would at least try.

Wouldn't he? But what if he'd agreed to come not to help her, but to help Mary?

Seeing all those guards at the gate reminded her of the danger. She shouldn't have asked him to take such a risk. But how could she not, when he was the only way to reach her daughter?

Good God, she was so anxious, she couldn't think straight.

Her gaze darted frantically to the courtyard, where the large traveling party appeared to have reached its final preparations.

Where was he? What if Joan was among the party?

She was being ridiculous. Lachlan was right. She could be anywhere. Besides, Bella hadn't seen anyone in the traveling party who looked familiar. Nor did she recognize the arms of the knights.

Her gaze swept over the crowd coming to a sudden halt. A group of finely gowned women appeared in the courtyard.

She stilled, feeling a strange tingle of awareness buzz down her spine. One of the ladies wore a dress of deep scarlet with a matching veil.

Bella gasped, her heart coming to a stunned stop. Her insides drained in a pool at her feet. She staggered, reaching for a nearby tree to steady her. Her legs had turned to jelly.

Red was Joan's favorite color. It had been since her father remarked how well it looked on her as a young girl. With her dark hair, fair skin, and crimson lips, the bold color emphasized her daughter's dramatic coloring.

It was Joan. She knew it was Joan.

And she was leaving.

Joan mounted her horse and started to follow the long procession out the gate. A bolt of panic shot through Bella.

She couldn't just let her daughter go without seeing her. Her feet started moving of their own accord. All she could think was that she had to get closer. *Just one look . . .*

Following the path that Lachlan had taken, she shot through the trees. A moment later she heard someone hard on her heels.

Sir Alex grabbed her arm, forcing her to stop. They were alone, as Boyd had taken the watch. "Where the hell do

you think you are going?" The young knight's face clouded
with embarrassment, realizing what he'd said, he amended,
"my lady."

Bella didn't care about blasphemies. Her only thought
was to reach Joan before she was gone.

"My daughter is leaving."

He frowned. "How can you be sure?"

"I saw her."

He shook his head. "Not from that distance. It's too far
to make out her face."

Bella's heart was racing. She didn't have time for this. By
time she made it down to the road through the village, Joan
would be gone.

She tried to pull away. "I didn't need to see her face. It
was her. I'm certain of it." She looked into his skeptical
eyes. "Don't you think I'd know my own daughter?"

She heard the rising hysteria in her voice but didn't care.

"It's been a few years," Sir Alex said gently. "She's probably changed—"

"It's her," she insisted, tired of patronizing men, even
those who meant well. "I know it's her." Tears shimmered
in her eyes. "Please, Sir Alex, I must . . . I have to see her
face. I won't get too close." She gazed up at him implor-
ingly, too frantic to care that she was begging him and taking advantage of his chivalrous nature.

He looked torn. "MacRuairi won't like it. He wanted
you to wait here until he got back."

"But he doesn't know she's leaving. He won't have found
her so quickly. He's going to miss her." She looked over
her shoulder, seeing the party moving through the gate.
"Please," she begged, tears streaming down her cheeks as
emotion rose inside her. "There isn't much time. I can't let
her go without looking at her face." Her voice caught. "I
haven't seen her in three years."

Sir Alex swore again. "Viper is going to kill me," he said

under his breath. "Very well, but don't move an inch from my side."

Bella would have thrown her arms around him and hugged him, but there wasn't time. She raced down the path, the grim-faced knight at her side.

When they reached the village, she feared she was too late. The crowd was so thick, it was hard to see the road.

Sir Alex grabbed her arm before she could go farther. "We stay here," he said firmly.

Bella rose on her tiptoes, trying to see over the deep crowd of villagers, but it was useless. She wasn't tall enough and the crowd was too dense.

She took a quick look around. The lad's garb was working; no one was paying any attention to her.

She couldn't stay here. But it was clear she'd pushed the young knight as far as he would go. Vowing that she would apologize later, the moment Sir Alex lightened his hold, she bolted through the crowd.

She received a few "heys" and "watch it, lads," but eventually she made it to the edge of the road where she saw that the procession had come to a stop. The loud disgruntled voices behind her she attributed to complaints about Sir Alex, whom she could hear plowing through the crowd in pursuit. Unlike a small lad, the big warrior's stepping in front of them wasn't appreciated.

He came up beside her. She didn't need to look at him to sense the fury emanating from him. "You and I are going to have a long talk if we make it out of this," he murmured under his breath.

Bella bit her lip, knowing she would feel guilty later, but right now she was too busy trying to find—

Her stomach knifed. A soft cry tore from her throat as her gaze fastened on the achingly familiar face of the lady in the scarlet gown.

It was her daughter. She'd *known* it, but seeing her face . . .

Her heart clenched. It was different.

Joan stood not a dozen yards away, deep in conversation with a merchant who was holding a stream of colorful ribbons to her head. She appeared to be amused by the old man's spirited attempt to sell her something, and a reserved smile tugged the edges of her mouth.

*Smiling.* Joan was smiling.

Some of the fear Bella had been holding inside let go. From all appearances her daughter was well.

But God, how she'd changed! The last time Bella had seen her, Joan had been like a colt: all long limbs and slightly too-large features, charmingly awkward as she stood poised on the cusp of womanhood.

But she'd still been a girl. Now she looked . . .

Bella's chest squeezed. She looked like a young woman. Though only four-and-ten, Joan appeared much older. The large features of girlhood now seemed refined and perfectly at place in her gently sculpted, heart-shaped face. With her big blue eyes, pale skin, dark hair, and regal features, her daughter had become a beauty.

The resemblance to her father was marked. In fact, except for her eyes—which were dark blue and wide set like hers—she looked nothing like Bella. She was even built differently. Whereas Bella was of middling height and until recently had always tended toward the curvaceous, Joan was tall and slim, her curves undeniably feminine but more modest in proportions.

Bella's heart tugged, realizing just how much she'd lost. More than she ever knew. Her daughter had become a woman, and she'd missed every blessed minute of it. Though achingly familiar in so many ways, the woman before her was essentially a stranger.

Sir Alex must have heard her cry and followed the direction of her stare. "Is that her?"

Something in his voice caused her to look away from her daughter a moment. The knight appeared stunned.

"Aye," Bella whispered in a deep voice. "It's her."

"She's a beauty."

Bella frowned, hearing the note of masculine appreciation in his tone. "She's four-and-ten," she replied, giving him a sharp look before turning back to her daughter. But Bella had been only a year older when she'd married Buchan.

The knight grimaced. "She looks older."

A man had come over and started to talk to Joan and the two young women standing with her. Bella didn't recognize him, but from his fine clothing and jewels, she knew he must be someone important. Who was he to her daughter?

Barely had the question formed when Bella's pulse jolted to a race. Joan was moving away from the merchant and returning to her horse.

She was going to ride away. Bella was going to lose her chance to contact her. To let her know she had never stopped thinking about her. Never stopped missing her. Never wavered an instant in her determination to get back to her.

It had been hard enough getting Lachlan to agree to come here; he would never agree to go after her.

Joan neared her horse. Bella froze like a deer in the hunter's sight. In a moment, her daughter would be gone.

Every instinct clamored to call out her daughter's name. To run to her, fold her in her arms, and carry her away from this nightmare.

But she couldn't. Dear God, she couldn't. There were too many soldiers. They would never be able to get away.

She looked around frantically. She had to do *something*. She couldn't just let her go.

A sign. She needed to give Joan a sign that she was with her. That she hadn't forgotten her.

She found it a few feet away, lying on a merchant's table. Would she understand?

Sir Alex had a firm hold of one of her wrists, not taking

any more chances on her getting loose. But the table was close enough for her to lean over and . . .

She snagged the pale-pink silk rose that had caught her eye and deftly slipped it off the table. The merchant, so caught up in the procession, didn't notice.

Sir Alex, however, did. "Damn it," he swore, reaching for it. "Don't do anything foolish."

But it was too late. Her brain had stopped working the moment she'd seen her daughter; she was thinking with her heart.

In one surreptitious motion, she tossed it between the crowd toward Joan. The pale-pink silk rose landed a few feet to her left.

"Ah hell," Sir Alex swore, seeing what she had done. He started to drag her away.

Bella kept her eyes pinned on her daughter. For a moment she thought Joan wouldn't see it. But then she jolted to a sudden stop as if she'd been struck by a bolt of lightning. Even in profile, Bella could see her face pale and her eyes widen. She understood.

Unfortunately, Joan wasn't the only one to notice. Though Bella had intended to catch only her daughter's attention, the distinguished lord walking ahead of her turned at the movement.

Suddenly, Bella had a bad feeling. Was the rose more of a sign than she realized?

Joan's gaze shot in the direction of the crowd. Whether their eyes would have met, whether her daughter would have recognized her in the lad's garb, Bella would never know. For at that moment, a man grabbed Bella from behind, tearing her from Sir Alex's grasp and hauling her up against him.

She'd been caught.

Lady Joan Comyn was enjoying herself. She'd never heard such ridiculous flattery in her life and couldn't help but smile at the man trying to sell her ribbons for three times the price she could purchase them for in London.

She'd had precious little to smile about in the few months since her father had died. Actually, it had been far longer than that, but she tried not to think of her mother—it was too painful.

Her life was in England now.

Of her new guardian, Sir Hugh Despenser, Joan didn't know what to think. Their interactions had been few, and when—such as now—he came to hurry them along, he seemed more impatient and annoyed than truly angry. Of age with her father, he was shrewd—his position as the king's favorite told her that—and she would not underestimate him.

As she and Margaret followed Sir Hugh back to their horses, Joan tried not to look at the crowd that was taking in their every move. But she couldn't help feeling self-conscious. Though she understood the fascination, she was naturally shy and reserved, and uncomfortable with people looking at her. With what had happened to her mother, it was perhaps understandable.

Suddenly, she sensed a movement out of the corner of her eye. When she looked down, it took her a moment to realize what it was.

Her heart slammed to a stop. Her breath caught in her chest with the force of a hammer.

Without realizing what she was doing, she knelt down to pick the item up, holding it almost reverently in her hand. Her eyes glazed with tears.

*Who . . . ? What did this mean?*

Instinctively, she turned in the direction where she'd sensed the movement. Her eyes scanned the crowed, looking for an answer. But there were so many people it was impossible to guess from where it had come.

Yet one golden-haired man stood out. He held a slim boy by the wrist and looked furious. It wasn't the anger that made him stand out, however. Tall, broad-shouldered, and lean, he was just about the most handsome man she'd ever seen. Although noticing men was something entirely new for her, once discovered it seemed she could do nothing else. She and her cousins had spent hours discussing the men at the wedding.

But none of them were like him. He was everything to make a young lady's heart race, and she was not immune.

She guessed him a few years past twenty, despite the stubbly beard on his boyishly handsome face that seemed intended to make him appear older.

She knew he was a warrior by the sword at his back and the simple leather war coat he wore as armor. But he wore no helm, and his sun-drenched hair shone like a cap of gold in the bright sunlight. Short and becomingly tousled, it made him look as if he'd emerged from a loch, shaken out the water, and ran his fingers through the thick golden mane as an afterthought.

Momentarily distracted by the handsome young warrior, it took her a moment to realize her reaction—and what had caused it—had been noticed.

"'Tis a pink rose!" She heard the hushed whispers filter through the crowd like the ripple of a stone tossed across a pond.

The villagers would not know her connection to the infamous Lady Isabella MacDuff, but they all recognized the traitor's symbol.

Unfortunately, so did her guardian. "What is that?"

Joan didn't answer. She saw Sir Hugh's eyes narrow and knew he recognized what it was. She let it fall from her hand.

He spun around, scanning the crowd as she had done. "What is the meaning of this? Who threw this?" He turned to the merchant who'd tried to sell her the ribbons. "Was it you?"

The merchant shook his head vehemently. "Nay, m-my l-lord," he answered, his voice shaking.

The morning had taken on an ominous cast. People shuffled uncomfortably, shooting furtive looks around.

Joan just wanted to leave. Anything that reminded her guardian of her mother was sure to cause her problems.

She ventured one more glance at the young warrior. What she saw then caused her blood to run cold. Another man had come up beside him to take hold of the boy. He, too, stood out for his height and muscular build. But it was his face that struck fear in her heart.

She'd been terrified the first time she'd seen him. It had been over two years ago, when the dark, menacing-looking warrior with the scarred face and eerie eyes had woken her as she slept in her chamber in Balvenie to explain why her mother had left her behind.

Except for her recent visit with William Lamberton, the Bishop of St. Andrews, it was the only direct information she'd had about her mother since she left. Her father's hatred for the "traitorous whore" who'd betrayed him had made the subject a closed one.

What was he doing here? Was it some kind of message?

Her heart started to pound frantically.

Joan knew what she had to do. Without another glance into the crowd, she lifted her chin and tossed back her head with all the disdain of the heir of Buchan.

Lifting her slippered foot, she place it atop the flower where it had fallen from her hand and dug the silken pedals into the dirt with her tiny heel. "It's nothing," she said to her guardian. "Nothing that means anything anymore."

Her mother was dead to her. She'd chosen her path, just as Joan had chosen hers.

But when she heard a soft cry in the crowd, her eyes went not to the handsome warrior, or to the terrifying one, but to the lad in between.

A chill tingled across her skin. There was something odd about him . . .

For a moment her heart died in a flash of absolute dread. But she forced herself to calm. Forced her lungs to fill and empty with air.

*It couldn't be.*

Feeling as if she'd just seen a ghost, Joan repressed a shiver and turned back to her guardian.

Lachlan was so furious he couldn't see straight. Seeing Bella in the crowd had been bad enough, but when she reached for that flower and he realized what she was going to do . . .

His heart stopped beating. Bloody hell, he wasn't going to kill her, she was going to kill him!

And she just might succeed if he couldn't think of a way to get them out of this. Fast.

He caught up to her a few seconds after Seton. If there was anyone he was more furious with than Bella, it was Dragon.

No one in the Highland Guard had taken longer to earn Lachlan's respect than the young Englishman. It wasn't because he suspected Seton had been chosen because of his illustrious brother; it was his attitude. Seton's rigid adherence to rules and the knightly code put him at odds with the pirate style of warfare employed by the Highland Guard. Half the time he walked around like he had a pike up his arse, something Lachlan didn't stop pointing out.

But Dragon's skill with the blade and stealth complemented Lachlan's skills, and they often ended up on missions together. Lachlan had thought he could rely on him, but he should have known better.

Snagging Bella's wrist, he hauled her up against him. Feeling her against his body, knowing she was safe if only for a moment, took just enough edge off his anger to stop him from doing all the things he wanted to do to her.

But when this was over . . .

He looked at Seton over the top of her cap. To his credit, the young knight met his gaze unflinchingly. His grim expression, however, told Lachlan that he knew there would be hell to pay for this.

After nearly three years of working together in situations where one errant sound could be the difference between life and death, they knew how to communicate in silence. A nod of his head and dart of his eyes told Seton what he wanted him to do.

Seeing that the younger man understood, Lachlan let her go. But it wasn't easy. Every primitive instinct clamored to hold on to her and . . . just hold on.

He had to stop himself from not catching her back to him when Despenser noticed what had drawn Lady Joan's attention.

Damn it, this wasn't good. Not good at all.

So much for remaining unnoticed. It seemed as though every pair of eyes in the retinue was turned in their direction. And in at least one pair he saw recognition.

He held his breath as the color slid from Lady Joan's pale face. Their eyes met for one long heartbeat.

Would she call him out? Identify him as a rebel and send him to his death?

She turned away. He breathed a ragged sigh of relief, thinking that the reports of her allegiance to the English must be wrong. But when she crushed the rose under her heel, he reconsidered. *Damn.* Her disavowal of her mother couldn't be any plainer.

*Ah, hell.* His gaze shot to Bella. Seton was slowly easing her through the crowd, but it wasn't fast enough. They'd managed to move only a few feet away. Any hope that she hadn't seen the crushed rose or heard her daughter's words fled the instant he saw her stricken expression.

He caught only a glimpse of her face in profile before Dragon pulled her away, but it was enough.

His chest tightened. Seeing her in pain . . . damn it, it pained him. He would have done anything to spare her from another moment of it. Lady Joan had crushed her mother's heart as surely as she had crushed that flower.

But if he thought the worst was over, he was wrong. A man who'd been riding ahead had come back to investigate and had noticed Seton and Bella. "You there. Where are you going?"

Lachlan swore. He wasn't a praying man, but if he were ever going to start, now would be the time. The man who'd noticed Bella was her former brother-in-law, William Comyn. Unfortunately, he wasn't a stranger to Lachlan. Indeed, in the long line of people eager to see his head adorning the gates of a castle, William Comyn would be standing in the front. Years ago Lachlan had humiliated him on the battlefield, and the proud nobleman had never forgotten it.

Lachlan tugged the cap he wore lower over his brow, though it was scant protection if Comyn turned his way.

But right now the danger was Bella.

Seton pulled her behind him and turned to face Comyn. Lachlan had never been so grateful to hear Seton's bloody English accent. "To the castle, my lord," he said. "The lad is supposed to be at work, not gaping at the pretty ladies."

Seton bowed, bestowing a dazzling grin on Joan and the other ladies, who blushed prettily.

Lachlan owed the knight an apology. It seemed all that gallantry and chivalry wasn't completely useless.

Comyn, however, was not impressed. His eyes narrowed. "You, boy, why are you hiding back there?"

Knowing there was no other choice, Seton eased Bella out from behind his back.

Lachlan stilled, his senses primed, ready to do whatever it took to defend her. *Bàs roimh Gèill*. Death before Surrender. It was the motto of the Highland Guard and one of the few things they all agreed upon.

She kept her eyes downcast, the cap shielding most of her face. That, coupled with the loss of weight wrought by her imprisonment . . .

He hoped to hell it was enough.

He glanced toward Despenser's group and noticed a furrow appear between Lady Joan's brows as she studied Bella.

Bella mumbled something in a low voice.

"What's that?" Comyn said. "Speak up, boy."

Seton backhanded Bella's shoulder—a little harder than Lachlan thought necessary. "You heard the lord," he said, then turned to Comyn apologetically. "He's shy, my lord."

Lachlan knew this couldn't go on much longer. That disguise wasn't going to hold up under scrutiny.

Joan put a hand on Comyn's arm. "Please, uncle, let the lad get back to work. He looks to be in enough trouble already." She gave a small laugh. "Lord Despenser is eager to begin our journey." She looked at the crushed rose. "I'm sure nothing was meant by it."

Comyn patted her hand indulgently, but he didn't turn from Seton and Bella, who stood unmoving in the crowd. A crowd that was only too grateful to have the attention turned on someone other than themselves. Lachlan had to do something to turn it on someone else—someone who was preferably not him.

He wished he had that pig. He looked around for something—anything—that could provide a distraction.

He didn't have a pig, but he had chickens. A few feet away were half a dozen hens in a temporary coop and tied beside it, one big, fat cockerel.

It was the cockerel that he focused on. He inched toward the rope.

Comyn opened his mouth to say something, his gaze still fixed on Bella and Seton, and Lachlan knew he'd run out of time. He pretended to trip forward, slicing through the rope with a dirk hidden in his hand as he crashed into the table to which it had been tied.

A table laden with baskets of eggs.

"Me eggs!" the farmer cried out.

Hell, "me eggs" were dripping down his damned face. Lachlan went to wipe it, but then stopped himself. Instead, he buried his face in some of the hay that had been cradling the eggs in the baskets. As disguises went, this one was bloody uncomfortable.

The absurdity of the situation was not lost on him; this day had taken on farcically disastrous proportions.

The crowd, startled by the sudden disturbance, started to chuckle. With him sprawled out in the dirt, covered in egg and hay, he didn't need to wonder why.

He pretended to wobble as he tried to get to his feet. "Sorry about that." He slurred his words slightly, hoping to give the impression that he was still drunk from a night of merrymaking.

But the farmer was no longer looking at him. Lachlan heard a few furious squawks, and a few seconds later: "Me cock!" the even more agitated farmer cried, pushing through the crowd after his fleeing bird. "Where's me cock?"

"It's the small, wiggly thing above your bollocks," a woman in the crowd yelled.

It was perfect. The crowd started laughing harder, exchanging a string of ribald jests at the poor farmer's expense.

But Lachlan wasn't taking any chances. He struggled to his feet again, this time going down hard on the wood frame of the temporary pen. The hens scattered. The people standing nearby rushed to try to capture them, and the crowd broke apart in disarray. The villagers who had carefully lined the street now flooded it.

Lachlan pretended to be dazed as he finally got to his feet. A woman nearby took his arm to steady him. He glanced in the direction he'd last seen Bella and Seton, but they were gone, having slipped away in the chaos.

Fortunately, Comyn didn't seem to have noticed. He and the rest of Despenser's party had moved out of the way to avoid the onslaught of clacking poultry. Lachlan didn't wait to see what would happen when order was finally restored.

Mumbling thanks to the woman who'd helped him stand, he thrust a few coins in her hand. "For the eggs," he said.

Then he did what he did best: He slipped away.

Or so he thought.

# Fourteen

They rode north, pushing hard to evade pursuit in the event anyone decided to come after them. But each time one of the men returned from scouting, they found no sign that they were being followed. It appeared they'd gotten away.

They were lucky, and Bella knew it. She'd never imagined, never intended anyone but her daughter to see the rose. It was only a decoration for a gown—nothing that should have drawn so much attention.

Her shoulders slumped. It was useless. There was no excuse she could conjure up that would make what she'd done anything less than foolhardy, risking not only her life but Lachlan's and Alex's as well.

They were furious with her. As they had every right to be.

And what had she accomplished? All she'd done was force herself to stand witness to her daughter's very public repudiation of her.

"*Nothing that means anything anymore.*" It seemed as if the words had been aimed right at her, every one an arrow to the heart.

There had to be some explanation. She didn't want to—couldn't—accept that she'd lost her daughter. That one act in crowning Bruce had already cost her so much. It couldn't cost her Joan.

Bella had wanted to do something important. To take a stand for something she'd believed in. To do her duty for her clan and country. Was it so wrong? Had her lofty ideals not been tested enough? Must they cost her everything?

Maybe Joan hadn't meant it. Maybe it was all a show to prove her loyalty to her uncle, and the man Bella had learned was Sir Hugh Despenser, presumably her new guardian.

But it hadn't seemed like a show. It had seemed quite real.

Not until she saw her daughter face-to-face would she know the truth. But how was she going to manage that?

He gaze fell on Lachlan. Actually, as he was riding ahead of her, it fell on his back. *He* could help her. Not that she'd think of asking him. He was so angry he would barely even look at her. Each time she'd tried to speak to him, he'd given her a harsh monosyllabic response and coldly turned away. The closeness she'd felt when riding with him was long forgotten. She contemplated sliding off her horse so he would order her to ride with him again.

Sir Alex wasn't much better—especially after she'd witnessed the heated exchange between him and Lachlan on their first stop to water the horses. From the looks of it, Lachlan had given him a tongue lashing the young warrior would not soon forget. Sir Alex had stood there silently, face red with anger, taking every blow without one word of defense. Only Robbie Boyd spoke to her in full sentences, but even he seemed disappointed in her.

It made for a long, uncomfortable, and lonely journey. They must have traveled twenty miles since leaving Roxburgh. The once promising day had turned to darkness a few hours ago.

When Lachlan finally called for them to halt, Bella could barely sit upright in the saddle. The events of the morning, the hard riding, the lack of sleep, and hunger had caught up to her.

They'd stopped in a grassy clearing at the base of a small brae. Though it was dark, she could make out a burn in the moonlight, running down the hill toward the River Tweed, which was just behind them. She was most surprised, however to smell the heavy scent of peat smoke in the soft breeze.

When Lachlan helped her down from her horse, despite the harsh set of his mouth, she ventured another question. "Where are we?"

"Peebles."

Her eyes widened. They had traveled some distance. Peebles was a royal burgh a little over twenty miles south of Edinburgh. They were nearly out of the Marches, but this part of Scotland was still under English control. Peebles Castle was sure to be garrisoned by King Edward's soldiers. Until now, they'd carefully avoided towns and villages of all sizes.

"Is it safe?" she asked hesitantly.

His eyes narrowed to dangerous slits of brilliant golden-green. God, how he could skewer with that gaze! "Far less dangerous than your trip to the market this morning."

Bella held her breath. She could feel the heat from the rage that he seemed a hair's breadth from venting. She almost wished he would. Just so it could be over with. "I'm—"

*Sorry*, she'd been about to say.

But he cut her off. "We need to change the horses, and you need to rest."

Before she could argue, he walked away. For someone who refused to lead his own clan, the man was a natural leader. He'd certainly perfected the ability to speak in edicts and commands.

While the men tended the horses, she sat down to eat. Even that took effort. The dried beef was hard and took a long time to chew. She did so carefully, having no desire to cause more trouble by choking.

She was nibbling on an oatcake when she saw Lachlan and Boyd disappear into the darkness. A few minutes later, Sir Alex strode toward her, a skin in his hand.

"Here," he said, holding it out to her. "It's probably stronger than you are used to, but it will help you relax. It's been a long day."

An understatement indeed. She took the skin and drew it to her mouth, wincing as the fiery amber liquid slid down her throat to sit and burn in her belly. But it left a pleasant warmth. After the first sip, the next couple went down considerably easier.

"You'd better give me that back," Sir Alex said, a hint of wryness in his voice. "I'll be accused of getting you drunk."

Bella bit her lip, looking up at him from her perch on a rock. "I owe you an apology." Heat rose in her cheeks. "I took advantage of your kindness, and I'm sorry for it."

He held her gaze steadily, then gave an indifferent shrug. "This war has separated too many mothers from their children. If my mother could see my brothers again, I know there is nothing that would stop her." Sir Alex had lost not only the famous Sir Christopher but another brother as well to Edward's barbarism. Both had been hanged, drawn, and quartered at Carlisle not long after Methven. He turned the subject back to her. "Seeing your daughter after so long must have been difficult."

"Aye," she said hoarsely, recalling the crushed rose. "More difficult than I expected. I'm afraid I wasn't thinking straight." She paused. "I'm sorry for any tension I might have caused."

He gave a bark of laughter. "Hell, there's always tension with MacRuairi. He and I have never been friends. Nor Boyd, for that matter," he added as an afterthought.

Bella frowned. "Yet you've fought together all these years, and work well together from what I can see."

It was true, she realized. There were subtle differences from two years ago when Sir Alex and Boyd had been with them on their journey to Kildrummy. If not exactly friendly, there wasn't the animosity she used to sense between the men. The warriors seemed more relaxed and comfortable together than before. She hadn't missed the looks, gestures, the silent forms of communication that they exchanged without thought, as if reading each other's minds. They worked as a team.

She suspected they liked each other more than they even realized.

Sir Alex shrugged. "It was necessary, but it won't be for much longer."

Her brows drew together. "What do you mean?"

He turned on her in surprise. "MacRuairi is leaving."

Her heart fell like a stone in her gut. "Leaving?" she echoed. *But I thought . . .*

"I thought you knew. His agreed-upon service is almost over. Rescuing you is his last mission for the king."

She felt a sharp pang in her chest. "I see."

But she didn't.

Her chest burned. *Leaving.* He was leaving.

God, why did it surprise her? He'd never pretended to be fighting for any other reason than money. But she'd hoped . . . she'd hoped time might have changed his mind.

She'd hoped *he'd* changed.

Why? He was wrong for her in every way, wasn't he? They had nothing in common. They were from two different worlds. She believed it was worth fighting for things you believe in, and he didn't think there was anything worth fighting for but himself. He'd told her so. She'd known it. But part of her had refused to believe it. Part of her had thought he wasn't as indifferent as he seemed—to the war or to her.

Lachlan strode back into the clearing. He glanced in their direction, and even from a distance she could see his jaw clench. He walked toward them, and she felt the strong urge to run.

"There's a shieling on the other side of the hill. It isn't much, but I can clear it of debris, and it should be comfortable enough for you to sleep in."

She blanched; the small amount of food she'd eaten suddenly seemed in danger of reappearing. A cold sweat beaded on her brow. The idea of sleeping in the small, dark stone shepherd's hut . . .

The blasted cage! God in heaven, would she ever be free of it?

"No!" she blurted. Then, getting a grip on her panic, she added more calmly, "It's a pleasant evening; I think I should prefer to sleep under the stars."

He held her gaze, his expression hard and impenetrable. But something made her think he'd sensed her reaction and knew exactly what she'd been feeling. And significantly, that he understood it.

Her eyes filled with tears. The unexpected empathy caught her off guard. Anger she could fight against, but the glimpse of gentleness and sensitivity stripped her defenses, leaving her feeling vulnerable in a way she'd never felt before. In a way she feared she could not protect against.

Thankfully, he did not press. "Very well. Get some sleep. We leave at dawn."

Lachlan wished he could follow his own advice. By necessity, warriors must be able to sleep anywhere for a short period of time, but his training wasn't helping him tonight. He was too damned restless—and too damned angry. Not even a dunk in the river had helped.

The immediate demands of getting them away from Roxburgh and through the borders safely had kept him focused, but once they'd stopped, it all came rushing back. He wouldn't have stopped at all, but he knew Bella needed rest. Despite the danger, he didn't want to push her. Only the fact that Bella was barely able to stand on her feet had kept him from telling her exactly what he thought of her morning foray into the streets of Roxburgh.

He got angry just thinking about it. Anger didn't bother him. That feeling was familiar. What he didn't like was this other feeling. A feeling he was pretty damned sure was panic.

If anything had happened to her . . .

Shite, there it was again. That *feeling*. The instant rush of icy fear mixed with helplessness.

Nothing was supposed to get to him. For years he'd made himself impenetrable. Invulnerable. Not caring about anything. But she was changing that, and he didn't like it.

Thank God this was almost over. Two more days—three at the most—and they would rejoin Bruce at Dunstaffnage. Then Bella MacDuff would be the king's responsibility.

But for some reason, that thought only made him angrier.

He sensed a movement behind him and stilled. Instinctively, he reached for the hilt of the dirk at his thigh, ready to spin and throw at the next sound. But the loud crackle of leaves underfoot made him hesitate. Though light of step, the person was making no attempt to keep quiet.

He stiffened again, this time with rage.

Slowly, he turned around. His fists clenched as he watched her approach.

By the time Bella stood before him, blood was pounding hot through his veins. He felt like a lion tethered to a tree, straining against his chains. One more foot and he'd be on her.

"Go back to bed." His voice came out like a low growl.

She didn't know how much danger she was in. Every pulse in his body throbbed, every muscle coiled, every nerve ending flared. He was riding the dangerous edge of control and didn't trust himself right now. Not with her so close.

God, he could smell her. The fresh scent of her soap mingled in the night breeze. Still garbed in the lad's clothing, she'd wrapped two additional plaids around her for warmth. Unfortunately, the plaids did nothing to hide the shape of the very feminine curves underneath.

She eyed him warily but did not heed his warning.

"I couldn't sleep," she said, looking up at him, her pale face bathed in the soft moonlight. "I wanted to apologize."

His jaw clenched. "For breaking your promise, disobeying my orders, or nearly getting us killed?"

Even in the moonlight he could see her cheeks heat. "For all of it. I don't know what came over me." She was fidgeting with her hands, something he couldn't recall ever seeing her do, and he realized how much distress this was causing her. It didn't make him feel any better. "I was watching for you to enter the gate when I saw her. I couldn't see her face, but I knew it was Joan. I had to see her up close. I thought you would miss her."

"I was about to pass her the note when I saw you."

Her eyes widened. "You were? I didn't think . . ." She bit her lip. "When I heard about Mary, I thought you might have agreed to go to Roxburgh for other reasons."

She hadn't trusted him. He'd given her no reason to, but still it stung. "I honor my promises, Bella. I might not make them very often, but when I do, I keep them."

She nodded. "I'm sorry."

"Maybe I could understand the desire to see her. But what in Hades could have possessed you to throw that flower?"

She winced, biting her lip and pleading with him silently for understanding. "I don't know. I didn't think anyone else would see or understand. I didn't realize the symbol was so well known. I couldn't let her leave without doing something."

"You didn't know the most widespread symbol of rebellion?"

She shook her head. "How would I?" she challenged.

Somehow his hands were on her shoulders, and he was shaking her, all of the fear and frustration pouring out in one blast of fiery anger. "Damn it, Bella, you could have been captured! Do you know how lucky you were that Comyn didn't recognize you? For Christ's sake, what were you thinking!"

"I wasn't." She shifted out of his grasp. "You don't have to bellow at me, I told you I was sorry. Why are you acting like you care, anyway?"

He should be glad she was still fighting after what she'd been through. Really he should be. But right now he wasn't in the mood for being challenged.

She tilted her head back and gazed up at him with that proud-countess, defiant gleam in her eye. "Or was it just your own skin you were worried about when you are so close to getting what you wanted?"

"What in Hades are you talking about?"

"This *is* your last mission, isn't it?"

"Who—?" He stopped, knowing exactly who. "Seton." He and that blasted knight were going to have another talk.

"Was it supposed to be a secret?"

"Nay." He'd just hoped to wait until he'd gotten her back to Bruce to tell her.

"So it's true?"

"Aye, it's true."

She looked at him as if she expected him to try to explain. He didn't have to explain anything; he didn't owe her any explanations.

"That's it, then? You are just going to sail off and not look back?"

That was exactly the plan, blast it. His teeth gritted together. "I agreed to three years, and three years is almost over."

She looked incredulous. "So you're going to collect your money and go back to selling your sword to the highest bidder?"

His face darkened, not liking the hint of scorn in her voice. "I have some debts." He couldn't bring the men who'd died for him back to life, but he sure as hell could provide for their families. The money from Bruce would be the last payment on a debt that could never be repaid. But what he intended to do with the coin wasn't any of her damned business. "Once they are paid, I'm done—with all of it."

"You are returning to your clan?" He didn't miss the note of hope in her voice.

His teeth grated together. "Nay."

"I don't understand you. I've watched you with these men. You are a good leader. Why are you shirking your duty to your clan?"

Good leader? He knew forty-four men who would disagree with her. "Leave it, Bella."

This time something in his voice must have warned her, and she wisely chose not to press. "Then why not stay and fight with Robert?"

It wasn't his fight, damn it. He wasn't supposed to care who won or lost.

*I don't.*

But he knew that wasn't quite true. He wasn't nearly as ambivalent as he wanted to be. Somehow, without him realizing it, he'd been caught up in the fervor and excitement of Robert the Bruce's impossible, historic, legendary rise from the ashes of defeat.

And though they might irritate him at times—some more than others—his Highland Guard brethren were the best warriors he'd ever fought alongside. Together they'd done things he'd never dreamed possible.

But it didn't change anything. "Bruce has his crown," he answered.

"But it isn't over. You know that as well as I do. Half of Scotland's castles—all the important ones in the south— are still controlled by English garrisons. Yes, Robert has his crown, but he rules over only half a country, and his reign is by no means secure. He has many enemies within who would be eager to see him fall. And Edward will not ignore Scotland forever. War with England is inevitable. There is still so much to be done."

The passion in her voice made him stare at her in disbelief. *No.* She couldn't . . . "You can't mean to get involved?"

She thrust up that chin and glared at him. "I will do whatever the king needs of me, once my daughter is out of danger."

His eyes narrowed. Obviously the crushed rose hadn't deterred her from trying to get her daughter back. The woman was as determined as she was stubborn. God's blood, what if she did something risky again? His pulse leapt before he brought it back down.

*Not my problem,* he reminded himself.

"After everything you've been through you still want to fight? Are you so anxious to be imprisoned again?"

She paled. "Of course not! You saw what it was like. It was horrible. The cold. The bars. The endless hours with nothing to do but try to prevent myself from going mad." She gave him a scathing glance, obviously furious at him for dredging up the unpleasant memories. "I can barely look at a closed door without feeling a shudder of panic. You saw it for yourself earlier with the shieling."

"How did you do it?"

Her eyes locked on his. "How did you?" she challenged softly. When he didn't say anything, she turned away with a shrug. "I thought of my family—of my daughter. I knew I had to get through it for her." She turned back to him, eyes flashing again. "Why are you asking me this? You know what it was like."

"Because that's exactly what you are facing if you continue on this quest." She needed to know the risks. "You've done enough, Bella. Take your freedom and don't look back."

"Don't you see, it isn't about me. It never has been."

He didn't see it at all. He never would. That was part of the problem. *Things bigger than yourself,* she'd said once. "Was it worth it?"

She flinched as if he'd hit her. The stricken look on her face almost made him wish his question back. Her chin quivered. "It has to be."

The desperate plea in her voice did something to him. For one moment he almost thought he could be the man to help her make sure it was.

Apparently, she was under the same foolish impression, because she would not relent. "I thought you were a man who finished the job, not left it half done."

The words pricked. She knew him better than he wanted to admit. *Not my fight . . .*

"I've done what I set out to do. It's over for me."

But not for her. She was a fighter. She would go on fighting as long as there was a breath in her body. Even for lost causes like him.

"So none of it matters to you?" she taunted. "You don't care about anything? Not whether Robert succeeds in freeing Scotland from England? Not whether your friends die?"

He just wanted to shut her up. He stepped closer, looming over her threateningly, fists clenched at his side. "They're not my friends."

"They aren't?" she challenged. He knew what she was going to say. *Don't say it.* "And what about me, Lachlan. Don't you don't care about—?"

He grabbed her before she could say it, backing her against a tree. He didn't want to care about her, about any of it. But she just kept digging and digging until she drew blood.

He'd had enough. She'd pushed him too damned far.

He pressed his body into hers, crudely wedging his cock between her legs. "You want to know what I care about, Bella? This is what I care about. I want to fuck you so badly, I can't think straight. I want to bury my tongue between your legs and lick you until you come against my face."

She gasped.

He sneered. "So unless you're ready to get down on your knees and wrap that incredible mouth around my cock, leave me the hell alone."

She should have told him to go to hell. That's what he wanted her to do. But Bella never did what she was supposed to do. Instead she smiled knowingly—as if she understood him. Which was impossible, since he didn't even understand himself.

"Am I getting a little too close to the truth, Lachlan?" The subtle taunt infuriated him. "Be as mean and crude as you like—you won't frighten me away."

His eyes darkened. Maybe not. But this sure as hell would. His mouth fell on hers in a rush of savage ferocity.

He'd warned her.

# Fifteen

❧

Bella had pushed him too far. Perhaps it was what she'd intended all along. This heat, this passion, this *madness* simmering between them had gone on for too long. She was done fighting it.

There was nothing stopping her. Buchan was dead. Her duty to him—if she'd owed him one—was gone.

Her long imprisonment, not knowing when or if she would ever be free, had taught her to take what moments of joy and pleasure she could eke out of life when she could. There might not be another chance.

And somehow she knew this would give her pleasure unlike anything she'd ever known. She wanted to feel passion just once in her life. Even if that were all that could ever be between them. His offer was clear—as it had always been. He'd never claimed to want anything more from her than this.

She didn't want anything more from him . . . did she?

On the surface nothing had changed. He was still a bastard. Still the man who was said to have betrayed his clan and murdered his wife. Still a ruthless mercenary who sold his sword to the highest bidder and claimed to care about nothing.

But he cared far more than he let on. His reaction to her

questions told her that. The meaner he got, the cruder he got, the more she knew she'd gotten to him. He used his forked tongue as a weapon and a shield—to push people away when they got too close and prevent them from looking at him too closely. But she sensed a deep sadness inside him. The blackness wasn't in his soul, but in the dark cloud hanging over it.

Still, his coarse words had shocked her. Of all the licentious acts her husband had forced upon her, he'd never done *that*. The thought of Lachlan's mouth *there*, his hot tongue probing her intimately . . .

She shuddered, her body quivering where he was so firmly notched against her.

The moment his mouth fell on hers, Bella knew there was no going back. His kiss was hot and hungry, every bit as raw and primal as the passion storming between them.

He bent her into him. Kissing her deeper. Molding her to the hard length of his body. She could feel every ridge, every bulge, every steely edge of muscle, as his body seemed to consume hers, melding together in a perfect fusion of heat.

His tongue circled against hers, urging—nay, demanding—her response.

She kissed him back, matching every carnal thrust with one of her own. His dark, spicy taste filled her senses, blinding her to anything but him.

This was no tender wooing, no smooth seduction, but a violent conflagration of desperate need between two people who wanted only one thing.

This fierce need, this desperation, this passion . . . she'd never thought to feel like this. Never imagined she could be so overcome. Never imagined she could feel this kind of connection to anyone. It seemed unreal that this could be happening to her. That the woman who'd experienced only coldness for years could find pleasure in the arms of one of the meanest, most feared and reviled men in Scotland.

But there was more to him than that. He was hard but not bad. Not as bad as he wanted to be, anyway. He'd just never had anyone to care for him. Never had anyone he could trust. She just needed to give him a chance. He was worth fighting for.

His mouth was so hot, each slanted movement, each swirl of his tongue stoking the flames a little higher. The heat of his kiss seemed to reach down to her toes, dragging her under. Her heart seemed slammed against her chest, fluttering wildly with every stroke.

She gripped his shoulders, her fingers digging into the studded leather of his *cotun*, needing to feel him even closer. He was so big and strong, and on some base level she needed that, his warrior's body as hard and unyielding as steel but as warm and comforting as the softest, warmest plaid.

In his arms, she would never be cold again.

She groaned when his big hands cupped her bottom, bringing her firmly against his hardness. A strange shudder trembled through her. Fear and excitement all at once. He seemed so . . . *big*. Every inch of the thick column of his manhood felt branded against her.

How would he . . . ?

She bit her lip. How would they . . . ?

Surely it would hurt?

But then he thrust against her, moving his hips in a slow, wicked rhythm that mimicked the movements of lovemaking, and she no longer cared.

Heat rose inside her. She felt the need intensify. Dampness flooded between her legs in a hot rush. Gathering. Concentrating. Coiling in a tight ball of restless desire.

Her skin flushed. Her breath hitched in uneven gasps.

He rubbed against her, increasing the friction, increasing her need.

She needed to move faster. Harder. She arched against him, feeling something strange come over her. She was climbing, reaching for something that hovered just out of her reach.

She didn't recognize the sounds coming from her. Urgent little moans she didn't fully understand.

He'd stopped kissing her. His mouth was on her neck, trailing down her throat, delving between her breasts. Ravishing. The scrape of his beard sending a delicious burn along the sensitive path of her skin.

He was groaning too, sounding almost as if he were in pain.

She sucked in her breath. Her body stilled, quivered, and then catapulted into a place of utter ecstasy. A place she'd never been before.

She cried out her pleasure, shattering into a thousand rays of shimmering light.

Lachlan didn't care that he had her pressed up against a tree. He didn't care that Boyd and Seton could return from the village with the horses at any time.

He'd lost the ability to think the moment his mouth had fallen on hers. Any hope that he could take this slow, that he might be able to exercise some semblance of control, died when she started to move against him. The proof of her desire was a powerful aphrodisiac. When he'd heard her little gasps of need turn insistent, heard her cry out her pleasure as her body spasmed against him, and knew he'd made her come . . .

He lost his mind. He couldn't think about anything other than getting inside her and making her his. *His,* damn it.

But it had been too long. He wasn't going to make it. Next time. Next time, he swore he would make it up to her. Next time he would make it good for her. Next time he would taste every inch of her. But right now he'd be lucky if he could get his braies open before he came.

Barely had the last spasm of her release ebbed when his mouth fell on hers again.

Leaving his chausses in place, he fumbled with the ties of his braies, pushing down just enough to spring his cock from the tight confinement. It bobbed hard against his stomach, the rush of cool air a blessed relief against the hot skin stretched painfully thin. He was as hard as steel, ready to explode at the barest nudge.

He didn't even take the time to touch her. He feared that one stroke of that delicate, silky pink flesh, damp with the evidence of her desire for him, would send him spinning in a whirlpool from which he would not be able to tear free.

He tugged the conveniently too-loose breeches down her hips and lifted her to position himself between her legs. Nudging her gently with the thick head, he groaned as the warm dampness of her release met the spongy sensitive flesh.

It was too much. His body shuddered, clenching hard to contain the pressure hammering at the base of his spine.

God, he wanted to come.

He couldn't wait any longer. Sliding his arm behind her back to protect her from the bark of the tree, he thrust into her with a hard slam of possession.

*Mine!* Finally. And nothing—nothing—had ever felt so good.

She gasped in surprise, her eyes widening on his. He held her gaze, his jaw clenched too tightly to talk or murmur encouraging words or apologies for taking her with all the skill of a squire with his first maid. But he told her with his eyes. They bored into her with all the intensity of the fierce emotions flaring inside him.

Emotions he didn't understand. Emotions that made his chest tighten as he looked into her eyes and filled him with a swell of something warm and soft. He wanted to hold on to her, make this moment last forever. But it had been too long. He'd wanted her too badly.

It felt too good.

*She* felt too good. Warm and soft, her body gripped him

like a fist. He held himself inside her, buried to the hilt, reaching for those last shreds of control, trying to fight the nearly overwhelming urge to thrust.

He kissed her again, trying to distract himself. But he was so hot. His skin was burning. Sweat gathered on his brow and blood pounded in his ears.

He wanted to thrust so badly he couldn't think.

He wanted to dig his fingers through her hair, letting the silky softness slide over him. But she still had her hair pinned up tightly atop her head in a plait for the cap.

She circled her arms around his neck, responding to his kiss with all the passion and enthusiasm of before.

Killing him with every eager stroke of her tongue.

He started to shake, his muscles trembling with the effort of keeping himself still.

He couldn't do it. The drive was too strong. He had to move.

He thrust hard and deep. He couldn't hold on any longer. It felt too good. He thrust again. "Oh God, I can't . . ." he bit out through clenched teeth. "Sorry . . . been too long."

He let go, sinking deep inside her one more time with a masculine roar of pure pleasure. Pleasure more raw, intense, and powerful than he'd ever experienced before. His mind went black as wave after wave of sensation exploded inside him. He didn't think it was ever going to stop.

He came back to consciousness slowly, his heartbeat and breathing a step behind.

*Jesus.* He didn't know how he was still standing, let alone holding her up. But he couldn't seem to let go, not ready to break the connection. Although God knew, it hadn't been a long one. He grimaced; even as a lad he'd had more control.

He pulled back a little to look into her eyes. They were still hazy with passion and he felt another twitch of pleasure.

"Jesus, Bella, I'm sorry."

He might have explained, or tried to make it up to her—he'd been serious about his eagerness to taste her with his tongue—but at that moment the hair at the back of his neck stood on end.

He heard a sound behind him.

Lachlan's exhausted limbs and aching muscles came instantly back to life, as the reflexive heat of battle surged through his veins. Every muscle in his body flared.

Connected as they were, Bella sensed the change immediately. "What's wrong?" she whispered.

He didn't have time to explain. They were right behind them. He lowered her to the ground, separating them. "Run," he ordered, a fierce edge to his voice. "Don't stop and don't look back. Just run."

Her eyes grew wide with fear. He couldn't look at her, knowing he had to act fast. If they caught her, he didn't have a chance.

He spun around, pulling up his braies even as he slid one of the swords from the baldric at his back. "Damn it, Bella," he jerked out his other sword, "run."

This time she didn't hesitate. He could hear the sound of her footsteps trailing away behind him as the first men entered the small clearing.

But any hope that she might have gotten away before they'd seen her faded when one of the men yelled. "Hurry, one of them is getting away!"

At least a dozen men on horseback headed off in her direction; the others—at least two times that many—headed for him.

Lachlan let them come.

He fought like a man possessed. One after another of the attackers fell under the skilled edges of his two swords. He blocked with one; sliced, cut, and jabbed with the other. No one could stop him. No one could beat him. He was indestructible. Invincible.

Almost.

But every man had his weakness. And when the men returned, one of whom was holding a wriggling Bella in his arms, a blade to her throat, Lachlan knew he'd found his. He'd thought his weakness was lust. He was wrong. His weakness was Bella.

"Drop your weapons," the man said with a sneer. "Or the lass dies."

Lachlan would die before he surrendered. But he would not watch her die.

One by one, his weapons clattered to the ground.

One minute Bella was overcome by emotions, wondering what Lachlan was apologizing for—although it had been over rather quickly, the feel of him driving inside her, filling her, claiming her in a way she'd never imagined, had been incredible. And when he'd made her come apart . . . she'd never felt anything like that before. The next she'd been captured by a vile group of ruffians and was being led into a guard room in Peebles Castle.

She was terrified. More so because of what had happened when they'd separated her from Lachlan than because she'd been captured again.

He'd managed to whisper something to her right before: "You don't know me."

She didn't even have time to ponder his words. They'd put him in chains and hit him so hard in the head with the hilt of a sword he'd crumpled to the ground like a big, armored poppet of rags.

"Don't hurt him," she'd pleaded. Assuming it was her they were after, she added, "I'll go with you willingly. Just please, don't hurt him."

The brute who'd captured her had given her a queer look. "What in Hades' bowels do I care if you come with us willingly? You'll come with us to encourage him to talk—willingly or nay."

Bella barely hid her surprise. Dear God, they didn't know who she was! It wasn't she they were after.

Then it must be Lachlan. But what could they want with him?

She didn't have to wait long to find out. Hands tied behind her back with ropes, she was pushed forward into the small room near the gate of the castle by a man leading her from behind. A few minutes later, Lachlan was tossed in after her. She lunged toward him, but another man grabbed her before she could reach him.

"I don't think so," he said, thrusting her onto a wooden bench.

Bella couldn't tear her eyes from Lachlan. Her heart rose in her throat. There was so much blood. It stained one side of his face and seeped from the big gash at his temple to pool in a puddle beneath his head.

Tears choked in her throat. He was so still. "You'll kill him if you don't stop that wound from bleeding."

The big, bearded brute of a man who seemed to be in charge laughed at her. "Don't worry, he'll live. At least until we get our reward," he added with an ominous chuckle.

He motioned to one of the three other men who'd crowded into the small chamber. About ten feet by ten, the room was well lit by torches on either side of the arched entry. She saw another door on the far side of the room, but as guard rooms also usually housed the pit prison, she didn't want to think about it. The man he'd motioned to lifted a bucket from the ground and poured the contents on Lachlan.

He immediately stirred, and she gave a little cry.

"Reward?" she asked their captor, while keeping her eyes fixed on Lachlan.

"Aye, three hundred marks."

She gasped, turning her full attention to the leader. It was a fortune. "But why?"

His eyes narrowed, under a heavy brow. "Who are you?"

"Isabella," she said, uncertain whether they'd heard her name. "Maxwell," she added, picking the first lowland clan that came to mind.

"And who are you to Lachlan MacRuairi?"

"Who?" she said, recalling Lachlan's instructions.

But she'd taken an instant too long to answer. The big man grinned, not fooled. "Obviously no regular whore if he was willing to surrender to save you." He shook his head, tugging on the tangled strands of his long, frizzy beard. "I couldn't believe my luck when I realized it was he at the fair this morning. 'What in the hell is Lachlan MacRuairi doing in Roxburgh?' I asked myself, with all of England hunting him—and half of Scotland, for that matter."

Bella bit her lip. Dear God, what had Lachlan done to draw such a bounty? And why hadn't he told her he was being hunted? No wonder he'd been so reluctant to go to Roxburgh.

"Leave her alone, Comyn," a voice rasped from below her. "She doesn't know anything."

Bella felt the blood drain from her face. Good God, Comyn! The brute must be one of her brother-in-law's men. Though she'd rarely crossed paths with Buchan's youngest brother, Sir William, it was a miracle none of the men had recognized her.

Yet.

The big, bearded man walked over to Lachlan and kicked him in the ribs like a dog. He winced but didn't make a sound. "So, you remember me, do you? I'll never forget *you*." He pulled off his helm. Bella smothered a gasp. Half his ear was missing. "As to whether the lass knows anything, we'll find out as soon as Sir William gets here. He won't be far behind. It took me a few minutes to convince him of whom I'd seen, but once I did . . . well, let's just say he's very anxious to see you. And wait until King Edward finds out he finally has one of the members of Bruce's secret army in his hands."

What was he talking about?

Suddenly, she stilled. Her gaze fell on Lachlan in wide-eyed shock. Margaret had told her some of the wild stories circling through the countryside about a pack of phantom warriors who fought for Bruce. Warriors who seemed to come out of nowhere, who dressed in black and blended into the night, with their faces hidden by ghastly blackened nasal helms. A highly skilled, elite group of warriors who were said to use war names to hide their identities.

Bella had dismissed the stories as fantastic. A product of some villagers' overactive imaginations.

*Viper.*

Suddenly the name came back to her. She'd barely noticed it at the time, but she distinctly recalled Sir Alex referring to him as Viper.

My God, was it true? Was he part of Robert's elite army?

He was. My God, he was. And he'd never said a word.

Bella stared at him. She'd taken him in her body, fallen apart in his arms, and felt closer to him than any man she'd ever known, but did she really know him at all?

He shot her a warning glance, and she lowered her gaze before anyone noticed her shock. But her heart was pounding in her throat.

Lachlan lifted his head from the ground and pinned Comyn with his piercing gaze. "Let us go now, and I won't kill you."

Given his position—trussed up in chains like a yuletide goose and lying on the floor with blood streaming down his face—the cold, matter-of-fact proclamation should have sounded ridiculous. But the malevolent gleam in his eye seemed to momentarily startle them.

It startled even her. This was the man reviled and feared across the seas. The pirate. The brigand. The heartless, predatory mercenary. If Viper was indeed his war name, it wasn't hard to guess why: He could be as mean and heartless as a snake.

Comyn recovered first. He laughed and kicked him again in the ribs—harder this time—but still Lachlan barely flinched. "You aren't in any position to be making threats. Not even you can kill four armed warriors with your hands chained behind your back."

Lachlan sat up quickly, and the other man instinctively moved back. Lachlan laughed, his mouth curved in a dangerous sneer. "You don't know what I can do."

Embarrassed to have betrayed his fear to the other men, Comyn laughed and kicked Lachlan again, this time under the chin. His head snapped back with a sickly thud against the stone wall. "Where you're going, the only thing you're going to kill is rats."

If Bella hadn't been watching Lachlan so closely, she would have missed the slight paling of his skin and the flash of fear in his steely gaze. They were gone so quickly, she almost wondered whether she'd imagined them. But then she recalled the same look two years ago, when they'd entered the tunnel at Kildrummy Castle, and knew she hadn't.

Unfortunately, their captor had picked up on it as well. His eyes gleamed with malicious intent. "Don't like dark holes much, do you?" To one of his men, he said, "Toss him in while we wait. Maybe some time down in the hole with the rats will loosen his tongue for Sir William."

The man started to pull Lachlan toward the door she'd noticed before. Past it, she suspected, was a hole in the floor secured by a wooden door or steel bars through which prisoners would be dropped to the pit prison below. But even chained, Lachlan put up a struggle. "I'm not going in there."

Another man had to help to pin him down. Together the two of them dragged him to the door. Bella felt his panic as clearly as if it were her own. She knew exactly what he was feeling. "Stop!" she cried out. "You can't put him in there."

It would drive him mad. As it would her.

She made an attempt to move toward him, but Comyn grabbed her and yanked her head back by the braided coil at the top of her head. He twisted her face toward the light. "You and I are going to get better acquainted." His eyes slid lecherously over her face. "At first I thought MacRuairi was buggering a lad. But you're a damned sight prettier than any lad." Bella shot him a look of furious disgust. When his dirty finger smoothed over her chin, she had to fight the urge to snap her teeth and bite. "A little pale and skinny, but aye, a real stunner with the mouth of a French whore."

"Put your hands on her and you won't die quickly." Lachlan hurled the threat over his shoulder as the men were trying to push him through the door. The closer he got to the pit prison the more frantically he fought, kicking, twisting, using his elbows, using whatever he could to slow them down.

Finally, the brute pushed her head back with a disgusted grunt. "Bloody hell, you can't control one chained man?"

He crossed the room in a few strides and grabbed Lachlan by the neck of his leather *cotun* to haul him up to face him.

The smile on Lachlan's face chilled her blood. "This is your last chance," he said idly. "Let us go or die."

Something in Lachlan's gaze must have warned him. Comyn thrust him away with a nervous laugh. "You must be mad."

Barely had the words left his mouth when Lachlan attacked. He spun around, untwisting the chains that were somehow no longer manacled to his wrists. In one smooth motion he tossed a loop of chain over Comyn's head, crossed his hands, and jerked them apart, snapping the man's neck before the other two men had a chance to react.

"Get down," he yelled to her, as he took another section

of the chain and looped it over the other two men, preventing them from reaching their weapons.

Bella dove to the ground and saw him slide one of the men's daggers from his belt and draw it across their throats. The men hadn't hit the floor when the knife sailed through the air and landed with a thud right between the stunned eyes of the last man.

In a matter of seconds, Lachlan had just killed four men.

His eyes found hers. "Are you all right?"

She nodded dumbly, still stunned by what she'd just seen and the unbelievable turn of events. "How did you undo the manacles?"

He shook his head. "Later. We have to get out of here—someone else could walk in at any minute." He was already going through the dead men's clothing and removing weapons. "The good news is we're close to the gate, and if they are expecting Sir William at any time, with luck the iron yett won't be closed. Here," he thrust a dirk in her hand, "do you know how to use it?"

She shook her head. "Nay, but I will figure it out if necessary."

He smiled, grabbing her behind her head to pull her in for a hard, fierce kiss. "That's my lass, always ready to fight."

Her heart squeezed. *My lass.* Of course, he didn't mean anything by it, but it filled her with an overwhelming sense of longing nonetheless.

He moved to the door, pressing his ear to the wooden slats before pushing it open.

"Finished already, Sir—?"

That was as far as the soldier got before Lachlan sank the steel of his blade into the side of his neck.

But he wasn't alone. "Watch out!" she cried, as another guard appeared from the other side.

Her warning was unnecessary. Lachlan had a dirk in his other hand as well and had already used it. He dragged both men inside the guard room they'd just vacated and closed the door behind him.

Holding his finger up to his mouth to indicate silence, he led her as they slipped along the side of the building, hiding in the shadows. The gate was not ten feet in front of them, at the end of the narrow passageway, one side of which was the tower housing the guard room. A similar tower opposite formed the other side.

At the end of the passageway was the iron yett and at least a half-dozen men-at-arms guarding the gate. But Lachlan was right—the yett wasn't closed. Still, she didn't see how they were going to slip past six armed guards.

Lachlan stopped about five feet from the gate. When one of the men started laughing loudly, he whispered, "As soon as I move, run. I need you out of the way."

She nodded, understanding. It was as before: Her capture had forced him to surrender. Lachlan could take care of himself. There was no question of that. It was she who hobbled him by requiring him to protect her. Bruce's secret army . . . Good God.

She didn't have time to think. In the next instant he moved and she followed right behind him, not stopping when he engaged the first soldier or the next. She ran past him, fending off a guard with a swipe of her dagger, and raced down the sloped dirt entry, not looking back. She barely flinched at the bone-chilling clatter of swords that reverberated behind her, shattering the quiet night air.

Suddenly, she heard the whiz of arrows fly over her head, heading not toward her but toward the castle. Two men appeared out of the darkness in front of her, slipping out from behind one of the castle's outer buildings.

Boyd and Seton—with the horses.

She was still a few feet away when she heard footsteps behind her.

Lachlan scooped her up and carried her the last few steps, lifting her onto one of the horses.

"Thanks for the help," he said dryly, hoisting himself up in his saddle.

Robbie grinned. "Took you long enough. I was beginning to worry."

Lachlan muttered something that sounded like "Sod off, Raider." But she couldn't be sure. They were already riding, racing for their lives, away from the castle that was stirring to life.

# Sixteen

Lachlan looped the drying cloth around his neck and made his way back toward the stable, carrying his freshly laundered linen tunic and braies over his arm. He'd let them dry a little by the fire before packing them in his bag.

God, it felt good to be clean! After nearly two days of hard riding, with only brief stops to water the horses, he hadn't been able to wait to find the nearest loch and wash the filth away. So much blood had caked on his head from the wound at his temple it had started to itch like the devil under his helm.

But they'd managed to evade their pursuers, and with any luck, by this time tomorrow his mission would be complete.

It was almost over. He'd done what he set out to do and rescued Bella. There was nothing left unfinished. He would claim his reward and end his service to Bruce with a clear conscience.

He should be thrilled. He should be anxious to get back as soon as possible. But he'd insisted they stop and not push forward to the coast.

It was for Bella, he told himself. He wasn't trying to delay.

He was still a short distance from the stables when the

wooden door flung open and Seton came storming out, a murderous look on his face.

"Where are you going?" Lachlan shouted from across the grassy field.

The young knight didn't stop. "To keep watch on the bloody hill." He headed off in the opposite direction without another word.

Boyd was sitting by the fire, sharpening his sword, when Lachlan entered. Reputed to be the strongest man in Scotland, Boyd was used not just for his hand-to-hand combat skills, but also to intimidate.

The big warrior's innocent expression didn't fool him. Tension thick enough to cut with that blade he was holding hung in the air.

"What the hell is the matter with Dragon?"

As if he needed to ask. Boyd and Seton had been an ill pairing from the first day the men chosen for the Highland Guard had gathered on the Isle of Skye for MacLeod's "training." Torture, was more like it. It had been the most grueling, brutal training regimen Lachlan had ever been through, including a weeklong trial through the pits of hell aptly dubbed Perdition.

After nearly three years, the English knight and fierce Scottish patriot had learned to work together, but tension had been building between them since they'd headed west out of Peebles, rather than continue north, in an effort to lose their pursuers.

Their journey through Lanarkshire and Ayrshire brought them deep into the heart of Wallace country. It was the place where the first seeds of rebellion had been born, where Boyd had fought alongside Wallace, and also, unfortunately, the place where Boyd had lost his father to English butchery. Boyd hated the English, and although Seton's family held lands in Scotland, they hailed from the North of England.

Boyd shrugged. "What's usually the matter with him? I offended his precious knightly sensibilities."

Seton had never fully embraced the revolutionary pirate style of warfare that Bruce had adopted: abandoning the knightly code to defeat the much larger and better-equipped English army. Tactics that had been used by the Highlanders and West Highland descendants of Somerled for generations. This new style of warfare was the very reason the Highland Guard was formed, and what made it unique: a small team of the best warriors in each discipline of warfare—irrespective of clan affiliation—who could get in and out quickly, utilizing surprise attacks calculated to impose maximum damage and fear.

Lachlan shot him a dark glare. "Meaning you provoked him."

Boyd's jaw locked. "He's lucky I didn't kill him for what he said last night."

The two warriors had nearly come to blows when they'd stopped for a quick rest to water the horses by Douglas Castle. Bella had innocently asked what had happened to the burned-out castle, the seat of Sir James Douglas, one of Bruce's closest household knights.

Seton had replied that it was the place where Bruce's men had forgotten their honor—a slight aimed directly at Boyd, who'd fought alongside Sir James Douglas the year before when they'd retaken the castle by capturing the English garrison stationed there, tossing them in the cellar before lighting it on fire. An incident that had spread fear through the hearts of the English soldiers stationed in garrisons all across the Southwest and Marches, irreverently known as "Douglas's Larder."

Honor had no place in war, but Seton held firm to some of the code of the past.

"Well, I need you both to help me sail the ship to get us out of here, so you'll have to wait to kill him until we get back. But if I were you, I'd make sure he doesn't have a dirk on him, or you might be the one trying to talk your way out of hell."

Boyd laughed. "Your mood has improved. Must be the dip in the loch?" He sniffed in the air. "Myrtle today, is it?"

Lachlan scowled and tossed the drying cloth that was around his neck at him, telling Boyd exactly what he could do with it. He used what soap was available, damn it.

Boyd laughed and continued sharpening his blade before the fire pit in the center of the old longhouse that now served as the stables and shelter for the farm animals when it got too cold. The family that was sheltering them for the night—the parents of a man who'd died fighting alongside Boyd and Wallace—resided in the newer stone cottage that stood at the base of Loudoun Hill just across the yard.

Though they weren't completely out of danger, and wouldn't be until they were north of the Tay, this part of southwest Scotland was much friendlier to Bruce than the Marches. Moreover, from the top of Loudoun Hill, the site of Bruce's near-miraculous defeat of the English last year on his return to Scotland, they would be able to see anyone approaching for miles.

It was safe enough to rest for a few hours, but they would leave for the coast well before dawn.

Bella hadn't been happy about it, but he'd insisted she sleep in the cottage. She needed a bed, damn it, even if only for a few hours. He could have forced her to ride with him again, but he didn't trust himself to hold her against him for hours. He might not want to let her go.

He wasn't avoiding her. Nay, he was just going to make damn sure they weren't surprised again. He'd been caught with his pants down—literally. He wasn't fool enough to say he regretted it—it had felt too incredible for that—but it had been a mistake. For more reasons than one.

If he'd hoped having her once would free him from this irrational infatuation, he'd miscalculated badly. It hadn't dulled his desire for her one whit. If anything, the too brief, too hurried, too frantic incident had only whetted his appetite for more. But he knew it was too dangerous. The danger wasn't from his enemies but from himself. If he touched her again it would only reinforce the irrational feeling that she was his.

Whatever this strange connection was between them, it didn't mean anything. He sure as hell wasn't fool enough to think it could be permanent.

Lachlan hung his damp clothes over a wooden post and sat opposite Boyd on a stool that he assumed was used for milking. He placed his weapons beside him and removed a steel padlock from his bag. MacKay had made it for him, and he'd yet to figure out the way to unlock it.

Boyd looked at him slyly over the flames of the fire. "You never did say what happened back in Peebles."

Lachlan quirked a brow lazily, poking the blunted iron nail in the hole. "I didn't think I needed to explain. I was taken by surprise."

"Hmm," Boyd said, studying him with a considered expression on his face. "I can't remember the last time you were taken by surprise."

Boyd was fishing, damn him. The arse had bloody well guessed what had happened, but Lachlan gave no indication he knew what Boyd was talking about. "It's been known to happen once or twice," Lachlan said dryly. "I can't be everywhere at once."

Suddenly, Boyd sat back in shock, staring at him as if he'd just glimpsed the Holy Grail. "My God, you like her!" He shook his head with disbelief. "I never thought I'd see the day, but you really like her."

Lachlan shot him a warning glare. "Of course I like her. How could I not? After what she's been through? She's a damned hero, didn't you know?"

That was part of the problem. She was a hero and he was a notorious, bastard mercenary who had more men hunt-

ing him than he could count. Her safety depended on ano-
nymity; with him she would always be in danger.

"So does this mean you've reconsidered?"

Lachlan's eyes narrowed. "What do you mean?"

Boyd shrugged. "With you and Lady Isabella . . . I
thought you might be thinking of sticking around a little
longer."

Lachlan stilled. For a moment he wondered . . .

Nay, it was impossible. Anger rose inside him. Damn
Boyd for trying to confuse him! He didn't need this shite.

"Just because I want to fuck her doesn't mean I'm going
to forget what I've worked for for three years. When the
king holds his council, I'll have my reward. Why the hell
would I stay?"

Ten years ago he'd had everything ripped away from
him. Now he had his chance to get some of it back. He'd
have a home, a place to call his own, and be truly indepen-
dent for the first time in his life. Answering to no one. Being
responsible for no one. With no ties and debts left to pay.
That was the only freedom for which he'd fought.

"You're a real arse, Viper. The lady deserves better." On
that they could agree. "But you know what I think? I think
she's gotten to you. Though hell if I know what she could
possibly see in you."

She didn't see anything in him. There was nothing to see.
"God's blood, Raider, when did you start sounding like my
cousin?"

If any more of the Highland Guard fell "in love"—
whatever the hell that meant—Lachlan wouldn't need to
leave; he'd swipe a dirk across his own throat just to not
have to listen any longer to the blathering virtues of having
a wife. Someone to take care of.

Someone to take care of him.

Someone who cared about whether he lived or died.

He felt a strange tightening in his chest, then pushed it
harshly away. Who in the hell would want that?

Suddenly, he turned at the sound of the door opening. Bella marched through, a determined glint in her eye.

"I hope I'm not disturbing anything?"

He and Boyd exchanged guilty glances, both of them wondering how long she'd been there. From her too-blank expression, he suspected longer than he wanted.

"Nay, nothing, my lady," Boyd said. "Is there something you needed?"

She lifted her chin. If it quivered a little, Lachlan told himself it was the flickering firelight. But it didn't stop the suffocating press of conscience against his chest or the ridiculous urge to pull her in his arms and tell her he didn't mean what he'd just said.

He *did* mean it, damn it. Maybe he wished he hadn't said it so crudely, but it was the truth. He wanted her, but a woman wasn't going to distract him. Not this time.

"I have some salve." She came over to Lachlan. "To tend your wounds."

He glanced up at her, surprised and discomfited by her thoughtfulness. He wasn't used to having anyone worry about him. It would be easy to . . .

Damn it, she was making him soft. He didn't need anyone. He waved her off. "I'm fine."

She looked down at him, her mouth pulled in a tight line of frustration, exasperation, and maybe even a little hurt. "Nails to the cross, Lachlan! Would it kill you to let someone take care of you for once?"

He arched a brow. Nails to the cross? She'd been around him long enough to pick up something better than that. Before he could reply that it might, she set down the armful of items she'd brought with her and turned to him with her hands on her hips. Shapely hips that were revealed all too well in those torturous breeches.

"I'm doing this even if I have to get Robbie to hold you down." She eyed the hulking warrior. "He certainly looks strong enough to do the job."

"Plenty strong, my lady," Boyd chimed in with a wink.

*Bastard.* Lachlan didn't need to look at him to know he was enjoying this. There were few men who would dare make that claim, but as Boyd was one of them, Lachlan decided not to put it to the test.

He put down the lock he had in his hand and smiled mockingly. "As you please, my lady."

She mumbled something under her breath that sounded remarkably like "why I bother."

Tilting his head toward the light, she inspected the gash on his temple. Her touch was soft and gentle. It felt good. A little too good. He jerked away.

She gave him an impatient scowl and pulled him right back. "You bathed," she said.

Lachlan heard a snicker coming from the opposite side of the fire. He shot Boyd a sidelong glare, but his dark head was down, pretending to be focused on his task. "I don't like being dirty."

He blamed the defensiveness in his tone on Boyd.

"I remember," she said softly, so Boyd couldn't hear. "It's nice. It was one of the first things I noticed about you. You smelled too clean for a brigand."

She'd bathed, too. He was trying not to notice how good she smelled, but she was standing too bloody close to him. His body heated with awareness. If Boyd weren't sitting there, he knew he'd be tempted to pull her onto his lap and take another stab at what they'd barely begun two nights ago.

"It's good," she added, running her fingers through his hair by his temple. "You managed to wash away most of the dirt and blood from the wound."

She reached down to pick up a swathe of linen and a clay pot.

He smothered a groan. Those damned lad's clothes were going to kill him. When she'd bent over in front of him, the gap in the linen beneath the tie at the neck opened, giving him an eyeful of one generously curved, softly rounded breast.

He was a man; he couldn't help himself. His eyes fastened on the place in the linen where her nipples jutted against the thin fabric. *Jesus.* His mouth watered, seeing the outline of delectable, hard, puckering flesh.

*Kiss her all over.* A promise he'd made to himself that he'd broken when Comyn's men had discovered them. But he was remembering it now. He wanted to strip her naked. Fill his hands with all that creamy flesh, bring it to his mouth, and suck each delicate pink nipple until it was berry red and throbbing tautly against his tongue.

He shifted, feeling a not-so-slow thickening in his braies. She was bent over him, her body achingly close, torturing him with her gentle touch. Her fingers smoothed the ointment over his wound, drawing small, caressing circles that only increased his ache.

Finally, when he didn't think he could bear her closeness, her touch, the warm fresh scent of her another minute, she wrapped a clean cloth around his head and stepped back.

He nearly sighed with relief.

Her flushed cheeks told him he was not the only one affected. "Are you hurt anywhere else?"

"Nay—"

"He has a cut on his arm and some nasty-looking bruises on his stomach," Boyd volunteered.

Lachlan shot him a death glare. He was going to kill Boyd for this. The bloody bastard knew exactly what kind of pain Lachlan was in right now.

Bella pursed her mouth. He couldn't tell whether it was in anger or reluctance. "Let me see."

He lifted his shirt to reveal the numerous blue, black, and red mottled bruises that had turned to one big, angry mass covering his entire right side.

She gasped, and then gave him a fierce scowl. "Why

didn't you say something? It looks as if you've broken some ribs. I could have wrapped them for you."

He shrugged, trying not to wince. They were broken, all right. "There wasn't time."

She reached out, gently skimming her fingers over the tender flesh. He flinched when her hand dipped low on his stomach.

Her voice softened. "I'm sorry, did that hurt?"

Aye, but not in the way she meant. His cock was pressing against the ties of his braies, doing its damnedest to inch closer and closer to her hand. "A little," he said gruffly.

She gave him a puzzled look. "I didn't think I touched you that hard." *Hard.* He groaned. *Don't say hard.* The throbbing increased. "I'll try to be more careful." She paused, hesitating. "If you take off your shirt, I can see to the cut on your arm and bind your ribs."

Lachlan swore he could hear Boyd smirking. "Are you going to sharpen that blade all night?" he bit out angrily. "Aren't you supposed to be finding us a boat?"

Boyd didn't bother hiding his amusement. He got to his feet slowly, sliding his sword back in the baldric at his back. "Aye, I'm going. It might take me a while," he pointed out unnecessarily.

Lachlan was already painfully aware that he'd made a mistake. Boyd's amusement was a hell of a lot safer than being alone with her. Before he could think of a way to call him back, the other man was gone.

Steeling himself for what was to come, Lachlan pulled his tunic over his head. The quicker this was over, the better.

She didn't make a sound but went perfectly still. Jaw clenched, he kept his eyes straight ahead. Horror. Disgust. Pity. He didn't want to see any of them. If she thought this was bad, she should see his back. But as it was, she stood in front of him and could see only the smattering of battle scars that crossed his chest and arms.

Growing impatient and wanting this torture to be over, he ventured a glance in her direction. It was a mistake. It wasn't the scars, the cuts, or the bruises that had made her hesitate.

She was . . .

Hell, she was staring at his chest as if she were starving, and he was a platter of marzipan.

He swelled harder. He couldn't take this. "Is something wrong?" he snapped.

She blushed and quickly averted her gaze. Picking up the salve, she began to tend the cut on his arm. It was a deep sword slice across his forearm from the Battle at Brander a couple of months ago, which had reopened at the hands, fists, and feet of Comyn's men.

Having her hands on him was no easier the second time around. His nerve endings snapped and fired with every touch. He felt as if he were jumping out of his damned skin. Especially when her finger started a slow trace of the mark on his arm.

A few days ago he would have taken care to hide it. The lion rampant, the symbol of Scotland's crown, set in a shield and encircled with the torquelike band of a spiderweb. It was the mark borne by all members of the Highland Guard. As many of the Guard had done, he'd personalized his, with two swords crossed behind the shield and a viper coiled in the web. She might not know it was the mark of the Guard, but the symbolism was clear.

"Why didn't you tell me?" she asked.

He met her accusing stare. "I took an oath. Besides, it was—*is*—too dangerous."

"You pretended to be nothing more than a hired sword, and instead I find out you are part of the most revered fighting force in Scotland? A member of the king's closest retinue. I thought you had no loyalty. I thought you'd betrayed me. And now I find out this? If you'd told me—"

"It wouldn't have changed anything."

"It would have for me. I might not have spent two years hating you for something you did not do." Suddenly, her eyes widened with realization. "Robert and Sir Alex? William and Magnus? The two men at the convent?"

"Stop!" he said, grabbing her wrist to pull her hand away from his arm. Fear made his heart pound. She knew too much. "Don't ask, don't even think about any of it. Don't you understand how dangerous knowledge is? Do you know what those men would have done to you if they thought you could tell them anything?" She paled. "Forget you heard anything they said."

He should have known better than to try to scare her. "Haven't I earned the right to know the truth?"

He clenched his jaw. "Not if it puts you in danger. Damn it, Bella, don't you understand? My former brother-in-law found out that I was a part of the guard, and now I have a price on my head to rival Bruce's. They will do anything to find out the names of the other men. Anything. It isn't just the other men at risk—their families will be in danger."

She lifted her chin, not backing down one inch. "I wouldn't say anything."

He nearly laughed. "Spoken like someone who has never been tortured."

"And you have?"

"Aye," he said bluntly. He hadn't broken, because at the time he hadn't cared about anything. He didn't have a weak spot. Then. "Care to see a sampling?"

He turned his back.

This time she gasped. Her eyes widened. He saw the horror that he feared, but also something else. Something unexpected. Something like admiration.

"My God, Lachlan." Her fingers ran over the jagged lines where the steel hooks had pierced and ripped his flesh, nearly to the bone. "To survive this . . ." Their eyes met. "What happened?"

Once he'd told her to ask him anything. He had no se-crets. He didn't care. His past was behind him.

But something had changed. Her care, her concern, her questions had opened old wounds.

And he feared it would reveal too much to a woman who had already gotten too close.

Bella knew he didn't want to tell her. He was pulling away from her, just as he'd been doing for the past two days. The closer they drew to safety, the farther away he seemed.

If she thought the way he'd avoided her and acted as if nothing had happened between them had hurt, it was noth-ing compared to the pain she'd experienced on hearing his crude disavowal to Robbie Boyd. Not until that moment did she realize just how much she'd come to care for him.

*"Just because I want to fuck her . . ."*

If he'd pointed an arrow at her heart it couldn't have been aimed more perfectly. Her chest squeezed and burned. To be an object of lust and nothing more. Dear God, would a man ever want her for something more?

She'd thought Lachlan was different. She'd thought . . .

What, that because it had felt special to her, it was to him? Had prison left her so desperate for a connection that she'd felt one where there wasn't?

No. She couldn't believe that was all it had been to him. He didn't mean it. He'd probably just been trying to stop Boyd's probing. Probably. But she couldn't be sure.

Perhaps his past would give her a clue. She wanted to know the truth, not what people said about him. She wanted to know everything about *him*.

"Tell me," she asked again. Knowing he hated being chal-lenged, she added, "I thought you had nothing to hide?"

He knew what she was doing but answered her with a shrug. "There isn't much to tell. My wife was very young, very beautiful, and very spoiled. I was infatuated with her."

Though he said it without emotion, Bella's heart pinched. It seemed so unlike him. "Within a few months, Juliana's ardor waned, and she regretted her impulsivity in marrying a bastard without much land to his name—even if he was a chieftain to a clan."

Bella paled. "You were chieftain?"

He smiled tightly. "Aye, for a while I did 'my duty,' as you call it. I was completely unaware of my wife's discontent, too blinded by lust to see what was happening right before my face. She devised a way to get rid of me—quite an ingenious little plan, actually—telling her brother that I intended to betray him. Unfortunately, Lorn believed her.

"At the time, King Edward was acting overlord of Scotland, and he was furious at Lorn and the rest of the MacDougalls for a recent spate of attacks on English soldiers. My brother-in-law decided this was a good opportunity to get back in the king's good graces. He needed someone to blame, and I was convenient. He sent me and my men on what was supposed to be a raid, but instead it was a slaughter—our slaughter. I alone survived. Forty-four men who'd followed me into battle never went home to their families."

She put her hand on his arm. God, no wonder he'd turned from his clan! He blamed himself for the deaths of all those men. "Oh, Lachlan, I'm—"

He ripped it away as if her comfort scalded him. "I'm not done. You wanted to know; now you'll hear all of it."

The mask of detachment had slipped. The fury of emotion revealed itself in the angry sneer of his mouth. "I should have died along with them." He pointed to a two-inch-wide circular scar on his shoulder. "Unconscious, with a spear pinned through my shoulder, the English left me for dead. Which I would have been in a few hours, had I not been found by my kinsmen—and enemies—the MacDonalds. I 'recovered' in a MacDonald prison for a few months, before my cousin, Angus Og, for reasons of his own, decided to help me escape. He was the one who asked me to join the Bruce," he said as an aside. "He tried to warn me about my wife, but I didn't want to listen. I didn't realize the truth until I returned to Dunstaffnage Castle, to find Juliana betrothed to another man—a much more rich and powerful man."

The lack of bitterness and emotion in his voice made her heart go out to him all the more. She wanted to touch him but knew that he wouldn't accept her comfort. Not now. Perhaps not ever.

"Juliana pretended to be glad to see me, right up to the point that her brother threw me in his pit prison and gave me these," he pointed to his back, "while trying to get me to confess my alleged betrayal." He laughed. "I think even he started to have doubts about my guilt after a while."

Horror washed over her at the calm manner with which he spoke of the cruelties inflicted on him. It was almost as if he were talking about someone else. She knew she was getting the barest sketch of what had happened and that he was leaving out things she didn't even want to imagine.

It certainly explained his reaction in the tunnel and to going into the pit prison at Peebles. She, better than anyone, understood that particular source of fear.

Their eyes met, and it was as if he knew what she was thinking. "Ah, yes, you discovered my little secret, didn't you? I've no fondness for dark holes."

He said it as if it should lessen her impression of him. But how could she not but admire him after all he'd been through? He'd been betrayed by those closest to him, had been imprisoned, and withstood suffering she couldn't imagine. He'd scraped and fought back after everything had been taken from him.

He'd survived.

Just as she had. "And I have no fondness for small rooms and bars." Their eyes held for a moment in shared understanding. She glanced down at the lock by his foot and understood something else. "The manacles. The lock in the tunnel. Is that why you are so good at getting past them?"

He lifted a brow in a mocking salute, obviously surprised that she'd made the connection. Reaching down behind his ankle, he slipped something from the leather sole of his boot and held it up for her inspection. It looked like a nail, but without the sharp tip. "I keep a spare in my boot, in case I am without my sporran. Unfortunately, working locks is a skill I learned only later. I escaped Dunstaffnage in a much less civilized way."

She tilted her head in question.

"There were so many rats they'd made wide holes under the walls. I dug my way out by following their path."

She shivered. Rats. She abhorred the vile creatures. One was bad enough, but hundreds? Good God, what must that have been like?

He stopped for a moment, but she knew he wasn't done. When she put her hand on his arm again, this time he did not shake her off. "What happened to your wife?"

"I should have just left, but I waited for her on a beach I knew she liked to walk on by the castle." Bleakness had crept into his matter-of-fact tone. "I confronted her. God knows what I was expecting. An excuse? An explanation? A denial? I was so angry, I needed *something*. She was shocked to see me, of course. I suspect she thought her brother had already had me killed. She feigned ignorance of my accusations, and God help me, I wanted to believe her. But as soon as my back was turned, she came at me with a dirk." Her gaze went to the jagged scar on his cheek. He smiled. "Aye, my reminder never to turn my back on a beautiful woman."

He said it in jest, but she suspected there was far more truth in it than he wanted to acknowledge. His wife's betrayal had molded him as much as his mother's rejection. Trust. Love. He knew neither. Anger and bitterness would have been easier to contend with. Cold acceptance was so much worse. How could he believe in something he didn't know existed?

"We struggled for the knife. I tripped and fell on her. When I stood up, the knife was lodged in her stomach. So you see, the rumors are true, at least in that respect."

"But it wasn't your fault! Good God, Lachlan, she was trying to kill you."

"She was a woman," he said tightly.

Bella stared at him in disbelief. "And so there can be no excuse?" She shook her head. "You claim to have no rules, no code but your own, but you are more conventional than you want to admit, Lachlan."

He gave her a sharp look, clearly not liking her observation. "When I returned home to my family at Castle Tioram, it was to find that I had been found guilty of treason, and my holdings, with what wealth I did have, declared forfeit."

"But surely your family—"

The muscle below his jaw jumped. "My family believed as everyone else."

"But didn't you explain?"

"Why? I realized my presence made it difficult for them, so I decided to go to Ireland and make what fortune I could as a gallowglass."

"So you expected blind loyalty from your family but won't give it yourself?"

White lines appeared around his mouth. "Leave it, Bella. Don't think you understand me; you don't."

But she couldn't leave it. For the first time so many things were clear to her. Why his reaction to her bothered him so much, and why he'd resisted it so strongly. He thought his feelings for his wife were to blame for the death of his men. That his desire for her—his lust—had made him fail his duty to his men.

It was clear he thought she posed the same threat. She understood why he didn't trust her. He'd known only unkindness and betrayal from the women who should have loved him. But she wanted him to trust her. "I'm not your wife, Lachlan. I would never betray you."

He laughed, making her feel naive again. "Everyone is capable of betrayal, Bella, everyone. It's only a matter of finding your weakness."

"So it's better to live your life in fear? To cut yourself off from everyone so that no one can ever hurt you?"

He gave her a hard look. "It's not me I'm thinking about."

*His men,* she realized. *He's still punishing himself for the deaths of his men.*

Her eyes widened. A mad thought stole into her brain. No. It wasn't possible. But the thought, once formed, could not be dislodged. It was something he'd said right before he'd shattered inside her. Something she'd barely noticed at the time but had recalled when he'd been talking about his wife.

She took a step closer, forcing him to look up at her. "Lachlan, when you said 'too long,' what did you mean?"

He turned away. His gaze fixed in the firelight. His voice was low and rough. "I haven't been with a woman for a while."

Her heart picked up speed. "How long is a while?"

He turned back to her, his handsome face painfully still. "Since my wife died."

"But that was . . ."

"Ten years ago," he finished flatly.

Bella couldn't believe it. How could a man who exuded virility have existed like a monk?

She must have voiced her question aloud without realizing it. He laughed harshly, giving her a pointed look. "There are other ways to find release." She blushed, realizing he was talking about pleasuring himself. "I was busy fighting most of the time. It wasn't difficult until recently." The heat in her cheeks intensified—he was talking about her. He shrugged. "It isn't all that unusual. There are the Templars, for example. Many warriors believe it adds to their strength."

He tried to fob it off as nothing, but she knew it didn't have anything to do with religion or his warrior's strength. "How long are you going to keep punishing yourself, Lachlan?" she asked quietly.

"I'm not punishing myself." He gave her a suggestive look. "Or don't you remember?"

"I remember," she said huskily. Only too well. Her body burned with the memory.

He held her gaze in the firelight. Night had fallen as they spoke, and the old stone building had grown darker. More intimate. More dangerous.

She was painfully aware of how close they stood, and how easy it would be to reach out and put her hands on his naked chest. A naked chest that had taken her breath away. She'd never seen anything so magnificent. Powerfully built from years of living by the sword, every inch of his lightly tanned flesh had been honed to perfection. Broad-shouldered, arms stacked with layers of bulging muscle, not an ounce of extra flesh marred the hard planes of his chest and tightly banded stomach. All she could think about was putting her hands on him and feeling all that strength under her touch.

Realizing she was staring, she lifted her gaze back up to his. His eyes glowed dangerously. "It's not a good idea, Bella."

The soft warning in his voice didn't give her pause. She thought she'd be content with passion, but she was wrong. She wanted more. Much more. He cared for her, and she intended to prove it. "Why?"

"I've nothing more to offer you."

But he did. If only he would see it. She put her hands on him, feeling a blast of heat shoot through her. Lightning. It was as if she were harnessing lightning. Her nerve endings snapped at the contact, the hard, warm flesh singeing her palms. She could feel the muscles straining under her fingertips. Fighting to be set free.

God, how she wanted him!

The muscle at his neck stood out like a taut rope. His fists clenched at his side. "It won't change anything," he warned.

But it already had for her.

She'd take the chance. Bella had never shirked from a fight, and she wouldn't start now. Without another thought, she leaned down and pressed her lips to his.

# Seventeen

He pulled her down on his lap and kissed her. Kissed her in a way that seemed to reach down to her toes, claiming every inch in between. It was both hot and possessive, less furious and frantic than before but every bit as passionate.

Bella gave herself over to his seduction. God, did he know how to kiss! Each skilled stroke of his tongue, each smooth caress of his lips, seemed calculated to draw her in deeper, eliciting every ounce of pleasure from her that he could and leaving her weak and boneless as a poppet of rags.

*Her* pleasure. A bubble of warmth rose and burst inside her. He cared about her pleasure. It wasn't just lust—not in the way she knew it. Tender was the last word she would use to describe Lachlan MacRuairi. Yet when he held her in his arms and kissed her, tenderness is what she felt.

She wrapped her hands around his neck, sinking into him, crushing her breasts against his magnificent chest. A chest that was every inch as hard and unyielding as it looked, but so much hotter. She could feel everything, the thin linen of her shirt a paltry barrier. But what would it be like to feel his skin on hers? To feel her nipples rake that hot, steely flesh?

She let her hands slide over his broad, muscular shoulders and down the rippling bulges of his arms. Her fingers clenched, unconsciously testing his rock-hard strength. His muscles flared, flexing even harder.

She shivered, a deep feminine thrill of appreciation shuddering through her. To be so beset by a few muscles— no matter how impressive—was really quite lowering. But there was something deeply arousing about his physical strength. About a man who was built not only to assail but to defend and protect.

She loved the way it felt to have those big arms wrapped around her, all those hard slabs of muscle cradling her softness.

One big hand was splayed over her bottom possessively. He pressed her closer, nestling her against him and letting her feel just how much he wanted her.

If the size of him was any indication, it was quite a lot.

Quite a lot indeed.

She squirmed. Moaned. A rush of heat pooled between her legs at the visceral reminder of just how good it would feel.

He groaned, and the sound reverberated down to her toes. His hand plunged through her hair to cup her head and bend her back. She opened her mouth wider. Drinking him in. Meeting the slow, insistent strokes of his tongue with her own.

They were drowning in heat, in desire, and in each other. She never wanted it to end.

Lachlan knew this wasn't a good idea, but he couldn't seem to stop kissing her. She just tasted so good.

*Lust,* he reminded himself. *It's only lust.* This tightness in his chest, this wave of warmth that came over him each time he looked into her eyes, the overwhelming need to give her pleasure, didn't mean a damned thing.

He'd always seen to a woman's pleasure. He'd realized as a lad that if he made a woman happy, she made him happy.

Very happy. But never had it seemed so *vital,* and never had a woman's pleasure increased his own.

It didn't mean anything, he told himself again. To prove it, he kissed her harder. Let his tongue delve into the delicious recesses of her mouth. Let his hands roam over every inch of her incredible body.

She was so sweet. Slim and delicate around her waist and back but generously curved in her chest and hips.

He slowed, weighing one of her breasts in his hand and savoring the heady sensation of holding all that soft, lush flesh. Squeezing gently, he caressed the taut nipple with his thumb as his tongue drew slow, lazy circles in her mouth.

*Fast and furious,* he reminded himself. But damn it, he didn't want it to end. He could go on kissing her forever. Her mouth was so soft and sweet, her responses so eager. And those soft little sounds of hers seemed to wrap right around his heart and make him want to hold her in his arms forever.

*Lust, damn it.*

But she was dragging him in. Taking him to a place he didn't want to go. Tempting him to gentleness with each tender, heartfelt stroke of her tongue, trying to wrest something from him that he didn't want to give.

And succeeding, damn it. His chest tightened. Squeezed. Filled with something warm and soft.

Whatever was happening to him, he didn't like it. He couldn't let it happen again. Hell, who was he kidding? Nothing had ever felt like this before. It wasn't just desire. It was something deeper. Something more intense. Something that wasn't for him.

*She* wasn't for him, damn it. She came with too many conditions—too many expectations.

He needed to get this back on the right track. He tore his mouth away.

She blinked, trying to see through the passion-filled haze that clouded her big, blue eyes. Her long, pale hair shim-

mered in the firelight, tumbling around her face in wildly
sensual disarray.

He clenched his jaw, steeling himself against the nearly
irresistible pull of her swollen, gently parted red lips and
husky little sharp intakes of breath.

"Take off your clothes."

She blinked again, fluttering her ridiculously long lashes.
"What?"

His eyes held hers. "I want you naked when I fuck you."

A small frown gathered between her brows. He steeled
himself against the stab in his chest. If she wanted this, they
were going to do it on his terms. In a way that could leave
no doubt of what it meant.

She hesitated. For a moment he thought she'd refuse, but
then understanding cleared away the confusion. She held
his gaze, eyes narrowed, silently challenging him with a
shrewd look that saw far too much. "That's how it's going
to be, is it?"

His jaw locked. "Aye."

She pursed her lips together and slowly began to take off
her clothes. He could tell by the stiffness of her movements
that she was furious. He didn't blame her. But she'd wanted
this, damn it.

Plaid, doublet, shirt, breeches, hose, shoes. One by one
they landed in a pile by his feet. His heart pounded faster
with every piece.

Finally, she stood before him proud, defiant, and completely, utterly, bewitchingly naked. She arched a taunting
brow. "I hope this meets with your approval?"

His mouth went dry. He held himself so still it felt as if
he'd turned to stone. God, did it. She was so beautiful.
Thinner and more delicate, but every bit as gorgeous as he
remembered. Big, round breasts, tiny waist, softly curved
hips, and long, lean limbs, with the most flawless ivory skin
he'd ever beheld, marred only by the faint bruises that still
lingered on her chest and neck.

The flash of anger at the sight of those bruises was swift and hard—he hadn't forgotten what the jailor had done to her—but it also filled him with a fierce wave of protectiveness. He wanted to pull her into his arms. Cradle her gently against his chest and hold her. Cherish and keep her safe forever.

He'd wanted to show her this was all about lust, but instead the odd mix of strength and vulnerability roused emotions in him that he'd never felt before.

His mouth tightened. He sounded like his cousin, MacSorley. Or MacLeod. Or Campbell. She was confusing him. Turning him into a lovesick fool. Filling him with crazy thoughts of things that were impossible.

Weren't they?

His eyes went back to hers.

"Your turn," she said. "If you get to look, so do I."

He could hear the challenge in her voice: How far was he going to push this?

"You do it," he said. He'd wanted to meet her challenge, but the huskiness in his voice belied the attempt. The thought of her hands on him . . .

Christ, he was in over his head.

She moved in front of him, holding her head up like a damned queen. A damned *naked* queen. He sucked in his breath. Her breasts were inches from his face. Her skin looked so soft and creamy, her nipples delicate pink berries just waiting to be plucked. He had to grip the wooden stool not to reach out and touch them.

He hissed when her hand touched his stomach. The muscles jumped. Everything jumped. She took her time with the ties. Exacting her revenge as she tortured him with light, achingly close brushes of her hand and fingers.

Her eyes widened when at last he was free. He felt himself growing even harder under her not-so-innocent stare.

Her tongue darted out to wet her lower lip. For a moment he thought she was going to put her mouth on him.

He gritted his teeth against the reflexive surge. Sweat gathered at his brow. The restraint was killing him. He wouldn't show her what she did to him. Wouldn't give her that kind of power over him. But he was fighting a war with himself that he couldn't win, and they both knew it.

She proved it with what she did next, showing him exactly who was in charge. Taking his challenge and answering it with one of her own. She rested her hands on his shoulders. Shock sizzled through him. His heart hammered in his chest. "Shall I ride you, my lord?"

His heart slammed to a stop, every muscle tensed with anticipation. Then, without waiting for him to answer, she straddled him and slowly lowered herself on him.

*Christ.* He sucked in his breath, holding her gaze as inch by agonizing inch he penetrated deep into her warm and welcoming body. He could see the pleasure infuse her features, see how much she liked it, and hear the soft gasps of her breath as he filled her.

He put his hands on her hips, gently guiding her deeper. *Oh God, yes.*

He forgot all about what he was trying to prove. She moaned, arching her back as he sank in as deep as he could go. He kissed her throat. Her breasts. Circling her nipples with his tongue before sucking them deep into his mouth.

It was hot. So incredibly hot.

She began to move. Riding him as she'd taunted. Lifting over him with slow, erotic little circles of her hips. Looking deep into his eyes the entire time.

It felt as if she were holding him by a string and cinching him closer and closer until the connection between them was so strong it seemed as if they were one.

He groaned, the sensations washing over him in a hot, drenching heat. The way she moved, the long, languid rhythm of her hips moving up and down, and the sultry heat in the stable combined in the most seductive, erotic dance of his life.

She started to go faster. Taking him in and out of her body at a wicked pace as her pleasure intensified, riding him with wild abandon. It was the most beautiful thing he'd ever seen. *She* was the most beautiful thing he'd ever seen.

She held her hands on his shoulders, using them for leverage as she thrust him deep into her body. Her face was only a few inches from his. Her breasts bounced against his chest. She held his gaze as she clenched around him, drawing him in with slow little pulls.

He'd wanted to show her that this was only lust; instead it had become the most incredible, intimate moment of his life.

He felt it again. That hard pull. That dragging under. That sensation of drowning in a whirlpool of something he didn't understand.

He was falling. Lost in sensation and the promise in her eyes. He couldn't seem to get close enough.

He slid his arm around her waist and kissed her fiercely, succumbing for a moment before suddenly jerking away.

Furious at himself, at her for doing this to him, he held her hips still. "Enough," he growled harshly. This position was too intimate.

The sudden curtailment of pleasure brought a confused look to her eyes. "What's wrong?"

"I want you on your knees so I can take you from behind."

He hated himself even as he said it. He was skating too close to what had happened with her husband and knew it. The base demand. Treating her more like a whore than a woman to be cherished.

Her eyes widened, and the look on her face cut him to the quick.

He'd gone too far. He knew he'd gone to far.

She would never forgive him for this. Maybe it was what he wanted. It would be better this way. Acid ate in his chest, settling low in his belly. It felt so wrong, but he couldn't seem to stop himself.

*Tell me no. Slap me like I deserve.*

"Well?" he threw down the gauntlet.

Part of him wanted her to put a stop to this. The other part feared she would.

"Am I supposed to run away now? Is this supposed to scare me off? You have no idea." She shook her head. "Why are you doing this, Lachlan? Why are you acting so mean?"

"I *am* mean. Haven't you figured that out yet?"

She held his gaze. She looked at him with compassion and something else. Something that made his heart flip over in his chest. "Aye, I've figured it out."

The understanding in her voice only made him angrier. "Do you want to fuck or not?" he snapped.

The vulgarity had no effect on her. She lifted her chin. "Is that what you want?"

He heard the challenge in her voice and knew what she was asking: Is that *all* you want? She wanted more from him. He gritted his teeth. "Aye."

Neither one of them believed it.

She shook her head as if he were a child who'd disappointed her. And hell if he didn't feel like it.

She lifted herself off him and stood. She was going to leave. He held his breath, a heartbeat away from stopping her. From calling her back. From drawing her against him and showing her all the gentleness and tenderness that she deserved. That he wanted to give her, damn it, but didn't know how.

He should have known better. Bella MacDuff was a fighter.

Slowly, she lowered herself to the ground, spreading out the plaid near the fire. Then, holding his gaze the entire time, she positioned herself on her hands and knees. His heart stopped beating. Not from the mouthwatering dis-

play of her sleek backside—although it was spectacular—
but from the trust shining in her eyes. Trust he didn't want,
damn it, and sure as hell didn't deserve.

He couldn't breathe through the tightness in his lungs.
She was so beautiful and defiant. Daring him to treat her
like this. Daring him to deny *her*.

Bella watched him struggle, knowing he was scared.
Knowing that he was battling himself, not her, and fighting
what she offered with everything he had. He lashed back
the way he always did, finding the weakness and going in
for the kill.

Did he honestly think he could get to her like this? She'd
been played by the master of cruelty and domination and
endured far worse than Lachlan could ever manage.

She hated that he used the pain of her past against her.
But even more, she hated that he was taking what they had
and trying to turn it into something base and meaningless.

But it wasn't. He was trying so hard to be harsh and
crude, but the very next minute his tender touch would
soothe the sting of his words. He cared. She was sure of it.
The way he looked into her eyes, the way he touched her,
left her no doubt. What they had was different. She just
needed to make him see it.

"Well," she asked softly. "Is this not what you wanted?"

Bella wanted him to tell her no. She wanted him to see
that he didn't need to do this. She wanted him to pull her
into his arms. To slide her down gently on the plaid and
kiss her until this was all forgotten. To make love to her
with all the passion and emotion she sensed burning inside
him.

To admit there was more to them than this.

But he clenched his jaw, banished his indecision, and
moved behind her. He was on his knees, his braies sliding
down around them, as he gripped her hips and positioned
himself between her legs.

But he didn't enter her.

Her body twitched nervously. She'd assumed this position many times before and had always found it particularly unpleasant—degrading and base.

But it wasn't, she realized. Not with Lachlan. She trusted him. He wouldn't hurt her.

He splayed his hands on her backside, moving them possessively over her buttocks. "You are so beautiful," he said hoarsely.

She felt strangely restless—as though she needed to move. His heavy erection pressed intimately against her, but all he did was touch her. And did he touch her! His hands caressed every inch of her. Sliding over her bottom, along her hips, and up to softly cup her breasts. When one big, battle-worn hand dipped between her legs she gasped.

He tucked her firmly against him, holding her close and cradling her bottom against his groin. The thick, hot column of flesh wedged against her. She could feel the light dusting of hair on his hard, muscular thighs against the back of hers. One hand plied her breast as the other slipped between her legs.

"Tell me if you don't want this," he whispered tightly in her ear.

He was giving her the choice. Her heart leapt. It was what she'd been waiting for. He wanted to bully and dominate, to turn this into something base and meaningless, but he couldn't.

He did care.

A rush of heat and dampness had gathered between her legs. His erection pressed more insistently against her backside. Nudging her. Giving her a heady taste of what was to come. In answer she pressed back against him, arching her back to the right angle to accommodate him.

Heat washed over her. She shouldn't be feeling this way. Eager. Aroused. Wickedly naughty. The thick head teased at her opening.

Aye, she wanted this. More than she'd ever imagined.

He made a harsh sound behind her, pinching her nipple with one hand as the other delved skillfully between her legs. He was opening her wider, using her dampness to ready her for him.

"Tell me," he demanded. "Do you want me inside you?"

She started to pant, writhe, pressing harder and more insistently against the tip of hard flesh poised achingly against her. He was so close, teasing her with his size.

His fingers stroked her harder, faster, deeper, bringing her to the edge . . .

"Yes. Please," she cried helplessly, knowing what she sought was close.

He swore, ramming into her in one hard thrust, filling her completely, and sending her careening into the mindless oblivion of pleasure.

She cried out, her body shuddering around him as he pumped into her at just the right speed, drawing it out. Slow and deep, long and tender.

"That's it, love, come for me. God, you feel so good."

*Love.* Her heart clung to that single word. Happiness bloomed inside her like a flower opening in the first rays of spring. New. Fresh. Beautiful.

He was holding her so close. Cradling her body to his. This was nothing like the animalistic mating she'd experienced before. She felt safe, cherished, protected.

Just when she thought it was over, he sent her over again. He sank into her fully, pulling her hard against him so it seemed as if he were touching the deepest part of her. He held her there, cradled against him, filling her from behind and grinding against her, as his fingers stroked her mercilessly from the front.

It was amazing. Beautiful. Tender in a way she'd never imagined.

She cried out, clenching, spasming, shattering, until he'd wrested every last bit of pleasure from her that he could. Or so she thought.

Lachlan couldn't stand it. The burning in his chest intensified. Hearing her cries of pleasure—knowing that he was the one responsible—and not being able to see her face was killing him.

Before he realized what he was doing, he'd turned her over, laid her down gently on the plaid, and surged into her again. This time, holding her tightly under him.

She gasped, eyes wide.

He stilled. "Did I hurt you?"

She shook her head, a joyful smile curving her mouth. She cupped his cheek in her hand. "Nay. I love how you make me feel."

*Love.* The look in her eyes . . .

Something shifted in his chest. Something he'd thought impossible.

Holding her gaze, he started to move. Long, slow, sensual strokes that dragged him deeper with every thrust. His jaw clenched against the raw pleasure surging inside him.

He was hot, heavy. Trying to make it last, but it felt too good.

Her lips parted. Her cheeks flushed. Her eyes fell to half-lidded slits. Her breath started to come in sharp little gasps. Her fingers tightened in his shoulders . . .

And then her hips started to lift, meeting his thrust with one of her own.

It was too much. Sensation surged hard inside him. He couldn't hold on. He pumped harder, grinding into her with each frantic stroke, needing to take her with him.

Her body arched. She started to cry out.

He let go, coming into her with a ferocity he'd never experienced before. Each pulse, each spasm, each sharp burst of pleasure seemed wrenched from the deepest part of him.

The entire time he was looking into her eyes. Being pulled in.

He barely had the strength to roll to the side before his muscles gave out. He collapsed beside her, breathing hard, more spent than he'd ever been in his life. Even being forced to run up the Cuillins during MacLeod's training hadn't taken so much out of him.

He was glad he was too exhausted to think for a while, because when he realized what he'd just done, the moments of sated bliss were all forgotten.

Shame burned in his gut. How could he have done that? How could he have tried to hurt her like that?

He'd played a dangerous game and lost. He'd wanted to prove to her that it didn't mean anything, but it was he who'd been proved wrong. He could no longer deny it: He cared for her. More than he'd cared for anyone in his life.

And still he'd hurt her. What the hell was wrong with him?

"I'm sorry," he said, his voice raw.

She rolled on her side, gazing up at him, with a sad smile that ate at his conscience. "I know."

She didn't know anything. She didn't understand him, damn it. She looked at him like he was someone he wasn't. Like she saw something in him that wasn't there. She expected too much from him. He could never be the man she wanted him to be. Didn't she know he would always hurt her?

A storm of conflicting emotions unfurled inside him. Longing. Resentment. Confusion. Anger. She was twisting him up in knots, making him forget what was important.

His jaw clenched. "This doesn't change anything."

She stared at him for a long moment. He steeled himself against the shadow of hurt in her eyes. "So it was just fucking, is that right, Lachlan?"

She threw the ugly word back at him like a taunt, daring him to agree with her.

His chest pounded. He felt as if the walls were closing in. As if he were walking into a dark tunnel. Why couldn't she stop pushing him? Why couldn't she just leave him alone?

*Freedom, damn it. No ties.*

He looked her right in the eye. "Aye."

She held his gaze for a long time. "You're a liar, Lachlan MacRuairi. You can lie to me, but don't lie to yourself."

Without another word, she picked up her clothes, pulled them on, and left him alone to the dark hammering of his own heart.


Bella waited for him to change his mind. From the time Sir Alex woke her in the early hours of the morning to ride the short distance to the coast, to the anxious minutes she waited in darkness while the men swam in the frigid waters of the sea to steal a galley out from under the noses of the sleeping English soldiers who commanded it, to the long hours being battered by the wind and waves as the three men struggled to man a ship usually sailed by ten times that number, she told herself Lachlan would admit the truth.

He cared for her. It wasn't just lust between them. She knew the difference, and what they'd shared was nothing like what she'd known before.

He pretended to be a mocking brigand who didn't care about anything, but she knew it was just a mask. He cared far more than he let on—about her and the men he fought with. He wouldn't turn his back on them.

Even when they finally arrived at Dunstaffnage Castle late that evening to a hero's welcome from Robert and a small contingent of his men, she convinced herself it wasn't too late. Lachlan wouldn't let her down. He wouldn't deny the promise of what lay between them. He wouldn't just walk away from her. Not after all they'd been through together. Not after what they'd shared. It wasn't lust, but two people making love. The connection was real.

This couldn't be the end.

He was scared, she told herself, confused. Just give him time.

But it turned out time was the one thing she didn't have.

They'd been ushered into a small solar off the Great Hall and given food and drink while Lachlan reported on all that had happened. In addition to herself, Lachlan, Boyd, Seton, and the king, four other men sat around the trestle table. The oldest, Sir Neil Campbell, one of Bruce's closest advisors, was well known to her from the months they'd spent in hiding in the hills of Atholl after Methven. The most forbidding, Tor MacLeod, a West Highland chief from the Isle of Skye, and the tall, devilishly handsome Norseman, Erik MacSorley, she recalled from that time as well. They'd stuck out as unusual, and now she could guess why. They must be part of this secret band of warriors.

The fourth man, Arthur Campbell, Sir Neil's much younger brother, was a stranger to her. Although he seemed to fit the imaginary criteria she'd constructed in her mind for Bruce's secret army: tall, muscular, and formidable-looking—not to mention unusually attractive—she couldn't be sure whether he was part of the group as well. From what she could gather, Sir Arthur had been fighting for the enemy and had been made keeper of Dunstaffnage Castle on his recent marriage to Anna MacDougall, the Lord of Lorn's daughter.

Lachlan did not leave anything out. Despite her protest, he assumed full blame for the disaster that had nearly befallen them in Roxburgh and their ensuing capture in Peebles. Though the king let him continue uninterrupted, Bella, who was seated next to him, could tell Robert wasn't pleased to hear what had transpired. All of the men exchanged uneasy glances when Lachlan spoke of the soldier's intention to question her about him.

"By the rood! What were you thinking?" The king was furious. "I knew it was a bad idea to let you go."

Bella tried to explain again. "I'm afraid I am to blame for what happened, Sire. I refused to return to Scotland until I'd seen my daughter. Lachlan ordered me to stay away from the castle, but I disobeyed him. None of this is his fault."

"He was in charge," Robert said angrily. "It was his mission."

She could see the big Norseman eyeing Lachlan speculatively. "I must say I'm surprised. It isn't like you to be so amenable, cousin."

Bella was surprised to hear they were kinsmen. Although they were of similar build, the two men couldn't have been more different. Blond, blue-eyed, and good-humored, with a charm that was unmistakable, Erik MacSorley was the light to Lachlan's dark.

Lachlan shot him a glare of warning, but the other man simply grinned.

Bella's cheeks warmed, guessing the cause for his amusement.

The king put his hand on hers, perhaps sensing her embarrassment. "We will speak of this later," he said, looking right at Lachlan. He turned back to her. "The important thing is that you are safe. For two years I have prayed for this day. Knowing what you and the others were enduring . . ." He paused, clearing the emotion from his throat. "Having you returned gives me hope that I will be welcoming the rest of my family home soon." His eyes darkened. "Edward will rot in hell for what he has done to you—and to Mary. I owe you a debt that can never be repaid. I would give you a celebration worthy of your sacrifice if I could."

Bella shook her head. "The fewer people who know of my release, the better. At least until my daughter is safely returned to me."

The king looked away uncomfortably. "You will stay here until we decide what is to be done," he said to her with a glance to Sir Arthur.

"I would be honored, my lady," Arthur said with a bow of his head. "My wife will welcome the company."

Bella nodded gratefully, hearing the sincerity in his voice.

The king stood, still holding her hand. It was as if he thought she might disappear if he let her go. She felt the heat of Lachlan's glare and glanced in his direction. The look of predatory intent was so fierce, for a moment she thought he would pounce across the table and rip her from the king's grasp.

But he quickly masked the emotion and looked away. Only the hard tic below his jaw betrayed his flash of anger. He was jealous.

"It's late," the king said. "You must be exhausted. We can speak more of this in the morning."

The rest of the men stood and followed them out of the solar. Bella warmed herself by the fire while Sir Arthur fetched a servant to see her to her room. One by one, the men came over to bid her good night and give her some combination of a welcome home and an expression of gratitude for what she'd done. All, that is, except for Lachlan.

This should have been a joyous occasion. For what was probably the first time since she'd left Balvenie Castle nearly three years ago, she was safe.

But she didn't feel safe, she felt lost. Even though they'd been in constant danger, hunted across the Marches and nearly imprisoned, she'd felt safe since the first time Lachlan had dragged her in the bushes and tucked her under his arm. He'd been her tether, the constant by her side, and without him it felt as if she were flailing in a storm-tossed sea. She'd come to . . .

Rely on him.

She was trying to concentrate on Sir Alex, thanking him for his part in her rescue, when out of the corner of her eye she noticed Lachlan speaking with the king.

"I don't know how to thank you," she said to the handsome young knight.

Sir Alex took her hand and gave her a gallant bow. "It was my honor, my lady. I only wish it could have come sooner."

She nodded. She did as well.

She would have said something else, but her attention was diverted to the opposite side of the room. Lachlan and Robert had finished their brief conversation and Lachlan had started to walk away.

*Leaving.* Without saying a word.

She didn't want to believe it. He couldn't be doing this. God, would she ever see him again?

Her heart lurched. A hard spike of panic rushed through her veins. Silently, she begged him to turn around. *Look at me. Don't leave.*

He kept walking. And somehow she knew if she let him go it would be too late.

"Pardon me," she said hastily to Sir Alex and darted after Lachlan.

She was aware the other men were watching but didn't care. Fear had swallowed her pride. "Wait! Lachlan, wait!"

He was nearly at the corridor when he came to an abrupt stop. Slowly, he turned around, his expression dark and forbidding as he watched her approach. He held himself stiffly—remotely—as if the distance between them were already insurmountable.

Aware of the eyes on them, Bella felt the heat rush to her cheeks. What had she intended to say? "Would you leave without saying goodbye?"

His jaw hardened at the subtle accusation in her voice. "It's over, Bella." Emotion twisted in her chest; he wasn't referring to the mission. "I've said everything that needed to be said."

If he'd been able to meet her gaze, the harshness of his tone might have discouraged her. "Have you?" She let the question hang before adding, "When will you go?"

"Soon."

The cold response cut like a knife. Why was he doing this? *Stay . . . Fight.*

"I don't want you to leave," she blurted.

He stilled, every muscle in his body drawn as tight as a bow. His eyes dipped to hers, two hard slits of piercing green. "What in the hell do you want from me, Bella?" The harshness of his voice took her aback. "An affair? Marriage?"

Her eyes widened. *Marriage.* Was that what she wanted? To be another man's chattel? To put herself at the mercy of another man when she'd just been freed? Could she ever trust a man enough to give him that kind of power over her?

Her heart started to beat very fast. She couldn't think. "I . . . I don't know."

She hadn't realized he'd been holding her arm until he dropped it. Her heart clenched at his stony expression; it felt as if she'd just failed an unspoken test. Had her hesitation hurt him? He'd caught her by surprise. He'd never hinted at a future, let alone one so permanent.

*So conventional.*

"You've been through a lot. It's not surprising that you would get overly attached. I tried to warn you. But it was my mistake. I thought you could handle it." He leaned down, his face cruelly mocking. "But just because you come a few times, it doesn't mean you're in love."

Bella sucked in her breath, feeling as if he'd just slapped her. Nay, not slapped her, something worse. Pitied her. Mocked her. For daring to try to care about him. For daring to think she could actually count on him. She'd taken a chance. She'd told him she wanted him to stay, and he'd thrown it back in her face.

Her cheeks heated with hurt and indignation. To hell with him! Nothing was worth this. She'd had enough cruelty in her life. She deserved more than this. She deserved someone who cared about her.

For years she'd been valued only for her body. She wouldn't—couldn't—let that happen again. If he didn't want her, didn't want to give them a chance, then that was the way it would be.

She was done making excuses for him.

She drew herself up, every inch the proud, disdainful countess. She'd had years of practice hiding her feelings, and she relied on every one of them right now. "Love?" She let out a brittle tinkle of laughter. "The thought never crossed my mind. I could never love someone like you. The man I give my heart to will be worthy of my love and be capable of loving me back. He won't be a mean, heartless bastard who would turn his back on his clan, friends, and country. It's no wonder that your wife left you, you're an—"

"That's enough," he growled. His eyes bit into her, his handsome face stark. "I think you've said enough."

She gasped, unable to breathe through the pain burning in her chest.

She'd done it. She'd finally managed to hurt him. But it gave her precious little satisfaction as she stood there frozen, feeling as if she were breaking apart, and watched him walk away.

# Eighteen

*Dunstaffnage Castle, November, 1308*

"You're sure you won't reconsider?" Bruce eyed Lachlan over the edge of his goblet. They were alone in the laird's solar of Dunstaffnage Castle. It was four weeks since Lachlan had been here last, and yet he could still hear the scorn in Bella's voice as she'd given him the set down he so richly deserved.

She was right: She did deserve better. He'd been trying to tell her that all along.

Marriage? What in Hades had possessed him to say that? Of course she'd hesitated. It wasn't her fault that for one moment he'd allowed himself to think . . .

He was a fool. The heroine didn't end up with the pirate. She needed a hero, not a villain. No wonder she'd laughed. He'd laugh, too.

Lachlan picked up his own glass and drained it. But the whisky did little to dull the burning ache in his chest.

He met the king's gaze from across the table. Though idly spoken, Lachlan knew the question was anything but an idle one. Robert the Bruce would keep his promise, but if there was a way he could honorably avoid doing so, he would.

Lachlan smiled just as idly. "Nay," he said with far more certainty than he felt. "I will not reconsider."

He'd left, needing to get away before he did something stupid. The exchange with Bella had left him angry, raw, his emotions frayed, unable to escape the gnawing feeling that he'd just made the biggest mistake of his life.

The time away was supposed to clear his mind. It hadn't. But as soon as Bruce paid him the rest of the money and signed the charters, he'd be on his way. It was why he'd returned. The king was holding his first council meeting at Ardchattan after the Feast of St. Andrew.

Hell, who was he kidding? That wasn't why he'd returned. He didn't need to be here for another week. He'd come back because he couldn't force himself to stay away a day longer.

He needed to make sure that she was all right.

He needed to know whether he'd made as big a mistake as he feared.

Not that it would make any difference. She would probably just tell him to go to hell the way he deserved. Now that she was safe, she'd undoubtedly realized that she didn't need him anymore. If she ever had.

Bruce's dark brows drew together in a scowl. "You are costing me a king's ransom. I hope you are putting it to good use."

Lachlan shrugged, having no intention of easing the king's curiosity. Nor would he feel guilt. He knew the king's coffers were depleted, but they would be filled up soon enough. "I thought your brother just returned from the south."

Edward Bruce, Sir James Douglas, Boyd, and Seton had led a party of warriors to collect the rents.

"Aye, but once again there is unrest in Galloway. I thought the resistance was put down last year, but the MacDowells and their allies are like weeds that refuse to die. I'm sending Edward back with reinforcements." The king watched him carefully. "The MacSweens are making trouble again, too. I have Chief and Hawk preparing the men to go on a moment's notice if they stir from Ireland. I've decided to put Hawk in charge of getting the team in and out—"

"Hawk? He's about as subtle as a battering ram. He'll get them all killed."

"It's only until we find a replacement for you. I was thinking perhaps my nephew—"

"Randolph?" Lachlan was incredulous. Sir Thomas Randolph, one of the most elite warriors in Scotland? "You can't be serious! He knows nothing about subterfuge. Half the time he has that sword stuck so firmly up his backside—"

He stopped himself. *Damn it.* His jaw clenched, knowing exactly what Bruce was trying to do. But Lachlan wouldn't bite. It wasn't his problem, and he wasn't going to get dragged into it. He had everything he wanted right at his fingertips.

"But I'm sure he'll figure it out," he added calmly.

Bruce lifted a corner of his mouth, but he didn't press. "I'd have thought you'd look more rested."

Lachlan quirked a brow.

Bruce tapped his fingers together. "After your time in the Isles attending to those personal matters you spoke of. Although I must say I'm surprised to see you. I wasn't expecting you for another week."

Lachlan's expression betrayed nothing, but he knew the king had guessed what had brought him back. "My plans changed."

Bruce wasn't fooled. "You look like hell. You might want to shave and clean up before you see Lady Isabella."

Lachlan stiffened at the mention of her name. "Why would I do that?"

Bruce's eyes narrowed. "I assumed it was for her that you went to Berwick." He slammed his goblet down and leaned across the table, all pretense of equanimity gone. "Damn it, Viper, I'd have thought you would have learned your lesson. I told you to lie low and stay clear of danger for a while, which doesn't include going on some rogue mission of vengeance, no matter how well warranted. To bloody England again?"

Lachlan's mouth curved into a sly smile. "I don't know what you're talking about."

"You know exactly what I'm talking about. I don't think it's any coincidence that a half-dozen men were killed in a strange attack at Berwick Castle a few weeks ago, including Bella's former jailor, who was found naked and hanging from the cage where she was kept."

He shrugged unrepentantly. "Sounds like divine justice to me."

"Don't you mean Highland justice?" Bruce scowled. "But how the hell did you get him to walk up there—" He stopped himself. "Never mind, I don't think I want to know." Bruce took another swig from his goblet. "You are lucky I still intend to uphold my side of our deal."

This time it was Lachlan who leaned over the table. "What are you talking about? I've kept my side of the bargain."

"Have you?" Bruce quirked a brow in challenge. "You agreed to be my man for three years, which means following orders. Something you seem to have a problem doing."

"I don't recall any orders."

Bruce's mouth thinned into a tight line. "You are trying my patience, Viper. Let me be perfectly clear: I don't want you anywhere near England or the Marches for a long time. I won't have the identities of my men jeopardized for any reason. Even a good one. Do you understand?"

"My service is finished," Lachlan pointed out. He didn't have to follow anyone's orders.

"Almost finished," Bruce corrected. "The council meeting isn't for another week."

Lachlan's jaw clenched.

"And I am still your king." Bruce sank back in his chair, with the generous smile of a man who'd won his point. "Don't worry, you will have your money and your island soon enough. Though what you're going to do with it all alone in the middle of nowhere, I don't know."

"Nothing," Lachlan said. That was the point, wasn't it? Peace. Solitude. No one to answer to. No one to be responsible for. A place to call his own. It sounded like heaven.

Didn't it?

His chest burned tighter.

She would expect him to stay. To fight. To bind himself to her and the cause. But he didn't believe in anything, damn it. She expected too damned much. She didn't even know what she wanted from him. Maybe nothing.

Damn it, why the hell was he thinking about this?

"Will you stay for Templar's wedding?"

He shrugged. "I don't know."

"He'd be disappointed if you didn't."

Surprisingly, Lachlan wanted to, but in some ways he suspected it would be easier if he didn't. A clean break was what he needed.

Wasn't it?

"And what of Lady Isabella?"

Lachlan tensed almost imperceptibly. Almost, but he suspected the king had seen it. Still, he couldn't prevent the anxious spike of his heartbeat. "She's well?"

"Well enough." A wry smile turned the king's mouth. "Better than you, from the looks of it."

"I'm glad to hear it." At least he should be. But part of him had hoped . . . what, that she'd been suffering the way he had?

"She's concerned for her daughter, of course," Bruce added.

*Not my problem.* But he found himself asking anyway, "Do you plan to send the team after her?"

Bruce shook his head. "Nay, the girl is safe enough where she is—"

They heard voices outside right before the door burst open. Lachlan's heart stopped when he recognized one of them.

"Damn," Bruce cursed under his breath, echoing Lachlan's thoughts.

Lachlan's reluctance to see her was understandable, but the king's was not. He frowned, wondering if something had happened between them.

"Robert, I—" She startled like a deer in the hunter's sights when she saw Lachlan.

He steeled himself, but it wasn't enough to prepare him for the gash of pain that dug across his chest when their eyes met.

A month hadn't been nearly long enough to clear his head. He realized a lifetime wouldn't be long enough.

Bella's heart lurched. Her blood, her thoughts, her voice, everything drained from her body. Except for her heart. That throbbed painfully.

After a month it shouldn't hurt so much. But seeing him again brought all those wounded emotions rushing back in full force.

"You're back," she said dumbly.

He stood up. "For the council meeting."

Of course. She hadn't expected anything different, had she? Her chest pinched. Only a fool would think he would have changed his mind and that she hadn't been the only one suffering these past weeks. She'd missed him so much.

Though he did look more disheveled and exhausted than she'd ever seen him. His hair was longer and one long, wavy lock slumped forward across his forehead. The hard, lean angles of his handsome face seemed sharper and even more predatory. A couple of weeks' dark stubble lined his jaw. Most surprising, however, was the layer of dust and grime that coated the leather of his *cotun*. She'd never seen him so unkempt. He looked as though he'd just dragged himself back from the battlefield. He was back to his ruffian ways, no doubt.

It infuriated her that it only seemed to make him more attractive. Weren't women supposed to be attracted to shining armor? How did he make rough, rugged, and gritty so appealing?

It didn't matter. She was done being a fool. He'd made his feelings—or lack thereof—painfully clear.

He'd left her. He didn't care enough.

"I wasn't expecting him for another week," Robert added.

She might not have attached any significance to the information had she not caught the sharp look Lachlan threw the king. Her heart leapt. Did it mean something? Had he come back for her?

God, she was doing it again. Looking for hidden meanings when the truth was plain to see. Would she ever learn?

She forced her thoughts back to the letter in her hand. "I'm sorry to disturb you. I can wait outside if you aren't finished."

"Is there a problem, Bella?" the king asked.

Bella nodded, tears filling her eyes, despite Lachlan's presence. "Aye, it's my daughter."

Lachlan took a step toward her. "What's—"

"That will be all, MacRuairi," Robert stopped him. "I will send for you if I need you."

It was almost as if Robert didn't want him to hear what she had to say. For a moment, it looked as if Lachlan might argue. But after a long pause, he nodded.

"Don't forget what I said," Robert added as he turned to leave.

Lachlan's mouth tightened, and he gave the king a curt nod before bestowing an equally curt bow on her. "My lady. I—" He hesitated. "We can speak later."

The words had an ominous lilt, but she knew it meant nothing. She stiffened, forcing a coolness to her voice. "That won't be necessary. I don't believe we have anything left to say."

She didn't want to talk to him. It hurt too much to even look at him. She might do something foolish, such as beg.

He gave her a long look, the muscle pulsing in his jaw. Then without another word he was gone, a whiplash of hurt and longing trailing in his wake.

Bella stared at the door for a moment, trying to fight the conflagration of emotions that had been unleashed inside her at the sight of him. The hurt was just as strong as it had been the night he walked away from her. She needed to put him behind her. That part of her life was over. Joan was all that mattered. Why was he doing this to her?

"Bella?" Robert prodded gently.

She startled, shaking off the smothering grip of melancholy. Her daughter needed her, and she wasn't going to let Robert put her off any longer.

For weeks, he'd avoided her questions about when she would be reunited with her daughter. The only time he'd discussed the subject was to bring her a letter passed on from Margaret, purporting to be from Joan. Her chest squeezed. The handwriting had looked like her daughter's, but in her heart she knew the words could not have been hers. *No further communication . . . Don't try to contact me again . . . Stay where you are.*

The last seemed like a warning.

She drew up her shoulders and looked the king square in the eye. "I need to go back to Berwick."

A frown gathered across his heavy brow. To his credit, he did not immediately refuse. "Why?"

She held out the latest missive from Margaret. This one had been brought directly by her mother, who'd arrived just a few days ago after being made aware of Bella's secret return. As happy as she was to see her mother, the news she'd brought had thrown her into a state of panic.

"It's from Margaret," she explained. "Joan, her cousin, and her uncle, William Comyn, are traveling to Berwick to see 'me'—Margaret—at the convent. They've been staying with Lady Isabel de Beaumont at Bamburgh Castle, and will travel to Berwick before returning south. You'll see from the date that they are expected by the end of the week."

There wasn't much time.

Robert's frown deepened. "That doesn't make any sense," he said, almost as if to himself.

"Not if you believe the first missive." Which Bella never had. "Something's wrong." She didn't know how to explain it; she just felt it deep in her bones. Her daughter was in danger.

Robert took the letter and scanned its contents. When he'd finished, he looked more perplexed than troubled. He dropped the letter on the table and gazed back up at her. "I know what you are thinking, but it's impossible. You can't risk going back to the convent."

"I have to," she insisted. "If Joan arrives with her uncle, everyone will learn that I've escaped. William Comyn knows what I look like. Margaret won't be able to fool him, and Joan's life will be in danger."

Robert shook his head. "It's too dangerous. Your daughter will not be harmed."

"You can't be certain of that."

He paused, debating something, seeming to choose his words with care. "Joan is being watched."

Bella's eyes widened. "By whom? Why have you not told me?"

"I can't say. You need to trust me. But I can assure you at the first sign of danger, I will know."

"But what if there is not time? What if they discover I am gone and decide to hurt Joan or throw her in prison immediately? I can't let that happen." She bent down, taking his hand to kneel beside him. "Please, Robert, if you will not help me get into that convent, then at least send some men to rescue her before the truth is discovered."

The king gave her a pained look. "I'm sorry, Bella, I wish I could help you, but it isn't possible. Not right now at least. We are too close to winning Mary's release; I can't risk doing anything to upset it. Not without more information. But I swear to you, at the first hint of a problem, I will do everything I can to get your daughter back to you safely. Until then, you will have to be patient."

Stung, Bella stared at him, tears burning her eyes and throat. She did not doubt the sincerity in his voice, but his refusal, even if well motivated, felt like a betrayal. She didn't want to listen to rational explanations. She just wanted her daughter back.

"I've been patient for three years," she said softly. It was a reminder—the only one she'd ever given him—of what she'd done for him.

Sad eyes met hers. "I know better than anyone what you have sacrificed, Bella—and how hard it is to wait. There is not a day that goes by that I do not long for my wife, daughter, and sisters." He squeezed her hand. "Just a little longer. This war can't go on forever."

It sounded as if he were trying to convince himself as much as her.

Bella nodded, but she knew she had to do something. Robert had a crown and country to think about, but she had only her daughter. If he wouldn't help her, she would find someone who would. Someone who could get her in and out of that convent without being seen.

Her stomach turned, knowing exactly who had the skills to do so. Lachlan. No doubt his ability to get in and out of places was what had made him so appealing to Bruce that he would be willing to pay him to fight in his elite group of warriors.

The idea of lowering herself to ask him for anything after what had transpired between them went against every bone in her body. But she'd grit her teeth, swallow the bitter taste in her mouth, and do it. For her daughter she would set aside her pride. For her daughter she would sell her soul to the devil himself if need be.

She only hoped it didn't come to that.

Lachlan MacRuairi was a mean drunk. As most of the time he figured he was mean enough already, he didn't usually drown himself in a big jug of whisky.

Tonight, however, he made an exception. Seeing Bella had unleashed all sorts of unwanted emotions, damn it, and he needed to get good and drunk not to think about it. She didn't want to see him. Didn't want to talk to him. Of course she didn't. Her cold reaction was understandable. It was what he'd expected, wasn't it? And it was sure as hell no less than he deserved.

When the drink didn't work, he turned to brawling. Drinking and fighting tended to go together.

It was Gordon who finally dragged him away from the table before he could inflict too much damage. "Damn it, Viper, what the hell are you trying to do? Do you want all three of them to kill you? You even managed to rile Hawk's temper."

"Must have lost his sense of humor along with his bollocks when he took a wife," Lachlan mumbled. "All of 'em did."

Gordon pushed him outside into the cold night air. Winter was in full force, and the icy mist hit him with a sobering slap. Or maybe he just wasn't as drunk as he wanted to be. He didn't stumble, lurch, or weave as Gordon led him across the darkened *barmkin* toward the barracks. And damn it, his head was much too clear.

He could see her in his mind, seated at the dais, not once glancing in his direction during the evening meal. *Over.*

*Done.* The finality hit him in the gut, churning unmercifully. It was what he'd wanted, wasn't it?

*Mistake.*

"Hell, if you talked about my wife like that, I don't think I'd show nearly that much restraint."

Lachlan lifted a lazy brow in Gordon's direction. "Haven't reconsidered yet? Not much time left to escape the noose."

An odd look crossed the other man's face before he shook it off with a smile. "Since my bride will be arriving any day, it's a little too late for that."

Lachlan thought about saying something, but showing unusual restraint, he bit his tongue. If there was something between MacKay and Gordon's intended, it wasn't his problem. If MacKay was too stubborn to say something it was his own damn fault. He would have to live with the consequences.

Just as Lachlan would. His teeth gritted together. He'd done the right thing, damn it—the only thing. But it didn't feel right.

"Are you all right?" Gordon asked. "You don't look too well."

Lachlan shook off the hand he'd held out to steady him. "A headache."

Gordon laughed. "I'm not surprised, with the amount of whisky you drank tonight." He sobered. "Did it help?"

Had anyone else asked, he would have feigned ignorance and told him to bugger off. But despite Lachlan's efforts to the contrary, William Gordon was a hard man not to like. "Nay."

"Anything I can do to help?"

Lachlan shook his head. Things had gotten so twisted between Bella and him, there was no way to untangle the mess—even if he wanted to. She'd made it perfectly clear that there was no future between them.

The only thing that was going to help was for him to get

out of here as soon as possible. Before he could inflict more damage on either of them. "Nothing that a dip in the loch won't cure," he replied.

Gordon shook his head. "That Viking blood must run hot in Islanders. Either that or you're all half-mad. I don't know why anyone would choose to swim in weather like this. Haven't you ever heard of a nice warm tub before a fire?"

"Tubs are for women," Lachlan replied. As he walked away to gather his things, he was surprised to realize that he was smiling.

His good humor didn't last long. Seated atop an overturned skiff that had obviously outlived its uses, he'd just finished pulling on his boots and fastening a plaid around his shoulders when he heard someone approaching behind him.

He stiffened, sensing her even before he turned to see her standing amidst the shadows of the moonlight. She didn't belong here. This place stirred too many bad memories. The last time he'd been alone with a woman on this beach, she'd ended up dead. Strange that he could think of it now with so little emotion.

Bella looked good, he realized. The weeks at Dunstaffnage had erased all traces of her captivity. A healthy bloom in her cheeks and a slight fullness in her face had replaced the gaunt pallor.

"William told me where I could find you."

*Bloody helpful of him.*

"I need to speak with you."

She shivered in the misty darkness, tightening the heavy fur-lined cloak she wore around her. He missed the breeches. In the lad's clothing, he'd almost convinced himself the distance between them was not so great. Seeing her in her finery only served to widen the divide. The pirate and the princess. The brigand and the heroine.

"Not now, Bella." Not here. Not in this place where he'd lost his soul.

"Please," she insisted. "It's important and cannot wait."

He should have just gotten up and walked away. But as he'd proved more than once, he was a fool when it came to Bella MacDuff.

She shivered again, and he clenched his fists to keep himself from dragging her into his arms. She was cold, damn it. He couldn't stand to see her cold, knowing that it reminded her of the hell she'd been through.

"Fine," he said angrily. "But we'll talk in there." He pointed to the wooden building that had stored the Mac-Dougalls' most prized *birlinns,* but which now housed the king's.

Getting up from the skiff, he grabbed the torch he'd brought with him and stormed up the sand to the storage building. It was pitch black, cool, and damp inside, but at least it was out of the wind and bone-chilling mist. Securing the torch to the iron bracket, he crossed his arms to keep them in place and turned to face her. "Well?"

She bit her lip, and he cursed the light. Not that darkness would help. He would still have his other senses with which to contend. Her intoxicating scent surrounded him. The soft hitch of her breath pounded in his ears. Every bone, every muscle, every fiber of his body was attuned to her.

"I need your help."

He was so shocked to hear those words that it took him a minute to process all that she was saying as she explained. But by the time she was done, any pride or happiness he might have felt in thinking that she'd turned to him because she believed in him, trusted him, cared for him, had died.

A hired sword. A man with no loyalties. That's why she'd come to him. That's how she saw him.

That was what he'd become. That was all he was to her. And he hated it.

"So you've come to me because the king has refused your request, and you think I will go against his command?" He shook his head. "I'm sorry, Bella. I know you are scared for your daughter, but the king is right. It's too dangerous."

He could see the rise of emotion in her face—her fear and desperation—though she fought to keep it at bay. It was clear she was doing her best not to argue with him but was finding it difficult. "I came to you because you are the only man who can help me. Because you have the skill to get me in and out of the convent without being seen. I came to you because you know how important this is to me." She looked into his eyes. "I came to you because you owe me this. You owe me my daughter."

The dart of her arrow hit him square in the chest, stealing his breath. It was his decision that had separated her from her daughter, and she'd never forgotten it. Neither had he. Deserved or not, guilt pricked his conscience.

He forced a mocking smile to his face. "You've changed, Bella. You've learned how to fight dirty."

She took a deep breath, as if the act pained her, and then thrust up her chin. "I learned from the best."

Aye, she had.

"I paid my debt by getting you out of that prison." He took a step toward her, fighting the heated emotions surging through his veins. "I was nearly imprisoned for you. Was that not enough? Do you want to see me chained to a rack?"

Bruce was right: He played a dangerous game of chance every time he stepped out of the Highlands.

The mask of control on her face crumpled and tears streamed down her cheeks. "Please, Lachlan, I know what I ask of you, but if I don't do something, they will find out I have escaped and take it out on Joan." He thought he was immune to desperate pleas. He was wrong. With her he'd never be immune. "I can't just leave her there, to the mercy of men who have none. I swear you won't hear a word of argument from me about anything—I will do everything you say. Please, Lachlan, I'm begging you. I need you."

*I need you.* The words bit into him. Digging. Penetrating. Threatening to break his resolve. He'd never wanted to give something so badly as he did at that moment. He would have sold his soul to help her.

But his soul had been sold a long time ago.

If he did as she asked and accepted this rogue mission, the king would be furious. The money and the land he was due would be in jeopardy. Everything he'd fought for, everything he wanted, would be at risk.

But it wasn't everything he wanted. That was the problem. He wanted her, and it seemed impossible to believe that she could ever want him.

He stared down into her upturned face, into the eyes looking at him with such trust and longing, and felt something inside him crack. His will breaking. "Bella, I . . ."

He stopped. *No.* He couldn't let his desire for a woman control his decisions. "I can't," he finished.

Her lush, sensual mouth twisted in anger. "You mean you won't!"

He grabbed her arm, preventing her from spinning away from him. "Nay, I mean I can't. Not until Bruce holds his first council."

"But that is too late." Her voice bubbled with hysteria. "We need to leave tonight, tomorrow morning at the latest. Even riding day and night we might not make it. Why—"

He heard her sharp intake of breath and saw her eyes widen on his face as the harsh understanding dawned. "Of course. The meeting is when Robert intends to bestow your reward." The scorn—the disgust—on her face ate like acid on his resolve. "Money. That's all this has ever been about to you."

He had to explain. He had to tell her why this was so important to him. Why he couldn't risk it. He wanted to help her, damn it, but he couldn't. Not if he was going to salvage what was left of his honor. People were counting on him. "Damn it, Bella, that's not all it's about. You don't understand—"

"I understand perfectly. How much will it take, Lachlan? I'll give you everything I have, although I'm sure it won't match the king's reward. With most of my husband's lands distributed amongst Robert's men, and my own unable to be claimed while I am in hiding, I'm afraid I've been forced to rely on the king's good grace. But when my lands are restored—"

He jerked her hard against him, fury racing through his veins. "I don't want your damned lands or your money."

Her blue eyes met his, flashing with angry challenge. "Then what is it you do want?"

He pulled her tighter against him, his body hardening at the contact. The battle raged inside him. What he thought he wanted. What he wanted. What he could have. All coiled together in a conflagration of pounding emotions he could no longer contain.

*You. I want you.* But he didn't know how to say it. How to give words to what he was feeling. How to make everything right.

And then everything went wrong.

# Nineteen

❧

"I know what you want." She moved her hips crudely against his hardness. "It's all you've ever wanted from me, isn't it? God, you are all the same!" She put her hand on him, molding it around his bulging cock. "If you don't want my money, then how about my body?"

A blast of heat surged through his loins. In her reckless rage she was the most seductive, irresistible creature Lachlan had ever seen.

"Stop it, Bella." He tried to unlatch her, but her hand held him firm. "That isn't what I want."

She laughed scornfully, the proof to the contrary hard in her hand. She stroked him, running her hand up and down his long length. She leaned closer to him, sliding her tongue over her bottom lip like a hungry cat. "Then what of my mouth, Lachlan? Will that convince you?"

It was no more than he deserved. He'd told her as much, but he'd lied then and sure as hell didn't want that now. Well, at least not like this. "No, damn it—"

He froze when she dropped to her knees before him and furiously started to untie his braies. "Jesus, Bella, stop! Don't do that!"

But his protest was weakened by what she was doing to

him. Her hand was on him, stroking him, milking him with a boldness she'd never displayed before.

*Wrong.* The knowledge blared like a flickering candle in his head. He should push her away. *This is wrong.*

But God, it felt good. He couldn't stop the groan as heat rushed to his groin. Swelling. Pulsing. Throbbing in her intimate grip.

*Wrong.* He grabbed the hand that gripped him, putting a harsh end to the sensual motion. "Damn it, Bella, stop!"

She looked up at him, her golden hair a blazing, tousled halo in the firelight. He jerked hard in her hand. Every muscle clenched against the temptation she presented. Those slanted, wide-set eyes, the plump, sensual mouth only inches . . .

Her eyes narrowed. He knew what she was going to do. Anticipation coursed through him in a hot rush, pulsing at the tip. He'd dreamed of this moment. It might be wrong, but he had.

She licked him. Dear God, she flicked out her tiny pink tongue and licked him. His knees buckled against the wave of pure pleasure, and he had to grab a wooden post to steady himself. The rush of heated sensation was unlike anything he'd ever imagined.

He must have made a sound because her lips curved in a slow, sensual smile. "I thought so."

She held his gaze, her tiny hand circled around him. His heart stopped, his breath caught, and his muscles tensed in anticipation as her mouth moved slowly over him. *Tell her no. Oh God . . .*

She took him in her mouth. Deep in her warm mouth. Her soft pink lips wrapped tightly around him. It was the most erotic thing he'd ever seen; his darkest fantasies come to life.

He knew he should push her away. If he were half the man she wanted him to be, he would. But any further protest was lost in the mindless state of sensual oblivion.

She took him mercilessly, ruthlessly, every movement calculated to bring him to his knees. The warm suction of her lips drew him deeper and deeper into the hot cavern of her mouth, the loving circle of her tongue swirling around his head, the soft hand at his base gently pumping . . .

It was unbelievable. Mind-blowing. She knew exactly how to taste him, how to suck him, how to drive him wild with pleasure. How had she learned . . . ?

*Oh hell.* He knew how.

He stiffened, pulling back. He might have found the strength to stop her, but she moved her hands around to grip his flanks, taking him even deeper. She sucked him harder. Faster. Milking him with her lips and tongue. Giving him no quarter.

Pressure gathered at the base of his spine. The sensations were too intense. He couldn't hold back. It was right there. Pleasure so intense nothing could have made him stop.

He gripped the back of her head, holding her to him as he came deep in her throat with a fierce roar of pleasure. *Jesus. God. Yes.* Wave after wave pulsed through him.

She kept her mouth around him until she'd wrung every drop from him.

But then it was over. Passion fled as quickly as it had arrived, leaving him as cold and empty as the room suddenly felt.

Her hands dropped from his backside. The icy shock of air hit him as she let him slide from the warm, wet embrace of her mouth. The enormity of what he'd done pounded through him unrelentingly. He felt ill. So ashamed he didn't even want to look at her. Honor? He had none.

He'd let her play the whore for him, giving proof to every bad thought she'd ever had about him.

He'd driven the only woman who'd ever tried to care for him to her knees, making her believe that was all he wanted from her. Any chance they might have had by his coming back was gone.

But the truth was far more bitter than that. Knowledge sank like a stone in his gut. It wasn't until he'd sunk to the lowest depths of depravity that Lachlan acknowledged the truth: *I love her.*

The sentiment he'd always denied, that he'd belittled others for succumbing to, crystallized in sharp awareness from the mass of confusing emotions that had been tormenting him from the first.

This hunger. This craving. This fierce intensity of emotion. This need to protect her. This overwhelming desire to make her happy.

This misery.

It wasn't just lust; it never had been. He loved her and had been fighting it from the start because it scared him to hell that she would never be able to love him back.

Now, he'd guaranteed it.

He looked down into her eyes, seeing the horror that mirrored his own. And worse, he saw the stark hurt and hollow disappointment.

He held her gaze, his heart burning a hole in his chest. He'd never hated anything as much as he did himself at that moment, seeing what he'd done to her. "I'll do it," he said stonily.

Even knowing it would cost him everything, he could not refuse her. He owed her that much.

My God, what had she done? Shame flooded Bella's cheeks.

She'd known that she was losing him. That he wouldn't change his mind. So panicked and desperate, she'd resorted to the one weapon she'd vowed never to use. She'd used her body, the skills forged at the hand of her husband's cruelty, to bend him to her will. She'd taken something that could have been beautiful and turned it into something shameful. She'd used his desire for her to get what she wanted.

She'd acted the whore.

Worse, he hadn't stopped her. How could he have let her do that? She'd thought . . .

She'd thought what they had was special. But it wasn't different at all. He was just like every other man. Lust was all he wanted from her. All she'd done was prove it.

He wouldn't even look at her. She didn't blame him. His agreement was cold comfort. She'd done what she needed to do for her daughter, but had sullied what was between them in the process.

The stoniness of his expression matched his tone. "Gather your things and meet me here in an hour."

"But—" Her hands twisted in knots. She should say something. But what? There was nothing she could say that would take away what had just happened.

He stood there stiffly, either not sensing or ignoring her distress. "You'll have to hurry if we are to leave before the gate is closed for the night. Find an excuse for your absence if you can. Anything to delay them." He looked at the ships crowding the room, seeming to speak his thoughts aloud. "We'll have to ride. Alone, I won't be able to sail fast enough to outrun my cousin."

Her eyes shot to his. "You think the king will send someone after us?"

He shrugged. "He might. He will guess where we are headed and won't be happy with either of us for disobeying him."

She bit her lip. Not for the first time, her conscience warred with her motherly instincts. She had to ensure her daughter was safe, but she knew what this was costing him. "Lachlan, I'm sorry. I wish there was another way—"

"Go," he cut her off; the time for apologies had passed. She'd forced him into this rogue mission and would have to bear the consequences. "There isn't much time."

She'd hated having to lie to Lady Anna, Sir Arthur's sweet-tempered young bride who'd been nothing but a

friend to her, but her claim that she was ill and would prefer not to be disturbed except by her mother bought them
some time. Her mother had reluctantly gone along with her
plan, recognizing the danger Joan was in.

They rode for nearly two days straight, stopping only to
change horses where they could and tend to their most
basic needs. With each mile, the pain and emptiness in her
chest seemed to grow, as did the distance between them.
She wanted to reach out but didn't know how. He seemed
so remote. So aloof. His expression painfully blank when
he looked at her.

She'd never seen him like this. Part of her wished he
would lash out at her again in anger. At least that she
understood—that she could defend against. But this stony
silence was so unlike him, she didn't know how to react. It
threw her off balance and gave proof to her fear that whatever had been between them had been irretrievably broken.

If the silence hurt, the strained attempts at conversation
were even worse. It seemed the only thing he could think to
do to break the silence was to point out every route marker
on the road and make her repeat over and over the direc-
tions to a safe house in Berwick in case anything happened
to him.

It was almost as if he were preparing her for something.

Though they were alone, they'd never felt more apart. It
was clear that he would rather be anyplace but here with
her. He took every opportunity to hunt, bringing her back
more grouse, pheasant, and partridge than they could possibly ever eat. Was he avoiding her, or was there another
purpose?

Finally, the strained awkwardness became so unbearable
Bella couldn't take it anymore. When Lachlan ordered her
to stop on the third night, telling her that they had to sleep
if only for a few hours, she knew she had to try to break
through this oppressive silence. She had to tell him that she
hated what had happened just as much as he did. That she

was wrong to have done what she did. That even after what had happened, she didn't want him to go. That she cared for him.

He might not return her feelings, but she had to at least tell him what they were.

She thought she had time. When she'd left to go wash by the icy river, he'd been collecting armfuls of heather—for what purpose she didn't know. But when she returned from tending her needs and washing as best she could, the heather had been dumped in a pile and he was gone.

It was nearly dark by the time Lachlan approached the small clearing by the river where they would camp for the night. They'd been fortunate not to have rain or snow the first two nights, but he could feel the dampness in the air and knew that a storm was on the way. A cold storm.

A miserable journey was about to get more miserable.

Though Bella hadn't raised a word of complaint, he wasn't going to put her through a night of riding in sleet and snow. They would have to stop to rest sometime, and tonight was as good as any. He hoped the storm would also slow down any pursuers. But if his fellow guardsmen—Bruce wouldn't send anyone else—had gone by ship, he knew they might well be ahead of them.

At least he and Bella had made it through the hills before the weather changed. Though the most difficult terrain of their journey was now behind them, leaving the highlands meant they were entering the most dangerous. English garrisons held all the major castles from here to Berwick. To have a chance at reaching the convent in time, they had to take the main road, increasing the danger.

Not wanting to test their luck by risking a night at an inn, Lachlan had decided to stop at the site of an ancient fortification known as Doune, just north of Stirling. The fort was in ruins, but there were walls enough to provide shelter for the night. Situated on a small rise, it would give him a good view of anyone who tried to approach.

He quickly scanned the area around the ruined stone-and-timber fort. It was bleak. Desolate. The russet heather-covered hillside was fronted by the dark, brownish-gray waters of the river. The landscape was as cold, dank, and forbidding as the skies. But it would serve their purpose, and he hoped be unlikely to attract unwanted company.

He'd been hunting longer than he intended. The animals sensed the storm as well, but he'd managed to trap a small hare. Maybe she'd like that better than the birds? He'd also collected enough wood to cook it and keep them warm for the night.

Bella had been washing when he left, and he'd taken care not to disturb her. Hell, he could still barely look at her without feeling the knife of shame twist through his gut. He had to at least try to apologize, even if he knew she'd never be able to forgive him. The tension between them had become unbearable.

He didn't know how to talk to her. All it seemed he could do was blather on about the roads. His attempts to show her how sorry he was had fared no better. She'd looked at him as if he was half-mad when he'd handed her the string of birds that he'd hunted for her. Then the heather he'd collected earlier to give her something soft to sleep on—women liked that, didn't they?—had been crawling with beetles.

He whistled the signal to let her know he approached, stilling when instead of a reply, he heard a soft sob.

His pulse spiked, senses flaring with alarm. *Bella!*

Heart in his throat, the hare and wood fell to the ground as he raced the last few feet up the hill into the small stone enclosure.

The cold, damp air hit him the moment he ducked his head under the low doorway. It was so dark that at first he didn't see her. He followed the sound to the back corner of the small room, loose pieces of stone crunching under his footsteps. She was curled up in a ball against the wall, her arms wrapped tightly around her legs and her face buried in her knees.

He rushed forward and knelt beside her. "Jesus, Bella, what happened?"

She lifted her head, blinking up at him as if she'd just realized he was there.

His eyes raked her face. Thank God, she appeared unharmed.

"Came . . . b-back . . . you . . . g-gone," she managed in between big, gulping sobs.

Lachlan felt some of the pressure in his chest begin to release. He reached out and cupped her chin, tilting her face to his. "Foolish lass, you couldn't have thought I would leave you?"

She looked so miserable his chest squeezed. He ached to pull her into his arms, but he didn't want to make it worse.

"Yes. No." She blinked up at him, the glare of accusation in her eye. "You did."

She wasn't referring to today, but to a month ago. *I tried.* "It mattered to you?"

A fresh flood of tears poured down her cheeks, but she glared at him with a mixture of exasperation and outrage. "Of course it mattered to me," she choked, before adding something that sounded like "you mutton-headed arse" under her breath.

He smiled. Even collapsed in a ball of tears, she still had spirit. To hell with it. He was done trying to fight this. If there was a chance in hell that something could be between them, he was going to take it. For the first time in days, he could see things clearly.

He took her gently into his arms, more than half-expecting her to push him away. When she didn't, a spark of hope fired inside him. "I won't leave you again. Ever."

He stroked her head as she sobbed against his chest.

Then, seeming to realize what he'd said, she looked up. "Y-you won't?"

She looked so stunned he couldn't stop a smile from curving his mouth. He shook his head. "Not if you don't want me to." He cradled her against him, trying to find the words to convince her. He'd spend a lifetime making it up to her, if she'd let him. "I know I'm an arse. I know I've hurt you. I know I don't deserve you, but for what it's worth, I . . ."

*Ah hell.* He'd never said these words to anyone in his life, and they didn't come easily. His heart pounded, but he forced himself to continue. There was no going back now. She could laugh in his face and grind his heart under her tiny heel if she wanted to—which was no more than he deserved—but at least he would have told her how he felt. He took a deep breath and spit it out. "I love you."

He heard her sharp intake of breath as she went still in his arms. For the longest time she didn't say anything, but simply stared up at him. He'd never felt so exposed in his life. His heart felt like a hammer in his chest, pounding hard and unrelentingly. At just about the point he didn't think he could stand another minute without squirming, she repeated hesitantly, "You *love* me?"

She managed to convey both wariness and skepticism in the inflection of that one word. He couldn't blame her. He wasn't all that comfortable with the idea himself. What the hell did he know about love?

He hadn't expected her to jump in his arms and declare her love for him—if she'd ever cared for him, he'd sure as hell ruined that—but it pained him to realize just how much cause she had to be cautious. He'd hurt her, and she feared he would do so again. "I know I haven't acted like it."

"No, you haven't," she agreed all too readily. "Why should I believe you?"

He should have known she wouldn't make it easy on

him. But he'd dug himself into this grave, so he needed to dig himself out. "I've never been so miserable in my life."

Her mouth quirked. "And this is supposed to convince me? I think you're going to have to do better than that."

For a man who'd never thought he had feelings, let alone tried to talk about them, he didn't know what to say. "I've never felt like this about anyone. You make me crazy. You make me happy. You make me want to be a better man."

A smile hovered around her lips. "That's sweet."

He nearly choked. "*Sweet?* Good God, don't let anyone hear you say that!" He'd never hear the end of it.

She eyed him expectantly. "Is that all?"

He gave her a sharp look. "This isn't exactly easy for me; you could show a little mercy."

She lifted an imperious brow. "Mercy? I didn't think you knew the word." She shook her head. "You know I'm beginning to doubt this fearsome reputation of yours. I didn't think you were scared of anything."

"I didn't think so either," he muttered under his breath. He'd rather take on an army of Englishmen with his bare hands—naked—then bare himself like this.

How could he find words to convey the enormity of what was in his heart? "You were right. I was fighting this. I was fighting you. I've done everything I could to make you hate me, but it wasn't until I succeeded that I knew what a damned fool I've been. I swear if I could take back what happened in that boathouse, I would." He dragged his hand through his hair, trying to find a way to explain the inexcusable. "I should have pushed you away, but I wasn't strong enough. Somehow it ended up all twisted. I tried to make myself believe that all I felt for you was lust, and I made you believe it."

"You didn't act alone, Lachlan. I should never have done what I did." Her cheeks flushed in the darkness. "It was wrong of me to try to persuade you that way. I didn't give you a choice to push me away; I wanted to make you weak." He felt her eyes on his face, as if she could dig the truth out of him. "But I don't understand. If you love me, why did you refuse to help me?"

He knew he had to tell her all of it. "You know I have some debts?" She nodded. "Some of the money is for the families of the men who died for me that day."

She gasped. Her eyes locked on his. "How much of it?"

He shrugged uncomfortably. "They had large families."

"My God, you've been supporting all those people for ten years?"

His jaw locked. "It's not enough." It would never be enough.

"Why didn't you tell me? How could you let me think you didn't care about your duty to your clan? How could you let me make all those accusations?"

"Because I didn't want you looking at me the way you are now. I'm not a bloody saint, but I pay my debts."

Her eyes widened with horror as she realized all the ramifications. "Oh God, Lachlan, I'm sorry. I swear to you I will find a way to make sure you get your money. If Robert won't . . . Somehow, I'll repay you."

He stiffened. "It's my debt, Bella, not yours. I don't want your money. I'll find a way."

"But—"

He stopped her with a finger over her mouth. "No."

Her lips pursed. "Do you always have to be so stubborn?"

He lifted a brow. "Do you?"

Their eyes met and her frown dissolved into a wry grin. "It would be much easier between us if we weren't."

"Aye, but I wouldn't want you any other way."

The broad smile that lit her face warmed his heart. "You wouldn't?"

He shook his head. "That stubborn pride makes you strong. It helped you survive. It brought you back to me."

He squeezed her harder against him. "I should have protected you."

"You did as much as was humanly possible. But no man is invincible—not even you. We were betrayed; there is nothing you or anyone could have done about that."

He started to argue, but this time it was she who put a finger to his mouth. "There are no one's hands I would rather put my life into, Lachlan. No one. I, too, wouldn't want you any other way."

He cocked a brow in silent challenge.

She bit her lip, trying not to laugh. "All right, maybe without the crude language."

He winced, recalling some of his more choice offerings. "I'm sorry about the things I said. I didn't mean them."

"I know."

"But they still hurt."

She nodded, eyes solemn. "A lot."

He squeezed her tighter against him, pressing his mouth against the soft silk of her hair. "I'm an arse."

Her mouth quirked; she shot him a sidelong glance. "You're starting to repeat yourself."

He smiled. That he had. Sobering, he took her chin once more between his thumb and finger and tilted her face to his. She was so damned beautiful. His heart seemed to have forgotten how to beat. "Have I convinced you?"

He sounded so hopeful, so eager for this to be over, that if it weren't so serious she would have laughed.

Was it possible he loved her? She desperately wanted to believe him. Looking at him it was hard not to. He looked so vulnerable, so uncertain. Two things she'd never thought to see on his face.

But years of disappointment made it hard for her to trust—especially with something as fragile as her heart.

Could she let herself love him?

She felt her heart swell in her chest as she gazed into his

eyes, and she knew the answer. What a foolish question! As if she could control her heart. Love happened whether she wanted it to or not.

Of course she loved him. This man who appeared so hard and uncaring on the outside but on the inside was filled with unexpected depths and contradictions. He was a man who'd bellow at her one minute and wrap a plaid around her the next. Who'd walked away from his clan but had done so out of a fierce sense of duty. A mercenary who'd sold his sword to the highest bidder to care for his clansmen. A man who exuded virility but had punished himself with celibacy for ten years. A man who'd claimed his friends meant nothing to him but would race into a burning building before he'd leave one of them die. A man who'd sacrifice everything he'd worked for to help her.

She'd loved him for a long time. She just thought she could protect herself by not admitting the truth.

A bubble of joy spread through her, putting a wide smile on her face. "Not quite yet, I'm afraid."

His face fell. He looked so crestfallen, this time she did laugh.

He frowned. "I'm glad you find this so amusing."

"Oh, I do." She grinned.

"I don't know what else to say, Bella. I seem to have exhausted my meager supply of love words."

She supposed she should be done torturing him, although she had to admit it was fun watching him wriggle and wince with each word like a lad in church clothes. Clearly, talking about his feelings didn't exactly come naturally to him.

She reached up and put her hand on his face, feeling the warmth seep through her.

"Perhaps you'd better show me, then," she said softly.

His eyes raked her face, as if he didn't quite trust his ears—or his interpretation. "Are you sure?"

She nodded, feeling suddenly shy. "I love you, too."

A fierce expression hardened his face. "You don't have to say that."

She smiled. "I know. But it's the truth." She paused. "I've loved you for a long time, but didn't want to acknowledge it because I was scared you would never love me back. And then when I thought you'd betrayed me . . ." Her voice drifted off.

He stroked her cheek with the side of his finger. "I'm sorry, love."

She shook her head. "It's in the past. All that matters is what we do from here. You're a hard man to love, Lachlan MacRuairi, but I do believe I'm up to the challenge."

"We'll probably argue."

"Aye, it seems likely."

"I have a bit of a temper when I get angry."

"I've noticed," she said wryly.

"I can be a mean bastard. I'll probably say something to hurt you."

She laughed. "Are you trying to scare me off?"

He gave her a rueful smile. "Maybe."

"Well, stop—it isn't going to work. I'm quite aware of your faults."

He frowned. "I didn't say they were faults."

She laughed, reaching up to twist the lock of dark hair that had fallen across his forehead around her finger. He was so heartbreakingly handsome, could she ever tire of looking at him? Their eyes met, and all jesting fell to the wayside. Suddenly, the air fired between them.

"I thought you were going to try to convince me," she said huskily.

He leaned down and kissed her, answering her command with the soft brush of his mouth. A kiss so tender and sweet it took her breath away.

He tore his mouth away with a pained groan. "I don't know what to do. I've never done this before."

She would have teased him, but she could see how much this meant to him. He wanted to get it right.

"Neither have I," she said softly. Like him, she knew lust, but not love—not tenderness.

Maybe if she had, her marriage might have been different. Her feelings for Lachlan had given her better perspective on her past and helped her to feel that she could put it behind her, where it belonged. Buchan seemed less the cruel monster of her memories, and more a man to be pitied. He'd wanted her so badly it had become an obsession. Looking back, she could see all the little places her marriage had gone wrong. He'd wanted her to respond, and her defiance only made him try harder. Until they'd entered a vicious cycle from which neither one of them could break free. They were both too stubborn to admit defeat.

"You humble me." His voice was gruff with emotion.

"And you me," she said, tears of happiness in her throat. She couldn't believe this was really happening. That something so wonderful was happening to her. Part of her feared that at any moment, someone would wake her up and tell her that it was all a dream.

His mouth fell on hers again, and she could feel the force of his emotion running through her.

It was all the reassurance she needed. She slid her hand around his head, running her fingers through his hair— which was far too soft and silky for a fierce warrior—to bring her mouth more fully against his.

She opened it, taking in the long, heartfelt strokes of his tongue. A delicious warmth spread through her. She'd never felt so safe. So secure.

So loved.

For a man who'd never done this before, he was doing an awfully good job of it.

He took his time. Teasing her. Tasting her. Stoking her passion one spark at a time. A stroke of his tongue. A touch of his hand. A soft groan of pleasure whispered in her ear.

Slowly, he eased her down on the ground under him, using the plaid she had wrapped around her shoulders as a blanket.

He lifted his head. "Are you cold? I gathered wood for a fire. It won't take me a minute—"

"I don't need a fire." She slid her hand under his shirt, feeling the heat of his skin radiate under her palms. He was hot enough for them both. She skimmed her hand over the rigid bands of his stomach. He sucked in his breath as the muscles clenched in response. "You'll keep me warm."

"I don't want anything between us," he warned.

His words only flooded her with more warmth as a flush of anticipation spread over her. Naked. Flesh to flesh. Skin to skin.

She nodded.

He began to remove his clothes. She felt she should look away. Surely it wasn't maidenly to be so interested. But she wasn't a maiden—and hadn't been in a long time. So she looked her fill. Holding her breath as piece by piece, his magnificent body was revealed to her bold gaze. Boots, weapons, plaid, leather *cotun*, chausses, and shirt were shucked off in a pile beside him. Then his hands moved to his waist. Her mouth went dry as he quickly worked the ties of his braies, releasing the hard column of his manhood. It was dark in the fort, but not too dark to see the massive size of him, and to remember how it had felt to take him in her mouth.

She swallowed, slowly.

"Keep looking at me like that, lass, and this isn't going to last very long." He slid out of his braies, tossing them in the pile with the rest.

Naked, aroused, every inch of his densely muscled physique bared to her view, he was magnificent. She told him so.

In response, he kissed her. She could feel his fingers working the ties of her shirt and breeches—she'd donned her lad's clothes again to travel—and feel his hands skim over her body as he helped her out of her clothes, but his mouth and tongue kept her so busy it wasn't until he broke the kiss that she realized she was naked. "It's you who are magnificent," he said, his voice filled with awe as his gaze skimmed over every inch of her naked flesh.

She blushed, feeling strangely shy. She'd been naked in front of him before, but this felt different. For the first time, a man's admiration of her body didn't bother her. Never had a man looked at her with such reverence—as if she were the most precious, beautiful woman in the world.

He reached out and gently cupped one of her breasts with his hands, running his thumb over the tight nub of her nipple. "I want to taste you, Bella."

She shivered at the husky promise of his words.

He leaned down, placing a tender kiss on the tip of her breast. She moaned, half-pleasure and half-protest at the all-too-fleeting touch.

He skimmed his finger over the heavy curve of her breast and down the flat of her stomach, his eyes feasting along the way.

He kissed her breasts again. Circling the nipple with long, lazy strokes of his tongue, while his hands continued to wreak havoc with her senses, sliding, teasing, trailing a feathery path along her stomach, hips, and thighs, until they finally dipped between her legs.

He released her nipple, looking into her eyes as he brushed his finger over her dampness. She shuddered, then squirmed as her body flooded with warmth. "Are you wet for me?"

She moaned, lifting her hips against his hand, silently begging for him to touch her and find out. But still he swept over her. His mouth slid down her stomach, pressing tiny kisses along the trail forged by his hands.

"I want to taste you right here." He pressed her intimately with his fingers.

*Oh God.* Her breath quickened in anticipation as she realized what he was going to do. What he'd threatened so coarsely to do before.

Should she stop him? Surely she should stop him. But her body was quivering, throbbing with need. And her hips—her hips couldn't seem to stay still.

"Do you trust me?"

His voice was husky with promise, a dark temptation too powerful to be resisted.

She could only nod. Words would not form. Anticipation beat in her like a drum.

He settled his dark head between her thighs, cupping her bottom to lift her hips toward his mouth, holding her gaze the entire time.

Oh God.

There would be no shying from this intimacy. But the wickedness, the wantonness, the naughtiness only served to deepen her arousal.

He seemed to be waiting for some kind of reply. Or maybe he was just prolonging the agony. "Let me love you, Bella."

And then he did. Kissing her. Tonguing her. Loving her with his mouth until she no longer knew her name. Until all she could think about was the exquisite torture he was exacting on her. Until the unbelievable sensations became too much.

She'd never imagined anything could feel like this. The pressure of his mouth. The flick of his tongue. The scratch of his whiskers against the sensitive skin.

She writhed. Moaned. Trembled.

He sent her tumbling over the edge, and then sent her over again. She cried out as wave after wave of pleasure spasmed through her.

He was inside her. Filling her. Taking her with long, tender strokes. Skin to skin. Their bodies melding in a fusion of heat and passion.

But when she looked into his eyes, she knew it was far more than that.

It was perfect. With each slow, penetrating stroke, she felt his love for her. And when at last they came together, she heard the words again, echoing in her ears.

The love and happiness that had eluded her for so long were finally hers. She savored every moment of joy, knowing how hard fought it had been won.

Hours later, after he'd built a fire, fed her, and loved her once more, she slept entwined in his arms, for the first time in years feeling hope in the promise of tomorrow. With Lachlan by her side, everything was going to be all right.

# Twenty

Lachlan didn't like it, but he didn't have any other choice. He drew the hood of the dark robe over his head and turned back to look at her standing in the doorway. God, he didn't want to leave her. "I won't be long," he said.

She put her hand on his arm with the unconscious ease of a woman who knew every inch of him and gave him a reassuring smile. "I'll be fine. After so many hours in the saddle, it will feel good to move around and stretch my legs."

He frowned. He didn't like leaving her alone, but he didn't have a choice. He had to scout the convent and find Margaret. She would be safe here for a couple of hours. "Don't stray too far from the cottage. Though there aren't likely to be any hunters or poachers at night, there are wild animals in the forest, or you could fall and twist an ankle—"

She stopped him with a laugh. "You sound like my mother."

His jaw clenched. "Damn it, Bella, I'm serious. Just because we've made it so far without any problems doesn't mean we're safe. We still have to get you in and out of that convent without being seen."

Not to mention getting out of England, through the

Marches, and back to the safe part of Scotland. His stomach knifed. What the hell were they doing here?

But she wasn't listening. Her mind had leapt beyond the "details" the moment they'd reached the outskirts of Berwick. As soon as he'd had confirmation from an informant whom the Highland Guard had used many times before that Despenser's party had arrived at the castle the day prior, Bella hadn't been able to sit still.

On their journey she'd confided more of the details of her imprisonment, including how they used the prospect of contact with her daughter to control her. He knew part of her had been protecting herself in case this was yet one more in a long line of disappointments. Once she'd learned Joan was close, however, there'd been no holding her back.

"I can't believe I'm going to see my daughter in a matter of days—maybe as soon as tomorrow."

The dreamy smile on her face made his chest tighten. He knew how much this meant to her, and he would cut off his right arm to make it happen, but she was getting ahead of herself. "*If* I can get you in there."

She lifted up on her toes to press an unfortunately chaste kiss on his mouth, which he suspected was merely to soften his frown. "Of course you'll get me in. It's a convent, not a heavily guarded castle, and it's protected by nuns, not soldiers. It will be child's play for you."

Unwavering faith wasn't something he was used to, and it made him bloody uncomfortable.

He didn't know what was wrong with him. So far everything had gone according to plan. But it was an adage among the Guard that the only thing you could count on in a mission was that something would always go wrong.

So far nothing had. The morning after the storm they'd woken to sunshine. The thin layer of snow hadn't slowed them down at all, and by the end of the morning had melted. They'd changed horses just south of Edinburgh and made it to Berwick on the fifth day of their journey—

nearly a half-day quicker than he'd anticipated. After the quick meeting with the informant to confirm Despenser's presence, they had gone to the forester's cottage by the stream that they'd used when they rescued Bella. Best of all, there had been no sign of his Highland Guard brethren.

Why couldn't he shake the feeling that something was wrong?

He knew why. He was too damned happy, and he didn't trust it. Happiness made him wary. And tentative. He didn't want anything to screw it up.

By unspoken agreement, he and Bella had avoided talking about the future for the same reasons. She needed to ensure her daughter's safety first, and he needed to ensure hers. There would be time when this was over. But the memories of what had happened the last time he'd mentioned a future still stung.

She was right. He was more conventional than he'd realized. He wanted her as his wife. But she loved him. It would have to be enough for now.

"It's not getting you in that I'm worried about," he replied. "It's getting you out. What if one of the nuns notices something and decides to look a little closer? What if Comyn does something? I don't trust him."

His words seemed to finally have the desired chilling effect. She sobered. "It's worth the risk, Lachlan. I have to try to do this." She put his hand on his cheek. How quickly he'd become used to the tender touch. To crave it.

"My vows—Margaret's vows—will protect me. And if not, I have you."

God, he wanted to be deserving of that faith. "I'm only a man, Bella—not a magician. There are some barriers even I cannot get past. You better than anyone know that."

She paled, the memories of her confinement too fresh.

He swore. "Ah hell, I'm sorry. I didn't mean to scare you. I just want you to be cautious. Remember, you did promise to follow orders."

Her mouth quirked. "All right. You win. I'll stay close to the cottage."

He smiled and dropped a kiss on her lips. "Now, there's an agreeable lass."

She made a face. "Go. Before I become very disagreeable."

He smiled and gave her another kiss, this one much more fierce, before reluctantly taking his leave.

As the convent was only a couple of miles away, he traveled on foot. This way he would attract less notice in the event anyone was nearby. He picked up the pace as he went, moving quickly through the trees and brush.

On some missions the members of the Guard would run like this for hours, across uneven terrain, up and down hills, in snow, rain, and sun. In one of their first training exercises, that sadist MacLeod had demanded that each one of them run fully armed from his castle of Dunvegan along the coast to the northern point of the Waternish Peninsula—a distance of about fifteen miles—in two hours. He'd let them rest all of five minutes before ordering them to run back.

Raised on the sea, and used to the quick Viking style attack of his forebearers, running came about as naturally to Lachlan as riding did to MacKay. The blasted Highlander could run for days. Though Lachlan had hated every minute of the training, he had to admit the endurance and speed had proved useful more times than he'd like to remember.

Now he could run for hours without thinking about it. But he'd still sure as hell rather be in a boat.

He slowed as he neared the convent. St. Mary de Mount Carmel was situated in a small forested glen in a remote area on the outskirts of town. Though it was quiet, and nothing appeared out of the ordinary, he intended to be damned careful.

He told himself it was just like any other mission. But it wasn't. He had Bella to worry about.

Emerging from the edge of the tree line, he scanned the area around the small walled enclosure. The moon was full, providing plenty of light. At least it did for Lachlan, who had unusually keen vision at night.

The convent consisted of three main buildings around a central cloister. To protect the nuns from the outside world, a ten-foot-high wall and a ditch had been built around the main buildings. But without guards and with only a locked gate to prevent entry, it was more for privacy than a defensive barrier. Hell, even an Englishman could breech these paltry defenses.

Lachlan figured his biggest problem was going to be staying hidden once he was inside. A man in a convent would stand out. The dark robe would help him blend into the darkness, but nothing could hide his size. And unlike other missions, he couldn't use his blade to cover any mishaps or surprises.

There were few things he refused to do, but killing women—nuns, no less—was one of them.

He waited in the darkness, watching and listening. Finally, about a half-hour after he'd arrived, the bell rang.

It was what he was waiting for. The call to evening prayers. All the women would be in one place.

He waited about ten more minutes, making sure everyone would be inside the church, and then made his move. He picked the darkest area of the castle—in this case the east side, which was shaded by the trees and mountain behind—and came out into the open. He'd be visible for about a hundred yards after he left the safety of the trees.

Dashing across, he made it without incident to the wall. Using gaps in the stones and jagged edges of the rock as finger- and toeholds, he climbed up a few feet until he could grip the top edge. From there he lifted himself up—not an easy feat, loaded down with armor and weapons. But pulling yourself up from a dead hang was another one of MacLeod's favorite training exercises.

Lying flat on the two-foot-wide platform, he stilled, getting his bearings. He was above what he suspected was the dormitory where the nuns slept. To his left in the center was the church, and opposite was the refectory.

He scanned the area for any sign of movement. Seeing nothing, he dropped down inside. As he wasn't familiar with the duration of church liturgies—hired swords didn't tend to spend a lot of time at church—he didn't know how much time he had. Moving quickly, he crossed the cloister, passing through what had to be a garden for the kitchens, before ducking behind an arched column of the walkway connecting the church to the refectory.

From here, he took some time to find the best position from which to watch the nuns emerge from the building. He needed to find Margaret as quickly as he could and follow her, or find a way to draw her away to speak to her privately. If he had to, he would wait until they slept and then sneak in and wake her.

It was imperative that he find her tonight. Margaret, with her knowledge of the layout and schedule of the convent, would be able to provide the best time and place to make the temporary switch before the meeting with Comyn and Joan.

Unfortunately, hiding places were limited. But he settled on a gap between the steepled roof of the church and the flat roof of the walkway. From the high position, he would have a good view of the nuns coming out of the chapel door. It was good and dark, with little chance of anyone seeing him. It also provided him with multiple escape routes, by traversing the roofs and dropping down on either side.

Once he was in position, it was just a matter of waiting. About twenty minutes later he heard the door open and the nuns began to emerge.

Although there was a nice beam of light from a torch to illuminate their faces as they stepped from the church, the women had a tendency to bow their heads as they walked. Combined with the veils and wimples that covered most of their faces, identifying Margaret was going to be more difficult than he'd realized.

He'd begun to think he might have missed her, when he finally saw her. Luck was with him. Not only was she one of the last to leave, but she also walked alone. If he could find a way to get her attention—

His head snapped around at a faint rustling sound behind him. His blood ran cold. He stilled, senses honed on the dark, surrounding countryside. It was probably an animal, nothing to worry about.

But then he heard it again. More distinctly this time. Closer. Muffled footsteps and the soft slink of metal. *Mail.* A soft whinny. *Horses.*

He muttered an oath. Something had gone wrong all right.

It was a trap. They'd been waiting for him. Which meant . . .

Bella! They must know she was free.

How didn't matter. Lachlan drew his swords out from under his cloak and crouched into position like a lion waiting to spring. He would get back to her even if he had to get through the entire English army to do it.

Bella washed, ate a few bites of cheese and oatcake, fiddled with the fire, tried to lie down on the old straw bed she'd covered with a plaid, and, having exhausted her options, began to pace around the old wooden building. As it wasn't much bigger than the ambry at Balvenie Castle, it didn't take more than a few strides to cross from one end to the other. Every few minutes, she would take a short detour to the small shuttered window and peer through the opening to see if anyone approached.

But it was so dark outside, all she could make out were the dark and slightly sinister-looking shadows of the trees.

She threw up her hands in frustration. This was torture. *Waiting* was torture.

Ever since they'd reached Berwick she'd been unable to contain her excitement. After so many years, she would finally be able to see her daughter face-to-face, to hold her in her arms, to hear the sound of her voice.

Lachlan would make it happen. Not once did she doubt him. She knew she could count on him.

The past few days had been fraught with danger, uncomfortably cold, and filled with mind-numbing exhaustion. But through it all, she'd been happier than she could remember in years. Although there had been no more opportunities to make love, she'd slept a few hours in Lachlan's arms in the saddle—he appeared to be able to go for days without sleep—and they'd talked whenever the pace allowed.

Despite the circumstances, their time alone had been wonderful. When her daughter was returned to her, her happiness would be complete.

She stopped before the window again and carefully lifted the wooden latch to open the shutter wide enough to peek outside. Shivering as the cold night air rushed into the room, she peered out into the darkness.

Nothing.

How long had it been? An hour, maybe longer?

She was about to close the shutter, when she caught a movement out of the corner of her eye. A branch swayed back and forth. It could have been the wind, but for a second she thought she saw the large shadow of a man.

Her heart jumped. Thank God, he was back!

She slammed the shutter closed, grabbed the oil lamp, and raced to the door. Tearing it open, she said, "Lachlan, I . . ."

Her voice died when a man stepped out of the shadows.

"Hello, Isabella."

Her heart plummeted to the ground. There, standing before her, was her husband's brother, William Comyn.

Instinctively, like a cornered hare, she looked around for a means of escape. But all thoughts of fleeing vanished, when roughly two dozen men emerged from the trees to encircle the lodge. One of them was the man whom she now recognized as Sir Hugh Despenser.

The happiness of the past few days, the excitement she'd been brimming with moments before, and all hope for the future died in the space of a cruel heartbeat, leaving nothing but despair and fear.

God in heaven, she'd die before she let them imprison her again!

It wasn't the entire English army, but it seemed like a good part of it. From Lachlan's perch hidden in the shadows of the church bell tower, he could see that the soldiers had surrounded him. Literally. There was a line of at least a hundred men all the way around the convent just beyond the ditch. He might be able to fight his way through, but without a horse, they would be on him like wolves.

A loud banging at the gate sent fissures of alarm running through the convent. He could hear the anxious shouts as the nuns retreated to the safety of the church. A few nuns with obvious authority—including undoubtedly the prioress—came to the gate. A moment later, soldiers flooded into the cloister.

He heard a commanding male voice. "Not harm you . . . looking for a rebel . . . search the premises . . ."

The nuns' outraged protests were to no avail.

Lachlan knew he didn't have much time. It wouldn't take them long to find him here. He jumped from the bell tower to the roof of the church below, then scrambled along the adjoining roof to a place he'd noticed before. A small, dark refuse area behind the kitchen.

If this didn't work, he'd have to take his chances fighting

his way out. But without a horse, he would be at a disadvantage. The hundred yards of open land loomed large.

He was in luck. Two men emerged into the small space below him and not three. Three men would have given them a chance to sound the alarm—he had only two hands.

He used them well.

Dropping from the roof, he took one man in a chokehold and stabbed the other in the side of the neck with the special dirk Saint had fashioned to pierce through mail. The steel blade was unusually sharp and thin—more like a narrow pick than a blade.

It enabled them to kill silently, which in circumstances like this was imperative.

A fraction of a second later, he slid the same dirk into the mailed back of the man he'd been holding around the neck.

After tossing the smaller of the two soldiers behind the fence of refuse, Lachlan set about removing the other man's armor, which bore arms he did not recognize—five lozenges in an azure fess.

He could hear other soldiers milling about in the kitchen and knew he didn't have much time before they came out to investigate.

The cloak, tabard, mail shirt, shield, and helm were the most important, so he focused on those. It took a few minutes of struggle to get the mail shirt over the dead man's head. Once removed, he had to get it over his own.

These bloody Englishmen were a short, small lot, but he managed to get the damned thing on. The helm, tabard, and cloak were much easier. Finally, his disguise was complete. After tossing the second man atop the first, he yelled into the darkness, "There, by the gate!"

As he'd hoped, the men went rushing out of the kitchen, and Lachlan followed behind them.

"Where is he?" he heard people yell. "I don't see him."

"Did you see him, Penington?"

He must be Penington. Lachlan shook his head and

moved off, following a stream of men that were passing through the gate.

His luck held for a few more minutes. But Penington's squire must have seen him emerge and brought him his horse. "Sir William!"

Lachlan turned. The lad's face paled. "You're not Sir William."

Before the lad could react, Lachlan grabbed the reins and pushed the boy out of his way. He was on the horse and riding as the cry went out behind him.

It didn't matter. He was nearly in the forest. It might take him some time to lose them, but he did not doubt that he would.

But the English would be scouring every inch of this forest. How long would it take them to find Bella? He had to get to her first.

Ice chilled every inch of her skin, penetrated her bones, and filled her veins, but Bella refused to cower or show them her fear. She met her brother-in-law's gaze unflinchingly. "What do you want, William?"

"You always were a proud lass. I told my brother it was a mistake to marry you." He shrugged indifferently. "But he saw I was right in the end."

"How did you find me?"

William shrugged. "It wasn't difficult. My men were watching the forest around the convent and alerted us when you arrived. We were expecting a larger party—it was nice of you to make it easy on us." He gave her an appraising glance. "Still wearing lad's clothing, are you? I must admit I never imagined it was you until one of my men said that MacRuairi had been traveling with a woman. When he described your mouth and eyes, I knew." He shook his head, tisking. "That was really quite foolish of you, attempting to see your daughter like that. We might not have ever known of your deception."

The ramifications tumbled through her mind. If they knew it was she, then the letter . . . it had all been a ploy—a trap. Her heart sank in despair. *Joan.* Where was her daughter?

"You've been a very naughty lady," Sir Hugh added. "But in the end it will all work out for the best."

"What are you talking about?"

He looked surprised that she hadn't realized it yet. "Why, MacRuairi. Surely, you've guessed why we've gone to all this trouble? We want the outlaw."

Actually, she hadn't. But her heart jumped to a hard thump. "I'm afraid you are to be disappointed. He's not here. Last I heard he was out west."

Her bravado was for nothing. Despenser's face hardened. "Do not take me for a fool, *Lady* Isabella—and I use that term very loosely. Right now your lover is cornered in the convent, with my men surrounding him."

Her heart jerked again, but she forced herself not to react, not to panic. Lachlan could take care of himself. He would find a way out. He always did.

Despenser must have guessed what she was thinking.

"And if he manages to slip through the net I have cast for him, you are all the bait I need to lure him into a second."

She blanched. "You must be mad to think I would ever let you use me to capture him."

"Even for freedom?" Despenser held out the bone. "For you and your daughter?"

Bella stilled. "You expect me to believe that?"

He shrugged. "You are not important to us, the brigand is. Sir William has graciously agreed to allow you to retire to his estates in Leicester with your daughter—at least until her marriage can be arranged. No one will know who you really are. Isabella MacDuff will be thought to be safely retired in a convent."

Bella looked back and forth between the two men. Even

if she could trust them—which was doubtful—she would never betray Lachlan like that.

She shook her head. Dread settled in her belly like a stone. But she realized she would face imprisonment rather than betray him. "You might as well take me back to Berwick right now; I won't do it."

Despenser smiled. "Such bold words. But I feared you might be difficult."

Sir William appeared distressed. "For once in your life be reasonable, Isabella. The scourge isn't worth it."

"Aye, he is," she said fiercely.

"Is he worth your daughter's life?" Despenser interjected softly.

The breath left her. She froze in abject horror. She turned on William. "You would do this? You would harm your brother's daughter to capture one man?"

"He isn't just one man," Despenser snapped. "He can lead us to many others. Men the king will be extremely grateful to know the identities of."

She should have known it would be Despenser's political ambitions at work. She pretended not to know what he was talking about and continued to stare accusingly at William.

"Of course I don't want to see the lass harmed," he assured her. "But you leave us no other choice."

"Where is she?" she demanded. "Where is my daughter?"

"She's safe. For now," Despenser said ominously.

But she could see from William's face there was more. "She's in the guard room at Berwick Castle."

*No.* Bella felt the ground begin to move. Her stomach knifed.

"I believe there's a cage free for her, if you refuse," Sir Hugh added.

*Oh God, no!* Horror rushed to smother her. Then everything went black.

* * *

It was a few hours before Lachlan could make his way back to her. He led his pursuers south for miles. After ditching both his horse and his borrowed, too-small armor near the sea—hoping they'd think he'd escaped by ship— he'd circled back on foot.

It seemed to take forever. His heart was pounding in his throat the entire time. If anything happened to her . . .

He tried not to think about it, tried to concentrate on his surroundings, but fear had wormed its way into his consciousness and no amount of force and determination would root it out.

Although there were still a few search parties concentrated in the area around the convent, the forest approaching the hunting lodge was ominously silent. His senses honed even sharper. Occasionally, he would hear a shout or the sound of dogs barking in the distance behind him, but it seemed the English had yet to extend their search this far out in his direction.

It was almost too quiet. He couldn't shake the feeling that something wasn't right. The dark feeling of foreboding weighed heavier with each step.

Though his heart urged him to race back to Bella as quickly as he could, he forced himself to proceed cautiously and be on the watch for any signs of danger. He couldn't afford to make any mistakes. He wouldn't let his emotions distract him—not this time.

*Please, let her be safe.* Lachlan repeated the prayer over and over in his mind. Though after so many years of disuse, he didn't expect anyone to be listening.

He kept to the shadows, darting through the trees and shrubs, pausing occasionally to listen and scout for any signs of a trap.

Nothing. Winter had deadened even the sounds of nature.

When at last the clearing and the old forester's cottage came into view, he could barely breathe. It seemed as if he'd been holding his breath for hours.

He scanned the moonlit landscape. Water on the right; horses tied to a tree exactly where he'd left them; wooden cottage a little farther away in the distance, slightly obscured by the trees, and dark but for the faint flicker of the oil lamp streaming through the cracks in the shutters.

He moved slower now, every nerve ending set on edge. Though his senses told him nothing was wrong, his instincts urged otherwise.

Suddenly, he froze at a cracking sound from above. A few moments later, he heard the sound of leaves rustling and realized it was an animal moving along the branches.

With a long exhale, he continued. Finally, he stood a few feet away from the lodge. Lifting his hand to his mouth, he hooted like an owl to let her know he approached and waited—heart hammering and blood pounding—for her response.

It came. The melodious call of the nightingale. The sweetest damned sound he'd ever heard. Thank God. All was well.

He bounded up the last few feet and pushed open the door, half-expecting her to be there to greet him.

He was surprised instead to see her seated on a stool before the fire with her back to him.

But it was she, and his heart sighed with relief to see her sitting there. "Bella?"

She turned only enough for him to see her profile, as if she couldn't bear to meet his eyes. Her face was as still and as pale as carved alabaster, and tears streamed down her cheeks.

A chill slid down his back. He lurched forward, taking her hand. It was as cold as ice. "What is it? What's wrong?"

Before the words were out of his mouth, he had his answer. His head jerked around at the sounds coming from outside as a swarm of soldiers descended around them like vultures.

*No.* His mind warred with his heart. He raced back to the open door, not wanting to believe what was happening.

But when he saw Despenser and Comyn emerge from the trees, he knew the inescapable truth: Bella had led him right into a trap.

Shock permeated every fiber of his being. But the pain of betrayal that followed cut like a knife through his heart.

*Not again.* He couldn't have made the same mistake again. She loved him; she would never betray him. There had to be an explanation.

As the men came forward to take him, he turned to look at her. "Why?"

If he hoped for a denial, he was to be disappointed.

"I'm sorry," she cried, her face crumpling in despair. "Oh God, Lachlan, I'm so sorry." The men grabbed him from behind. He let them drag him away. *It was true.* "They have Joan. They have my daughter!"

# Twenty-one

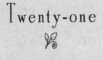

They'd lied to her.

Bella thought the moment they dragged Lachlan away, seeing the shock of betrayal written on his face, was the worst moment of this hideous nightmare. But being brought back to Berwick Castle, tossed in the guard room, and told she would not be reunited with her daughter after all—that her daughter didn't even know she was here, and that it had all been a lie to trick her into betraying Lachlan—made it so much worse.

Her daughter had never been in danger. According to William, she rejected any connection with her mother and enjoyed her position in England. Bella was relieved to know her daughter was safe but refused to believe the rest.

She was ashamed by how easily she'd been duped. How once again they'd used her fear for her daughter to control her, this time inducing her to betray the man she loved.

The look on his face when he'd realized what was happening would haunt her for the rest of her life. She sank back against the stone wall. However short that life might be.

Despair flooded through her. To have found happiness after all these years and have it wrenched away so cruelly was a crushing blow. Lachlan would never forgive her. Just like his wife and mother, she was just another woman who'd betrayed him.

Even knowing she hadn't had a choice didn't make it any easier. He had a chance in prison; her daughter didn't.

He was right. Everyone was capable of betrayal because everyone had a weak spot. And they'd found hers.

She bowed her head on her knees, her heart twisted with anguish. Where was he? What was happening to him? Were they hurting him? Was he cursing her name right now for what she'd done to him?

She couldn't bear to think about it.

Tears streamed down her cheeks, burning like acid. God, how miserably she'd failed! Not only Lachlan but her daughter as well. Now they were all at the mercy of Edward and his men.

Dear God, what would become of them?

The English were taking no chances of his escape.

The last thing Lachlan remembered before being doused with cold water was Bella's anguished face as he was being dragged away. They'd manacled his hands, and then he'd felt an explosion of pain behind his ear. From the violence of his headache, he gathered a war hammer or the hilt of a sword had struck him from behind.

The ice-cold water brought him harshly back to consciousness. He sat up, only to feel his head explode in pain, followed by a surge of instantaneous nausea. Rolling over, he retched uncontrollably on the damp ground beside him. His vision blended into doubles.

"Looks like he's awake," he heard a voice above him say.

He looked up, seeing a man peering down on him from a square opening about ten feet above him. It was the only source of light in the dark pit, and Lachlan took a moment to memorize as much of the room as he could before responding, knowing that as soon as the guard closed the door it would be as black as Hades in there.

Bile threatened again, but Lachlan refused to let himself think about it. He needed to keep the panic at bay. But it snapped in the back of his mind unrelentingly.

The walls seemed to be closing in around him. He was choking, and he had to force even breaths through his lungs.

The pit was ten feet by fifteen of solid, jagged, rough-cut rock that had been built by God, not man. The floor was sandy dirt and rock. Bones, pieces of old straw, and hardened human excrement appeared to have been pushed to one corner by the last occupant. Though he saw no evidence of rats, he could almost hear the squeaks and scampering.

Sweat gathered on his icy brow. *Stay calm. Think.*

He found what he was looking for in the far corner.

When Lachlan didn't respond, the man threw another bucket of icy water on him.

This time he realized the full horror of his predicament. The water hit naked skin. Before they'd dropped him in the pit, they'd stripped him of every last piece of clothing. He didn't have his tools, his weapons, anything.

How the hell was he going to get his hands free?

Reflexively, he pulled against the manacles pinning his hands behind him. The iron bands suddenly felt tighter—stronger—now that he knew he wouldn't be able to unlock them.

Panic snapped a little louder, a pack of rabid dogs just waiting to be set free.

He shook his head to clear it of those thoughts, spraying droplets of water from his sopping hair. "Thanks for the bath," he replied. "Next time would you mind sending down some soap?" He sniffed. "It stinks down here."

The man chuckled. "After a while, you won't notice. I'm glad you are in such good humor. You'll need it. They're bringing in someone special for you." He paused for effect. "The Extractor. I'm sure you've heard of him?"

Lachlan's blood went cold. The Extractor was the King of England's most feared torturer, known for being able to extract information from even the most unwilling of prisoners.

Lachlan's mind filled with images—memories of what he'd gone through before and things he'd learned of since.

But he gave no indication of the effect the words had on him. "You can save him a journey; I've met men of his ilk before."

Though his features were largely masked by the shadow cast by the light behind him, Lachlan could see the guard smile. "We've heard you can be difficult. But he's not coming all this way just to meet *you*." He turned his head. "Bring her in."

*God, no!* Lachlan's heart hammered. Every muscle in his body flared with the urge to fight. But he knew he couldn't react.

"Stop!" Bella shouted. "Where are you taking me?"

The fear in her voice cut at his heart. But he knew he couldn't do anything.

He heard the muffled sounds of struggle from above as two men dragged her in. He forced himself to lie perfectly still as they forced her head down into the opening where he could see her.

"Lachlan! Oh, God, Lachlan is that you? What have they done to you?"

His mouth curled in anger. "Get that bitch out of here."

She gasped, recoiling in shock. "Lachlan, please, I'm so sorry. There was nothing I could do."

"Do you think I want to listen to your explanations? You betrayed me," he spat malevolently. "Get her the fuck out of my face!"

He heard her broken sob as the men pulled her back. His chest burned. When the original guardsman's face appeared again, Lachlan added, "I'll be looking forward to watching what your visitor has in mind for that bitch. When he's done, I want a turn."

Her soft cries tore at his heart as they led her away.

The guard frowned, as if that hadn't gone as he'd planned. "I thought you were lovers?"

"She's the reason I'm here. Do you think I give a shite what happens to her?"

It was obviously not the reaction the guard had been expecting.

Which was exactly what Lachlan was hoping for.

The guard shook his head. "You're a cold-blooded bastard, MacRuairi. But you'll have some time to think about it. The Extractor won't be here until tomorrow night."

And before Lachlan could say anything more the door slammed shut, sending him into a sea of blackness.

Lachlan knew he couldn't count on them to believe what he'd said about Bella. The thought of what they might do to her to get him to talk . . .

His gut twisted. He wouldn't last long. He could hope to delay them with lies, but for how long? How long before he was faced with the choice of watching the woman he loved suffer agonizing pain or betraying his friends?

He should have known better than to offer bold proclamations of his ability to withstand any kind of torture to Bruce. Everyone had his breaking point. Even he.

Bella's was her daughter. How could he blame her for what she'd done? When faced with an impossible choice, she'd chosen to protect her daughter. The moment of betrayal he'd felt had turned to understanding when he'd learned the truth. He could only imagine what they'd threatened to get her to agree.

And what was she going through now, being imprisoned again?

He needed to get out of here as soon as possible. His mind went to work in the darkness. It was so pitch black he couldn't see his own feet. There was one good thing about learning from the guard what they intended: Lachlan's fear for Bella had outstripped the panic of being in another dank hole.

He scooted around the perimeter of the room, inching toward the pile of bones. It wasn't easy with his hands chained behind his back, but he dug through the grisly pile, tossing aside anything that was too big. Eventually, he found a piece that might work—it was about the size and length of his little finger.

He stood. After finding a rock at the right height, he held the bone as firmly as he could and banged his hands backward. He swore when the impact caused him to lose his grip. He had to sweep his hand around in the dark a while to find the bones. But the second time, it worked. The bone splintered in half.

He examined both pieces and chose the sharper of the two, which he honed further by filing it for a while against the rock.

When it was about the right shape and size, he carefully went to work on the manacles. It took him an hour, mostly because he didn't want to rush and chance the bone snapping off in the lock, but eventually his hands were free.

Feeling around in the dark was easier now, and he worked his way around the room until he found what he'd noticed before: a small rectangular drain.

Berwick Castle had been built on a motte adjacent to the sea. At one time, part of the motte had been surrounded by water. The drain had been necessary to prevent the chamber from flooding with water. An iron grate covered it, but if he could work it free he might be able to squeeze through it and find his way out.

He worked for hours on the grate. Using the chain between the manacles that had bound his hands, he wrapped it around the grate and pulled. But the damned thing seemed welded into the rock.

He pulled and dug until his hands bled. God, what he would have done for Boyd's additional strength!

It was one of the most satisfying moments of his life when the bloody grate broke free.

Ignoring the demons of panic roaring in his head, Lachlan forced himself to squeeze into the tight hole. There was barely an inch to move around him. He wound like a snake through the rocky maze, contorting his body into the narrowest shape possible and praying he didn't get stuck. Jagged pieces of rock tore through his flesh, but he could hear the sound of water below and knew that he must be close.

But then his luck ran out. The drain took a sharp turn down, halving in size. The sea and freedom lay a tantalizingly short distance beneath him—no more than forty feet—but he'd gone as far as he could go.

He let out a string of blasphemies that would have sent him straight to hell if he wasn't already there.

He wouldn't give up. Not even when they came for him. But Lachlan knew that right now, his best chance was to pray for a miracle.

# Twenty-two

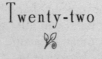

His miracle arrived that night.

Lachlan was ready for the door to open. He'd spent hours gathering what weapons he could: a half-dozen rocks of various sizes chipped from the walls of the drain, the manacles and chain, a larger piece of bone sharpened to a point to use as a crude dirk.

At the first sounds of someone fiddling with the lock, he stood with his back against the wall in the darkest corner. He would need time for his eyes to adjust to the sudden blast of light, and he wanted to draw the guard's head down into the pit.

The guard seemed to be having an unusual amount of difficulty with the lock. Lachlan could hear muffled oaths coming from above.

Finally it opened.

The narrow beam of light was blinding. As soon as he saw the guard's head descend, he took aim at the blur and fired, throwing the piece of steel as hard as he could.

Hurling stones into the sea as a lad had been a favorite pastime of his, and it came to great effect when he heard an oath and the guard tumbled forward into the pit. The guard was unusually big for an Englishman, and he landed with a resounding thud.

Lachlan ignored his angry cursing and focused on the hole above, waiting for the next guard to come forward.

"Damn it, Viper," a familiar voice said from above. "What the hell did you hit him with?"

Lachlan's stomach pitched forward. *Ah hell.* "Hawk?"

His cousin's grinning face peered down at him. He winked. "At your service."

Lachlan started over toward the body moaning on the ground. "Who did I hit?"

"Chief."

He groaned, realizing the leader of the Highland Guard was sitting with his helmed head between his hands. From the dent on the nasal guard and the blood running down his nose, it looked like the small piece of metal between his eyes had saved him from much worse injury.

"I feel like a damn church bell," MacLeod groaned. "My head is ringing. What the hell was that?"

Lachlan grinned. It wasn't often that he had the chance to best Tor MacLeod, but he savored it when he did. "A piece of my manacle." He smirked pointedly. *"Bàs roimh Gèill."* Death before surrender, he reminded him.

"Nice shot," MacLeod said with another wince as he wiped some of the blood from his face. "You've learned a few things after all."

Lachlan held out his hand and helped him to his feet. "I wasn't expecting you."

MacLeod gave him a dark look. "Forget what I said. You haven't learned shite."

"Couldn't leave you here to rot, cousin," MacSorley said from above. "Next time you might try asking for help before you go running off on your own."

Lachlan's jaw clenched as he looked at MacLeod. "I assume you know this mission wasn't exactly sanctioned by the king."

"Aye, we'll have a little talk about your problem following orders later. But Hawk's right. Next time don't go off on a rogue mission without help. It took a hell of a lot of work to find you—not to mention trying to get you out of here. We had the devil of a time with the locks." He gave him a hard look. "And don't forget I've had an unsanctioned mission of my own."

Lachlan knew he referred to the rogue mission on the castle where MacLeod's wife was being held. A mission they'd all joined in.

Lachlan had underestimated them, and he knew it. He nodded in acknowledgment.

MacLeod turned up to MacSorley. "Hawk, throw down that bloody rope."

While his cousin took turns lifting them out of the pit prison, Lachlan explained what had happened, and MacLeod gave him a quick summary of how they'd managed to get into the castle. It was similar to how they'd entered on the first attempt to free Bella. Boyd and Seton had snuck in earlier in the day with a supply cart and hid in the granary until nightfall. To provide as much time as possible, they'd waited for the guard at the postern sea-gate to change, and then made their move: eliminating the soldiers, donning their garb (much as Lachlan had done), and assuming their position on the wall. They'd signaled MacLeod and the rest of the Highland Guard, who were waiting on a beach nearby.

Swimming in the darkness, they'd approached the castle by sea, using a rope and grappling hook to scale the wall. MacLean, Lamont, and MacGregor had joined Boyd and Seton in their post at the sea-gate, while Gordon and MacKay prepared a distraction in case it proved necessary closer to the main gate of the castle. MacLeod and MacSorley had been charged with finding him.

Lachlan didn't need to ask how they'd gotten past the soldiers watching him; their bodies were strewn across the floor in the guard room.

"You didn't have any problems?" Lachlan asked.

"Sneaking into one of the most highly defended English castles on the Marches? Nothing to it," MacLeod said sarcastically. "Hell, Viper, why don't you get yourself imprisoned in the Tower of London next time and make it interesting."

MacSorley was keeping watch by the door. "Speaking of, we don't have much time. It's the middle of the night, but there are enough soldiers out there to celebrate May Day. We need to find Lady Isabella and get out of here before someone comes to check on them." He indicated the men on the floor.

Lachlan recalled what she'd said of her initial captivity. "They kept her in the east tower last time." Before and after her imprisonment in the cage.

"Good," MacLeod said. "It's close to the sea-gate and not as heavily guarded. We want to avoid the constable's tower and donjon near the front gate. It's lit up like the fires of Beltane out there."

Lachlan grimaced. MacLeod wasn't going to like what he had planned.

The greatest swordsman in the Highlands cursed and argued, but Lachlan knew it was mostly for show. MacLeod loved the challenge just as much as he did. And what he intended certainly qualified.

"You have an hour," MacLeod said. "We can't wait any longer. When the guard at the sea-gate changes we need to be gone."

Lachlan nodded. "We'll be there."

He started to leave.

"Cousin."

Lachlan turned to see MacSorley holding up his clothing and armor. "You might want these."

Lachlan grinned. He'd forgotten he was naked.

Bella lay huddled in her plaid on the crude straw mattress. Her tears had been spent hours ago. Though she was exhausted and drained, she couldn't sleep or stir from the waking nightmare of what had befallen them.

Over and over she replayed what had happened. Despenser and William's trap had been perfect. They knew she would return to the convent to see her daughter and prevent her escape from being discovered, and they'd guessed from their previous involvement that Lachlan would be with her. Ironically, love had doomed them both. The love they had for each other, and the love she had for her daughter.

It didn't help that she knew she couldn't have done anything differently. She just wished she hadn't dragged Lachlan along with her.

God, how he hated her! Even in the horrible darkness of that pit, the venom in his gaze had sparked like green fire.

She couldn't blame him. He had to be going mad down there, facing the demons of his own personal hell.

*"I'm sorry,"* she whimpered miserably. *"I'm so sorry."*

The single candle flickered at a shift in the air. The door.

She glanced over her shoulder and gasped. Her heart slammed into her chest. Standing there, filling the doorway, Lachlan loomed in the shadows like some kind of terrifying phantom in black leather and steel. Piercing green eyes found hers from beneath the brim of his nasal helm.

Instinctively, she sat up, tucking her feet underneath her, retreating against the wall.

As if that could protect her.

"How . . . ?" She didn't finish the question. How he managed to escape no longer surprised her.

He held up his finger to his mouth, closed the door behind him, and crossed the room in two strides.

She held her breath, not knowing what he intended. The things he'd said, the hatred in his eyes . . .

He pulled her into his arms, crushing her against his chest and cupping her head with the palm of his hand. "Jesus, Bella, are you all right?"

The emotion in his voice confused her. She pushed back enough to look up at him. "I thought you hated me."

He smiled, sending a pang right to her heart. "I was trying to protect you." He stroked her cheek tenderly. "I hoped that if they thought I blamed you, they would not try to use you to get to me."

Her breath caught in horror, realizing what he meant. She bit her lip, looking up at him hesitantly. "You were very convincing."

He laughed and dropped a soft kiss on her mouth. "I'm sorry."

Her composure crumpled. "Good gracious, Lachlan what do you have to be sorry for? This is all my fault. I told you I would never betray you, but you were right— everyone is capable of betrayal."

He tipped her chin, forcing her gaze to his. "I was wrong. I made it seem black and white. What you did wasn't a betrayal. They gave you an impossible choice and you chose the less terrible of the two."

"They told me they would put her in the cage." He muttered a vile oath, and tears streamed down her cheeks. "I couldn't let them do that, Lachlan. I couldn't let them put my daughter—"

"Shhh," he stopped her, soothing her with his gentle embrace. "Of course you couldn't. It's over. Don't think about it." He comforted her for a few moments, but then pulled back, looking into her face. "We don't have much time. Are you ready?"

She nodded. Though she knew it was ridiculous, and that every minute they lingered only added to the danger, she couldn't help the irrational pang of disappointment in knowing that her daughter was so close.

But she might as well be a kingdom away. A kingdom separated by hundreds of soldiers and masses of thick stone walls.

If he guessed her thoughts, he didn't say anything. Instead, he arched a brow. "Aren't you going to ask how I escaped?"

She shrugged. "I figured you found a way to unlock the door."

He shook his head. "You are a hard lass to impress. You do realize the door was more than three feet above my head—and the lock was on the outside."

"You scaled the walls? Flew?"

He laughed. "Not quite. They came for me."

She heard the note of pride in his voice and realized of whom he spoke. Their eyes met, and she smiled. "I'm not surprised."

"Bruce will be furious."

"Aye," she agreed.

"I'll probably have to work out a new agreement."

Her heart thumped erratically—hopefully. "Does this mean you've decided to stay?"

He nodded, pulling her into his arms once more. "I meant what I said. I won't leave you again. I'll stay even if I have to fight for free." She beamed at him, joy surging through every corner of her heart. "But don't tell Bruce that."

She laughed. "I won't."

He dropped a kiss on her nose and pulled her to her feet. "Good, then we'd better go. Someone is waiting for us."

The dramatic turn of events could have been overwhelming, but as soon as they entered the corridor, danger and the threat of discovery became Bella's immediate focus.

Good God, how did he do this all the time? Her heart was fluttering as frantically as the wings of a butterfly. Every noise, every flicker of light sent her into a cold panic that they would be caught.

Lachlan seemed two steps ahead of her. By the time she recognized the threat, he'd already dealt with it.

He didn't need to ever worry about impressing her. She was in awe.

There hadn't been an opportunity for her to question him about his plan, but she was surprised when after exiting the eastern tower, he led her around the barrack full of sleeping English soldiers to the castle church.

She tugged on his hand in question.

He shook his head, telling her silently not to worry, and pulled her through the back door of the small church. It was deathly quiet; a few candles flickered by the altar where they'd been left after prayers.

"Why are we here?" she whispered, sensing it was safe to talk.

"I've brought someone to see you." Suddenly, he looked worried. "Listen to what she has to say, love. I'll be here when you are done."

The blood drained from her face, and her eyes widened with disbelief. *My God!* He hadn't. He couldn't. But he had.

Lachlan opened the door to the vestry, and there, standing in the middle of the room where the priest's robes were stored, was her daughter.

Lachlan caught her from behind when her legs gave out. "Joan!" After three years, the soft cry was all she could manage.

The beautiful girl—nay, woman—looked back at her uncertainly. "Hello, Mother."

Bella composed herself and turned to Lachlan, tears glistening in her eyes. He'd given her the greatest gift in the world. He'd given her back her daughter. Her heart squeezed. God, how she loved him! "Thank you."

He nodded.

"Are you ready?" Bella asked excitedly, stepping forward but stopping when Joan took a step back. The subtle rejection stung. *Give her time. It's been so long.* But Bella ached to take her into her arms. Covering her hurt, she asked, "Did you have time to gather what you needed?"

Joan exchanged a look with Lachlan over Bella's head. He shook his head. "I'll be waiting outside."

Before Bella could construe what that meant, she was alone with her daughter.

"I'm not going," Joan said.

Bella's heart stopped. Her mind closed; she knew she didn't want to hear this. "I know it's been three years. I know you must think I left you—"

Joan shook off her attempt to explain. "I know you intended to take me with you. I don't blame you for what happened. You did what you had to do. What you believed in. I could never blame you for that."

Bella's heart crumpled. Who was this quiet, self-possessed young woman? This stranger? Where was the girl who'd huddled with her in bed to hear stories, who'd run to her when she'd scratched her knee, who'd *needed* her?

"Then, why?" Bella choked. "Why do you not wish to come with me?"

Joan put her hand down on a small table as if to steady herself—the only outward sign that this might be difficult for her. Her expression was so composed and serene. So *determined.*

"My life is here in England now with my cousins and uncle."

Bella felt her heart breaking. "But it could be dangerous for you."

Joan lifted a wry brow, the movement so mature it cracked Bella's heart a little more. "More dangerous than Scotland?" She shook her head. "I think not. MacRuairi told me what they threatened you with, but I assure you I've never been in any danger. King Edward favors me. I think . . ." Her voice caught a little. "I think he is ashamed of what his father did to you. Sir Hugh is fond of me as well. He's promised to find me a husband soon. A powerful man who can help ensure my claim to the earldom."

Bella looked at her daughter in shock. It wasn't uncommon, of course, but . . . "You wish to marry? But you are only fourteen!"

"Not right away, perhaps, but soon. I merely wish to explain to you why I cannot go. Why I will not go. You chose your path, Mother; now I must choose mine."

Something wasn't right. Or maybe she just wanted to tell herself that. "But—"

The door opened behind her.

It was Lachlan. "I'm sorry, Bella, we have to go. They'll be changing the guard soon."

But her legs wouldn't move. After all these years, the one thing that had kept her going was the moment she would be reunited with her daughter. She'd never imagined Joan would not want to go with her.

"My life is here, Mother," her daughter repeated quietly.

Bella felt her shoulders shake, felt herself begin to crumble. But Lachlan was behind her. Steadying her. Holding her up.

She let herself lean on him. God knew she needed his strength.

"If that is what you wish," she said, her voice trembling.

Joan nodded solemnly. "It is." She was not as unaffected as she seemed. Bella could see the stiffness in her arms and shoulders. She was holding herself very tightly.

"May I write to you?"

Joan looked down, refusing to meet her gaze. For the first time, she resembled the child Bella remembered.

"It would be better for me if you didn't."

Bella tried to swallow, but the lump stuck in her throat. "I understand." It would be safer for her daughter if everyone believed them estranged.

Sensing her anguish, Joan offered, "Perhaps when the war is over."

Bella nodded, forcing a smile to her face. "Then I will pray for a swift end."

Joan smiled tentatively back at her. "As will I."

They shared a moment of silence, a shared prayer for tomorrow.

"I'm sorry, Bel," Lachlan urged softly from behind. "We have to go."

"But—" Bella stopped herself, trying to get her emotions under control. She took a deep, ragged breath, fighting the burning in her chest. "Goodbye, Jo."

It was what she'd called her as a child.

Joan lifted her eyes to hers. It seemed to take her some effort to respond. "Goodbye, Mother."

There was something in her voice. Something in the depths of her eyes that told her Joan was not the stranger she seemed. That her daughter was still there. Hidden by years of separation, but still there.

Bella couldn't stop herself. She closed the distance between them and pulled the stiff girl into her arms, hugging her tight. For a moment, Joan sagged in her arms. But then she stiffened and pulled away.

Bella took her by the shoulders. "Swear to me if you are ever in danger you will send for me."

Joan nodded. "I will. I promise."

She unfastened the brooch on her cloak and handed it to her daughter. "I want you to have this."

Joan's eyes widened when she realized it was the MacDuff brooch. "I couldn't—"

She tried to hand it back, but Bella shook her off. "Please. I want you to have it. It's part of who you are."

Joan nodded, her eyes conspicuously shimmery. She looked to Lachlan helplessly.

He gently pulled Bella away. For the second time, Bella slipped into the darkness, leaving her daughter behind.

It was a long time before she had a chance to speak with Lachlan, but his solid presence at her side as they escaped the castle with the rest of his brethren helped keep her on her feet, helped steady her when she wobbled, and helped soothe the pain of her daughter's choosing a future that didn't include her.

Hours later, wrapped in the comforting warmth of his arms so she could try to sleep while they rode, she let her tears finally fall, mourning the loss not of her daughter but of their life together. It was a day every mother knew would come, but hers had come too soon. Sons were forced from their mother's arms as boys to be fostered or squired to a knight. But daughters . . . her daughter should have been hers until she married.

"I'm sorry, love," Lachlan said gently.

Bella nodded. Seeing how worried he was, she managed a small smile. "Better not let your cousin hear you say that."

He frowned. "Hawk can go bugger—" He stopped, giving her an apologetic wince. "I don't care what he thinks."

"Really? From those looks you were giving him a while back, I thought he seemed to be bothering you quite a bit. What did he say?"

"Nothing," he said too quickly, but then reconsidered when she gave him an admonishing lift of her brow. "Let's just say he's enjoying the fact that I've softened my tone on marriage."

"You have?"

"Aye . . . well . . . damn it, Bella, I want you to marry me. I know I don't have anything to offer you. That you'd be a fool to get wrapped up with the likes of me, but—"

"If this is a proposal, you might want to stop telling me all the reasons I shouldn't marry you."

He scowled—a little petulantly for a man named after a deadly snake, but she'd remind him of that later. "I just wanted to make sure you knew what you were getting into."

She laughed. "I know exactly what I'd be getting into.

But I think you left out the most important part." He seemed confused, so she gave him a little help. "The point where you declare your undying love for me."

"I thought that was obvious."

"It is. But as this is a marriage proposal, I think I should like to hear it again."

He tilted her chin and looked deep into her eyes. "I love you, Bella. I will love you not until my dying day, but from the heights of heaven or the depths of hell until my soul ceases to be."

He was getting quite good at this. She put her hand on the familiar stubbled cheek. God, she loved him. "I'd be honored to be your wife."

He grinned, the sweetest, happiest grin she'd ever seen on his face. He drew her into his arms and kissed her. Telling her with the soft strokes of his tongue and mouth exactly how deeply he loved her.

When he finally broke the kiss, she was breathing hard and wishing they weren't riding on a horse in the middle of the night through the forest surrounded by ten very interested, smirking Highlanders.

Her thoughts must have been plain to see. He chuckled, whispering, "Later."

The sensual promise in that one word sent shivers of anticipation shooting through her veins. She nodded and sagged back against him.

"She'll be safe, Bella. As safe as anyone can be in this damned war."

How well he knew her. He'd guessed the direction of her thoughts. "She seemed quite certain about her uncle and Sir Hugh's fondness for her."

Lachlan was quiet. A little too quiet.

"What did you do?"

He shrugged. "I simply made sure Sir Hugh didn't forget it."

Her eyes flew to his. "You snuck into his chamber?"

"I had a few extra minutes."

She shook her head. "And how did you convince—" She stopped herself. "Forget it, I don't want to know."

Lachlan grinned. "Let's just say, I put the fear of God in him."

"Or the fear of the phantom Guard, you mean."

He laughed.

"What the hell is that sound?" MacSorley said from behind them.

"Sod off, Hawk," Lachlan said fiercely.

Bella grinned. "Your cousin really is amusing."

Lachlan groaned, along with the other men close enough to hear. "God, don't let him hear you say that."

But it was too late. Hawk took the opportunity to regale her with just how amusing he could be—much to Lachlan's annoyance. But after a while, he gave up trying to shut him up and even managed to get in a few digs of his own.

Much later, when Tor MacLeod had called an end to the "chatter," Bella sank back against him and closed her eyes.

"I know you were hoping for a different ending," Lachlan said quietly.

This war had already exacted so much from her. But Bella refused to let it cost her her daughter. "It's not the end, it's only the beginning."

With Lachlan by her side, she would fight to the end.

# Epilogue

❧

*December 1314, Benbecula, The Western Isles*

For six years she'd waited for this day, and now that it was finally here, Bella could barely contain herself.

She waited anxiously by the window in the Great Hall of the magnificent tower house her husband had built for her in paradise—or their little corner of it, anyway. The small isle of Benbecula, straddled between North and South Uist, was remote, private, and as beautiful as the Garden of Eden, with its long stretches of sandy dune beaches, lush green grasses, and wide-open vistas of sparkling blue waters.

In spite of the king's anger at their unsanctioned mission all those years ago, Robert had kept his promise and awarded Lachlan the lands and coin he'd earned for his service. Whether it was Bella's urging, Lachlan's vow to serve the king until the end of the war, or his young sister Mary's release from prison a few weeks after their return that was responsible for the king's change of heart, she didn't know.

But the families of Lachlan's clansmen who'd died fighting for him had their security, and Lachlan had the quiet, peaceful home he'd worked so hard for. Especially now that he'd returned for good. The elite warrior had fought his last battle in June. The war was over. A war that had demanded so much of them all. But they'd done their part and survived.

Yet as full as her heart had been these past years, there had always been an empty corner. Today it would be filled.

She gazed out the window, scanning the crystal-clear horizon, her hands twisting anxiously in her skirts.

She glanced over her shoulder, her heart catching as it always did every time she looked at him. Lachlan was even more handsome now than the first time she'd seen him. The fierce brigand had been transformed. He was just as physically imposing, but the cruel lines around his mouth had softened. Smiles, once infrequent, now came easily. Their happiness had been hard won, but it had been won.

"Are you sure it will be today?" she asked.

One of those easy smiles curved his mouth. "Aye, just as I was sure the last five times you asked me. Don't worry, Bel. She'll be here. Hawk said by around midday."

He stood from his chair beside the fire and came up behind her, wrapping his big arms around her waist and nuzzling her neck. She squirmed, giggling like a girl and not a woman of six-and-thirty. "That tickles." She turned around and playfully tugged the square of stubble below his lip. "You and your cousin come up with the strangest ideas."

This one—a contest of sorts—was for the most unique beard. Bella had to admit, she looked forward to seeing what they came up with. Lachlan's most recent was a small square patch just below his lip. Somehow, rather than look silly, it only seemed to make him even more wickedly handsome.

He arched a brow. "I thought you liked it."

She blushed at the memory of exactly when she'd told him how much she liked it and gave him a playful shove. "You're incorrigible."

He spun her back into his arms and kissed her. "And you're beautiful."

She melted into him, sliding her hands around his neck, and savored the long, slow strokes of his tongue.

"Ah hell, they're doing it again."

Bella shot Lachlan a glare that only grew sharper when she saw how hard he was fighting not to laugh. "I thought you were going to try to watch your language."

He gave her a boyish shrug. "I am—trying."

Bella turned, putting her hands on her hips to admonish the five-year-old interloper, who not only looked but sounded exactly like his father. "Erik, what did we talk about?"

The dark-haired, green-eyed charmer graced her with a dazzling smile. "My, you look beautiful today, Mother."

Oh, God help her!

Bella shot Lachlan another glare when she heard him laugh.

"Don't look at me," he said. "You're the one that wanted to name him after Hawk."

He might look and sound like his father, but Erik MacRuairi was as charming, roguish, and irresistible as his namesake. It was impossible to stay angry with him. He had her wrapped around the hilt of one of his tiny wooden swords. He insisted on two. Just like his father's, each was engraved with the words *"usque ad finem."* To the very end. Again, just like his father's.

Lachlan crossed the room and knelt beside his firstborn. Despite his amusement, he managed an impressively stern frown. "Remember our talk, son?"

Erik nodded, a disreputable wave of dark hair falling across his forehead.

"I'm disappointed in you," Lachlan admonished gravely. "It's not polite to curse around ladies."

The miniature Lachlan frowned, seeming to consider this for a moment. But then he smiled. "All right, I'll just curse around the men. But you might want to tell Tina—she was cursing something fierce a few minutes ago when Ranald stopped her from taking your *birlinn* out with Robbie."

"What!" Bella cried.

This time it was Lachlan who cursed.

Erik looked at them as if they were addled. "That's what I came to tell you," he explained patiently. "Tina wanted to take Father's *birlinn* out to meet Uncle Erik, but Ranald wouldn't let her."

"For God's sake!" Bella exclaimed, covering her mouth in horror.

Erik tugged on his father's sleeve. "Isn't that a blasphemy, Father?"

"Don't worry," Lachlan said to her, saving some kind of explanation to Erik for later. "I'll take care of it."

Bella nodded, collapsing in the nearest chair. The four-year-old blond-haired, green-eyed pirate-in-the-making thought she could sail a ship—with her two-year-old brother Robert, no less, as her second-in-command. She could probably do it, too. The little termagant would be the death of her. Their daughter had been named after both her famous Aunt Christina of the Isles as well as Tor MacLeod's wife, who'd become one of Bella's closest friends in the past six years, but the Viking blood of her ancestors coursed strongly through her veins.

Hand in hand, father and son strode out of the hall. Lachlan with the predatory grace she'd always admired, and Erik with a swagger that in not too many years would break countless hearts.

How she loved them. After years of hardship, fortune had smiled on her indeed. She'd thought when she hadn't quickened with child for so many years after Joan that she was barren. But she'd discovered that she was pregnant with Erik not long after they'd returned from Berwick.

At the time, the little boy had been a ray of light in more ways than one.

She pushed aside the sad thoughts and walked back to the window. She smiled, seeing Lachlan tossing Robbie up in the air with Erik and Tina chasing circles around him in the sand. So much for the new clothes she'd dressed them in. Unable to resist the lure of her family and a rare sunny day in December, she hurried out of the Hall to join them.

But as soon as Bella stepped out of the entry, she caught sight of the sail. She froze at the top of the stairs as the *birlinn* with its hawk-carved bow sailed effortlessly into the sea-loch.

She was here. Bella closed her eyes, giving a silent prayer of thanks. After all these years, Joan was finally here.

The swell of emotion hit her hard, landing with a thud against her chest. Tears glistened in her eyes.

She gripped the wooden rail like a lifeline as she slowly descended the steps. But when Joan stepped onto the jetty and began walking toward her, Bella gave up all pretense of composure. Tears streamed freely down her cheeks as her legs carried her faster and faster.

Joan looked up. She was so beautiful. The promise of beauty had been fulfilled in the gorgeous young woman who met her gaze. And when a broad smile of joy broke out across that serenely beautiful face, Bella knew that everything was going to be all right.

Her daughter had come back to her. A daughter who was more like she than she'd ever imagined. Perhaps better than anyone, Bella understood the choice Joan had made. Why she'd done what she had. But nearly ten years of sacrifice was over; the rest of their lives would be for them.

Dropping the hand of the man at her side, Joan ran the last few feet and launched herself into Bella's arms.

They laughed, cried, and experienced every kind of joy in between.

They had so much to say to each other, but it could wait. They had time.

Eventually, Bella held her out to look at her. "You are well."

Joan smiled. "Very well."

Bella didn't miss the glance she gave to the man who stood beside Hawk on the jetty. She was relieved to see there didn't seem to be any lingering animosity between the English knight and the *Gall-Gaedhil* seafarer. She hoped Lachlan, too, would keep his promise to be nice.

The children peeked out from behind Lachlan's legs, not quite knowing what to make of the scene.

"Why is mother crying?" Tina asked her father.

"Because she's happy." Lachlan's eyes met hers, and he smiled. "Very happy. Come, little ones, it's time to meet your sister."

As Bella watched her children come together, at long last her happiness was complete.

It had all been worth it.

# AUTHOR'S NOTE

The character of Lachlan is a compilation of the actual Lachlan (or Roland, as he is sometimes called) MacRuairi and his brother Ruairi—both bastard sons of Alan of Garmoran. Historians seem to agree that the MacRuairis were the wildest and most lawless of the descendants of Somerled, who'd inherited the "piratical tendencies of the Vikings" (R. Andrew MacDonald, *The Kingdom of the Isles*, Tuckwell Press, 2002, pg. 190).

Lachlan is referred to as "a 'sinister figure,' and a 'buccaneering predator' who 'played solely for his own hand.'" (See MacDonald, pg. 190, and G.W.S. Barrow, *Robert Bruce*, Edinburgh University Press, 2005, pg. 377.) As Barrow describes him: "A shadowy figure, Lachlan flits in and out of the record of the Anglo-Scottish war, always in the background, always a troublemaker. He defied in turn and with impunity King John, Edward I, the Guardians and the earl of Ross. In his own esteem he may well have ranked as a king of the Isles . . ." (Barrow, pg. 377).

With references like that, it was hard not to be intrigued. Talk about the makings of a perfect "bad boy" hero!

Lachlan was said to be married to John of Lorn's daughter, whose given name is not known. In keeping with my attempt to use appropriate clan names, I borrowed the name Juliana from her aunt who was married to Alexander MacDonald (Angus Og's brother).

The battle at Kentra Bay in 1297 was reputedly fought between Lachlan MacRuairi and the English. The setup by John of Lorn, however, is my invention. Lachlan did spend some time in a MacDonald prison, and the MacDougalls gave him refuge after he escaped. But sometime shortly afterward he switched allegiance from the MacDougalls to the MacDonalds, which got my imagination going. It sounded like the perfect makings of a betrayal.

In contrast to the piratical MacRuairis, Isabella MacDuff, Countess of Buchan, has gone down in history as one of the great Scottish heroines. Married to John Comyn, the Earl of Buchan (who was decades older than she), at an early age, she escaped from her husband (some say on his stolen horses) and raced to Scone to crown Bruce, arriving a day late. A second ceremony was indeed held, demonstrating how important tradition was to establish the legitimacy of Bruce's claim.

Technically, the chief of the Clan MacDuff had the right to enthrone Scotland's kings by leading them to the stone of destiny (which had been removed by Edward I). Significantly, crowning was not part of the ceremony prior to this time. The absence of a coronation in the ceremony along with the king not being anointed were arguments used by Edward to show that the Scots were sub-kings to England. For simplicity, I used crowning and enthronement interchangeably.

Why Isabella risked so much for Bruce is unclear. There were rumors, as I alluded to, of her being Bruce's lover. I suppose it's possible, but it seems more like English propaganda to me, especially since the queen and Isabella were traveling together when they were taken. But Bruce did have a number of bastards.

When Bruce's fortunes fell after his loss at the battle of Methven, so, too, did Isabella's. Most historians agree that the women were with Bruce until the battle of Dal Righ, where he ordered them to the safety of Kildrummy while he and his men fled west. Why the women left Kildrummy is unclear, but they were captured in Tain, betrayed by the Earl of Ross, who violated sanctuary to take them.

Kildrummy Castle fell not long after the women escaped. As I described, the garrison was betrayed by the blacksmith who set fire to grain that was being stored temporarily in the Great Hall. Nigel Bruce was captured, as was Robert Boyd, who apparently managed to escape. Nigel, however, was executed (the third of Bruce's brothers to be killed in a year). The English did indeed pay the blacksmith his gold by pouring it down his throat.

For her part in Bruce's coronation, Isabella MacDuff was imprisoned in a cage and hung from a tower at Berwick Castle. Those who read French can see a link on my website to Edward's actual order for imprisoning the women.

How long Isabella was forced to endure her cruel captivity is not known, but it might have been as long as four years. She was eventually transferred to the convent at the monastery of Mount Carmel, but what happened to her afterward is unclear. Most likely she died in the convent, as she was not returned with the other women after the war. I did find one account of an escape, however, which I thought the most satisfying, if not the most likely, of endings for such a great heroine.

Although there was no evidence that Buchan attempted to divorce Isabella, it doesn't seem illogical. He made no attempt to influence Edward to lessen her punishment. Indeed, some sources suggest he wanted her executed. The dissolution of marriage in medieval times is an extremely complicated subject, with experts disagreeing on just how prevalent it might have been. You can read more about it if you are interested in the "Special Features" section of my website.

Isabella and Buchan probably didn't have any children,

although I did come across one instance of a daughter named Isabel. Conveniently for my story, Buchan died in 1308 while Isabella was still in captivity. Although the connection with Lachlan is fiction, I thought she deserved a happy ending.

The fate of the other women is much clearer. Bruce's sister Christina (the widow of the Earl of Mar and Christopher Seton) was taken to Sixhills nunnery. Queen Elizabeth got off fairly easy—probably because of the influence of her father, the Earl of Ulster—and was placed under house arrest in Burstwick. Bruce's young daughter Marjory, by his first wife Isabella of Mar, was originally slated for a cage in the Tower of London. When Edward relented, she was taken to Walton priory. Mary, Bruce's young sister, suffered a similar fate to that of Isabella, ordered to a cage in Roxburgh Castle.

Why was Mary Bruce imprisoned in a cage when the others weren't? I don't know, nor was I able to find an explanation for why she might have been singled out among the others for such cruel punishment. At the time, she was probably only thirteen or fourteen.

Mary was released in 1309, but the rest of the women were not returned to Scotland until after the end of the war in 1314. Mary married the much older Neil Campbell (Arthur's brother in *The Ranger*) and then, after his death, Alexander Fraser (Christina's brother in *The Chief*).

For more, please visit my website at www.monicamccarty .com.

Read on for an excerpt from

# THE SAINT

by Monica McCarty

Published by Ballantine Books

*Inverbreakie Castle, Ross, Scottish Highlands, August 1305*

Magnus MacKay caught the movement out of the corner of his swollen eye, but it was too late. He couldn't get the studded leather targe around in time to shield himself, and the war hammer landed with full, bone-crushing force across his left side, sending him careening headfirst into the dirt. Again. Albeit this time with at least a few broken ribs.

Behind his own grunt of pain, he heard the collective gasp of the crowd, followed by the anxious silence as they waited for his next move. If he had one.

A broad shadow fell across him, blocking out the bright sunlight. He gazed up into the menacing visage of his enemy.

"Had enough?" the Sutherland henchman taunted.

Every inch of him had had enough. Magnus hurt in places he didn't know he could hurt. He'd been bruised, battered, and hammered to a bloody pulp, but he wouldn't give up. Not this time. For five years he'd suffered defeat at the hands of Donald Munro, the Sutherland champion. But not today. Today he fought for something too important.

Magnus spit the dirt out of his mouth, wiped the blood and sweat from his eyes, and gritted his teeth against the pain, as he dragged himself back to his feet. He wobbled, but through sheer force of will steadied and shook the stars clear from his vision. "Never."

A cheer went up from the crowd. Or half the crowd, that is. Like the rest of Scotland, the clans gathered to watch the Highland Games were divided. But it wasn't Robert Bruce and John Comyn that men took sides with today (though both of Scotland's claimants to the throne were present), but between an even older and bloodier feud: the MacKays and the Sutherlands.

"Stubborn whelp," the other man said.

Magnus didn't necessarily disagree. He lifted his targe in one hand and his hammer in the other and prepared for the next blow.

It came. Again and again. Like a battering ram. Munro was relentless.

But so was Magnus. Every time the fierce warrior knocked him down, he got up. He refused to give up. He'd be damned if he'd come in second to the braggart again.

The Sutherland henchman had been a thorn in his side since the first Games Magnus had competed in five years before. He'd been only eight and ten and besting the heralded champion, who was five years older and already in the prime of his manhood, had seemed an impossible task. Then.

But Magnus was no longer a stripling lad. In the last year, he'd added considerable bulk and strength to his lean, muscular build. At a handful of inches over Munro's six feet, Magnus had the advantage in height. The scales were no longer so unbalanced.

He'd already acquitted himself well at these Games, winning the footrace and sword challenges—although the best swordsman in the Highlands, Tor MacLeod, was absent—and placing among the top three in the other competitions with the exception of swimming, which was to be expected. Magnus hailed from the mountains of Northern Scotland, and the Islanders—Erik MacSorley in particular—dominated the water events.

But this was the challenge Magnus had to win. The hammer event belonged to Munro. He'd dominated it for nearly ten years. It was his pride and dominion. And wresting the crown from his nemesis's head to claim victory for the MacKays would make it all the more satisfying. Hatred ran deep between the two clans, but Munro's arrogance and disdain had made it personal.

But it was more than hatred and clan pride fueling Magnus's determination to win. He was deeply conscious of one set of eyes on him. One big and crystal blue set of eyes. Helen. The girl—nay, woman (she was *finally* eighteen)—he intended to marry. The thought of losing to Munro in front of her . . .

He couldn't. Damn it. He *wouldn't*. How could he ask her to marry a man who came in second? Victory would be a sign that the time was right.

He blocked another powerful blow with his shield, his muscles flexing to absorb the shock. Steeling himself against the burning in his side, he took the full weight of his opponent's momentum on the shield and managed a swing of his own hammer. Munro twisted away, but the blow that Magnus landed on his shoulder was more than glancing.

It was the first crack. The look of fury on his opponent's face couldn't mask the frustration. Munro was tiring. The fierce attack and repeated swings of the heavy weapon had taken their toll.

This was it. The opening he'd been waiting for.

Magnus caught the scent of something that revived his aching body like nothing else: victory. With a sudden, inexplicable burst of strength from the very bowels of his determination, he took the offensive. Pummeling with his hammer and thrusting with his targe, he drove his surprised opponent back.

Munro stumbled, and Magnus seized the advantage, wrapping his foot around the henchman's ankle to knock him completely to the ground. Kneeling on his chest, he thrust his shield against his enemy's throat and lifted the hammer high above his head.

"Yield," he bit out forcefully, his words carrying across the silent arena. The stunning reversal had struck the crowd dumb.

Munro tried to fight back, but Magnus was in control. He dug the edge of the targe deeper, crushing his throat and cutting off his breath.

"Yield," he repeated. Rage surged through his veins, the brutality of the fight having taken its toll. The urge to finish it rose up hard inside him. But these were the Highland Games, not the life-and-death games of the gladiator.

For one long heartbeat, however, it might have come to that. Munro refused to yield and Magnus refused to let him go until he did. Despite the temporary truce of the Games, the hatred raging between the two proud Highlanders threatened to destroy it.

Fortunately, the decision was taken from their hands.

"Victory to MacKay," a man's voice rang out. Baron Innes. The holder of Inverbreakie Castle and the host of these games.

A cheer rang out. Magnus lowered his hammer, pulled back his targe, and released Munro. Standing, he thrust his arms out wide, basking in the cheers and savoring the rush of victory.

He'd done it. He'd won. *Helen*.

A swarm of people gathered round him. His father, younger siblings, friends, and a fair number of pretty young lasses.

But none were the lass he most wanted to see. Helen couldn't come to him. And as much as he wanted to see her right now, he dare not seek out her gaze.

For his Helen was none other than Helen of Moray, the daughter of his greatest enemy, the Earl of Sutherland.

* * *

Thank God it was over! Helen didn't think she could bear another minute. Sitting there, watching Magnus get beaten to within an inch of his life, and not being able to react, being forced to smother every flinch, every gasp of horror, every whispered prayer for him not to get up, as the man who was like a brother to her pummeled him to the ground, had been pure agony.

Magnus was too tough for his own good. The stubborn ox didn't know when to give up!

She was going to kill him herself for putting her through that. Magnus knew she didn't enjoy the violent competitions in the Highland Games—why men beat each other senseless in the name of sport, she would never understand—but for some reason he'd made her promise to be there.

"Are you all right?"

Helen tried to force her heart back down to her chest, but it seemed lodged permanently in her throat. She turned mutely to her brother.

Kenneth frowned, his gaze flickering over her face and down to her hands, which were still clenched in the soft wool folds of her skirts. "You seem distressed. I thought you were going to faint for a moment."

Her pulse quickened. He was far too observant. She *was* distressed, but she dared no let him suspect the reason. Her hot-tempered brother despised the MacKays, and Magnus most of all. The two were of age, but Magnus had gotten the best of him in the competitions since they were lads. If Kenneth found out about them . . .

He wouldn't. He couldn't.

"I didn't expect it to be so . . . *intense,*" she said, which was the truth. "And of course, I'm disappointed." Belatedly she recalled her family loyalty.

He eyed her suspiciously, as if he didn't quite believe that was all to it. She held her breath, but then the crowd roared again, distracting him. His face darkened as he took in the glee of the Mackays. "I can't believe he won." He shook his head with disgust. "Father is going to be furious."

A different kind of alarm shot through her. "Perhaps it would be best if we did not tell him? Not right away, at least."

Kenneth's eyes met hers, his expression suddenly grim. "Is it that bad?"

"He will be fine," she said firmly. Of course he would. It was the only possibility she would consider. "But I do not want to distract him. He needs all his strength to fight the illness."

But each time the lung ailment came back it seemed worse. She probably shouldn't have come, but Magnus had made her promise. And the thought of not seeing him for another year with the threat of war swirling all around them . . .

She couldn't stay away.

It was only a week. Her father would be fine without her for a week. She'd left precise instructions for Beth, the serving lass who helped her care for her father, and Muriel had promised to check on him. It was she who'd taught Helen everything she knew about healing.

Kenneth's jaw hardened, his expression grim. "Then perhaps you are right." He took her elbow and nodded in the direction of their fallen champion. "Come, you'd best see to Munro. Although it appears it's mostly our champion's pride that has taken a beating." A wry smile turned his mouth. "Perhaps he will learn a little humility."

If her brother didn't sound all together displeased at their champion's loss, Helen didn't wonder why. He'd suffered many defeats at the hand of their champion.

As soon as her brother looked away, Helen stole one last glance toward Magnus. But he was surrounded, lost in the crowd of cheering admirers, his enemy's daughter undoubtedly far from his mind.

She sighed. Soon he'd have crowds of ladies following him about like Gregor MacGregor and Robbie Boyd. The famed archer with the face of Apollo and the strongest man in Scotland had taken on a God-like status at the Games and had a bevy of starry-eyed young women hanging on their every move.

She followed her brother and pretended not to let it bother her. But it did. She wasn't jealous—not really. Well, perhaps more jealous of the freedom the women had to talk with him in public than of the women themselves. Although the curvaceous blond attached to his arm had been quite pretty, she recalled with a pang.

Why did everything have to be so complicated?

The first time they'd met, she'd never given a second thought about sneaking away to meet him. The feud hadn't mattered to her. All she'd been thinking about was that she liked him. That for the first time she'd met someone who seemed to understand her.

When she was with him she felt unique, not different. He didn't care that she didn't like sewing or playing the lute. That she dozed during Father Gerald's sermons and didn't pray as much as she should. He didn't care that she'd rather wear a simple woolen kirtle (more often than not tied up between her legs) than a fancy court gown. He hadn't even laughed the one spring she'd decided to cut her hair because it kept getting in her eyes.

But the constraints of the feud had begun to chafe. Stolen moments a couple times a year—sometimes only once—were no longer enough. She wanted more. She wanted to be able to stand by his side and have him smile down at her the way he did that made her insides melt.

If a little voice in the back of her head that sounded like her father said, "Perhaps you should have thought of this in the beginning, Helen lass?" she quieted it. It would be fine. Somehow they would make it work.

She loved him, and he loved her.

She gnawed on her lower lip. She was almost certain of it. He'd kissed her, hadn't he? It didn't matter that barely had their lips touched and her heart finished slamming into her chest, when he'd set her harshly away from him.

Part of her sensed his feelings ran just as deeply and passionately as hers. And despite the danger, despite the knowledge that her family would consider her actions a betrayal, she couldn't stay away. It was foolish—impossible. But also exciting. When she was with Magnus, she felt freer than she'd ever felt in her life.

How could she not take what they had and hold on tight? As Horace said, *"Carpe diem, quam minimum credula postero."* Seize the day, trusting as little as possible in the future. She might not have been much of a student when her father had brought in tutors for her, but she remembered that. The words had resonated.

It seemed to take forever to tend Donald's wounds, if not his tattered pride, but at the first opportunity she snuck away and waited for Magnus to find her. It didn't take him long. Usually making him work to find her was part of the fun. But she was so anxious to see him, she made it easy on him.

The snap of a twig was the only warning she had before two big hands circled her waist from behind and snatched her down off her perch.

She gasped as her back met the hard planes of his chest. Her cheeks flushed with heat. By saints, he was strong. The lean frame of youth was now stacked with layer upon layer of hard, steely muscle. The changes in him had not gone unnoticed and being plastered so intimately against those changes sent a strange warmth shimmering over her and a flutter of awareness low in her belly. Her heart quickened.

He spun her around to face him. "I thought we agreed no more climbing trees?"

Agreed? Ordered was more like it. She wrinkled her nose. Sometimes he could be just as bossy and overprotective as her brothers. "Ah, Helen," they'd say with an indul-

gent sigh. "What have you gone and done now?" They
meant well, but they'd never understood her. Not like
Magnus did.

Helen ignored his frown and gasped as she gazed up into
the familiar, handsome face. The boyishly strong, even features had been bruised and battered almost beyond recognition. He'd bathed and made some attempt to tend his
wounds, but there was no washing away the big red and
purple mass covering his jaw, split lip, broken nose, and
large cut near his eye. She traced the area around it lightly
with her fingers, seeing that someone had already tended it.
"Does it hurt horribly?"

He shook his head, capturing her hand in his to draw it
away. "Nay."

"Liar." She pushed him away, hearing the grunt of pain
and realizing she'd forgotten about the ribs. She put her
hands on her hips. "It's no more than you deserve after
what you did."

His brows furrowed in befuddlement. "I won."

"I don't care if you won, he nearly killed you!"

He folded his arms across his chest, a decidedly cocky
grin on his face. For a moment her gaze snagged on the
bulging display of muscle in his arms. Lately it seemed she
was always noticing things like that at the most inoppor-
tune times. It flustered her. *He* flustered her. Which was
disconcerting, since from the first she'd always been comfortable around him.

"But he didn't," he said.

The arrogance of his pronouncement distracted her from
her distraction. Her eyes narrowed. Men and their pride.
Nay, *Highlanders* and their pride. They were a special
breed of proud and stubborn. "You don't have to sound so
pleased with yourself."

He frowned. "Aren't you pleased for me?"

Helen nearly threw her hands up. "Of course I am."

The frown deepened. "Then why are you so upset?"

Were all men obtuse? "Because I don't like seeing you get hurt."

He grinned again, snagging her around the waist as she tried to spin away from him. It was a playful move— something he'd done many times before—but there was something different this time when he dragged her up against the long length of his powerful body. Something hot and dangerous crackled in the air between them.

She gasped at the contact, feeling every solid inch of the steely chest and legs plastered to hers.

He looked down at her, his warm, golden-brown eyes darkening. "But I have you to take care of me, don't I?"

The huskiness in his voice sent a shiver running through her. She blinked up at him, surprised at the change that had come over him. He never flirted with her like this. It was strange, exciting, and a little intimidating. He was a man, and suddenly she was achingly aware of it. A warrior, a champion, not the tall, lanky lad she'd first met.

She tilted her head back, her lips parting in some instinctive response. She could see the desire swimming in his eyes and sucked in her breath in anticipation.

He was going to kiss her. God, he was *really* going to kiss her.

Finally!

Her heart hammered in her ears, as he lowered his head. She could feel his muscles tighten around her. Feel the pounding of his heart against hers and sensed the passion surging inside him. Her knees weakened as desire shot through her in a wave of melting heat.

She sighed with pleasure at the first contact, at the sensation of his soft lips pressing against hers. Warmth and the faint tinge of spice infused her, flooding her senses with the heady taste of him.

He kissed her tenderly, dragging his lips over hers in a gentle caress. She sank into him, unconsciously seeking more.

*Show me how much you care for me.* She wanted throes

of passion. She wanted heartfelt declarations of love. She wanted it all.

He made a pained sound, and for a moment she wondered if she'd hurt his ribs. But then his arms tightened around her. His mouth hardened, pressing against her more fully. The taste of spice grew deeper, more arousing. She could feel the tension in his muscles, feel the power surging through him, and her body melted in anticipation, when suddenly he stiffened and pulled away with a harsh curse.

He released her so suddenly, she had to catch herself from stumbling. Her legs seemed to be missing the bones.

Her eyes widened, shocked and not a little disappointed. Had she done something wrong?

He dragged his fingers through silky-straight, sandy-brown hair. "Marry me."

She gaped at him in astonishment. "W-what?"

His gaze locked on hers. "I want you to be my wife."

The spontaneity of the proposal was so unlike him, at first she thought he must be jesting. But one look at his face told her differently. "You're serious?"

"Aye."

"But why?"

He frowned. It was obviously not the response he'd hoped for. "I would think that would be obvious. I care for you."

Not "I love you." Not "I can't live without you." Not "I want to ravish you senseless."

There was a tiny pinch in the vicinity of her heart. Helen told herself she was being ridiculous. This was what she wanted, wasn't it? He'd told her how he felt—even if it wasn't exactly with the flourish she'd hoped for.

He was so confoundingly *controlled*. Not cold and unfeeling, but calm and even-tempered. Steady. A rock not a volcano. But sometimes she'd wish he'd explode.

When she didn't respond right away, he added, "Surely this can't come as a surprise to you?"

Actually it did. She bit her lip. "We never talked about the future." Perhaps because they'd both been trying to ignore the realities.

*Marriage.* It was the only option for a woman in her position. Then why did the very idea strike fear in her heart?

But this was Magnus. He understood her. She loved him. Of course she wanted to marry him.

But what he was asking was impossible. "Our families will never allow it."

He didn't bother arguing with her. "I'm not asking our families. Run away with me."

She sucked in her breath. A clandestine marriage? The notion was shocking. But also, she admitted, oddly appealing—and undeniably romantic. Where would they go? Perhaps the continent? How exciting it would be to travel across the countryside with only each other to please. "Where would we go?"

He looked at her strangely. "Strathnavar. My father will be angry at first, of course, but my mother will understand. He'll come around eventually."

Northern Scotland, not the continent. The MacKay lands were in Caithness, which bordered Sutherland.

"And where would we live?" she asked carefully.

"At Castle Varrich with my family. When I am chief, the castle will be yours."

Of course. Silly lass. How could she have thought differently? His mother was the perfect lady of the castle. Naturally, he would expect as much from her. Her breath squeezed.

"Why now? Why can't we wait and see—"

"I'm tired of waiting. Nothing will change." His jaw hardened, an unfamiliar glint of steel in his eye. He was growing impatient with her. For a moment she thought he might lose his temper. But Magnus never lost his temper.

Sometimes she even wondered whether he had one. "I'm tired of sneaking around, not being able to speak or even look at you in public. You are eighteen now, Helen. How much longer before your father finds you a husband?"

She blanched, knowing he was right. She'd escaped a betrothal this long only because her father was ill and needed her.

Her heart stopped. Oh God, who would take care of her father? She looked at him helplessly, the enormity of the decision making her hesitate. She loved him, but she loved her family, too. How could she choose between them?

He must have read her indecision. "Don't you see, this is the only way it can be. What we have . . ." His voice dropped off. "What we have is special. Don't you want to be with me?"

"Of course, I do. But I need some time—"

"There isn't time," he said harshly. But he wasn't looking at her. A moment later, she knew why.

"Get the hell away from her!"

Her heart dropped. Helen turned around to see her brother flying toward them.

Magnus saw the blood drain from Helen's face and wished he could spare her from this moment. But it had been inevitable. They'd been fortunate to escape discovery for so long.

Although, if they were going to be discovered by anyone in her family, he would rather it be her eldest brother William, the heir to the earldom. He at least wasn't a complete arse. If there was anyone he disliked more than Donald Munro, it was Kenneth Sutherland. He had all the arrogance and all the snide mockery of Munro, with a hot temper to boot.

Instinctively, Magnus moved around to block Helen. He

knew she was close to her brother, but he wasn't taking any chances. Sutherland was unpredictable at best, rash at worst.

Magnus caught the other man's fist before it could slam into his jaw and pushed him back. "This isn't any of your business, Sutherland."

Her brother would have come at him again, but Helen stepped between them. Next to her oaf of a brother she looked as diminutive as a child. Her auburn head barely reached the middle of his chest. But she wasn't a child. For two long years Magnus had been waiting for her to turn eighteen. He wanted her so badly he couldn't breathe. This impish, fey creature, with her big blue eyes, freckled nose, and wild mane of glorious deep red hair. Hers was not a conventional beauty, but to him, there was no one more breathtaking.

"Please, Kenneth, it's not what you think."

Sutherland's eyes sparked with anger. "It's exactly what I think. I knew there was something wrong at the competition, but I didn't want to believe it. I didn't want to think you could be so disloyal."

Helen flinched, and Magnus swore. "Damn it, leave her the hell out of this. If you want to take your anger out on someone, take it out on me."

The other man's eyes narrowed. "With pleasure." He reached for his sword. "I'm going to enjoy killing you."

"A bold claim for someone who has never bested me in anything."

Sutherland snarled with fury.

Helen cried out and launched herself at him. "No, please," tears were sliding down her cheeks, "don't do this, I l-love him."

Magnus had been reaching for his own sword, but her words stopped him. His heart slammed in his chest. She loved him. She'd never said so before, and after their recent conversation he hadn't been so sure. Warmth settled over him. He'd been right. They were meant to be together. She felt it, too.

With more gentleness than Magnus would have thought him capable of, her arse of a brother said, "Ah, Helen." He stroked her cheek fondly. "You don't know what you are saying. Of course, you think you're in love with him. You're eighteen. That's what young girls do, they fall in love."

She shook her head fervently. "It's not like that."

"It's exactly like that," he said. "You love to love. Every day is like May Day to you. But how well can you know him?" Suddenly, his expression narrowed. "How long have you been meeting like this?"

She flushed, looking down at her feet. Magnus felt his anger rise, seeing her guilt.

"We met at the Games at Dunottar," Magnus interjected. "By accident."

Kenneth spun on her. "Four years ago?"

He swore when Helen nodded.

"By God, if he's disgraced you, I'll string him up by his bollocks and see him gelded—"

"He's done nothing," Helen interrupted. "He's treated me with perfect courtesy."

Magnus frowned, hearing something odd in her voice. It almost sounded like disappointment. "Have care what you say, Sutherland. You have a right to your anger, but I will not allow you to impinge your sister's honor or mine."

It might have taken every last shred of his control, but Magnus hadn't done more than kiss her. He wouldn't dishonor her like that. He'd wait until they were married, and then he'd dishonor her plenty. The sweet taste of her lips on his still haunted him. But it had been as much care for her innocence as lack of confidence in his own control that had caused him to pull away.

Sutherland's face darkened, as if he knew exactly what

he was thinking. "It'll be a cold day in Hades before you get the chance." He shot Magnus a look that promised retribution and took his sister's arm. "Come, Helen, we're leaving."

Helen shook her head and tried to pull away. "No, I—"

She looked to Magnus helplessly. His mouth tightened. She only had to say the word, and he'd claim her right now. He'd defeated the Sutherland champion—her brother would not stand in his way.

Sutherland grabbed her by the shoulders and turned her to face him. "What were you thinking, lass? Your eyes are so filled with sunshine, you think it shines as brightly for everyone else. But you aren't going to be able to make this have a happy ending. Not this time. Surely you didn't think anything could come of this?"

Magnus had had enough. "I asked her to be my wife."

Sutherland's face turned so red with anger, he appeared to choke. "God's blood, you must be mad! I'd sooner see her married to old longshanks himself than to a MacKay."

Magnus's hand closed around the hilt of his sword. "It's not you I've asked."

Both men's eyes fell on Helen, whose pale face was ravaged by tears that looked so wrong on her face. Helen never cried, that she was told of her deep distress. She looked back and forth between them.

Magnus clenched his jaw, knowing how hard this was on her. He knew what he asked of her. But she had to decide. It was always going to come down to this.

Sutherland did not show such restraint. "If you marry him, it will start a war."

"It doesn't have to," Magnus said.

Sutherland acted as if he hadn't spoken. "You would turn your back on your family? On Father? He needs you."

Her tear-stained eyes grew enormous in her pale face. She looked at Magnus pleadingly and he knew. His chest started to burn.

"I'm sorry," she said. "I can't . . ."

Their eyes met. He didn't want to believe it. But the truth was there in stark, vivid blue.

*Jesus.* His gut twisted. He couldn't believe . . . He'd thought . . .

He stiffened and turned brusquely away, holding himself perfectly still so he wouldn't do something to shame himself like beg. The worst part was how badly he wanted to. But he had his pride, damn it. It was bad enough that Sutherland was here to witness his rejection.

Sutherland folded Helen into his arms. "Of course you can't, sister. MacKay couldn't have expected you to agree to this. Only a romantic fool would have thought you'd agree to run away with him."

Magnus could hear him laughing at him. He clenched his fists, wanting to smash the taunting smile off the bastard's face.

Had he really expected her to run away with him?

Aye, fool that he was, he had. Helen was different. Helen wasn't bound by convention. If she'd loved him enough, nothing would have stopped her.

He would have given up everything for her, if she'd only asked.

But she never did. The next morning he watched the Sutherland tents coming down. They were leaving. Her brothers weren't going to give her any chance to change her mind.

Robert Bruce, the Earl of Carrick, approached him with Neil Campbell just as Helen exited the castle. Her face was hidden in the hood of her dark cloak, but he would know her anywhere.

Magnus barely listened to their proposition. Barely heard the details of a secret group of warriors being formed by Bruce to help defeat the English. He was too caught up in Helen. Too busy watching her leave him.

*Turn back.* But she never did. She rode out of the gate, disappearing into the morning mist, and never once looked back. He watched until the last Sutherland banner had dis-appeared from view.

Bruce was still talking.

He wanted Magnus for his secret army. It was all he needed to hear. "I'll do it."

He'd do anything to get away from here.